CW01192474

The Metanatural Adventures of Dr. Black

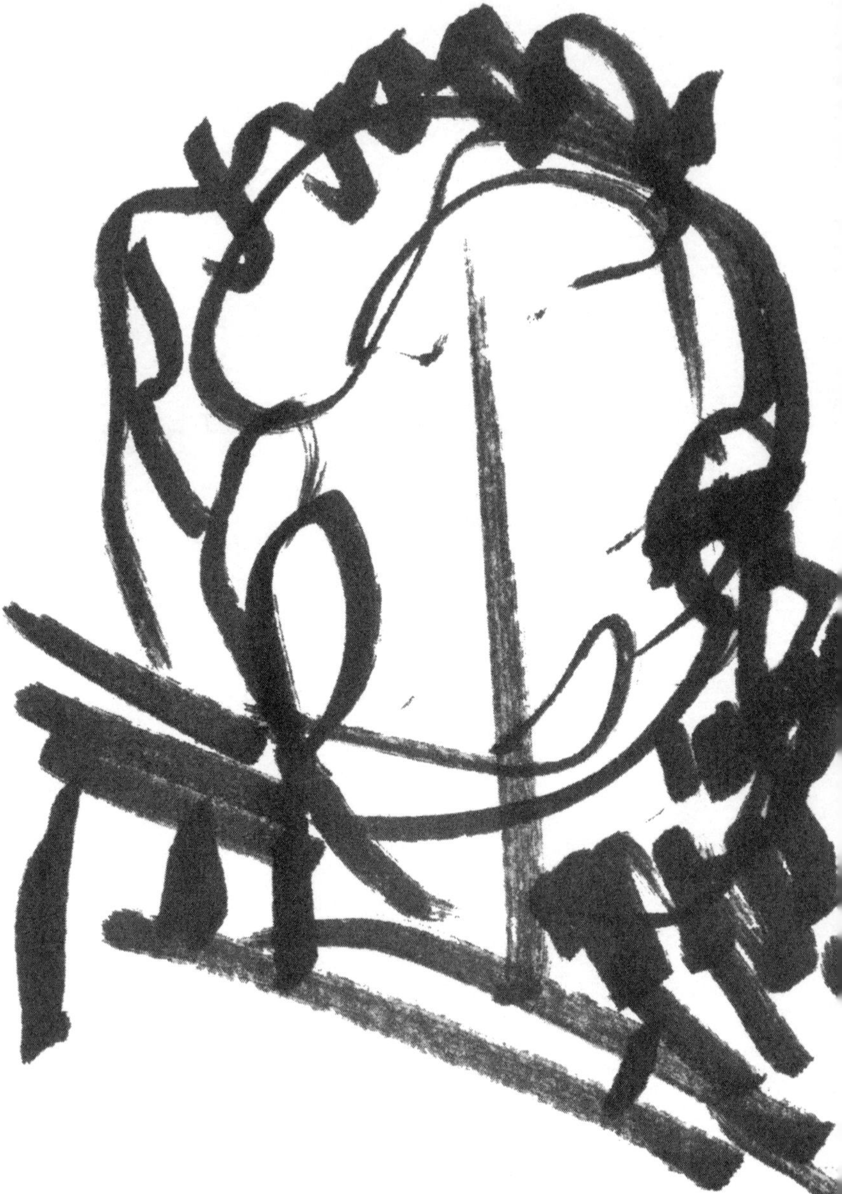

The METANATURAL ADVENTURES OF DR. BLACK

BRENDAN CONNELL

INTRODUCTION
BY JEFF VANDERMEER

The Metanatural Adventures of Dr. Black
Copyright © 2014 Brendan Connell

Introduction
Copyright © 2014 Jeff VanderMeer

Cover Art
Based on a photograph of Kenzan clay tile,
Kenzan Co., Inc., used with permission

Interior Illustrations
Copyright © 2014 The Estate of John Connell

The right of Brendan Connell to be identified as Author of this Work has been asserted by him in accordance with the Copyright, Designs and Patents Act 1988.

Published in August 2014 by PS Publishing Ltd. by arrangement with the author. All rights reserved by the author.

FIRST EDITION

ISBN
978-1-848637-53-5 • 978-1-848637-54-2- (Signed Edition)

This book is a work of fiction. Names, characters, places and incidents either are products of the author's imagination or are used fictitiously. Any resemblance to actual events or locales or persons, living or dead, is entirely coincidental.

Design and layout by Alligator Tree Graphics.

Printed and bound in England by T.J. International.

PS Publishing Ltd
Grosvenor House • 1 New Road • Hornsea, HU18 1PG • England

e-mail: editor@pspublishing.co.uk   *Internet:* http://www.pspublishing.co.uk

The Metanatural Adventures of Dr. Black

fully revised and restored
with copious footnotes for the layman

Supervisor
Prof. Ivy Sultan

Honorary Member of the Asiatic Society of Nicosia and the Société Académique de Léon and President of the Executive Committee of the Fitchburg Historical Society. Corresponding Member of the Königliche Gesellschaft der Wissenschaften zu Göttingen. Foreign Member of the Szczecińskie Towarzystwo Naukowe. Vice-President of the Philadelphia Latin Club. Reviser of the Mongolian Old Testament and Moravian Missionary on the Sikkim-Bhutan Frontier.

BIBLIOTHECA GRECO-METAPHYSICAL SERIES NO. XXIX

Chief Editor: *Prof. Samdhong Kai*
Professor of Bodo at Gauhati University
and author of "A Journey to Dambuk,"
"Manual of the Lechitic Languages," &c., &c., &c.

Printed at Qumin's Offset Printers, Shoe Lane, Oxford

60% subsidised by the United Centre for
the Commission of Languages with
further assistance provided by the
Council for the New Megatherium Club

Sāsanā: 2558   2014   Burmese Era: 1376

5774

Subscribers
to the First Edition,

which was distributed at the Annual Spring Meeting of the Society for Independent Savants in July of the previous year.

*Imperial Paper.

R. Allen, Esq.
Mr. Big
Mr. W.H.P. Capps, Litt.D.
Miss Melissa Chowdry*
Mons. Cornwallis, Col. au service de leurs Majesties Imp.
Mr. K. de Falco
Prof. Galassio*
Doctor Grunje, *4 copies*
Mr. Z. Holland, Distributor of Stamps
Miss Agatha Innsworth
Mr. James
First Counsellor and Guide Lenny
Mr. Longwall, Drugger
Mr. Morris, C.L.M.
Mr. and Mrs. Alberto Nessi
Mr. O.T. Ogilby, Procurator Fiscal*
A. Paretti, *6 copies*
Mrs. Price
Honourable Dr. Q.
Dr. Rod, *2 copies*
The Duke of Rutland
Sir N. Ruxby
The Duchess of S.
Mr. Thimbley, Papyrologist
Tracks of a Large Animal, *2 copies*
Lord Viscount T.
Rev. Mr. Rime
Mrs. Rodenbach, F.S.*
Anna S., Mistress of the Household
Prof. Tomo
Mr. Jakob F. Vane, Gentleman
Mr. K. Vernon, Agrologist
Hank Yu*
Miss Zinny

Contents

Introduction / xi
A Season with Dr. Black / 3
Fragment Group A / 45
Dr. Black and the Guerrilla / 53
Fragment Group B / 113
Dr. Black in Monte Carlo / 119
Red-Haired Man in a Sweater,
From the Private Papers of Dr. Black / 163
Fragment Group C / 185
Dr. Black and the Village of Stones / 191
Dr. Black, Thoughts and Patents / 227
Fragment / 273
Dr. Black in Rome / 277
Fragment Group D / 313
Dr. Black at Red Demon Temple / 319
Variety / 359
Suggested Reading / 363

Dr. Black: A Brief Reverie
by Jeff VanderMeer

WHAT TO MAKE OF DR. BLACK, NOT PARTICULARLY THE MOST orthodox of heroes or anti-heroes? As written by Brendan Connell, Dr. Black seems to have always existed and yet be utterly unique. He is simultaneously learned and, in certain environments, a bit of a fool. He has some tastes that are quite normal and others that are outrageous. There is always a bit of comedy as a sting in the tail of the more serious stories, and a seeming encyclopedic knowledge on the author's part of the comic pratfalls of yesteryear in others.

We encounter Dr. Black at his most vulnerable in the opening story, "A Season with Dr. Black," and at his quirkiest, too. A kind of stream-of-consciousness patter is interwoven with the events occurring in the foreground. We see the limits of his experience and discover that despite his vast array of eccentricities, which at times seem to have formed a hardened carapace around him, Dr. Black also displays a touching kind of naivety and trust. (It doesn't hurt that he tends to be surrounded by rogues who are far easier to map with a moral compass ...)

One of the doctor's most endearing qualities is how he continues to offer up the unusual and yet relatable. In "Dr. Black and the Guerillas," facing a firing squad, he divulges to us, not his interrogators, a collage of experience that showcases Connell's comfort both with the character and language: "childhood = Alabama (to the sounds of Sweet Nadine: huge. crowned with red hair. her beautiful voice + his own father: a thick and elongated torso; great-great-great-great-grandson of noted physician and chemist Joseph Black = discoverer of carbon dioxide *of a gentle and pleasing countenance. performed on the flute with great taste and feeling* her voice ringing out inviting his mind inquisitive wanting to acquire feasting always on digits and alphabets small particles and the stars dry-embalm that potato or burn with magnifying glass) + the boy doctor himself making: a diffusion cloud chamber / an electric lemon / a snow-storm in a can; incidents of life = emotions & operations for the purpose of testing certain principles."

This is a rather remarkable re-interpretation of "his life flashed before his eyes," taking what in the abstract would seem destined for cliché and rendering it fresh and almost startling. Which then, in a lovely demonstration of the way in which Connell manages to shift tone, to pivot without effort, pratfalls into the absurd, and yet no less detailed: "the construction of a massive umbrella with which he was able to jump off the roof of a five-storey doll factory in Williamsburg, Brooklyn / if he were killed he would sorely miss the chicken heart back at his laboratory on Long Island which he had kept alive for twenty-seven years pulsating in a solution of sea salt."

What are we reading here, in these "adventures"? They contain grotesqueries galore, certainly, in the most delicious way. You could say that Huysmans and other Decadents exist as amiable ghosts here, along with hints of a more surreal Max Beerbohm. But this is not pastiche, merely an indication of predecessors: Connell presents something fresh, new, and with a more modern outlook. The prose is at times reminiscent of Vladimir Nabokov in its complexity, but a kind of raw earnestness not present in Nabokov manifests here, too. In short, the issue of influence is an elusive one, relegated here to the status of an idle pursuit following immersion in these pages. What *is* clear is that Dr. Black could not be quite so expressive, nor so learned, nor so assimilated in terms of influence if the author himself was not learned, expressive, assimilated.

The fascinating Dr. Black, brought to life in such a way, is the plot upon which Connell successfully hangs many interesting set pieces and descriptions that in lesser hands might be rendered inert upon the page. Please don't go looking for the ordinary in these stories, because you can find the ordinary in quantity in other places, and at a discount. Appreciate instead, for the example, the magnificent food descriptions in "Dr. Black in Rome," which do much more than lie there like tempting appetizers on a restaurant table. The story is cleverly structured around

Introduction xiii

menus. *"Fregula with mussels. Spaghetti alla Eros. Zuppa alla Valpellinese."* Dr. Black, following a lecture at the University of Rome, where he gave a paper on "canine sexual dimorphism in Egyptian Eocene anthropoid primates," now sits at dinner with similarly erudite companions, including a man who has written a book entitled *A Brief History of Bivalves*.

The genius of the conversation that follows is how Connell mixes the sublime with the trivial, and the exalted with the earthy; one could say that the entire point of the story, plotwise, is to conceal an elicit assignation. Or, perhaps, to act as a delicious delivery system for some enticing facts about Rome: "The City of Rome emerges from the banks of the Tiber at a distance of 1,867,214 inches from the mouth of that river, which makes a profound furrow in the plain which extends between the Alban hills." But, in fact, those 1,867,214 inches are simply a circling back to Dr. Black as well, because Connell so perfectly re-creates a sense of interiority, of perspective, that any facts about Rome are also clues to how the good doctor sees the world.

The story perhaps sums up the allure of this collection in the way that it emanates an exuberance and curiosity about the world, a kind of questing that allows for both the sincere and the cynical. Connell sends up the pomposity of academia but also celebrates intellectual pursuits, examines carnality with a kind of dispassionate eye in a story that is also unabashedly sensual. There is also an effect of pulling back to a wider view, within Dr. Black's perspective, as when during a comedy of errors involving a tryst he sees his lover as also "merely a conglomeration of constantly changing atoms." This widening reverie, which also perhaps freezes in place an essential arrogance on the doctor's part, is juxtaposed against the present moment in such a way as to create an intense gravitational pull, an awe-inspiring long view that adds even more texture and layering. And, yet, Connell cannot quite let us have the stars without reminding us of the gutter, his reverie in this case anchored in such perfectly un-enchanting details as "the latrines of Lepcis Magna."

Details make these stories glorious. Where else can you read the words "the butt of every space cowboy's disdain" adjacent to the words "*a)* Hasdrubal the Boëtharch with no rhomboid crystal hammer," without the result reading like disjointed and disintegrating mumblings?

The sharpness on display makes a fair amount of fiction seem like a photocopy of a photocopy, with no true connection to the real world or to even the underlying abstract concepts that help us create that world. (As if to underscore that point, clichés are offered up *as such* in the Dr. Black stories: "*Stock footage of: Circus of Maxentius, cork trees, Tomb of Cecilia Metella, Aurelian's walls, Roman traffic, the Colloseum . . .* ")

"People always cry nihilism when they are confronted by a system of assessment that refutes conceptual thought that they can't quite grasp," Dr. Black says at one point during a conversation. Whatever might be refuted, assessed, or not quite grasped by the people in these stories, Connell has created a character unique in the history of fiction, and one whose misadventures will fascinate the reader.

The Metanatural Adventures of Dr. Black

A Season

with

Dr. Black

I have heard that Aconite
Being timely taken hath a healing might
Against the scorpion's stroke.

Ben Jonson, *Sejanus, His Fall*

I.

Dr. Black, at 4 feet, 11 inches, was taller than a midget. His neck, equal in circumference to that of the average bulldog, supported a cranium of vast ability, a thinning corruption of growth combed back over its surface; a black and frothing monument adhered to his chin. The eyes of a priest or judge. The head of a buffalo. Legs absurdly svelte. A torso profound in its girth.

Mr. Clovis drove the car with arms taut, motions mechanical; the decorum of the well-paid servant. His eyes followed the curvature of the road, the play of light patching through the apple trees, and the cows, to his left, which bent over green pasture. Occasionally he glanced in the rearview mirror, more to ascertain the well-being of the doctor than to appreciate the lack of approaching traffic.

"Eyes on the road, Dick," the doctor grunted.

"Yes, Doctor."

The car, like the shadow of some imperious, savage bird, drifted across the countryside, shaping itself to the protuberances and declivities that lay in its way, its presence, and the presence of its adherents, strangely out of place amongst the wealth of life that painted the landscape.... At the dirt drive it turned in, to the left. Mr. Clovis, briefly removing himself from the vehicle, opened the rustic, corral-style gate. The tires ground along the narrow and arboured way, the thick neck of Dr. Black turning from left to right, in observation of the springtime of his estate.

The mansion, a structure built some two hundred years earlier by a wealthy and retired merchant, stood quaint against the backdrop of orchard and blue, cotton-spotted sky. Mrs. Clovis, brought down some three days earlier to get the establishment in readiness, stood arms akimbo on the front steps, her healthy chest and stomach thrust forward by way of greeting.

"It's about time you got here," she said to her husband as he extricated the valises from the trunk of the car. "His tomato soup has been ready for thirty minutes."

II.

THE DOCTOR ENJOYED HIS TOMATO SOUP VERY MUCH AND THE next day requested that a plate of the same fruit be brought to him, fresh and seasoned with balsamic vinegar, salt and fresh basil.

"Alfred brought me a whole box of these yesterday when he heard you were coming," Mrs. Clovis said, setting down the plate. She expounded on the hospitality of country folks as opposed to city dwellers and then, seeing the doctor's attention drift decidedly toward his meal, commented: "He has a greenhouse-full over at his place. He seems to have it in his mind to make money off them."

Dr. Black slightly rotated one of the ruby red disks with his knife and fork before slicing off a portion. Lifting it to his mouth, he noted a sunken lesion, which marred a small area of the skin.

"Anything wrong?" Mrs. Clovis asked, seeing his eyebrows contract and fearing she had made some careless mistake in her culinary preparation.

Without reply he examined the tomato more carefully and then finished his lunch, his appetite apparently unhindered.

Later that afternoon he made his way over the field of new alfalfa, which lay beyond his own backyard, and along the creek-side until he reached Alfred's residence. It was obvious at first glance that the man had been busy since the year before. A long, stretched-out greenhouse lay on the side of the old farmhouse and others, in mid-construction, skeletal forms of plastic sheeting and pipe, were stationed in the near vicinity. In front of the house was a dusty yard strewn with tired discord: a roll of chicken wire, some rotted lumber, a wheelbarrow settled with rainwater and lively with nesting mosquitoes. The barn was on the other side of the yard, the door open. A man sat in the hay-strewn dirt, his body half in and half out of the structure, tinkering with a fishing rod and reel.

He looked up and the doctor could not help but notice the low forehead and rather broad zygomas—a skull structure not necessarily of the most advanced variety. With a certain degree of disgust Dr. Black considered that, after all, this specimen before him might be decisive proof that mankind descended from the hippopotamus rather than the agile ape.

A dog, of the miniature and hairless variety, impeded the doctor's grim meditation with its bark and snapped at his legs. As his foot lifted the creature up, making it temporarily airborne, he considered how right Galileo was to disprove Aristotle's theory about a heavy body descending faster than a light one, for, as a projectile, the dog acted verily the same as any stone shot from a catapult.

The two men exchanged greetings. Alfred, showing the hospitality of a country man, invited his guest into the house for a glass of cider.

"No, thank you," the doctor said firmly and explained his mission: "Though I do indeed owe you a social call, at present I have come regarding your tomato plants—a predicament which I am sure, in the long run, you will find much more beneficial than any unguided table talk we might share."

"So you don't care for a glass of cider?" Alfred asked with a bewildered expression.

"No my friend, I have come to see your tomato plants," the doctor continued undaunted. "You brought me my lunch which, to colloquialise, was 'right neighbourly' of you, and I intend to repay the favour. You reportedly have the notion to subsist, at least in part, off of the proceeds of your crop. I will not venture to comment on the practicality of this projected means of livelihood, but merely wish to visit your greenhouse."

Scratching his head, Alfred led the way.

For a half an hour the doctor examined the plants, now turning over the leaves of one, now caressing another's filamented stem. Alfred stood silent, with arms crossed, awaiting the unasked for verdict.

"I am afraid your entire greenhouse is suffering from the early stages of anthracnose," Dr. Black said gravely. "As you can see, the fruits are infected with these small, water-soaked indentations. On some of the lesions there are even masses of blooming fungus. As the situation progresses, the mildew which feeds on this decaying matter will undoubtedly penetrate the fruit and completely destroy it."

"I see a few little spots on a tomato or two," Alfred said with a surly twist of his lips, "but I'm not so sure it's such a big problem." The presence and threatening tone of this hunkered down, big talking urbanite put him on his guard and he was not immediately ready to accept his prophecies.

"The fruit may be infected when small," the doctor persisted. "At this stage its appearance is relatively benign, the lesions not appearing until they begin to ripen. The tomatoes you brought me were not seriously wounded, but, from my observations, I can guarantee you that your entire crop is extremely susceptible; and as this harvest approaches maturity——Trust me my friend, a preventative fungicide is in order, as well as an entire restructuring of the soil so as to allow adequate drainage. And crop rotation, possibly with basil—this is your only hope."

III.

CAPARISONED IN A SMOKING JACKET OF HUE TO MATCH HIS NAME, Dr. Black sat in the library, eyes journeying back and forth between the pages of *The Journal of Mixoscopic Introversion* and the promontory of his pipe, which exuded a sleepy blue coil that rose and mated with the high rafters of the ceiling. These were the leisure hours, when his mind might sponge up information according to its own whim, while darkness coated the trees and fields, and his digestive organ slowly processed the repast of the hour previous. This organ, assisted by the occasional ablutions administered from a goblet of brandy, seemed, on this occasion, to be uttering slight hogs of dissatisfaction. The doctor listened, his face assuming the annoyed expression of a judge tolerating the introduction of a surprise witness.... There was sound indeed.... He examined its mode of resonance, the bubbling and protruding cantata, its irregular scramble. It appeared, on more subjective discernment, to be generating from outside his intestinal scope.... Yes, there was little doubt that its source lay not only beyond the ramparts of his belly, but beyond the very walls in which his entire composition abided.

"Go in and tell him," were the half-muted words that came from the hall.

"But you were the one that said she could stay!"

"Don't be a coward; tell him!"

After a few whispers and whines of uncertain phrase, a tap sounded at the door, which forthwith creaked open, revealing a quarter slice of Mr. Clovis, his mien especially grave, a pallor whiting his temples.

"Yes?" the doctor asked, setting down his intellectual equipage.

The door opened further; Mr. Clovis stepped in.

"You know the road?" he asked meekly.

"The one at the end of the drive?"

"Exactly."
"Well?"
"You know the road?"
"Where cars go?"
"That is my point entirely, Doctor!"
"That there is a road?"
"Yes, and that cars go along it ... and ... "
"And?"
"And ... and sometimes they break."
"So, our car broke?" the doctor asked rather curtly, flinging back his head.
"No, not ours."
"Then?"
"Hers, Doctor."
"Your wife—a car?"
"No."
"Pardon?"
"The young lady."
"Yes?"
"Yes."
"And this young lady is?"
"She is sitting in the dining room."
"And what is she doing in the dining room, might I ask?"
"Eating a sandwich, Doctor."
"So?"
"It is ham and cheese."
"And ... so?"
"So ... you refuse to have a phone line put in!"
"And where there is smoke there is fire?"
"Exactly."
"Which means?"
"Which means that Georgia is preparing the spare bedroom at the end of the hall."
"And you are asking my permission, or demanding my compliance?"

"Your permission, Doctor."

At that moment the doctor could not help but pity the broad range of mortals who suffer from the disease called marriage.

IV.

*N*OCTURNAL POLLUTION TO THE IMAGE OF A WALLOWING SWINE, erotic zoophilia; or, for a certain nun, the sight of an ape, contact with a priest's hand, contemplation of the crucified Christ, or demon (such as with the head of a fish, or serpentine, pronged member—hell being a river of asps—coupling with the horns of the bull moose), the presence of flies in contact—The other boys hunting raccoons and opossums (to deliver, sell at the black cabins that which they themselves would not eat); him, alone, pursuing the mysteries of the Alabama cane break pitcher plant (mouths agape, bodies waxy, sinister without thought or particular will),—Others which might imbibe small reptiles, scorpions and frogs— pasty mucilage—(Francis Darwin growing his two colonies of sundews), Dr. Black thinking of the garden of the retired savant: Drosera rotundifolia, Drosera binata, and the great staghorn sundew with its twenty-three-inch leaves, or the Brazilian Drosera villosa, or the beautiful black-eyed sundew, and the tree-like giant sundew. ... A malicious hothouse: The huntsman's cup, the king monkey cup, Nepenthes ampullaria, which, with no difficulty, could digest rats—White trumpet, hooded trumpet, yellow trumpet, sweet trumpet; and maybe a small pond of piscivorous plants— bladderworts; dropwort wreathing the water's edge, hemlock, you umbelliferous wonder, dead tongue, the silence of Socrates; or in cultivating some poisonous patch, take, as Hecate did, the foam of Cerberus (thrust upon the aged men of Ceos when their usefulness had expired), that fleshy, spindle-shaped root: monkshood; the juice of which, applied to an arrow's tip, was mentioned by Diocorids as being used to kill wolves, Aconitum lycotonum; thus wolf's bane; tongue and mouth tingling, ants madly crawling over flesh, pains epigastric, lightness of head, staggering, breath laboured, halted.

Science: The art of intellectual cannibalism.

He sat with his back against a well-measured past, an intricate codex memorised by rote (his own mythology being more strange and dangerous than any of Hercules' tasks). There were experiences wrought, and discoveries, beneficial as locusts, piled up along the semi-material trail of his person, made apparent by hints and feelings and effects and after-effects that might not be felt in their full measure till one hundred years hence.

V.

The next morning brought with it, aside from the doctor's fried egg and half a cantaloupe, an image jointly stirring and fantastic.

She appeared in the door of the dining room wearing a pair of rather sheer pyjamas which, together with the early rays of light, accented her figure in a provocative manner. She stretched her long limbs and yawned; ran a hand through a spume of wild golden strands; blinked (robin's eggs on an outstretched sapling limb); and laughed.

Dr. Black rose from his seat, a spoonful of melon frozen in one hand, and greeted her with a rather severe degree of decorum.

"Oh, thank you so much for the bed," she replied, rushing forward and seizing the free hand of her host. "It would have been so awful to have had to sleep in my car all night!"

"Apparently it was my pleasure," he replied in a gruff voice. "You may sit down if you wish."

She did wish, and sat directly across from him.

"Do you like eggs?" he asked, eyebrows inclining darkly.

"If they are poached. . . . If they are poached I like them."

"And might I ask the name of my guest who likes poached eggs?"

"Tandy," she replied, her face opening up into a fresh smile.

"Georgia!" the doctor bellowed, turning his head toward the kitchen door. "A poached egg for Miss Tandy!"

He then lowered his visual apparatus, and resumed operation on the half cantaloupe.

Mrs. Clovis brought Tandy two poached eggs, two slices of buttered wheat toast, and a cup of creamed coffee, which the young woman consumed with an appetite.

VI.

SHE OBSERVED HIS ACTIVITIES WITH DISCRETION, TIMIDLY circumambulating his vicinity. Occasionally he would raise his eyes from the tome before him and observe the shadow flit by the door, the sweep of golden hair that moved past the window.

Mr. Clovis was convinced that they need not commandeer a tow truck. He had offered his services as mechanic and could be seen in the drive, buried from waist to head in the hood of the car, or sucked beneath it, feet wagging under the bumper, the sound of grunts and thrash of wrench echoing from that region.

"You just make yourself at home," Mrs. Clovis told Tandy. "Don't mind the Doctor's ways. He seems rough on the outside, but I can tell he doesn't mind one bit having a pretty young lady like you around."

Tandy gave a cute shrug of the shoulders and demonstrated how naturally her lips could pout. She turned and walked toward the apple orchard (wearing simple shorts, a blouse, elegant summer apparel). A few soft clouds hung above the trees, and a few globes of unripe fruit beneath, or from. A blue jay rocked on a branch and then, at her approach, flew off to a more discreet location.... Something else fluttered aside from those wings. She sighed, the subdued cursing of Mr. Clovis painting a shadowy backdrop to that article, like a landscape by Leonardo da Vinci, or Giorgione (serration and mystery of cold mountains making the valley's tranquil tints all the more profound, endowing the stationary female figure with a kind of kinetic energy).

"Place your foot upon me, your slave," she whispered, and let the sound dissipate in the still air, while the quivering of her lips by no means cut short the rose that blossomed within her, a dark maroon, with glistening thorns.

VII.

"It is amazing that they could sit in the same room for so long without either one speaking hardly a word," Mr. Clovis observed, shovelling a forkful of apple pie into the damp cave of his mouth.

"Either one?" his wife chirped. "The poor girl has tried, but he is so stone cold, it scares her. She thinks he wants her to leave."

"Well, maybe he does."

"Dick—sometimes you amaze me. For a man, you know so little about men."

"You don't amaze me, Georgia. Women always think they understand men, and when they realise that they don't after all, it's too late."

"Is it too late for me, Dick?" Mrs. Clovis asked with intimidating drollery.

He shovelled another forkful of apple pie into his mouth.

Her sole occupation was the observation of the ash at the end of Dr. Black's corona. It grew, millimetre by millimetre, in train of the smouldering cherry, and then, all at once, was dislodged with a powerful gesture of its master's wrist. He read. He cleared his throat. He wet it with brandy. She watched. She waited. With the red of her tongue she navigated the fullness of her lips. He did not look up. She did. He turned another page. She threw herself back into the unsympathetic luxury of her chair. He crossed one svelte leg over the next.

"Do you always read?" she ventured.

His eyes consummated the paragraph at hand, and he then slowly looked up, with an expression both sharp and languid, or annoyed.

"Do I always read?" he mirrored. "Do you never read?"

"I like to read *Cosmopolitan*," she replied, tucking her legs under her and curling, retreating into a corner of the chair. "Sometimes I also read books. I read F. Scott Fitzgerald."

"F. Scott Fitzgerald you say? . . . Do you also enjoy walks on the beach in the moonlight, foreign films, and horseback riding by candlelight?"

"Why, yes! How did you know? . . . I mean, all but the horseback riding by candlelight. I haven't had that pleasure yet." She smiled.

He bookmarked his literature. "Oh, I am sure you will," he said, laying it aside.

His composure impressed her. The very immobility of his bearing carried with it a certain audacious element that made her feel as if she were in the presence of one much more powerful than herself; a lichen-coated stone or petrifying, oxidized log of ancient redwood which, once dislodged from its precarious ledge, could very well break her tall, thin form—smudge its submissive fragility—the fragility of living flesh.

For several minutes he looked at her in grave silence while she pursed her lips prettily. It was obvious that he was positioning his rooks and knaves, lowering the bucket of his will into the deep and chilly well of his intelligence.

He got up.

She angled back her head upon its stem and cast out the blue petals of her eyes. The emotion she felt, when he chucked her under the chin, straddled the territory of both danger and longing.

VIII.

Web of skin,
Network of bones,
coated pliant,
quivering,
pleading negative taut as the drum of some animistic peoples, who stare into the wild of night, absorbed by the ancient and slowly-moving glacier of birth feeding on birth, the statue marble, Venus ground to dust, mixed with the humus within which he could stretch his roots, absorb the nutrients to feed those sticky tentacles.
 "No?"
 "Yes."
 "No?" he laughed.
 "Yes, yes, yes!"
 Later, running one hand through the axe of his beard, he remembered the words of Baudelaire: Cruelty and sensual pleasure are identical, like extreme heat and extreme cold.

IX.

"Well, it's none of your business."

"I never said it was," Mr. Clovis replied, watching his wife dice a red onion. "It was an observation, that's all."

"What, you don't think I have ears as well?" She scowled, turning, the knife flashing in one hand and tears rolling down her cheeks. "I have eyes and ears just like you. I simply choose to keep them in their place."

"Yes. . . . Yes, Georgia."

"You should be happy for him," wiping the tears from her eyes. "Find a little companionship. . . . Man doesn't always have to be alone."

"No Georgia. . . . Apparently not."

"What did you say?"

"I said yes, Georgia. . . . I'm going into town; to the auto shop."

"You're trying to hurry the job, aren't you?"

"No, Georgia; I'm taking as long as I possibly can."

"Well. . . . Fine. . . . And remember to pick up some chives while you're out."

She continued to dice the onion, which was destined to animate the body of a tuna fish salad. Ten minutes later, Alfred knocked at the screen door which was situated so as to give access to a small back porch where firewood was stored. He stepped in, his left hand gripping the neck of a duck which hung limp, its tail feathers almost touching the ground.

"I brought this for the Doc," Alfred said, holding up the fowl. "I wanted to leave it for him for thanks. Shot it this morning. . . . He was right you know. He was pretty right about that fungus."

"He usually is," Mrs. Clovis said. "Wonderful!" she cried, taking up the bird in her plump hand. "Sit down and let me get you a glass of something. . . . Some nice red."

Alfred took hold of the back of a chair, knit his brows, and then plunged his buttocks down on the seat, obviously unused to stationing himself upon furniture.

She did most of the talking, Alfred only occasionally articulating a few words between sips of his wine. He was hesitant with his speech, as are many men used to being alone, not fully trusting their tongues to act in strict accordance with the wills of their brains. As much as he liked the occasional caress of human contact and the light, comfortable kitchen filled with appetizing aromas, there was no question that he would have been relieved to be back home in the company of his dog and tomato plants.

The door that led to the dining room opened and Tandy stepped in. She wore tight jeans and red leather boots. Her t-shirt was stretched over her full bosom.

"I came to get the Doctor a cappuccino," she said. And then, turning to Alfred, she raised her hand and said, "Hi, I'm Tandy."

Alfred rose from his seat and muttered something inarticulate.

X.

THE SINGLE GRAIN OF MILLET SAT POISED ON THE LIP OF THE porcelain dish, which, in its turn, rested upon the tabletop in the backyard. Dr. Black stood at his study window, his hands wrapped around a pair of binoculars. He watched with earnest patience as a group of sparrows hopped around a section of the lawn, following the line of birdseed. One, more eager than the others, made a brief foray up to the sprinkled table top, pecked a few morsels, and then descended once more to the grass.

"Damn him," the doctor breathed.

His vexation however was soon appeased. Another sparrow, less cautious, took its colleague's place, eating the scattered seed and turning with clipped motions around the shore of the dish. Dr. Black raised the binoculars to his eyes, adjusting the focus. The grain of millet sat alone on the porcelain lip. The bird observed it briefly, and then pecked it up and into its little beak.

"Good," the doctor said, with composed excitement, removing the watch from his breast pocket and noting the exact time.

The sparrow chirped pitifully, took a hop, and then flew off the table's edge. In mid-air, approximately two metres from the earth's surface, it plummeted, and briefly palpitated on the grass.

"One fifteenth grain in fifteen seconds," Dr. Black said. "I will get Mr. Clovis to fetch it for weight."

The room above the study was that which harboured Tandy. She too was framed by a window, the slight shiver that coursed through her nervous system juxtaposing a dampness which arose from her skin; a languid and uncertain horror, desire.

The apparatus (well-oiled, diabolic, a veritable stallion of cast iron, Trojan in its mythopoeic tragedy) roared, rhythmically, flywheels

A Season with Dr. Black 23

turning, pistons playing in and out of cylinders; the deliberate thrust of machination: lameness, squinting, paedophilia, necrophilia, presbyphilia, pygmalionism—these under the heading *Abnormal Attraction*—and—and algolagnia; he could not forget that.

Through diverse experience he had found that to use his own self as the substratum for experimentation was, though dangerous, the best method by which to observe the psychological, even psychophysical, effects of morbid positionings and affinities. The true way to determine the effects (microcosmically) of thieving was to thieve: in order to clarify the impact of murder, one must turn murderer. Criminal behaviour was a mildew; the latent need for incision, humiliation, consumption of still bleating sauce of flesh, vertigo of deviations resembling a tribe of monkeys springing through the trees: This binary space on which all combinations were transposed (even if subtly) aroused the doctor's attention.

XI.

THE DAY WAS ESPECIALLY NICE AND THE AIR WAS STILL AND QUIET, sometimes stroked by the sound of a large fly descending on some small and rare spot of filth. Mr. and Mrs. Clovis were at the town which lay a few miles away, her buying provisions, him a few mechanical items.

The full afternoon light fell on Tandy's back. Her knees and hands pressed against the twig-covered earth, the raiment of maize-coloured hair falling over her face. She twitched in anticipation, in the distance the hills, some areas covered with small forest, rolled away, seemingly shy to witness that human episode. Then the extent of the cane played in the air, described a few delicate, spiralling circles before descending, rattan cutting, whistling, giving the donation of localized, bodily suffering—And nature hid her face; the spirit of trees, oceans and wind recoiled at the sound of irreverent snarls, blaze of tormented lust, and pule of hammering detumescence.

Later, the western light solemnised the patch of ground, like the sleeping place of a dog, rubbed raw as an infected and itchy wound.

There were flashes, glimpses of life through a horrific, existential lens: the two of them, as if painted by Arcimboldo; her, a haunting, beautiful form, hair the flowing of an orange sulphur, face a cabbage white splayed over an orange jezebel, the brush feet of the Marpesia marcella marking her slim eyebrows, eyes themselves denoted in the blue eyespots of the Australian Tisiphone abeona morrisi—Let her exoskeleton be that of a giant swallowtail, veins of the pearly eye (the cute little proboscis of a Coenonym phadorus raised in the air).... For him, his head the Callipogon barbatus beetle, a Metrius contractus representing his beard, the longhorn, California prionus, that North American spiny-necked giant would constitute his forearms, hands and fingers, the menacing jaws of the Dorcus titanus his mouth, the violent pincers of the Taiwanese male Dorcus sika his extended feet, cruel, prehensile—torso the two-tone Goliathus regius of the Ivory Coast, elytron, forewings extended, like a flapping, open blazer.

XII.

H E PROJECTED, LOGIC SOMEWHAT ANAESTHETISED, HIS OWN vision of the future, its possibilities—those delights sitting beneath a playful veil, the hand of the tamer needing to merely tug it away....Of course, bearing within his person a rather granite streak of genius, he was not altogether unaware of the folly: metaphorically, he slept with one eye open—or the lid slightly elevated at least.

Our first impressions of people may or may not contain a degree of accuracy; but our perceptions, meted by familiarity, certainly relay a far different signal. A man's silence we might initially judge as gravity, only later to denounce as mere stupidity; after acquiring a taste for snails, they are much enjoyed—to juxtapose the idea that familiarity breeds contempt, let it be said that familiarity has the ability to add entrancing gloss (and contempt is the bread eaten by the subdued, the infatuated).

The notes that he kept on their relations began to have hints of poetry—the pedantic stiffness of his style often reflected whispers, shimmerings of something not unlike the *Remedia Amoris* of Ovid. At first Tandy was referred to simply as "my subject." Later however he began to jot down her actual name—an aberration, unprofessional to the highest degree, which he had never before permitted himself. After having made the blunder a number of times he drew his attention to the subject and filled a page full of observations, in his close, spidery hand on what he believed to be the cause.... Still the trick persisted. But, instead of breaking himself of the habit, he indulged further, finding it easier to trust in his eventual triumph than deal fully with those minute discrepancies of reason as they arose.

They walked in silence, Tandy a few paces behind him. Though her legs were the longer, they were kept in check due to a certain wariness, subjugation. She had many things to say, but emotions, tending towards awe, stitched her swollen lips shut—Fear (nocturnally applied) could lubricate those bands of flesh, split them into a punctured heart and drag forth the howl, scream of tortured ecstasy. And wax (soft yellow substance of bees, honeycomb cells), remembered, as it flowed over her breasts, stiffening in combination with the rosette petals to be traced by the grim fascination and tapering muscle of a dwarf.

He walked on with deliberation, eyeing the ground and noting the grasshoppers as they propelled from the weeds along his path. As a boy he had made study of such insects, dislodging their jack-knifed legs and caressing their quivering and tragic antennae. Butterflies skewered, set upon cardboard sheets and beetles snatched from their gentle perambulations to be labelled, categorised, brooded over. And, it is said, men are simply boys of a larger dimension (that cranium swollen with incubating theories, gut blooming like a near-hatched egg). Aware of the apparition behind him, he walked on, blind to the incoming clouds as they blotted out the afternoon sun.

Respecting his abstraction, Tandy kept quiet, even as they mounted the low hill covered with a thin maple forest which rose up like a fallen mantle of rusty green above the rich knot of the valley, drops of rain ticking against the network of leaves. The drops came at first scattered and pleasant, then, as Tandy and the doctor achieved higher ground, advanced in distance, the shower fell melancholy, heedless, plastering down the hair of the man's head and beading through the frothing monument which adhered to his chin. The female's hair gained depth of tone; her clothing, saturated, did what could only be described through cliché, the descending liquid dispelling any loose folds of silk or cotton. Dr. Black's svelte legs became pronounced, comic, ridiculous beneath that mammoth torso which was, in turn, capped by a bony and throbbing mass, bridge of genius.

"Should we turn back now?" his companion asked timidly.

The doctor gave no indication of having heard. The ends of his trousers dragged through the mud; unsure, noir, the parallel bands of his legs advanced the grimly ludicrous man to the hill's summit, where he stopped, legs bowed, straddling the very earth.

"Come here," he sniffed, and turned, producing a length of cord from the breast of his jacket.

"Where should I go?"

"Over here—up against the trunk of this tree."

"But you don't seem to be in any state——"

"Move, slave!" he wheezed, blinking away the drops of water which rolled over his eyelids.

"Are you sure?" Tandy asked quietly. "Wouldn't you rather go back and have me make you a cup of tea with lemon and honey?"

He moved towards her with a kind of knotted exasperation. It was a bit too much—A bit too much to have to hear of the acid juice of a pale yellow fruit infused with the sticky sweet nectar of bees—She could stand prone and helpless, without the will to say no, yet the other would need the stamina to say yes. The rain came, heavy, morphing, its gloom washing away the stoic armour, that layer of grease which sealed out the cold.

"You're mine," he said, trying to operate.

A cryptic utterance of desperation.

XIII.

"He is normally so healthy—just like a rock."

"Yes," Mr. Clovis replied.

"I can tell you have your own opinions on the subject," his wife said, ladling out a bowl of steaming chicken soup patterned with celery.

"I still have a right to my opinions I suppose."

"Do you?... Well, you don't have any right to dislike her."

"I never said I disliked her."

"Well, you are jealous then."

"No, just a little worried—worried that he is getting carried away. He is not a young man you know."

"And he is not an old man. He is two years younger than you."

"But I don't chase after barely legal women."

"Do your job and take up this soup," Mrs. Clovis concluded, shaking her head—a motion that did not terminate with the departure of Dick and the broth, but accompanied her solitude (the solitude of a woman confident in the truth, the accuracy of titles, labels and their inherent reliability—the solitude of a woman who does not mind viewing her husband's opinions through the bars of a cage, but would prefer not to see them clawing clumsily over foreign soil and likely to cause localised regret).

XIV.

WITH CATARRH OF BOTH NOSE AND THROAT (FLOW OF LIQUID; dulling, dimming of the mental organ) he lay, incarcerated by his bed—the lukewarm bed of a single man, not much regretted when born as the only possible sphere of normal rest, but gravely lamented and seen as cold comfort to the alternate animal (substantial, primal, void filling) heat that raised him from being not only a man in name, but a man in function. So one might try the narcotic drug heroin once for the experience of it, and try it a thousand times again, still claiming the experience while the underlying reality exists, in nomenclature akin to fact, as little more than the stereotypical junkie—though in the doctor's case he was far past the frontier of stereotype, and the symptoms of addiction from which he suffered were not brought on by any sap of glorious poppy, were injected by modes other than those intravenous (that warm, kind *brutal* feeling of fondness *suppurating or carbonised lust* graspable as ghost; melting point of a phantom) *because when lay that way could see and see could feel soft substance between bones skin pulpy feel with upper limbs shoulder to hand palm. fist. finger an anatomist stepping from star to star of that body of that body breath through the trachea see diaphragm move take up the science. chain up the notes all while not knowing but being realising cannot really both know (formulaically— pragmatically) and feel too quick you writhing snake—if mastery not much more than a diurnal offspring of villainy disguised in garments or raging genius, plethora of zigzagging appellations, well furnished dungeon of fence or chicken wire, thought trail of breadcrumbs or candy all children really fear to be eaten alive, for what is creature woman (levelling all pyramids of intellection), step on me kick my rib and there and there (pressure of heel, retrograde of calf) strappado oh you condiment you condiment for my hot meat*

XV.

His flesh was alive with cold shivers. An obnoxious taste, almost herbal, lined his nostrils. He was aware that the order of his mind was disturbed and he mentally applied himself to a few relatively basic mathematical equations, with unsatisfactory results.

"Poor dear," Tandy said, petting his forehead. She ran her hand over his chest, letting her nails trace furrows in the skin, breaking the elastic substance in the last lingering pressure.

"Another mouthful of soup. . . . . Go on."

He tilted up the bulk of his head and let the spoonful of soup be inserted above the growth of his beard, beneath the arch of his moustache. He knew very well that a damaged constitution often arose from causes hyper-mental rather than strictly physical, but lacked the energy, the dynamism of will required to trace and track the origin of the current unsettling of his system. There is an inherent difficulty in being both doctor and patient, just as an executioner is not so good at simultaneously playing the part of the very man he executes, the condemned.

Verily a *Danaë* of Correggio (for she was no plump Rubens or stomachy maiden of Boucher), and if she lacked the ability to go beyond simple premise, basic syllogism, she was still loaded with instinct and could appropriate more with an erotic smirk than another might with the composition of compendious volumes or years of astounding revelation. So, if he recklessly crawled on all fours:

"Just go ahead and whip me!"

"I don't feel like it."

"Oh God!" scratching at her nadir, wetting with tears the sole of her foot.

And her:

Laughing, turning, walking away, not a follow me hither so much as knife twist of growing disdain, as if he were some crude though rich morsel which found its way to the pharynx, pushed through the esophagus, and then sat troublesome at the pit of her stomach, refusing to either advance or retreat, suddenly ugly as a court jester, she, amused as a lowbred woman observing a show of most unusual persons of abnormal form, towing with chains still violent for all their lack of visibility, a savant or buffoon, great sir or midget stumbling, slithering in her wake.

And he:

Perversely relishing his new role—the lush drums of desire beating in the curtained epicentre (punctuated by the spine traversing trilobite of fear, more ancient than the sea dwelling stromatolites), a variety of panic ensuing, destructive as locust or berzerking gypsy moth, he negotiates, like a subterranean rodent, the symbiosis of man (glint of steel restrained by scabbard), and woman (jellyfish), primordial vestment, as the bound marsupial is born still half embryonic to wallow in the temperate pouch.

XVI.

He had been sedulously avoiding all serious intellectual pursuit, all labour. Tandy insisted that he not alter his habits because of her presence. She said it would make her feel bad. He attempted to comply, locking himself in his study for a regulated period each day.

Tandy, who was an energetic young Homo sapiens, went for walks on these occasions:

She walked along the country road, the colours all around vivid, hues as pure as paint. The lines of the tree trunks rose up, leading the eye into their clouds of pale, rustling green. The cows in the meadows were a chocolate brown and the perfume of the grass they chewed was delicious.

Tandy sucked in the air through her small, elegant nose.

The purr of a motor sounded from behind her and, as she proceeded, grew into a low roar. She turned and watched the tractor slowly bounce along the road and advance towards her. She waved at the approach.

"Hi!" she shouted.

The tractor slowed and halted quite near. A low forehead sat beneath the straw hat; two blinking eyes appeared above those rather broad zygomas.

"How do you do, ma'am?" Alfred blushed.

"I love your tractor!"

Swallowing: "Thank you ma'am."

"Where are you going?"

"Taking these tomatoes to town."

A trailer of tomatoes was in tow, the fruits red as blood.

XVII.

"She took the car and left."

"She did not say why?" the doctor said with concern.

"I didn't ask."

Later, that evening, when he saw her at the dinner table, he thought her countenance looked particularly bright.

"You look very beautiful tonight," he remarked.

"Thank you." She put a shrimp in her mouth.

"Where were you today?"

She did not answer, but proceeded to serve herself a portion of tossed salad.

"What a wonderful salad. I love the spinach."

"Where were you today?" he repeated, setting down his knife and fork.

"Oh . . . I had to . . . go . . . to the doctor."

"Is something the matter with you?" he asked, his brows corrugating.

"Are you not aware that I have a license to practice medicine?"

She stopped chewing, swallowed, and took a sip of the white wine that sat by her side.

Her eyes opened wide.

"I'm pregnant," she said.

Dr. Black was stunned. This was far more momentous than the growth habits of any Byblis gigantea or Utriclaria. Quarks and neutrons were indeed small things, as were the expanding and contracting spasms of the universe, compared to this titbit of information.

He arose from his seat, approached her with solemn strides and, leaning over, applied a kiss to her forehead.

During the days that followed he doted on her. She was moody. He was gentle. He began to wear a yellow tie and print shirts. Her breasts appeared especially full, her lips especially lush.

XVIII.

She suggested that they go down to the basement.

"May I ask why?"

"Oh, you know how I am," she replied. "I like things to be dark and cool."

The note of mockery in her voice, so it seemed to him, was one of flirtation. He followed her down the steps and noticed with distaste the untidy state of the basement. A single unshaded bulb, which was the only source of light, vaguely illumined a dusty chamber scattered with various useless items: a few broken pieces of sheet rock, wine bottles, a large oaken barrel, probably a century old, a coil of rusted chain, etc.

It had always been the doctor's intention to have the place put in order and made use of.

"I will get Mr. Clovis to begin cleaning down here tomorrow," he said and kissed Tandy's hand.

She smiled as she looked down at the bald spot on the head before her.

She gripped his hair with her five free fingers and then let them drop to the back of his huge neck, which she stroked.

"Oh, you beauty," he thought, and clung to her.

She made a suggestion which somewhat startled him.

"Blindfolded?" he said. "With what?"

A pair of sleeping patches dangled from her poised thumb and forefinger.

"You would like that?" he asked, rising to his feet.

"And why not?" she counter-questioned haughtily. "Are you telling me you wouldn't?"

"I would," he replied quietly and stroked his beard.

Laughing, she put the blinds over his eyes and slapped him on the face. He was in darkness and heard her movements with amorous anticipation. The familiar rattle of chains met his ears.

"What is that dear?" he asked, knowing full well the answer.

"You'll find out," Tandy replied.

He felt weight applied to his shoulders, snake around his chest, and then bind his hands.

"You little vixen," he chuckled with the slightest hint of excitement.

"Are you my slave?" she asked.

He tried to move his arms but could not.

"I suppose, being bound to serve you," he replied, "I am your personal property—but I must say, my higher reason objects.... Proceed."

He felt an immense crack to his jaw, which sent him reeling two steps back, where he knocked his head against the wall.

"Tandy!" he yelled. "Not so rough!"

"This is better than horseback riding by candlelight," she giggled, in her most silvery voice. "On your knees, dear."

He felt himself gripped and pushed down and experienced a mingling of fear and admiration for this previously unknown strength of hers.

"Oh, you beauty," he thought and then groaned as blow upon blow fell on his back.

"Take it off," he cried. "I want to experience you exerting force. My God, but it hurts!"

The blinds were removed. To his horror it was not Tandy who stood before him, but Alfred, with shirt off and bare, virile chest, strongly reminiscent of the cave dwelling ancestors of man.

"Alfred!" the doctor gasped.

A female laugh came from one shadowed corner of the basement. Her outline could be seen, bow-shaped, with pale highlights and seemingly quivering.

"I hate to do this, Doc," Alfred said, taking him by the chain that bound his hands and yanking him to his feet.

The aperture of the wooden barrel enveloped him just subsequent to the painful kick he felt applied to his backside. His head knocked against the inside of the barrel and then, as it was heaved upright, he contacted the bottom, limbs tangled. The lid was applied and nailed shut, throwing him into complete darkness. Those familiar, erotic giggles came to him, pricking like thorns.

"What should we do with him?" she laughed.

"I guess that's up to you ma'am."

"Why don't we roll him down a hill, like in the cartoons?"

"It's whatever you want," Alfred replied. "But... "

"But? You have reservations? You don't want to obey me?"

"It's not that I don't want to obey you ma'am. It's just that his advice, honest to God, probably saved my tomato plants. They weren't getting proper drainage."

"You're such a good boy, aren't you?" she sighed.

Then there was a silence, one which the doctor could hardly be grateful for, and noise, which sickened him.

XIX.

HE STOOD, MUTE AND ABJECT IN HIS STUDY, THE SOUND OF HER laughter filtering through the book-laden walls. She was speaking to Mrs. Clovis, telling her how grateful she was about Dick and the car, the work he had done—the helpfulness of them both. There is little more cruel than to flaunt kindness to others before the despised, to parade aloof smiles before the dejected who feel a marked claim to affection.

His short stature swayed. He stepped to the window and leaned against the sill. He could hear the click of her heels on the parquet floor of the hall. Her fist knocked on the door.

The doctor cleared his throat. "Come in," he said.

Turning his head, he saw her, sheathed in a leather jacket and trousers, heels, high, ominous, like balancing daggers. Her yellow hair swept over her shoulders and her face was the blank plastic of a doll's.

"Well, the car is running fine," she said.

"I see," with a slight tremor in his voice.

"Mr. Clovis did a wonderful job."

"Yes." The doctor stared out the window. A brown leaf fell from a tree, floated slowly to the ground with pendulous motion. "He is an excellent mechanic."

Silence.

"So, I guess this is goodbye," she said lightly.

Dr. Black spun around and advanced a stride. "Why?" he groaned. "I don't see why it has to be that way."

"Because."

"Don't you think you are being a little too cruel my dear?"

"For a man who poisons small birds, that statement seems out of place."

"I . . . I am a scientist."

"And I am a woman."

He had to bend his neck back in order to meet her eyes, which glowed, dominant, a foot above his own.

"Oh, God!" he moaned, burying his head in the palms of his hands.

Later, he heard the car door slam, the wheels grind out the driveway. His hazy sockets watered with a flash of self pity, and then contracted, lids half lowered, iris, pupil, like rosary peas, Abrus precatorius, shiny red and black; toxicity at fifteen ten-thousandths a human subject's bodily weight; the drear of the book-laden study slithering over the cornea, penetrating the optic nerve. Indeed, to be strangled with strands of silk was more painful than with a rusty circlet of strong wire. All the facts, the weight of his intellect suddenly crushed him like so much baggage of granite and marble; and pinched, as a swamp of dull scissors might; ego under the strain of rejection, cast off from the clouds into the worm infested soil, to sharpen its fangs and lash out, gaining nourishment by whatever means it might. His lips curled with bitter amusement and quivered, the flavour of abasement still coating his tongue. There were those memories, like frescoes of hell; her leg raised, the ball of her foot balanced on his bowed head; and fantasies, what should have been   *him crucified on an obscene gesture of her hand, the nail, like a sharpened spade, piercing the back of his neck, slicing through his brain, which is dulled to the state of a mollusc, a limpet, while his arms are stretched, broken on her protruding and strained knuckles   naked, manacled, restrained in a dungeon, head pushed against antique stone secreting liquid filth, back lashed by her hair done up in a vicious and snapping braid   imprisoned in a minute and frigid cage, his ample flesh pushing through the tight constraint of bars—she sits atop the grill and laughs musically, her naked buttocks press through to his palpitating   whinnying form; he pushes a tremendous ball of near molten iron (glowing orange and orchestrating sizzling sounds upon his skin) up an almost perpendicular hill, her in the rear—she pokes him with her toe, teases his sparse head of hair, makes lisping promises as fire hiccoughs from the earth   him, hands and feet stapled together in the position of a roped calf, her searing, branding his side with the seal of her perversion   violent and abrasive amphibians gnaw at his limbs, entwine them with their tails, as she giggles, rocks with liquorice merriment, naked, one leg draped over the next   skew-*

ered, secured upon a red hot metal spit which she turns with a single outstretched finger, orange and blue flames crackling below, a squadron of meat-hungry, burly and stupid men form a semicircle around the scene, licking their oleaginous lips.

XX.

THE WEATHER GREW COOLER AND THE WOODED HILLSIDE BEGAN to gain tints of yellow and a deep, sad red. The creek was almost dry and its banks of smoothed stones and coarse sand took on a rich, golden colour in the early fall light.

Alfred could be seen across the field of ripe, mellow alfalfa, busy with his tomato plants, which were prospering and bursting with fruit. The dog, a mere spot at his heels, turned and barked at the house opposite, the sound carrying through the still air, shrill, defiant.

Mrs. Clovis sat on the passenger side of the front seat and watched as her husband transported the luggage down the steps and loaded it in the trunk of the car. The forest of apple trees sat to her left, the fruit ready, and much of it damaged by the society of crows and other birds that rattled in its branches. She had a small bag of profound red spheres at her feet, and another of granny smiths, green and slightly bitter, which she would transform into a set of pies once they returned home.

The doctor walked out the front door, steps somewhat unsteady, his head covered by a black felt hat which, due to its newness, was strangely incongruous with the grey batch of face beneath it, beard draping sombrely to his chest. He locked the door and strode down the steps.

"Everything in order?" he asked.

"All gassed up and ready to go," Mr. Clovis replied, slamming the trunk of the car shut. His manner had a sort of tight joviality to it, consistent with what was unsaid but was undoubtedly thought.

Both husband and wife had always viewed the doctor with a mixture of awe and indulgence: awe due to his obviously superior intelligence, social standing, and the fact that he paid their wages and therefore, to a certain extent, held their lives in his hand. There was however the other side of the coin: Dr. Black was a man so absorbed in his mental world that he might very well starve to death without someone to cook for him, and would undoubtedly be condemned to go about on foot without Dick there to perform the mundane but necessary task of keeping the car with gas and oil.

At the moment, the moment of crisis, they felt, to some extent, superior to the Doctor who had let himself be jostled by a common emotion; an emotion Mrs. Clovis had previously felt, if he were ever susceptible to, would certainly be in the position of commander-in-chief, not cast aside subordinate.

"It's disgusting," Mr. Clovis had said to her when the situation became obvious.

"Yes," she had replied, "it is disgusting to see a man let his spine be plucked out when a woman is just begging to be made to feel like a woman!"

The wild, predatory look in his plump wife's eyes had made Mr. Clovis hasten to the nearby woods, where he spent a good deal of time gathering kindling for the evening's fire.

Now the season was over. The Clovises awaited him, both positioned in the front seat of the large, American car; Mr. Clovis upright behind the steering wheel, his wife across from him, her eyes peering out the window. With a sigh the doctor took a farewell look at his country property, with its calm fall beauty. Buildings/vehicular emissions/racket and a good deal of labour awaited him, which might very well be the balm he so needed for his gored vanity. He breathed in deeply through his nose, letting the intake expand the oxygen loving organs of his chest, and then, firming up the musculature of his face, opened the door of the car and climbed into the backseat.

Mr. Clovis started the car, let it idle for a moment, and then pulled out of the driveway. The soft light filtered through the trees and patterned out over the car seat and Dr. Black's trousers and jacket. The car hit pavement, turned to the right, and purred down the road, off into the hills, a long, dull shadow stretching behind it and seeming to remain a great while, even after the vehicle had disappeared around the bend. Gravely, the sound of the motor withdrew into the distance.

Fragment

Group

A

I.

There were no dreams within those walls—only nightmares;—the living entombed like the dead. In shadows like toads; mould growing on breasts cultivated rancour spilling savage devotees of an angry God. They screamed infinite times, vomited out tones of mortification; spines writhe like snakes; spasms of hate steeped in the excrescence of bees.

"Love is my assassin."
"Love is hate."
"The day is black."
"The night is like a torch."
"Filthy water."
"Pure blood."
"Wicked prayers."
"Crime excellence."

II.

Beards

Small frail beards should be ignored. Beards should be full, vast—items around which mist gathers and pilgrims voyage to see. Beards should be long enough that they can be used as belts to hold up the trousers
black and golden beards
or
black bound
in platinum thread
orange beards
bright as hot plasma braided with
magnetic fields.

III.

THOSE THREAD-LIKE GROWTHS, WAVE AFTER WAVE, DARK NOT white yet frothy as sea foam, fell into the sink, victim of blades, first scissors then razor. The doctor was merciless; with the latter instrument he made the skin of his face smooth. His left hand was a blur as he cranked the water faucet on. He rinsed and then, looking in the mirror, saw his face round and the colour of alabaster.

"Just like a little boy," he murmured to himself, running the fingers of his right hand over his left cheek and then jaw.

He turned, let his gaze rest for a moment over the rolling hills green with grapevines; the dramatic blue sky in which he could imagine his own head floating, endowed with a pair of rainbow-hued wings, mouth open in sweet song: Dr. Black, Cherub. Then, after letting his right hand caress the rotundity of his belly which was bisected by a stripe of thick black hair, he took up the cloth, the wimple, and put it over his head, drew its folds about his chin. He then sheathed his body in a navy blue full-length skirt with elasticated waistband and a long-sleeved bodice of the same material with round-neck and hook-and-eye fasteners at the front. A starched white collar completed the costume. He turned back towards the mirror, opened his eyes wide, delighted with the vision of the plump and sober nun before him.

IV.

"Poverty, chastity and obedience," he said in an altered voice, soft and exaggeratedly effeminate.
"I have looked over your paperwork... letters of recommendation."
"I hope they satisfy you."
"Your history appears to be exemplary."
The doctor bowed his head.
"Our convent however is different from others. Life here is far from easy. Once you enter our numbers, you are dead to the outside world."
"So much the better."
"And we require a high degree of allegiance. The abbess is not to be trifled with. Obedience and loyalty are our creed. This place is for the chosen few, the elite of woman kind."
"I long for regulations."
"Now here—sign this contract in your blood." And taking out a little pen-knife, she pierced the doctor's fingers and handed him a quill.
He signed: Sister Nero.

V.

The abbey was situated against the Valdez mountains: rocky spikes three-quarters submerged in pine forest. Behind high and massive walls, protecting it from the intrusion of seculars, from the rays of the sun, lay the huge, rambling building. It had a cruciform church with a nave of nine bays/extensive cellars/scriptorium/chambers/calefactory/vestiarium. buildings for the most part combined, with just a few detached. bakehouse. infirmary. barns. To the east many acres of ancient orchard: half-rotten trunks which bled green shoots. The main entrance, on the north side, was defended by three separate iron doors.

"Sister Martinez will show you to your quarters."

The doors closed behind him. Now there was no turning back.

He was led through the cold and empty hallways of the convent, up and down steps, around numerous corners, to the northern cloister. A low door let out a short, shrill cry as she opened it.

"You will find your schedule pinned to the door," she said.

The doctor looked in her eyes, which were like dead coals, bowed his head solemnly, and entered.

He looked about his cell: a wooden box-bedstead with woollen blankets, and a mattress of straw, a table for meals, a single straight-backed, hard-bottomed chair. A large wooden crucifix was affixed to the wall above the bed. That was all.

He sat down and let out a sigh.

"Knowledge comes at a dear price," he thought.

He stroked his naked chin; lower extremity of the face pathetic as a shaved dog.

*Dr. Black
and the
Guerrilla*

I.

THE MOUNTAINS WERE THE COLOUR OF CHRYSOPRASE. THE TRAIN rattled over the joints of the tracks, passed through fincas sprinkled red with coffee beans and over precipitous bridges, the white froth of rivers raging far below. The windows of the carriage were all half down. The doctor relaxed his gaze on the luxuriant countryside. The delicate murmur of Spanish reached his ears.

"Sí, así és..."

"...Oh no, no tienen nada en contra de las ideas; solamente a los que las divulgan."

"Las ideas son peligrosas..."

"Claramente."

"....mejor aún...la Guerrilla de la Luz Ardiente..."

Clickety-clack.

He had an attack of drowsiness. When he awoke the sun was setting. Evening swept over the jungle and it changed; into something perilous— a whispering mass of black waves which lurked beneath primordial orange, the newborn sky of night. The carriage was dark and the people within were silhouettes and shadows; a few murmured together in low, indistinguishable tones; he heard an old man's voice, which was like rust[1].

At Los Moscadinos, the doctor took up his duffle bag and deboarded, as did a few other passengers, who then quickly disappeared into the dark. The station was empty; huge moths beat against the single light

---

1. He, Dr. Black, polymath and great phytographist, foremost of amateur nephologists, etc., is in San Corrados, where he is conducting researches for his mammoth study *A Key to All Gods*, id est, he is attempting to locate the Yaroa tribe and investigate their practices regarding the deity Apozitz.

that illuminated the signboard. Orthopterous insects crunched beneath his feet. He made his way onto the street, which was paved with bricks. A few men were sitting in front of a shop opposite him, on empty crates, smoking cigarettes and muttering together in low voices.

He approached and smelled the stale smell of drunkenness.

"Does anyone know which direction to take for the Hotel San Salvador?" he asked.

Eight malevolent eyes looked at him.

"Hotel San Salvador," he repeated.

"Not... goddamned Oficina de Turismo," one man grunted.

"Forty pesos," said another.

"... part of Trujillo's death squad," said a third.

The men were drunk on aguardiente; martyring themselves on the public street in the name of poverty and hopelessness while their wives and mothers wept at home, praying to Our Lady of Desperate Hours in the shape of six peso reproductions (40 x 50 cm framed matted prints, and 25 cm cold-cast resin statuettes) inspired by the miraculous picture kept at La Cienega[1].

The doctor looked at the fourth, an emaciated and ragged individual whose tongue was pressed delicately between his teeth, as if he were caught frozen in the process of lisping.

"The Hotel San Salvador," Black asked; "tell me amigo, where is it?"

The man did not answer, but simply pointed up the street; and the doctor turned and walked in that direction, hearing laughter behind him. In San Corrados there were many kinds of laughter. There was the laughter of joy and the laughter of derision. There were loud bursts and soft chuckles. The girls laughed flowers, and the politicians laughed

---

1. This village, 20 miles north of Los Moscadinos, claims that its icon of Our Lady has been repainted by the touch of the Supreme Being. After some of the paint on the icon in the local church had been removed for restoration, it was miraculously repainted in the middle of the night by a hand so expert that all who saw the work called it unearthly. Villagers believe the painting is protected by divine power. Tradition has it that a band of the country's worst thieves and drunkards once tried to steal it, but suddenly broke down in tears, and thereafter lived the lives of honest citizens.

venom. The rich men laughed with self-satisfaction, and the poor gave the laughter of misery, of resignation; and then there was the laughter of defiance.

Black himself, when he finally found the Hotel San Salvador, let go an audible expulsion of air from his lungs,—but not laughter. He sighed as he looked up at: a seedy and ill-kept edifice; peeling pink paint and cracked walls. A vague light crept through curtained windows which were shielded by iron bars. The doctor rang the bell. A few moments later a man in a wheelchair, with a face like a chisel, opened the door.

"I believe you have a reservation; for a Black,—Dr. Black."

The man paused for a moment and stared penetratingly into the doctor's eyes, before replying. "Yes," he said, "we have a room with a bed."

He back-wheeled, and Black entered.

"Alejandro!" the man called out, and an instant later an obsequious and dirty looking youth made his appearance and showed the doctor upstairs. A white door with a brown patch of dirt around the handle. When the light to the room was turned on, he saw a mouse scurry across the floor and disappear into a small aperture in the wall. The only furniture: a single chair, a zinc-topped table and a bed. It was a room, still tainted by the spirits of dead love-making, bed-wetting and probable suicide.

"It is not unlike a jail cell," the doctor thought, and then said aloud: "Is this the best chamber in the castle?"

The young man shrugged his shoulders and gave a meaningless smile. After receiving a few coins, he turned and left. Black set down his duffle bag, unbuttoned his shirt and lay upon the bed. His forehead glistened with sweat. From somewhere in the night he heard the sound of a badly played guitar. He stared up at the yellow stains on the ceiling: one was in the shape of the Hebrew letter *lamed*, another a Stillson wrench. He closed his eyes and experienced the residual movement of the train: as often occurs upon the termination of a long rail voyage, he still felt as if he were physically in motion; and the gears of his mind were turning. Thoughts flowed in layers, arranged themselves in his brain in classificatory divisions, beginningless ideas and images and endless conceptions. Adhering strictly to fact, the moment was for him a large pad containing a framework of metal springs which supported his reclining body, yet San Corrados was for his imagination, which was the revelation of science and as profound as the human soul, still a banquet of wonderful things:

1. Anthropological and archaeological studies
   a. Local divisions of aboriginal peoples
      i. In preparation for marriage, the females of the Vacotocha tribe are placed in baskets in the huts of their future in-laws and must remain suspended over an open fire of jacaranda wood unceasingly for a period of three months. The Vacotocha are known for their use of a number of hallucinogens in magico-religious practices. They have a rich and complex set of theological concepts and believe that every human being is endowed with three souls.
      ii. The Guaya live in the south-western region of the country, along the Río de la Muerte and its tributaries. The men wear loin cloths dyed red from the onoto berry. Their peculiar wardress consists of grass skirts and long blond (zeñojañe) grass wigs. Their diet is made up in a large part of the succulent, greasy larvae of Caryobruchus known as 'etéme', which they skewer or wrap in leaves and gently roast, or, occasionally, consume raw. Guaya marriage restrictions include sib and phratry exogamy. Since the first European contacts, the population of this tribe has diminished disastrously (new diseases, deliberate campaigns of extermination).
      iii. The Ajaja Muajaja, or Monkey Sucking Tribe, live only in a few remote villages of the rain forest of San Corrados. Only a handful of outsiders have come in contact with them. Communication is difficult as their language consists of a series of whooping sounds, which have never been properly researched by anthropologists. They are a matriarchal society. Each female, of child-bearing age, wears, almost by way of decoration, a baby monkey on each breast. They have also been known to breastfeed small pigs and raccoons. Communities range in size from 8 to 100 people. Though in previous times they ate their dead, as a way of keeping their loved ones with them forever, their

current custom is to store them in large jars placed inverted in the earth.
    iv. Most importantly, the Yaroa: little studied, reputed worshippers of the god Apozitz, that mysterious senior deity. Their language is closely related to Jorá. As yet, their only contact with white men has been limited, for the most part, to the occasional killing of rubber tappers, gold-prospectors and missionaries.
  b. Flagelantes
    i. Maria of Monte Carmelo: pleasure and delight, thoughts on love while whipping herself with leathern thongs / two raw red patches / Sisterhood of Penance.
    ii. The Brotherhood of the Iron Candle flagellate themselves twice a day. Discalced, they proceed gradually to the public square, where they strip to the waist and prostrate in a large circle—each one, by his posture, signifying the nature of the sins he wishes to expiate, the murderer lying on his back, the adulterer on his face, the bearer of false witness on one side holding up three fingers, etc. First they let themselves be beaten by the Master, and then, after rising to their feet, stand in a line and scourge themselves ruthlessly, crying out that their over-hot blood is being merged with the cooling Blood of Christ and that their penance is the only thing preserving the whole world from the flames of absolute destruction.
    iii. The Disciplinaries of Christ Jesus/auto-flagellate/butterfly-shaped bruises/faces covered.
    iv. Brotherhood of the Purple Silence/my father beat you with whips, but I will beat you with scorpions/strike themselves solely with glass-laden wooden paddles/occasional ritual crucifixions.
2. The broad range of nature
  a. The giant tree rat of San Corrados, a pale grey animal, streaked with white from head to snout and belonging to the abracomid family (a peculiar bouquet of frantic mammals). These are, it would seem, the same creatures which were kept as pets by the ancient Incas, their skeletons having been found in the tombs of their owners.

b. mountains / frozen cones of fire ...... / ...... waters[1]
c. Plasmodial slime moulds
> (*The scene occurs upon a vast expanse of decaying leaves and bark, rich in both perfume and colour.*)
> *Ceratiomyxa fruticulosa* [in the form of a poroid crust]. x*YzzPy*!
> *Physarum cinereum.* Ks ... ss ... *k* ... ss*k* ... ss.
> *Ceratiomyxa fruticulosa.* P*y*! P*yzzzzzzzzzz*!
> *Physarum cinereum.* ss*k*?
> *Ceratiomyxa fruticulosa. zzzzzzzzzzzz*!
> (*Enter stage left* LICEA OPERCULATA, *extraordinarily long of stalk, and sporting chestnut-coloured sporocarps.*)
> *Licea operculata.* rrrrrrrrrrrrrrrrrrrj. mmRj. jm. jm.
> *Ceratiomyxa fruticulosa*: z*Pz*! [*Aside.*
> (*Enter stage right* PHYSARUM SUPERBUM, *bright and eye-catching with golden-orange plasmodiocarps;—permiscuous.*)
> *Physarum superbum.* eeeiiooyioyoyeeaaayooyooiyuuyyyaaiio-iaiao ...
> *Physarum cinereum.* Ks ... ssk*ss*.

... The concentrated sauce of his ideas.

---

1. flowwefallcontinuecontinuouslytocascadefrotharoundrockswetsofsosweetlyt-musical ...

II.

THE NEXT MORNING THINGS SEEMED SOMEWHAT MORE CHEERFUL. His bus did not leave for Azúcar until 11:30 a.m., so he had time to expend....

Children played in the streets and stern-faced women could be seen making their way up to the church, to pray to Our Lady of Perpetual Hope[1]. The doctor breakfasted on café con leche and pan dulce. The coffee was sweet and good and the pastry fresh, with a crust of pink sugar on its surface. He then walked along the main street and smoked a cigar, an object of curiosity; circumnavigated the plaza, letting his vision drift over the giant and luminous blooms of the datura with which that public square was adorned and the pigeons strutting over the cobbles.

---

1. The image of Our Lady of Perpetual Hope is a mere three inches high, and is carved in a simple, almost naive manner from a dark, fine-grained steatite. The statuette is displayed in a large silver monstrance which magnifies its appearance. While searching for edible mushrooms outside of the then small village of Los Moscadinos, on the 4th of October, 1702, a poor mestizo woman by the name of Maria Martinez found this little image of the Virgin sitting beside the footpath. She brought it home with her, but it soon vanished, only to be rediscovered later at its original location. After the statue had repeated this behavior sixteen more times the inhabitants of the area finally took this to mean that Our Lady wanted a shrine built there, which was done, and it is today visited by thousands of pilgrims each year.

III.

THE BUS, DASHBOARD DECORATED WITH A BRIGHTLY-COLOURED statuette of St. Jude and garlands of latex flowers, was crowded. The vehicle drove madly along a poorly paved and precipitous road. They drove past fields: men on horseback moved through cows and half naked children waved from the front of half dilapidated cottages. The smell of manure, drifting through the open windows, invoked a vivid memory: his uncle's ranch in Wyoming, where as a boy he sometimes spent his summers.... And then there was the smell of isoamyl acetate. He turned his head. A woman next to him was eating a banana.

The bus passed a huge patch of brown dirt, a mining operation, where the forest had been bulldozed away to expose bauxite deposits. The massive naked roots of great tropical trees hung out along the edge of the clearing like the arteries from the neck of a slaughtered cow. Huge yellow vehicles, like fantastic beasts, moved through the earth and gnawed at the forest, as if famished. The doctor inhaled the smell of upturned earth, heard the sound of distant chainsaws. Then the bus turned and rolled along the side of a hill, past a rocky cliff face and then into the town which sat at the bottom of in a declivity, a nest of shacks and newly constructed, concrete domiciles. It was dirty and sad. An unwholesome odour hung in the air: one of liquor, cheap tobacco, excrement of livestock and sour poverty. It was a place where the only flourishing enterprises were prostitution and shops catering to miners and adventurers; a place where humans rotted, putrefied in the overhumid air of the jungle, beneath the sharp arrows of the sun.

When he got off the bus the doctor stood and waited for Díaz, who was to be his guide. Jack Brown[1] had recommended him as an admirable backland expert, and the doctor had great faith in Jack.

---

1. A good friend of the doctor's. Much mentioned in his private papers.

Dr. Black and the Guerrilla 63

He lit a cigar; made a few notes in his diary; ran a hand through the thicket of his beard; bought a slice of watermelon and ate it; composed an intricate mathematical equation with a stick in the dust; rubbed his eye-sockets; and asked his way to the house of Díaz, carrying his duffle bag: weary and rationally downcast. An air of squalor and poverty pervaded every street and every house that he passed.... Then he found himself at the edge of town......The words 'The Devil Lives Here!' were spray-painted along the side of an abandoned shack. His shoes squeaked as he walked and he could feel his socks falling down his shins; he heard the sucking sound of an airplane, a jet in the distance.... He found the street and then the house. A few chickens scratched in the yard. He knocked on the door. A fat woman dressed in black answered.

"Excuse me Señora," he said. "Is this the house of Casildo Díaz?"

"It is."

"Is he at home and, if not, do you know when he will return? I spoke with him on the telephone a week ago, so he should be expecting me. I am a client."

"He is dead. He was shot three days ago. The guerrillas shot him." And, in a sorrowful voice, she told her story, not at all uncommon, of how the guerrillas, the Flaming Light Guerrillas, had tried to recruit her husband, but he had refused. As a revenge, she claimed, they gave his name anonymously to the police as a rebellion conspirator and the police, a highly immoral body, had come to his house and arrested him.... "He was found in a ditch a few days later."

The doctor solemnly offered the woman his condolences. He then explained his own position: as a man without a place to stay, in need of someone to assist him to travel through the jungle, to reach and contact the Yaroa tribe.

"Come in," she said. "I have a sick child in the house. And it is a house of mourning. You can sleep here tonight. But tomorrow you must go."

The interior was dark. A portrait photo of a handsome man with a large jaw was set amidst flowers and burning candles. A child yanked at the doctor's pant leg, and he gently brushed it aside. That evening he ate blood sausages with Señora Díaz and her offspring: the small one, a healthy little girl, maybe six, the older a feverish boy of twelve, thin and pale, who smiled weakly as he sipped at a broth specially prepared for him. Later Black examined the child, and questioned the mother, thereby finding out that he was employed as a part-time worker at a relative's sugarcane plantation at the edge of town.

"I believe your son is suffering from some sort of pesticide related illness. Probably from some mixture of glyphosate and Cosmo-Flux 411F.... RoundUp Ultra.... Toxic stuff.... This is no flu.... Have him stay away from the plantation. He is an intelligent boy, and that is not the correct work for him."

He slept on the couch, the flicker of the candles of mourning illuminating the room throughout the night...... wavering shadows...

IV.

"YOU NEED A GUIDE. THERE IS A MAN NAMED JESÚS CHUAYO IN town who sometimes worked with my husband. He has his problems, but is honest. It is Saturday, so you will surely find him stationed in front of the Bar Rita, with all the other backlanders."

It was Saturday and the town was full of drunk aluminium miners and Indians from the interior selling their produce: chayote, bitter manioc, squash, bunches of sugarcane, citrus fruits and tobacco—the whole making up a mass of colourful spots, like a painting by Seurat. A young boy sold caged parrots. At the livestock market pigs squealed and goats bleated. Men on cross-country motorcycles roared up and down the road and others, shirtless, leaned out of the windows of brothels, moustaches limp, cigarettes dangling from passion-coated mouths.

The doctor passed by a withered old curandera, selling love potions, charms to ward off evil spirits: asafoetida powder, dried seahorses, bottles of dove's blood, candles, green, red and white, painted with magico-religious symbols; an antifertility potion made from the bark of the icoja tree; and then picho huayo, the leaves of Siparuna guianensis to be used as an aphrodisiac.

His eye was attracted by a group of half a dozen men, walking down the road two abreast, bare to their waists. One of the foremost bore a great wooden cross on his shoulder while the others, like weakened debauchees wishing to goad on their diminished power, whipped their own backs with knotted scourges, chanting together a melancholy canticle of the Passion of Christ while blood coursed from their flesh. These were the Disciplinaries of Christ Jesus making their way from village to village. He followed their movements, watched as they walked past a whore house, a Chinese restaurant, and then past a group of aboriginal looking men standing in front of a bar. The doctor raised his eyes and saw the lettering: Bar Rita.

As he approached, a stoutly built individual with a hatchet face and long, oily hair stumbled up against him, breathing out anise-flavoured breath and murmuring words of melancholy inebriation. Black contemptuously pushed the man away and stepped towards the group.

"I am looking for Jesús Chuayo," he said, speaking in a profound voice and stretching his little legs so as to appear taller.

The men laughed.

"Señor, Jesús is drunk on aguardiente. He is the man you just passed."

The doctor turned his head and saw the man stumble along, back bent, arms slackly hanging at his sides.

"Does he normally drink so early?" he asked.

"You better ask him, Señor. Around here we don't talk about our friends to strangers."

The doctor took a few paces in pursuit of the receding drunkard, in a slow gait began to follow, not at all sure if he even wanted to catch him. The smell of frying tucumanas. The sound of a spirited avocado vendor. And then, appearing before him like a jack-in-the-box, was an individual with a large chest and a picaresque smile, one of those Indians who moments before had stood before the Bar Rita.

"Señor . . . !"

"Yes?"

"I am Júnior."

"And?"

"Do not trust that man. Do not trust Chuayo, he is a drunkard and a thief."

"I thought that, in this area of the world, it was inappropriate to talk about one's friends to strangers?"

"It is. But Chuayo is not my friend."

"I need to find an honest guide."

"I am an honest guide," the man said. "I am from the Grilled Cat tribe. My people do not lie and steal like these others. If you trust the other he will rob you, maybe even kill you in the night. But I am from the Grilled Cat tribe and like white people. . . . And I have letters of recommendation.... And, anyhow, as you can see, he is too drunk to be of service to you now."

The doctor, though certainly putting no faith in the man's credentials, did see his logic regarding Jesús's inability to function and did also very much want to be on his way. He invited Júnior to a restaurant where, over fruit juice and chupe, they reached a price for services. With the Indian's help, the doctor later that afternoon purchased two good stout mules and laden them with provisions: with food, blankets and rifles.

That night he slept at the whore house, the colourful language of San Corrados drifting through the thin walls, occasional cries of intoxicated passion piercing them.

Early the next morning they set out, making their way along a narrow dirt road and then a footpath that led through an upland meadow dominated by large dew-covered herbs of the genus Stegolepis in the monocotyledonous family Rapateaceae. The doctor felt exhilarated to finally be on his way to the interior, into the clean tropical forest and away from the seedy squalor of the towns. He stopped, looked over the mist-filled valleys and breathed in the fresh air which was perfumed with the vapours of myriad living organisms.

"That is the bush," Júnior said. "No more civilisation. A white man could not survive there alone. He could not survive without a good guide like me."

"Júnior, I am not attempting to passively exist in the jungle. I need you to lead me to the village of the Yaroa, not rate my skills as a survivalist."

The Indian shrugged his shoulders and continued walking. Then, as if to himself: "Still, many kidnappings, untimely disappearances."

And they descended from the hilly uplands into the vast ocean of green; away from the advanced and clamant states of human society.

V.

THE DAYS GO BY...

Dr. Black's head ducked under branches, the narrow bands of his legs carried the bulk of his person through land striking in appearance (strange / glamorous).

Dense, often nearly impenetrable vegetation, would give way to rolling plains and this again would be swallowed up by jungle lush and alive with thousands of plants and murmuring insects. Visual perfume: creepers hanging down from the tall and purple-flowering Caesalpiniaceae, forming a complex network of fibres; flowers shaped like hearts, others like estoiles; the moist surface of brightly-coloured frogs, there in almost biblical numbers, and growing from the forest floor delicate mushrooms with fimbrillate caps. Trees raised themselves out from dead trees; some clubfooted, others saddlebacked; the bentlimbed and hunchbacked, then strange spindly giants; the sound of water dripping from so many, which were full of birds, peach-fronted parakeets and helmeted manikins; from canopy to base: a vast assortment of small air-breathing arthropods. Clicking. Chirping. He marvelled at a yellow mombin tree, upon which he found a full thirty-six species of ant. There were black-water rivers along the banks of which grew many varieties of superb orchids. They passed by roaring waterfalls and over precarious bridges made of woven grass.

Júnior, with his rifle, shot an ant-eater. They picketed the mules on a grassy hillside.

Darkness falls...

Júnior roasted the flesh of the ant-eater over the fire and served it with slices of lime and boiled yucca. The doctor ate with a good appetite and after dinner lit a cigar and drank from a flask of rye whisky.

"Do you want a drink Júnior?"

"No, thank you patrón. I do not drink while working."

His smiling face was red in the glow of the flames and reminded the doctor of one of those bizarre demons by Stefan Lochner. The doctor felt mellowed by the heavy food, the whisky and the grey mixture of gasses and suspended carbon particles resulting from the combustion of his cigar.

"It is a beautiful night," he murmured. "Wonderfully peaceful."

"Yes," said the Indian. "It is on such nights that the kharisiri come out."

"Kharisiri?"

"The predatory ghouls that live in this forest."

The doctor chuckled. "And what do they do, these ghouls?" he asked with a smile.

"They are blood stealers. They steal people's blood and sell it to foreigners."

"Charming.... Maybe I will purchase a few centavos worth."

"Originally they were noblemen who died in childbirth. They stalk travellers and they are horrible to look at, with shrivelled flesh that is as white as chalk and they have death's heads tattooed on their thighs."

Black's cigar was smoked half way through, its flavour no longer fresh. He threw the remaining half onto the coals of the fire and Júnior deftly snatched it up. As he puffed at the butt, a dense cloud of smoke momentarily concealed his face.

"There are many spirits in these forests," he said. "There are spirits of black stones, of plants and many types of animal spirits.... A cousin of mine found trouble with one—when he was walking home... after dark.... He met a group of merry bats, and they invited him to drink aguardiente with them in a bacurí tree and he accepted. One of their number was a female of great beauty. He was attracted to her and came back the next night and drank with her and flirted and kissed her lips and touched her face.... So every night he would go and flirt with her and he began to fall really in love—slowly changing all the while, with a bat's head and claws ... ears. ... And finally, his wife, who understood what was happening and was a proud woman, built up a fire under the tree, burning it down and killing both her husband and the bats. A year or so later she ran off with a garimpeiro and is now living in Los Moscadinos, shaming herself in whoredom."

The doctor curled up in his blanket, looked up at the sky, at the throbbing stars, and listened to the sounds of the jungle. Demons, spirits, exsanguinating ghouls? He did not know. He slept; entered upon the gallop of his dreams.

Next day ...

He awoke in the pewter light of morning, and was surprised not to detect Júnior preparing breakfast, not to smell coffee brewing ...

"Lazy ... " he murmured.

He felt his own tongue in his mouth, thick and dry like a piece of driftwood.

... His mind cleared, his consciousness emerged from the residue of sleep. He sat up and looked around himself. There was no Júnior. ... The area was still and empty. Aside from the blanket he had been sleeping under, and his own pants, shirt and jacket, which he had used as a pillow, all the gear of the little camp was absent.

He sat up and scratched two or three areas of his body, then arose and dressed.

"Júnior!" he called out in a hoarse voice.

There was no reply. Dr. Black strode to the grassy slope. The mules were no longer there. Guns, equipment, food (even the remains of the roasted ant-eater),—all were gone. The Indian had bolted.

"My cigars," the doctor murmured. And then, "... the snake would not drink with me, I suppose, because it would have been a bond of friendship. ... If I could just give the thief a good inguinal kick!"

And it was quite obvious, at least for the present, that he would have to give up on his project. Charting that deity of the Yaroa would have to wait for a more propitious time. He did not know the jungle. Finding his way back to civilisation, to a serving of pique macho and a cold cerveza,

Dr. Black and the Guerrilla 71

was the main priority. Using his Swiss army knife, he cut a slit in the middle of the blanket, slipped his head and beard through the opening, and wore it as a poncho. He found his walking stick leaning against a tree and took it. For a moment he stood and looked at the dead ashes of the campfire. Then he grunted and turned, his slender legs proceeded to take him through the jungle; survival the order of the day:

Navigating by the sun,

Sucking liquid from water vines.

"The pleasures of travelling," he murmured as he made his way through an area of marshy grass, phlebotomic insects, jejéns and maraguís, yaguasas and mosquitoes buzzing in his ears, biting the back of his neck.

He felt hunger and came to a considerable-sized, pyramidal-crowned abiu, a tree heavy with elliptical yellow fruit, ripe and ready to be eaten. With the aid of his walking stick the doctor managed to knock several down. He laid out his blanket against the base of the perennial plant, sat and proceeded to eat that perfectly ripe and deliciously sweet tissue, caramel flavoured, peeling away the skin and revealing the fragrant white pulp in which sat four oblong seeds, brown, with a pale hilum on one side of each.

His hunger in some measure satisfied, he closed his eyes, let his thoughts wander over the tracts of his intellect. . . . . . . Grown weary, he napped.

―――――

"I may be somewhat behind on my ophiological studies, but none the less I believe I would be correct to say that I am in the grip of a python."

VI.

Apido's Narrative

I LEARN MEDICINE FROM THE SPIRITS OF THE PLANTS. I HEAR THE souls of the trees. I am the headman, the doctor of my people.

The purgative taught me. The roots taught me. Green organs, they taught me.

Ayahuma, the plant spirit without a head, told me to go. He told me to go out and trek half a day's journey and look near the black water of the river.

Together with Quispe, my apprentice, the second cousin of my wife's brother, I went. He knows the tongue of the civilizados. I know some tongue of the civilizados. But only we. We, the henchmen of Apozitz, are knowledge built.

Along the way I forested. I picked the sacred honi xuma, the vine of souls, while Quispe sang the song of the erectile-crested seriema. The day was good and full of beauty. Squatting in the sun, we lunched on stpaykt[1]. The water whispered and we lunched on his stpaykt.

We then walked. We walked a great many steps. We walked and came to a secluded glade.

Against a cauje tree the stranger sat. His neck was as thick as its trunk. He was interwrapped by Anaconda who wanted to steal him bodily. She wished to swallow him and take him to her world beneath the water. His face was covered with hair and his body, which was thick as the belly of a pregnant matron, was covered in a sand-coloured skin like those worn by the people of the cities and the people of the mines.

Quispe, with a projectile from his blowgun, his faithful slave, pierced

---

1. The aquatic larvae of dobsonflies.

the neck of the Anaconda. The muscles of its body relaxed; I witnessed its spirit leap from its eyes and travel across the thread which bound it to the river.

And the man arose from the coil of flesh offering with his hand the sign of universal peace. I offered up prayers to Apaec, the deity of the serpents, and asked for forgiveness for the slaughter and received in return the auspicious sign of the bird in the sky. We led him back to the village; and all the eyes of my people were on him. At my hut I invited him to sit and called on Ka'ata, the third daughter of my brother's wife's cousin, to come and pick the lice from his hair; but at this he grew unpleasant and uttered words in a voice like thunder.

VII.

M<small>EANWHILE</small>...

Júnior made his way merrily along the bank of the Rio Meixueiro, puffing on the doctor's cigars and sipping at his whisky. Certainly his people of the Grilled Cat tribe—the greatest group of thieves in all of South America—would be proud of him, for having stripped the gringo so clean of his possessions.

...... startled ......

... an erroneous move would result in a lethal shower of darts delivered by the world's most skilful dart-blowers....

Fade to: Primitive housing. Small garden plots. Two stout young men (warriors), wearing only the G-string, with labrets on the lower lip, forcefully escorting Júnior to the hut of the village headman. His, Apido's, face was a labyrinth of wrinkles and he wore a necklace made of beetles. Dignified, he stood with Dr. Black.

Júnior gave a forced laugh. "Señor Doctor," he said. "Finally I have found you."

Apido pointed to the backland expert. "He killed the sacred ant-eater," he said. "He has been discovered in our forest with the flesh of the sacred tapir, the flesh of my people, who upon demise are reborn as tapirs. He has revelled in sin against Nuxi, and the Yaroa people, and according to our tradition, he must pay the ultimate penalty."

"Death," the doctor murmured gravely, recalling how the ancients of that region treated their victims: skinning them alive, draining and drinking their blood ... sometimes one would be tossed in an open pit, left to be eaten by ants and flies ... at others they were dismembered, their limbs scattered over the landscape, or sometimes used as trophies.

"No," said Apido, "my people only put those we honour in some degree

Dr. Black and the Guerrilla 75

to death. We will not stain our soil with blood of weakling. This man, this vehicle of evil, will suffer the fate he deserves for his sacrilege."

"Patrón," Júnior cried out in horror, "you have to save me!"

"My dear fellow," Black responded coolly, "I believe you seriously exaggerate my moral obligations to you, as, from the moment you made off with my cigars and whisky, you terminated any of those implied contractual commitments which exist between employer and employed. From my informed and experienced, though at this moment admittedly biased point of view, the village headman here has a point when he refers to you as a vehicle of evil deserving of a certain dishonourable fate; and indeed I must refuse to interfere with the aboriginal traditions of his tribe."

Apido prepared a brew of three parts the powdered iridescent blue wings of the male Morpho menelaus butterfly, one part the red seeds of the shrub Bixa orellana, and one part a variety of stramonium called yawa maikiua;—all boiled together with mishquipanga fruit.

"What is he doing?" the doctor whispered to Quispe.

"He will change him into a dog," the other replied.

The tribesmen held Júnior down while a truly awful practice was enacted: a mangy and miserable dog was brought forward and slain by Apido, who drove a dagger into its breast and tore out its heart, which he forced the Grilled Cat Indian to eat. After stripping the canine of its hide and tying it to the back of the malefactor, the shaman then poured the potion down the latter's throat, one of the young warriors having violently forced open his mouth. Apido murmured under his breath, made signs with his hands, and engraved a picture of a dog on Júnior's chest.

That evening: a young woman wearing a banana-leaf bra and a grass skirt dyed bright crimson with the juice of the achiote berry as well as a garter of parrot down around her knee signifying her virginity served the doctor boiled muscovy duck and air potatoes seasoned with ají. He slept in a hut thatched with fronds of the cohune palm and could hear the coquí (tree frogs) sing. In the days that followed: He taught Quispe how to tie a

Matthew Walker knot, while the young man in turn demonstrated how to make that velvet-black juice called curare from the barks of *Strychnos toxifera* and *Chondrodendron tomentosum, and then the fish poisons: timiu and masu, a*s well as elaborate traps for birds. The doctor took notes of the daily habits of the tribe, indulged himself in anthropological recreations, gravely watched the women prepare yucca and their local beverage: a drink made from peach palm fruit (Bactrix gasipaes); them giggling under the glint of his eyes; certain maidens, slim grasshoppers, sending his way dazzling ultratropical smiles. He composed a brief vocabulary of the Yaroa language, heavy in frictionless continuants and flapped palato-alveolar consonants, as well as ingressive, implosive speech sounds produced by suction occlusion and plosive release, which facilitated him in basic communication with the tribespeople.

VIII.

"Where is Quispe?"

"He cannot leave his hut."

The doctor made his way there, curious as to why he had not seen the young man, whom he had grown very fond of, for several days.

The young Indian lay on a bed of foliage with his hands on his belly and legs spread wide apart. He panted and breathed heavily. The doctor questioned him and noted the man's symptoms which consisted of: leg cramps, mood swings, dizziness, nausea and abdominal pain.

"I hurt here," the man grunted, pointing to his swollen belly.

Apido entered the hut. "His wife is giving birth," he said gravely. "She is at the residence of her mother."

The doctor was fascinated by Quispe's reaction to his wife's parturition and recalled Professor von den Steinen's studies of the couvade.

"He is asserting his paternity," the doctor thought; and then asked aloud: "Why don't you get up my friend?"

"No," Quispe murmured weakly. "If I walk, I will trample on the head of my unborn child.... If I hunt, I will slaughter it."

"You are weak, you need to eat properly"

"No, if I eat the meat of the water-haas, my son will be born with buck teeth.... If I eat the rhinoceros beetle, he will have too big a nose...."

He began to howl. A young girl came running to the hut and informed those present that Quispe's wife had just given birth to a boy. Apido went off and returned a short while later with the baby in his arms. He showed the child to Quispe and then, taking out his dagger, made an incision in the right forearm of the latter. He drained off a quantity of blood and rubbed it on the child after which the father seemed much appeased.

IX.

BLACK WAS INSTRUCTED IN RITUAL, UNDERWENT INITIATIONS; A long exposure beneath a roaring waterfall; ceremonial wrestling; and viewing of the sacred musical instruments: a horn made from the arm bone of some ancient enemy, shrill and mournful of tone, the kespix, the bull-roarer which breathed sounds which excite men, and the two-holed flute, the sight and noise of which was forbidden to females and children. And for three days he was only allowed to eat food prepared by a postmenopausal woman.

"You wish to meet Apozitz?"

"Very much," the doctor said.

"Come."

Apido led him through the jungle—really but a short way, to an area thickly overgrown with bush.

"The Temple of the Under-River," Apido said.

The doctor looked at the pyramidical stone structure, interwrapped, strangled by jungle vines—obviously very old indeed; and he could tell at a glance that the bulk of it lay beneath the ground, having been buried by time, by layer upon layer of vegetable matter. It seemed to have been constructed more or less on the system of the Pirca, using some variety of glue-like argillaceous earth to join the stones. To find such a building in the midst of those pluvial forests was certainly noteworthy.

After lighting a balsa–bark torch, the headman led the doctor through an opening in the side of the structure. They walked through long galleries, the walls of which were covered with intonaci of red clay, red pigmentation. The place was a veritable maze, with hallways stretching in all directions. It was obvious that a whole network of underground passages existed beneath the jungle.

"In the golden age," Apido explained as they walked "the gods inhabited these forests. They ruled over my people, endowed us with great knowledge, and made us lords of the land. And so we prospered.... There was much corn; the people wore rich jewellery; our warriors went to battle dressed in garments of vicuña.... Then, in the year zero, the year 9,063 BC according to the calendar of you white barbarians, the gods for the most part left...."

The two men now stood in an arrow-shaped chamber which was decorated with vibrant frescoes of vicious dwarfs and strange deities with serpentine hairdos. The room had a distinctive single sustaining column, carved in monolithic stone, placed in its centre.

"At present," Apido continued, making a broad gesture that seemed to indicate some powerful and near distant force approaching: "At present your people drill under the mountains and rise into the sky in the stomachs of great white vultures.... You cut down the forests. Sometimes I send spirits after the loggers. In this manner they are occasionally run over by their own bulldozers, or crushed under the very trees they sever.... But my powers are limited, and if things do not change eventually your people will dig up the whole earth; they will even discover our tunnels and caves, which reach from one end of the country to the other."

He turned and walked on, leading the doctor down a long narrow stairway, talking all the while:

"The gods for the most part left, as I said.... But Apozitz did not leave. He stayed, and my people, the Yaroa, were put in charge of him. And it is I, as one-with-knowledge, as headman, who am in charge of him."

They reached the base of the stairway, turned to the right, and were in a largish gallery, the walls of which were lined with a series of quadrangular niches and decorated with ivy-shaped tablets and mosaics. At one end, seated on a throne of andiroba (*Carapa guianensis*) supported by stone jaguars, sat Apozitz, next to him a large ant-eater, the divine sidekick Nuxi, carved in stone and bearing traces of blue and green pigment. The body of Apozitz was stuffed with earth and covered with ash paste, the whole coated with black manganese paint. A wig of brilliant red hair was pasted to its skull, and very long red eyebrows above its eyes.

Dr. Black had not the equipment to perform radiocarbon dating, but his belief was that the mummy before him was a good seven or eight thousand years old, if not older; as the methods used in the mummification process were nearly identical to those of the Chinchorro,—of which he had adequate knowledge, having just recently spent several days studying the fine collection of Chinchorro mummies stored in the vaults of the Monte Carmelo Museum of Archaeology.

"I am in charge of clothing and feeding him," Apido said.

What does he eat?"

"Moonbeams."

X.

The next evening...

An adult moon. Apozitz was carried, paraded through the village, Apido stalking before him, chanting, recounting myth and calling forth a feast of beams. Women and children retreated to their huts. Men, all males over the age of 14, gathered, some wearing headbands of bright orange toucan plumage, others armbands of yellow and red macaw feathers. The doctor was bathed in chanviro water, his back and shoulders painted with a perpendicular and oblique lined pattern, given wind-dried tobacco to chew and then, to take into his stomach through his throat, virola pellets, that sacred semen of the sun, which Apido shook out onto his hand from a wooden muhipu-nuri. Melodies and invocations. (Sound of sacred drum. Rattle-lance.) Yaroa cosmovision: Celestial Grandfather, mythic circles, rhythms of time, male = land of four corners; Mars = eye of anu-branco bird; bright stars = older brothers, dim = younger siblings. Chills, cold sweats, heavy tongue.

"Sometimes one must lay aside the microscope and look through the kaleidoscope," the doctor thought.

The veins stuck out on his bull-like neck.

He heard a rush of air.

"What is that?" he asked.

"It is the milky way," Apido answered gravely.

(Visions of jaguars and snakes); the men around him changed: monstrous snouts, heads prancing around on elongated legs, men belching emerald smoke and laughing fire.... He felt spasms begin to course through his body, jets of pain roll along his spine. He was shocked. A brief, sudden burst of bright light; his life displayed instantly, like a logograph seen *en silhouette*; other images—(him peeling his mother's kisses from himself and placing them in his heart, tokens of tender devotion)—and of a sudden his limbs were transformed into oblong bands of some highly elastic substance and he was a projectile. It was as if his entire body were being forced through a tube, ejected with great velocity. On the other side he was nothing but a great, pulsating mind, an abstract of himself, an intellect without concrete reality that soared like a cyclone through a turquoise sky which shimmered as if it were composed of billions of sequins. Far, far below was a great blanket, green with patches of blue; equatorial diameter of 7,926 miles, polar diameter of 7,900 miles—(then thickly populated areas in the midst of contrasting countryside, suburbs, houses, the doctor's Long Island residence: Mr. Clovis, that valet, driver, door porter washing the large, American car: a voice in the background of a bickering and unhappy Georgia Clovis...

The doctor looked up. In an instant his vision covered the 92.9 mean miles to the sun, which spat golden fire and was carried aloft by a network of numerous wings, so many of which flew towards the doctor, yellow eagles.

"We will take you to where the world ends," they said, and proceeded to drag him with their claws, push and buffet him with their beaks, to: a great porphyry-like mass; spiralling structures; miraculous staircases to right and left; he glided through a forest-like garden of dark dew-kissed blooms, past the tombs of deceased philosophies, through stellar gates and then massive doors which sang balsam-scented melodies on their hinges; corridors and passageways, the walls of which were decorated with plentiful portraits, beautifully painted, as if by the hands of some Venetian master—Giovanni Bellini or Lorenzo Lotto—though the subject matter had all the eccentricity of the works of Hieronymus Bosch. There was a horrible winged creature with snake hair and the beak of a bird, her face wearing a look of tranquil cruelty, which the doctor recognised as the Etruscan demoness Tuchulcha. He saw the thirty-horned Yehwe Zogbanu, as well as personages with faces on their bellies, others hirsute.... Then, into a large and pale chamber which seemed to hum. There were numerous fantastically shaped items arranged in a glass case in the centre of the room: an icositetrahedron, a twenty-four-faced lump of what appeared to be some vaguely alive variety of mineral;

a truly bizarre sepia-coloured irregular polyhedron; a bright-green dodecahedron, covered with spikes like those of the sea porcupine; these items, like strange astral funguses, appeared incredibly rare and precious.

Footsteps.

"Welcome Doctor. I am Nuxi."

The deity had the head of a large, tropical American edentate (Myrmecophaga jubata) attached to the pale body of a man of affairs. He spoke, not in English, but rather in a variety of Pennsylvania-German-Pali-Middle-Mexican-Persian which the doctor, an able linguist, could perfectly understand.

Black inquired as to the significance of the objects in the glass case.

"Those are your sentiments Doctor," the deity replied.

"My sentiments?"

"Your sentiments."

"And what are my sentiments doing here, might I ask?"

"This is the Heaven of Metanatural History, and it is where all the nonmaterial parts of Earth's imminent scientists are kept for both study and display." The deity scratched its snout and then rolled out a long protrusile tongue.

"It is all very odd.... Is this a variety of religious experience?"

"It is not the insanity of genius if that is what you are implying."

"Nor am I suffering from pathological unhappiness."

The deity shrugged its shoulders. "I am not here to make a convert of you Doctor."

"Then...?"

"One of these specimens, one of your sentiments is mildly damaged."

"Not good."

"No."

"So?"

"If you want to repair it, the first step you will have to take is to visit the shrine of Our Lady of the Rains in San Corrados."

Sound. As breath substituted for phonation.

A great shadow passed over the room and the doctor felt fear.

His body was covered with dirt and sweat. Apido leaned over him.
"Good," he murmured. "You have met Apozitz."

"It was Nuxi."

"But the shadow..."

Dissolve to:

That night the men of the village celebrated the doctor's induction by performing the dance of the centipede and drinking abundantly of manioc beer. (The doctor sat cross-legged, solemnly before the fire, with a blanket wrapped around his bare shoulders, the linked column of men slowly winding around him, their legs moving in unison as they chanted: chü-chü-chü-cha, hejabingin heja heja, chü-chü-chü-cha.)

Júnior lay in the dust, at the periphery of the scene, gnawing on a bone.

XI.

D<small>R. B</small>LACK WALKED THROUGH THE DEEP SHADE OF BROADLEAF evergreen trees.

He could not say that he was happier than he had ever been, because that was not true; but he could honestly admit that he had never known such peace. He was accepted by the natives, who were for the most part not taller than him and, indeed, he could have no regrets as to his stay with them. The information he had gathered there in that small isolated village, where he had undoubtedly been the first white man to have taken part in a Yaroa ceremony, would be a valuable edition to his *A Key to All Gods*.

"Maybe it would be better," he said to himself, "to remain here, quietly going about my research, in peace, rather than in the great world, where I am all too well known, and yet not adequately appreciated.... A native wife, an aboriginal romance ... a suitable setting ... walking through the virgin forest of love ... as many great men have done: Gauguin ... Papillon ... "

"But perhaps I am being too simple," he thought, wondering if he could ever relinquish being the man-numeral he had seemingly always been and abide as a mere human creature treading over the earth....

He strolled deep into that tract of extensive wooded area, stick in hand, gazed at its floor, at fallen leaves and mosses, termites and snails as big as his fist. Then the golden darts of the sun began to pierce through the now dwindling trees, the country opened up before him, and there was a meadow, lush with waist-high grasses. Butterflies fluttered through naked daylight. Baths of brightness and festivals of colour. A bare-faced curassow burst out from the greenery and flew back towards the forest while the doctor made his way forward, in the direction of a natural elevation in the near distance, pear-shaped and scarred with white rock formations.... His specimen bag was half full (detritivorous insects + tail feather of a hyacinth macaw + several cylindrical bodied terrestrial arthropods + a poculiform fungus)....

A little later...

The hill was covered with mushroom-shaped stones, and he hopped from one to the next....

From behind a crop of rocks leaped four armed men. One, apparently the eldest, wore a thick fan-shaped beard and carried an old bolt-action Mauser and a pistol in his belt. Two others carried Kalashnikovs and had moustaches jutting from their faces, while a fourth, a clean shaven and very young man, had a Mitchell's Saber semi-automatic shotgun trained on the doctor in a significantly threatening manner.

Shouted one: "Halt! How many in your party!"

"One. I am alone."

"A capitalist?"

"No. I am a scientist... a polymath."

"He is a spy."

"... sent by President Trujillo."

"No, he is CIA. A goddamn American agent."

"I assure you, my friends, that you are mistaken," the doctor murmured, taking a step forward.

"Stay a little back or these guns might go off!"

"I'll shoot him," the younger one said, thrusting his semi-automatic shotgun towards the doctor's head.

The heavily bearded individual, who had been silent until then, intervened. "Better not Xefe," he said. "El General might want to interrogate this one. We had better bring him back to camp. There will be time enough to shoot him later."

"Alonzo is right. And it would be unethical for us to blow his brains out without torturing him first."

Dr. Black's hands were tied behind his back with his own shoelaces. He was marched down the hill, over an expanse of field and then to the east, through the jungle.

The camp was set up in a clearing and was composed of about twenty

Dr. Black and the Guerrilla

tents concealed beneath camouflage netting. Men carrying Kalashnikovs and Winchester Model 70s sat on the grass or leaned against trees, smoking hand-rolled cigarettes. A few played cards in front of their tents. Three or four marksmen could be seen perched in the branches of trees in case of emergency.

Dr. Black was taken before a tent somewhat larger than the rest. Alonzo entered and came out a moment later accompanied by a short man with a sensual nose, a romantic moustache and a huge, heavily shadowed chin. The thick hair on his head was made manageable and lustrous with brilliantine and combed with religious care. He stood erect, as one who both deserves and receives respect; obviously a superior of some sort.

"Who is this?" he asked.

"A spy."

"Evidence?"

"He was snooping around the observation point."

"Did you search him?"

"Yes."

"And?"

"He had a cientipedoro."

"The white thief would look best with a corte corbata," commented Xefe sullenly.

"Shut up," the superior said, and then turned to the doctor: "Señor, I am General Hector Pineda, head of the People's Revolutionary Army of San Corrados. You are currently being held as an enemy combatant on charges of spying and knowingly attempting to gather information for the enemy. Do you have anything to say in your defence?"

"The Flaming Light Guerrillas," the doctor thought, and then said aloud: "General, I am a scientist and in no way involved in any form of espionage. My name is Black. Dr. Black. For the last six weeks I have been staying with the Yaroa tribe, engaging in anthropological studies. If you would send one of your men to the village, I am sure you could easily confirm this information."

The general made an indulgent gesture.

"I believe you and am sorry for the mistake of my men.... I know quite certainly that it is impossible to obtain a position as an undercover agent for any of the 193 nations of the world if you are under 160 cm.... Unfortunately you will have to be shot anyhow, as the location of our camp has been revealed to you."

XII.

Eleven o'clock. Night. A single candle. Sacks of yucca were piled up on one side and strings of garlic hung from above. The tent functioned not only as headquarters of the revolutionary movement, but also as Pineda's bedroom, and an all-purpose storeroom.... The general's mouth clenched. Six of his baluster-shaped rooks sat ranged at the fingertips of Black, who was now thoughtfully meditating on whether he should continue with his careful and slow manoeuvring or turn swashbuckler. Finally:

"Señor Doctor," the general said in exasperation, "I believe it is your move."

For one condemned to die the next day at dawn, the doctor was exceptionally relaxed. He put more material in position, deflected while the general jettisoned. Tranquilly Black double attacked; tranquilly he finished his opponent.

General Peneda rose from his seat, a look of agitation distorting his features.

"Xefe, guard him," he said, pointing to the doctor. "I need to take a leak!"

The next day at dawn...

Pale but calm, the doctor stood in an open clearing, with his hands tied behind his back. His short body cast a long shadow beside him. Six men, bearing arms, stood in a row before him. Two others, with tri-fold military entrenching shovels, squatted against the foot of a nearby tree. Alonzo approached from the direction of the camp.

"It is time to get real," he said.

"Real," the doctor murmured, wondering whether this was:

a. simply a statement from the lexicon of machismo
b. something that existed independently of ideas concerning it

or,

c. something that existed independently from all other things and from which all other things derive: (a conception of the supreme being?)

"Would you like a blindfold?"

"No. I would prefer, at the moment of dissolution, to have my visual awareness entirely unimpaired."

The other bowed stiffly. "As you wish." He turned to the gunmen. "Ready!" he cried, opening an enormous mouthful of yellow teeth.

The doctor considering how *a bullet can contain a supper of roast game...freedom...a river of sadness...the end of a noble career...travelling at 2,000 feet per second...with rifles positioned about 30 feet away...upon being fired...the projectiles would arrive in about twelve thousandths of a second...but taking into account air-resistance...partial differential equation...*

"...Aim!..."

seeing: childhood = Alabama (to the sounds of Sweet Nadine: huge. crowned with red hair. her beautiful voice + his own father: a thick and elongated torso; great-great-great-great-grandson of noted physician and chemist Joseph Black = discoverer of carbon dioxide *of a gentle and pleasing countenance. performed on the flute with great taste and feeling* her voice ringing out inviting his mind inquisitive wanting to acquire feasting always on digits and alphabets small particles and the stars dry-embalm that potato or burn with magnifying glass) + the boy doctor himself making: a diffusion cloud chamber / an electric lemon / a snowstorm in a can; incidents of life = emotions & operations for the purpose of testing certain principles: in China he pumped blood from a living dog into the decapitated head of a murderer three hours after execution (eyelids twitching, trembling lips forming unspoken words) / the construction of a massive umbrella with which he was able to jump off the roof of a five-storey doll factory in Williamsburg, Brooklyn / if he were killed he would sorely miss the chicken heart back at his laboratory on Long Island which he had kept alive for twenty-seven years pulsating in a solution of sea salt.

"This is unpleasant," he thought.
He stuck out his chest.
"Halt! Halt damn it!"
The general appeared. A long strand of brilliantined black hair hung over his right eye. "Rematch!" he shouted. "I demand a rematch!"

XIII.

"YOU WILL NOT ALLOW ME TO BEAT YOU."

"As a matter of principle, I would not allow a 6-year-old child to beat me."

"These principles..."

They christened their friendship with a bottle of singani.

Though most of the guerrilla group was made up of San Corradans, there were a number of foreigners: a few Peruvians and Bolivians, a Colombian, and even a Scandanavian-Argentinian woman, a slender and silent creature whose bruised eyelids were the decoration of ardent glares. These foreigners were the real backbone of the movement, as several of them were linked to funding from outside sources desiring to see the overthrow of the current government.......

The two men strolled through the camp, the general with his hands clasped behind his back.

"My gear and notes are back in the village of the Yaroa," the doctor said.

"I will send one of my men to fetch them."

"There is a box of Cerdans."

"Oh!"

"Yes. And when I have them, I will be happy to share them with you. In the meantime would you mind letting me have another one of your Dzilawó Fuentes[1]?"

---

1. The Dzilawó Fuente is a cigar made in Remedios. The factory was originally a hospital of the Spanish colony. In 1854 it was turned into a prison and later, in 1931, a School of Modernist Poetics was established there by the great San

Dr. Black and the Guerrilla

"My cigars are yours," the general said, drawing two robustos from his shirt pocket and handing one to Black.

The doctor ran the cigar under his nose, appreciating its earthy aroma. The two men now walked, puffed meditatively on their tobacco.

"Your situation..." the doctor said.

"Mmmm..."

"President Trujillo wants your head."

"Damn Trujillo..."

"He is in power."

"Trujillo.... From him the people get nothing but tear gas and privatisation. He would have them trade their liberty for designer jeans and sunglasses." The general made an imperative gesture. "When I was 10 years old I had a dream that I would liberate the people of San Corrados. It is my destiny. The government accuses us of kidnappings and narco-trafficking. They say that my followers are nothing but a bunch of left-wing peasants. The farmers no longer have any land of their own. The big plantations and mines are owned by only a few, who keep all the wealth of the country for themselves." And then he grew expansive, opened his arms as if he were embracing the whole country, went into his grand vision: equality for all, the education of the peasants, the streets paved with corn, and chickens ready roasted and dripping with plum sauce springing from the earth. The children, instead of playing in pools of malarial mud, would dance around puddles of cocoa butter and the poorest family would be able to eat veal cutlets off silver plate and wash it down with good Spanish wine.

"And Casildo Díaz?"

"Díaz...?"

"You knew him?"

"I know everyone."

"He was found dead in a ditch."

Corradan poet Diego Raíz Diego. Today it is the home of a small production factory whose cigars, though not particularly well known in connoisseurs' circles, have been a local favourite for generations.

"He was your friend was he?"

"He might have been."

"The police... they killed him."

"Did your men not try and recruit him, and when he refused, leak his name to the authorities as a conspirator against the government?"

The general chuckled. "Recruit him? Hell! he was with the Revolutionary Army for years.... One of my best men!"

"That is not what his wife said."

"A true San Corradan woman will not easily reveal the treasures of her heart... to the police... or the gringo."

They continued to walk, the general enlarging on his revolutionary projects: seizure of outlying farms and ranches / criminal landowners see the colour of their own blood / workers expelling the bitter taste of hatred from their mouths.

"We have armed propaganda teams in all the villages," he said from behind a thick cloud of smoke. "We must appear before the people, giving them support with our weapons; that will give them the message of the struggle."

"I wish you success."

Pineda now stopped walking, turned and, after looking thoughtfully at the doctor, the great chess player, proceeded to press him to reveal his skills as a theoretical strategist, because, as the general put it, the PRASC had plenty of bodies but very few minds. Black at first refused, on the grounds that he was, essentially, a person opposed to war, to all varieties of mass violence, and furthermore had no desire to be a carpet general.

"Come now, Doctor. Carpet general? In the jungles of San Corrados, where the revolutionary army operates, there are no carpets. Every man has his function, and you Señor would function importantly.... Join the revolution, Black. We will succeed, we will be victorious, we will accomplish the feat!"

"Your revolution is not mine, General."

"There is only one revolution, Doctor. Can't you see our need? Do I have to speak hammers to you?"

Then the general went into his mode of persuasive language, beginning in soft tones, expressing the affirmative by the negative of its contrary, his voice a well-oiled instrument for playing the tunes of delib-

Dr. Black and the Guerrilla

erative oratory. He used metaphors of: making love on green grass, horses galloping, birds in flight, employing beautiful imagery to justify boiling landowners in pots, skinning the president alive, setting fire to the headquarters of police and foreign corporations and painting the hillsides red with soldiers' blood. The doctor shook his head and was on the threshold of response when General Pineda, a veritable modern Cicero, had recourse to prolepsis, cutting off future objections, spicing his words with subtle dashes of irony and even throwing in a rather striking hypallage to bring home his point. Inspired, his voice gradually gaining in volume, he personified the revolution, with rapid strokes of his tongue drawing a portrait of some great and noble entity, some hazy and not quite graspable being, embodying all noble qualities which he expressed by linking several subordinate relative pronoun clauses prozeugmatically with a yoking noun. In bugle-like tones he expressed moral exaltation, joining decorum to trenchancy of language, finally descending into a mode of linked antitheses, his beautiful and emphatic speech having all the art of poetry, and all the charm of a song by Irving Berlin interpreted by a choir of twelve-pound cannons. The doctor's eyes began to be clouded over with the mist of imagination. He envisioned himself radiating masculine authority, a bandana wrapped around his forehead, at the front of the revolutionary army, peasants with machetes and pitchforks, bludgeons and butcher's knives, ranged before him by the hundreds of thousands.... Cries of hunger, violent demands for justice on their lips.... And did he not after all have ampliate knowledge concerning strategy and politics? Had he not read Miyamoto Musashi's *Gorin no sho* in the original Japanese and studied in depth the writings of Vegetius?

So, by the time the general had exhaled his final epanalepsis, Black was recruited.

In the days that followed, he drew up plans to:
A) Destroy military and police installations
B) Cut off lines of communication: cables, radio, messengers
C) Set up ambushes
D) Kidnap officials and agents
E) Rob banks

XIV.

Raids and Penetrations

(secret, loud, dangerous) destruction-producing abstraction
an orchestra of gunshots
(intrepid, virile) a stick of dynamite lit with the end of a cigar
sound—fire—smoke
they blew up bridges / railroad lines / and sabotaged mines
......devoting themselves to the trinity of violence, chance and reason...

XV (1).

Xefe had been shot in the leg. Dr. Black inspected, stuck his index finger in the wound, and the young man gave out a white-hot scream.

"Damn this fool," Xefe thought.

"It looks bad," the doctor said, drawing his Swiss army knife from his pocket. "I am afraid I am going to have to amputate."

"Amputate?" Xefe said. "What the hell do you have to amputate?" Beads of sweat appeared on his forehead.

"I hope you don't mind the pain. It has to be cut off." The doctor winked at General Pineda.

The general gazed mournfully down at the leg. "Yes," he said. "It looks bad."

Everyone burst out laughing. At first Xefe was mortified, briefly enflamed with rage. But then, seeing that the joke was broadly enjoyed, he was filled with a sudden admiration for the doctor.

XV (2).

At one point they entered the town of Saavedra disguised as flagelantes, masked, whipping themselves and crying out.

...... incendiary bombs......

"Shoot damn you!"

"But they are flagelantes—Disciplinaries of Christ Jesus! How can I shoot a Disciplinary of Christ Jesus?!?"

"Damn it, they are guerrillas!" Captain Ladros cried, pulling out his pistol and firing after the rebels, who laughed as they rode away.

"Everyone okay?" Alonzo asked.

"Not so good," said Xefe. "I have been hit."

When they were a safe distance from the town, they abandoned the stolen jeep and made for the backlands, Xefe being carried.

...... Dr. Black inspected, stuck his index finger in the wound, and the young man gave out a white-hot scream.

"Damn this fool," Xefe thought.

XV (3).

"KITAKAKITA."
"Ah! Ah! Ah! Ah!"
"Papel higiénico ... japonés ... "
"Ah! Ah! Ah! Ah!"
Captain Ladros roared with laughter.
Bauooooom!
"Oooooh!"

...... incendiary bombs......
"Shoot damn you!"

XVI.

"WE ARE DOING EXCELLENTLY!"

"Excellently?" said the doctor. "Maybe, but at this rate it will take years to overthrow the present government."

"What are a few years when liberty is concerned!"

"They may not be much to liberty, but to myself they are a great deal.... I have much work to do.... *A Key to All Gods*: it is a project I should complete while I am still at the top of my game."

The general made an indulgent gesture. "If you have a suggestion that might help to expedite matters," he said, "I am prepared to listen."

"It is clear that we must take the capital."

"The capital! But man, these days Trujillo has it practically surrounded by concertina wire... checkpoints... soldiers like ants..."

"I believe I can get you into Monte Carmelo without being detected."

"If you could do such a thing, the Revolutionary Army would be eternally grateful."

The doctor looked at him and said thoughtfully, "But there are certain conditions."

"Conditions?"

"Yes. You would need to give your word that you would terminate all mining and logging operations in the country."

"Terminate? Well... I would certainly terminate them as private entities.... Yet, as state-run projects I see no reason why——"

"General, I can get you into Monte Carmelo, but, in order to do so, I must have your express assurance that you will do as I request. Otherwise, I can do nothing for you."

XVII.

Q UISPE, TOGETHER WITH A HALF-DOZEN YAROAS, LED THE general's party of picked men through the passageways of the temple. The former were armed with blow-guns and darts dipped in 'one-frog-leap', a variety of curare so potent that, when tested on one of those tailless amphibians, it would only be able to jump once before it was paralysed.

They made their way in single file through the great hallways, up and down long series of steps, through bottle-shaped chambers, some engraved with effigies, others with great heads tenoned into the walls, with pottery, exquisite aryballos and clay masks piled in the corners. At first all preserved a respectful, awed silence, but after a period they became more used to their unusual surroundings. Jokes were heard. The occasional ringing of laughter.

"Who is that sniffing at the General's heels?"

"Oh—some damned Grilled Cat Indian who thinks he is a dog."

They walked on until the man-made walls gave way to cave walls, painted in many places with zoomorphic and anthromophic motifs, parallel lines, spots and spirals. They were led through a grand rift-passage and then past rimstone pools. A vast cavern opened up before them through which a calm, gurgling river flowed.

"Our transport," Quispe said, pointing to a dozen dug-out canoes beached on the sandy bank.

"Brilliant!" the general cried with delight, his voice echoing through the cavern, bizarre, almost spectral. "If all my revolutionaries were as efficient as this young Yaroa..."

The men piled into the bongos and began to paddle downstream. The water, looking like a river of oil, was exceedingly cool and the adventurers, with one lantern per boat, appeared as a string of slowly and fluidly moving lights. Their way led them through canyon-like passages and massive cathedral-sized chambers—mile after mile of underground wilderness, keyholes, waterfalls of stone, perfectly cylindrical phreatic tubes. The Yaroas proved themselves to be masterful oarsmen, controlling the crafts with remarkable precision, around sharp bends, through shallows and mazes of bamboo-shaped rocks. There were incredibly fine-grained sand beaches where the party would stop and drink maté, eat food. At one point Júnior jumped into the water, paddled around and splashed. He got out, shook himself off, deposited an eyeless white fish at the feet of the general, and then barked.

"Fish for supper!" said the general.

The men gathered around.

"Look, the water's full of them!" shouted Alonzo.

"There are a few troglobitic crayfish too," said the doctor, shining his flashlight into the gurgling liquid.

Later they grilled their catch on the coals of a small fire, while the Yaroas, who refused to eat what came from the underground river, satisfied themselves with large white spiders which they gathered from the cracks of the cave walls. Weary, the men played tic-tac-toe on the sand; then flashlights were extinguished and they slept, the darkness only interrupted by the occasional glow of a cigarette or cigar, and fading embers.

... would sing in a low and sweet voice ...

... the doctor found many bones, some of extinct animals, one of an unknown bovid ...

Further on, the cave roof became so low that they were forced to duck as they paddled and finally, just when it was becoming impossible for them to proceed any further, Quispe signalled and they parked the canoes in a kind of harbour that existed off to one side and there left them,—the group now squeezing through a narrow and low opening in the cave wall.... Many heads were bumped.... The air was thick and uncomfortable.... The passage gradually opened up and they were able to walk upright. And then, of a sudden, they found themselves in an immense cavern—so vast in fact that their flashlights were unable to penetrate the darkness.

"Be careful," Quispe said, pointing to a chasm which opened up to their left. "There are many bottomless pits."

And indeed the cave floor was pitted with a surprising number of forbidding black holes, around the edges of which Júnior scurried, excitedly sticking his nose within.

"How beautiful!" sighed Hulda, the Scandinavian-Argentinian, her flashlight shining on a sparkling gypsum crystal which grew from the cave wall.

Black was otherwise diverted. He had caught sight of a magnificent hydromagnesite balloon.

They were soon going through a near museum of such speleothems;—some curling like giant overgrown toenails, others appearing as flowers—in dazzling white, orange and green. Soda-straw stalactites, golden clusters and colonnades. There were contorted ramshorn objects, others which seemed like balls of fur, or then again beards that dripped from overhead. It was as if they were walking through an exotic garden, with delicate needle-like growths of calcite; helictite bushes whose branches were twisted, gnarled.

... And then the floor began to even out, was paved with large, smooth blocks of stone. To one side was a honeycomb of dark cells.

"What is this place?" the doctor asked Quispe.

"This is the jail where we keep the gods of peoples conquered ... once upon a time."

The doctor peered into some of the compartments and saw: a human head and hands emerging from a turtle shell carved out of alabaster.... In another a giant flea with a human face. There was Ka-Ata-Killa, the moon goddess.... Huaillepenyi, the god of fog.... Gnome-like beings secured with ropes.... A figure with eyebrows like mountains and wearing a feline headdress.... Fanged mouths, huge, wing-like ears.... And then a shackled image of Christ—a very old statue, obviously dating from the time of the early missionaries.

They moved on and presently found themselves in a type of temple complex.

A giant head, solemn, monstrous, was carved out of the rock. The walls were covered with sophisticated pictographs and diagrams. Then, in the centre of an especially large chamber, a chamber whose walls were frescoed with vivid blue and green designs, sat a bench-like throne 9 feet wide and 5 feet deep in vermilion painted limestone adorned with hieroglyphs and sculptured portraits. Layer upon layer of yellowing sheaves were stacked in shelves nearby.

The doctor took notes vigorously.

"What are they?" the general asked, flipping through the integumentary leaves.

"Human skins," said Black pointing to a nearby tripod-vase out of which bristled the blades of numerous sacrificial knives.

———

More walking: through hallways and chambers; then a slow ascent through a narrow, zigzagging passageway. They began to climb a great stairway—a stairway that seemed to go on endlessly. Occasional channels would open up to the right and left, but these Quispe avoided. Weariness. The joviality of the first day had entirely disappeared. There was some grumbling heard. "A hell of a lot of steps." "Damn it!" "Whoever doesn't like it can stay behind." "A real pain in the ass."

———

Liquid oozed from the walls.

"What an awful stench."

"It is sewage," Black said.

"Sewage! Then we are . . . "

"We must be near the surface."

Quispe turned and looked at the two men gravely. "We are just beneath the centre of the city."

"The city?"

"Monte Carmelo."

———

. . . verticality. . . . . . .

"This stone," Quispe said, pointing overhead.

"Should we not move on?"

"Apido, who speaks with the shadows, said here."

"We must remove the mortar." This was the doctor. "Feel it;—it is very soft from the moisture!"

Several of the men commenced the somewhat tedious work of chipping away at the mortar with their pocket knives.

After several hours:

"Look, we can move the stone in its socket!"

Thirty minutes later they were able to completely dislodge it, lowering it to the floor.

"Lead on," the general said to Quispe.

"We Yaroa cannot go any further."

"... Then I shall go."

"Would you not prefer to send forward a reconnaissance party?" asked Black.

"That is us Doctor!"

The general went through the hole. A number of strong arms hoisted the doctor up after him.

———

It was quite warm. They turned on their flashlights. They were under a projecting hood of stone ... and then, stepping forward, in a large, sumptuously decorated chamber: walls covered with velvet, a thick carpet on the floor. To one side of the room was a great Italian gothic chest and a French armoire of the XVIth century. To the other, raised on a dais, was a large four-post bed with an elaborately carved cornice and *colones torses* enriched with gilding. A hoarse sound, which the doctor immediately recognised as being caused by the vibrating of a soft palate, came from that area. The general looked at Black and silently put his finger to his lips. The two then tip-toed towards the bed and peered inside. A figure was curled up under the bedding, under a magnificently embroidered coverlet. General Pineda shone his light on it. A face appeared. A figure sat up, and rubbed its eyes.

"What—what is this?" the man, who looked like Joe E. Brown with a moustache, asked in stupefaction.

"Good evening Trujillo," the general said. He spoke with cold, almost hostile politeness

"Is that—Is that you Peneda?"

"It is I."

"Who—Who let you in?"

"Do not be concerned. Do not shout or cause alarm or I will kill you."

"What do you want?"

"For you to get out of bed and put on your pants."

President Trujillo got out of bed and put on a pair of black linen trousers.

"Now," said the general, "you will do just as I tell you."

"I will not do anything he tells me," Trujillo thought.

"You will call General Moncho Sisneros, head of your army, and have him direct all military forces from the city to Yánez, in the distant province of Almedina. Afterwards, you will call the head of your police force, and have him temporarily disband his men."

Trujillo protested. "And what reason should I give for these orders?"

"You are President of San Corrados. That is reason enough."

The room was now filling with Flaming Light Guerrillas—rough looking individuals, well-armed, who emerged from the depths of the great fireplace.... Trujillo looked around him; his mouth puckered... and he did as he was told.... After which:

"Señor Trujillo," Pineda said boldly, "I hereby officially remove you from office."

At 5:12 a.m. Dino Martinez, of the Servicio de Noticias del Tercer Mundo, reports from Monte Carmelo:

"With the dawn just hours away, San Corrados has announced a new Military High Command for the transition to a new Presidency of the Republic. At 4:30 a.m. SCT Hector Pineda was named as Army CIC as well as the interim president of San Corrados...."

Pineda, leader of the Peoples Revolutionary army of San Corrados, appeared at dawn on the screen of Radio Monte Carmelo Television asking the forces of Trujillo not to resist him.

......Xefe led a band of 18,000 armed bandoleros into the city..........

.........The poor came down from the hills and filled the streets.......

...... In the provinces a few gunshots rang out. The soldiers lazily surrendered... police replaced the pistols in their holsters with bottles of booze..........

———

There was much open-air celebration: music and cross-gender dressing, guitars and banjos and red-hot cries. Butchered pigs adorned with dead chickens, colourful ribbons and bottles of aguardiente were paraded through the streets while people performed vigorous triple-metre dances, bodies like jelly, and sang with exaggerated tone colour.

XVIII.

SEVERAL WEEKS LATER, AT THE PRESIDENTIAL MANSION IN MONTE Carmelo...
Severely sumptuous. Deep red hangings. A portrait by Inza. A painting by Jose del Castillo. Júnior was curled up before a log fire. The rich smoke of cigars. An amphora-shaped decanter decorated with quadruple spiral ribbing. Two glasses of Scotch whisky. President Pineda, elegant in a perfectly pressed charcoal grey suit of wool and viscose, the left breast embellished with a self-bestowed medal of the Order of the Merit of San Corrados, sat in a leather armchair, one leg hooked over the next, the doctor heavily sunk in a plush armchair opposite him.

"Come Doctor, my country needs men like you."

"In what capacity?"

"Scientific work... weapons program... and you can catalogue our fauna..."

"I am afraid I will not be able to help you, General. Like all mortals, my days are numbered, and I must dedicate my allotted time for the most part to already scheduled activities."

"All the same my friend—I will have a bronze statue of you erected on the Plaza Alcalde,—on top of a big pillar—like Balzac."

"But if you really wish to please me..."

"Yes?"

"If you really wish to please me General, instead of having my likeness cast in bronze, you will help the family of Casildo Díaz.... See that his son receives a proper education... and his wife a reasonable pension...."

[*Portrait by Inza.* Damn if he isn't... sentimental....

Decanter of Whisky. But you must understand, that he drank my blood...]

And then the weather changed...

The mist rolled in and settled over the mountains and between the hills, white and mysterious like an ocean of phantoms; and the rains came; at first in a mere drizzle; and the foliage, the surrounding hills were dazzlingly bright like emerald. The street vendors, those who sold papaya with lime and peeled cucumbers sprinkled with chile, disappeared, and shop doors closed. The liquid began to fall with great force. Round faces stared from rain-blurred windows. The doctor stayed indoors, smoking and reading exotically bound books from the presidential library.

One evening, at dinner, the doctor said to the general:

"I believe it is worth mentioning that, if this rain keeps up, your city stands in danger. To the north of us, thousands of acres of forest have been cleared away for mining. For the past 7 days it has been raining at a rate of about 2 inches per day, every inch of rain adding about 5 pounds of water to every square foot of soil—which means in an area, of let us say, 50 x 100 feet, we have a daily weight of 50,000 pounds of water being added to the soil. At present I estimate that 175 tons of water have been added to every such parcel of land. The weight of all this rainwater might very well make the shifting of soil particles exceed the combined resistance of the soil particles clinging to one another and the bedrock to the point where shear stress takes over."

General Pineda shrugged his shoulders and, after swallowing a mouthful of sirloin said, "Doctor, you most certainly exaggerate the danger.... Because, you see, it is not that I deny there being a danger, it is merely..." His lips wrapped themselves around the rim of his wine glass.

Later Black listened to the sheets of rain sweep against the courtyard outside his window; he went over his notes, those he had gathered amongst the Yaroa—those vastly important records and comments which would amply add to *A Key to All Gods*.... He then rose and stretched himself, took up a rare volume by Diego Raíz Diego; stroking his beard read the poem which begins:

Under the carob tree,
in whose shade I bathe,
my mind thinks of long things,

and then he raised his head, saw through the pane of glass: high upon the hill, a great electrically illuminated cross: symbol of what exists beyond the visible world (operating through faith or intuition): remembering the Heaven of Metanatural History and the words of Nuxi.

The next day he visited the shrine of Our Lady of the Rains[1].

The liquid grumbled against his umbrella as he entered the presidential limousine....

There:

...The constant clicking of beads.... Indian and Mestizo women were crouched before the icon, their lips murmuring prayers.... He seated himself in a pew, and gazed up at the high altar, the famous image of Our Lady of the Rains, to the right of which was a painting by Murillo, to the left a golden reliquary in which was held a relic, an atomic segment

---

1. On November 11th, 1713 the Blessed Virgin, dressed in a costume of brightly-coloured bird feathers and a cloak of burlap, appeared to a 92-year-old neophyte named Tomás Garcés, who was on his way to hear Mass in Monte Carmelo. She sent him to Bishop D. de la Gala with a request to have a temple built where she stood. The bishop, as may be imagined, was not convinced by the old man's testimony and requested that the woman, if she was the genuine article, perform a miracle, show a sign, or do something especially interesting. Tomás returned to the Blessed Virgin and repeated the bishop's words. After hearing the report she told the neophyte to go and gather asparagus for the bishop's dinner table and handed him her cloak to use as a basket. Tomás, though he had never in his life even seen asparagus, and though asparagus does not grow anywhere near Monte Carmelo, yet still came across a beautiful patch of the vegetable, which he gathered in the folds of the cloak. Appearing before the bishop, he emptied the contents of the cloak upon the table, and on the cloak itself was now painted a life-sized figure of the Virgin Mother glowing in a rainbow of gorgeous shades. In 1964 Pope Paul VI declared the shrine a basilica.

Dr. Black and the Guerrilla 111

of the True Cross (item no. 786 in Rohault de Fleury's catalogue). The doctor glanced over. Next to him, on the pew, was a magazine someone had apparently forgotten. He picked it up. It was a Bolivian tabloid. Impulsively he flipped through it. Then, there she was, her long blonde hair falling across her naked shoulders like the rays of the sun; the caption: 'Millionaire Playboy Brock Rutter lives life to its fullest'.

And the very next morning Black took one of the few commercial flights available out of San Corrados.

Flight: Edgard International flight 34 on an Airbus Jet
Depart: Monte Carmelo, San Coraddos (MCL) at 8:50 a.m.
Arrive: Caracas, Venezuela (CCS) at 3:35 p.m.
Stops: None

connecting to

Flight: Air France flight 461 on an Airbus Industrie Jet
Depart: Caracas, Venezuela (CCS) at 6:00 p.m.
Arrive: Paris de Gaulle, France (CDG) at 8:15 a.m.
Stops: None

connecting to

Flight: Air France flight 7704 on an Airbus Industrie Jet
Depart: Paris de Gaulle, France (CDG) at 10:35 a.m.
Arrive: Nice, France (NCE) 12:10 p.m.
Stops: None

XIX.

The rain continued day after day. The rivers were swollen. Río de la Muerte broke forth from its banks. Trees were uprooted. The songs of the Vacotocha could be heard rising up out of the jungles.... White flashes of fire scarred the sky. The mines turned into great mudslides; the wet soil moved downhill, picking up loose rocks, vegetation, more soil, and boulders, which ground together and roared. Men and donkeys were buried up to their necks. In the capital, a faint rumbling sound was heard, which increased in volume as the mud, like a living mass of brown flesh, moved towards the city. It swallowed up the northern suburb, taking with it mansions and rose gardens, and then, following the path of least resistance at a rate of 17 km per hour, moved into the slums of La Avenida de los Dolores, where it sucked up corrugated metal, outhouses and typhoid fever—balls of poverty, incest and murder.... The population fled to the south and watched as the mass of wet, soft earth filled the streets. The Plaza Alcalde was a great tobacco-coloured lake... and riding on the waves of mud in coffin-shaped curator-quality cardboard boxes were the Chinchorro mummies, swept out from the vaults of the Monte Carmelo Museum of Archaeology,—like a fleet of vessels arriving from the netherworld.

Fragment

Group

B

I.

Inv. No: 675.4
Material: Scratched on a potsherd
Provenance: Found during an excavation outside Latakia

Written in the in the Ugaritic alphabet, the inscription reads:

charm of hog's teeth

Inv. No: 675.4
Material: Papyrus
Provenance: Unknown

Letter from a friend in Alexandria of acute tediousness told in the grossest language.

Inv. No: 675.4
A small quarto on paper, containing 34 leaves neatly written in the 18th century.

Describes cases of melancholia in Belgium. Composed by Dr. L. Stieglitz, renowned expert on encephalic nervous textures.

Inv. No: 675.7
Material: Papyrus, six leaves, burned at the edges

Recto in phonogrammatic writing:

Flower land wet sky foreleg of ox jackal cow

Verso:

Reed mountain god

II.

Mr. Peneda was born into a peasant family in a coffee-growing area of west-central San Corrados. The oldest of seven children, he received an elementary school education before going to work as a woodcutter, butcher, baker, and candy salesman. When he was 19, he represented San Corrados at the Olympic Games in fencing.

In January of 1972 he, in order to win a wager, drank eighty cups of coffee in seven hours and fifteen minutes and then, emboldened by the beverage, led a silent anti-government protest of 100,000 people through the streets of Monte Carmelo. He was arrested and tortured with the pimentinha, but upon his release, was immediately acknowledged as a leader of the people.

III.

THE DOCTOR FOUND THEIR DOCTRINE FASCINATING. IT WAS THE doctrine of Christianity stripped of all its beauty. A raw, bleeding wound bound in black leather and seared, branded in flaming letters.

He recalled the words of David Hume: "Is He willing to prevent evil, but not able? Then He is impotent. Is He able, but not willing? Then He is malevolent."

"But then," the doctor thought, "Hume was but plagiarising Epicurus.... The premise of it all lying in the idea of an omnipotent, omniscient and benevolent God. If God were benevolent, then he would prevent evil, eliminate it completely. And since the world is full of evil.... So the good sisters have solved the problem by worshipping a god who is both omnipotent and omniscient, but lacks any form of benevolence.... Conveniently, they have completely ignored Leibniz and his *Essais de Théodicée sur la bonté de Dieu, la liberté de l'homme et l'origine du mal*, but such convenient oversights are the nature of all formalised religious systems.... It seems that these women are worshipping some sort of Demiurge, a Samael rather than Christ, a malevolent architect who has constructed the universe as a giant torture chamber which grinds infinite numbers of sentient beings into pain-laden beef."

Some of the books he found on the shelves were of extraordinary interest:

The Life of Eve
The Virtue of Dread
The Love letters of Paul the Apostle
The Second Life of Lazarus
The Early Years of St. Mary of Egypt

Dr. Black

in

Monte

Carlo

I.

Italic-Slavonic-West-Germanic language mix oral Waldorf salad old debauchees silk dresses naked arms reveal cinnamon and cream-coloured flesh oozing over croupiers shouts piquant money odour Gianni Vivé Sulman perfume sweat gland secretion. Dubious looking gentlemen with wilting moustaches flitted from table to table—ghosts of millionaires past—those who had long ago lost their fortunes at the casino and now haunted it—a few low-value chips clinging to their moist palms. A woman with an enormous bosom engulfed in two sequin-smeared shells slithered by, the aftermost part of her hull seeming an animal apart from the rest of her person. Then a long-limbed female crowned by a spume of golden strands, her eyes robin's eggs on an outstretched sapling limb, her form a vase of a thousand mysteries, a veritable Ludovisi throne, the woman's contours an alphabet of everything enticing, recalling Nike adjusting her sandal, a portrait of Spring, the goddesses from the east pediment of the Parthenon, a picture painted in white ink.

"Ah—there's an attractive piece of woman flesh!"

"She arrived with Brock Rutter. Is considered the beauty of the season."

"Delicious!"

"She is certainly gorgeous, but I imagine also dangerous to touch."

"Don't be silly. Any man would throw his life away for a chance at that."

These comments came from the mouths of two men, both under 30 years of age, who stood, arms behind backs, observing. One of them had worked at the casino for years; the other had been hired only a few months before. The first, who went by the name of Guy Pérès, was said to have been an exceptional tennis player before——Well, no matter, since both he and his friend merely have bit parts, are possessed of just a few sparkling lines, in this tale ...

An aged, million-wrinkled gentleman was rolled about in a wheelchair by a well-dressed young lackey. A wool blanket covered the former's lap, and upon this lay a rack of 500 euro chips.

"Look at that one," the young man who we have declined to name said, nodding towards the old man. "He has the face of one of those renifleurs one always sees milling about women's restrooms at Paris train stations."

"That is the Count Igor von Buxhoeveden, probably one of the richest men in the world. He has had thirty-two wives, and as many divorces."

"Money attracts women," the other said sententiously.

"I don't know. When he was younger he was said to have been remarkably handsome."

"But he is no longer young."

"Well, he must have some secret, for even at his age he still manages to make new conquests."

The eyes of the nameless one widened.

"And this fellow! That morphology."

"I have never seen him before."

"A dwarf!"

"He looks like a sadist to me."

They gazed at the short black figure, engulfed in a mist of cigar smoke, beard protruding before it like a giant and somewhat blunted obsidian arrowhead as it passed them by.

"In the casino there is never a shortage of interesting faces!"

The doctor strolled through the crowd, took in the varied physiognomies, the patterns of certain handsome females, studied them as he might have a group of chemolithoautotrophic Archaea;—with great interest, on the lookout for certain already known features—not absolutely immune to the many other fleshy charms through which he waded.

When he saw her, he was surprised how little it did affect him. There was no sudden acceleration of heart beat, no gasping for air.

"It seems that either I have previously underestimated my own coolness of mind," the doctor thought, "or I will in the future be witness to some variety of delayed reaction."

She was there, near a roulette table, her shapely body gilded with a golden dress.

Sensing his presence, as a wild animal—not tamed, not easily domes-

Dr. Black in Monte Carlo

ticated—does that of man, she turned, impaled him with her sharp blue gaze.

He stepped up to her, caressing the carpet with the soles of his small shoes, inhaled her silently for a moment before letting a few words drift out of the depths of his beard.

"Good evening. I believe we have... met before?"

"Have we?" she said coldly.

"I never forget a former patient."

"That is odd—I always forget my former doctors."

"Then I take it you have had many?"

"General practitioners, witch doctors, quacks—the world is full of men with therapies."

"You seem very disillusioned."

"Not in the least. I would not part with my illusions for anything."

"I am delighted to hear it."

"Thanks," she said. A hint of a smile. "Now if you would get me a drink."

"If you asked," he replied, "I would get you one thousand."

"A single white Russian will do."

"You are a monogamous drinker."

"One never sleeps and dines in the same way."

Rubbing his hands together, he slipped off to the bar. When he returned Tandy was standing with another gentleman—tall; long-shanked; healthy; teeth dazzlingly white and skin the colour of an alloy of 91% copper, 9% tin; scrupulously shaven chin clefted and his body as if sculpted by some Hellenistic artist of questionable importance, the clearly defined ridges of the muscles somewhat exaggerated, obvious even when covered with an exquisitely expensive suit of Italian make.

This was Australian millionaire-playboy Brock Rutter. He was a man who enjoyed hang-gliding, racing his yacht and flexing his muscles in public places to the click of the paparazzi. Made confident by money, the specious good looks of the amateur bodybuilder and an above average intelligence untainted by wisdom, he was like a modern Hercules ready to perform great deeds, to make conquests, financial, physical, and romantic.

"Your drink," Black said, handing Tandy the glass.

"And get me a gin and tonic," Brock demanded.
"I am afraid you will have to ask the waiter for that."
"Then who are you?"
"This is my doctor—former doctor."
"The young lady and I go back a good ways," Black added majestically.

Brock scowled, had an ominous look in his eyes, but nonetheless offered Black his hand, squeezed the latter's fingers tightly between his own.

"Well," he said with an ironical hint in his voice, "any friend of Tandy's is a friend of mine."

The doctor winced—as much from the pain caused by the man's cliché as from that caused by his over-forceful grip. He felt awkward, wondered what spiritual madness had led him to Monte Carlo, to attempt to dive once more into the chasm of this woman's heart.

"Well . . . " he muttered and, for one of the first times in his life at a loss for words, contented himself by stretching his lips and showing his teeth.

"Yes, well," Brock responded. "It would be a pleasure to continue talking to you, I'm sure, but we have other things to do. So, if you would excuse us . . . "

The man slipped his arm around Tandy's waist and led her off. Black gazed after them, briefly envisioning himself and Brock stripped naked, wrestling, biting each other's flesh in a battle for a beautiful pink gobbet of Tandy's love, her lust; he stood
immersed in that kingdom of catacombs
catacombs of organisms
mechanical bread and
old debauchees
silk dresses and
oozing croupiers
croupiers sweat gland secretion
catacombs neither whorehouse nor slaughterhouse
gongs
gunshots
dice thrashing themselves till they spit out teeth.

Black extracted a cigar from his jacket, lit it, ordered a between the sheets (8 ml triple sec, 8 ml curacao, 22 ml light rum, 22 ml cognac, shake with ice and strain into a chilled cocktail glass, spray with fresh lemon juice) from a passing waiter.

Fortified, he went forth. The sights and sounds of society. Naked shoulders glistened beneath the chandeliers. Dice rattled. Cards fluttered about like great moths.

The roulette tables attracted his attention.

"Ah," he thought, "the 'small wheel' invented by Blaise Pascal (father of the probability theory, first man to wear a wristwatch) as a bi-product of a machine for perpetual motion. A real tool of the devil, for add up the numbers and what do you get, a beastly 666.... The houses edge is 2.7%.... But look how people are attracted to it, like certain hymenopterous insects to a flower!"

The tables were indeed crowded. A garden of blooms around which well-tailored gentlemen and nervous women stood.

One table seemed more lively than the rest. Amongst the personages surrounding it was Count von Buxhoeveden, lodged at the forefront in his wheelchair, his attendant Ivan[1] standing gravely behind him. The aged Russian gentleman was causing a small sensation. He was losing disastrously, and with each loss he only increased his stake, teeth clenched, lips bent back in a bestial grimace.

"Red!" the count cried, thrusting several stacks of chips on that colour.

"If that old scoundrel is betting red," the doctor thought, "then you can be sure I will place my money on my own namesake."

He laid a 100 euro chip on black.

The wheel spun, a blur of colour.

"Black 20!" the croupier shouted.

The count scowled; then his lips twisted upward, squirmed slightly. From the bottom of his throat came a strange cackling laugh.

---

1. Ivan Edzhubov was a man somewhat shorter than average with a rather large nose that sat close to his face. He had a high forehead, blue eyes, and a stocky body.

"Take me back to the hotel Ivan. Enough of this caprice for the evening."

"And I should probably do likewise," the doctor thought, recalling Einstein's very apt remark about roulette.

For the evening, he had won 100 euros.

II.

He awoke the next morning in good spirits. She had not absolutely repulsed him, which he believed meant that she was not impregnable to his murky charms. After all, they had shared many delicious moments together—moments of amorous humiliation such as create bonds difficult indeed to completely dissolve;—and though the pursuit of her person might be termed a mild form of madness, the doctor thought it better to indulge than negate this whim, lest it mutate and grow into some bizarre force truly destructive to his splendid ambitions.

He was staying at the Hôtel Hermitage, on the Square Beaumarchais, enjoying its discreet luxury. He sat on the balcony in his bathrobe, breakfast set out before him on a small, glass-topped table. The dazzling multi-shaded blue of the Riviera stretched out below, sprinkled with sailing boats and yachts. He took a sip of strong coffee; dipped his spoon into a poached egg, let his eyes swim over the bright gold of its yolk and ate as only a confident man can.

Lifting them from this miniature Morro Velho, he saw, in the park of the hotel below, a man doing jumping jacks. It was Rutter—going through some sort of morning aerobics routine.

Not long later, as a small man with a miniature moustache (room service) was removing the breakfast crockery, he asked:

"So, is Brock Rutter staying here?"

"He is indeed, Monsieur."

"Ah!"

"In the suite duplex."

"Alone?"

"Indeed not Monsieur. A man like Monsieur Rutter never sleeps alone."

"I see," the doctor said, his eyebrows bumping into each other.

After showering and dressing, he made his way out of his room, let his legs, which were only 67/108ths the mass of his arms, carry him down the magnificent staircase. In the lobby he passed by Count von Buxhoeveden. The two men's eyes met momentarily.

"Eyes of jade," the doctor thought, recalling those 8,000-year-old artefacts found in the Inner Mongolian Autonomous Region, around the Xinglonggou Ruins of Aohan Banner in Chifeng City, those bits of the substance implanted in one of the eye sockets of the dead before they were buried speak to heaven through pi disk old nephrite dragon; swift indeed he deposited his key at the desk, exited that temporary domain,

like an old chestnut tree his frame,

a hive of numbers his mind,

beard dark, mind clear,

he reflected, "I must pursue her person with at least some measure of vigour, for this young lady is already in the grip of another man. My nature is naturally aloof, but strategically..."

He walked through the front door; was in that mythic and highly cultured place, between the Alps and the Mediterranean sea, where dreams are whipped up from the cream of reality. There was the Museum of Prehistoric Anthropology with its Neanderthal, Cro-Magnon and Grimaldi remains; the Exotic Garden and the Observatory Cave; the Musée des souvenirs Napoléoniens et collections des archives historiques du Palais; H.S.H. The Prince of Monaco's Collection of Classic Cars; Zoological Gardens; or...

A bellboy came running up beside him, spoke in a loud voice to an awaiting driver:

"Monsieur Rutter will be down in ten minutes. Have his car ready. He wants to take his lady friend to the Musée des poupées."

"Well, that answers that," the doctor thought as he climbed into a cab. "To the Musée National des poupées et des automates d'autrefois."

"Avenue Princesse Grace."

"Precisely."

III.

THE NATIONAL MUSEUM OF DOLLS AND AUTOMATONS OF Yesteryear. The doctor had not been there for more than a quarter of an hour before the others arrived. At first he concealed his presence. Hiding behind animatronic cowboys and automatic fortune tellers. And then he let himself be seen near a pair of elegant mannequins.

Brock gave a subdued snarl. The face of the woman by his side was as emotionless as the dolls all around.

"Ah, you here!" the doctor said, giving a bizarre smile; an avalanche of teeth between an anemone of black whiskers.

"Yes, it seems we have the same taste in sightseeing," said Tandy.

The doctor thought he detected irony.

A smile skimmed over her lips and he saw
woman from the roots of her feet to the soles of her hair
[82 kisses x 5 = a midget paradise]
[She: an artificial equipment / execute task / command: novemdecillion[1]]
[He: a richly decorated game paddle]
[Black = spirit of sprouting maize[2]]

Brock dragged her away.

The doctor subsequently spent around three quarters of an hour in the museum, looking at its offerings, meditating on automatons, what he saw, but even more so what he wished to see / a mechanical trumpet player signed Johann Nepomuk Mälzel / a jar of mechanical worms / Baron Wolfgang von Kempelen's chess Turk / mechanical cloud, grey in

---

1. Her hair in maiden whorls,
   mouth a nozzle from which spewed filth
   the colour of flowers.
2. Drunk on meat-flavoured liquor.

colour, which flashes lighting, produces rain and strong hail/Charles Gumpel's Mephisto. Exiting the establishment, he decided to stroll towards his lunch. Long limousines glided past him and expensive sports cars stuffed full of gorgeous individuals were seen zipping around tight corners. Money spent putrid luxury velvet stained feuille de rose with brains rusted breath corrupted puke in lukewarm sprays of English suicide ripped up eyelids crowing million bellies cement-hearted slouching swine curl of tongue over arching spine mink séance à trois.

The following internal dialogue took place:

"There must be a way to win her over that does not cause great labour or discomfort."

"If she doesn't hate you that is."

"Even if she does hate me. After all, hate has never been an impediment to love."

"An example please."

"Empress Theodora. She seemed to have hated almost every man she loved, if we are to believe the *Historia Arcana* of Procopius."

"Very well, you've made your point. But what about Tandy?"

"As far as I can see, the task is simply to make myself firstly agreeable to her, and secondly desirable, a being that she feels compelled to long or crave for."

"Invert the order."

"Yes, right."

"And then there is a little matter which we haven't yet addressed."

"Rutter."

"Precisely."

"What can she possibly perceive in him?"

"Aside from him being rich, handsome, intelligent and intrepid, nothing. He is a complete buffoon, not utterly coarse, but certainly far from refined."

"Love is not logical."

"Yes, the girl did already throw you over for a farmer of solanaceous perennial plants."

"That was the dominatrix in her."

"So you need to try and appeal to her kinder, gentler side."

"Hmmm. I don't know about that. I think the endgame is simply to repair certain sentiments I hold for her, in whatever manner I am best able."

He lunched alone in the dining room of the hotel on la verdurette croquante à l'huile de noix et foie gras de canard with pain de seigle et citrons, l'émincé de queue de lotte rôtie au coulis de poivrons doux with pommes compotées au pistou, les fromages affinés de maître céneri.

The doctor was just about to summon the dessert cart, when Ivan approached.

"Excuse me Monsieur."

"Yes?"

"Count von Buxhoeveden has sent me to ask you if you would care to join him for coffee."

The doctor turned his head, saw the count at another table waving him over, and rose from his seat.

The count was a man of refined manners who spoke exquisite French, more than adequate English and German, but managed to stumble over his native Russian as if it were a foreign language. A large burgundy cravat was wrapped around his delicate throat; his hands were like desiccated lilies; his lips had a haughty, sarcastic tilt to them, sculpted as they were (like pebbles in a stream) by a good seventy years of bon mots.

The two men shook hands.

"I am always interested in making the acquaintance of a celebrity."

"Come Count—my background is hardly popular science."

"Ah, but you cannot be modest with me Monsieur Docteur for I have read your articles[1] and I trust that I am very close to the mark when I say that they are a good deal more insightful than those of Lydston, Legrand, Contarano or Tardieu."

---

1. Some theories regarding heavily-tainted men, *Acta Extraniologica, Vol. 95, No. 3*, 244-297

    Handkerchief thefts and other bobbery: their relation to the continuance of the human species, *European Journal of Anarchic Psychology, Vol. 37, Issue 5*, 44-49

    The romantic inclinations of Tiberius, a medico-forensic study, *Behaviour Experts' Digest, Vol. 2, No. 6*, 4-38

"But the items you are, I believe, referring to," Black said, taking a seat, "are mere psychological studies, words I composed in moments of trite apathy, and I myself put very little stock in them."

"That is wrong of you, for the most important thing in this life is man's relation with the opposite sex."

"Some would disagree with you. Some would point to God,—to religion."

"Religion!... Love should be the only religion of a gentleman."

"A most remarkable assertion coming from a man of your time of life."

"Well, what sort of swine would I be if, after living the happy existence of an atheist, I suddenly threw myself into the arms of the priests at the first whiff of the tomb?... No, I will not play the hypocrite.... Anyhow, a man's amorous capabilities are very much like a good cheese. They are not fully ripe until they begin to rot."

The doctor inclined his head. "I bow to experience."

"Yes, experience! Sometimes I feel as if I should take up a pen and, like Casanova, compose my memoirs."

"To instruct future generations?"

"No. To relive the romances of my past. After all, pleasure is so cerebral..."

"Then, do goats feel pleasure?"

"Not half as much as man I imagine."

Their coffee was brought and the good doctor managed to extricate a délice au chocolat en sauce douce from the dessert cart.

The count satisfied himself with a spoonful of balsamo di Gilead di Salomone[1] mixed in with his coffee, after which:

---

1. If you say yes, you're lost; if no, a million miles away.
   The Formula:
   Cardamon ... gram. 30
   Cannella ...   "   30
   Balsamo della Mecca 2
   Tint. di Cantaridi gram. 1
   42 proof alchohol 100
   Sugar 250

"Would you care to go for a stroll in the garden? I enjoy a bit of sunshine after lunch."

"As you wish."

"You may go now Ivan, the doctor, I am sure, will be kind enough to take charge of the chair for a brief period."

The servant took his leave. The doctor got up from his seat and wheeled the count out onto the terrace, and then into the garden.

The sunshine was dazzling. Down below they could see the ocean upon which played the sails of boats.

There were blooms of roses in almost sickening abundance, the sweet reek of fecundity. An occasional bee swam through the air, hovered about a flower, sucked at its nectar. An indistinct smile, that of a man smelling memories, indulging in fantasies, being whispered to by ghosts of love played on the count's lips.

He had the doctor stop for him to dip his nose into a flower.

"Ah," he murmured, "the perfume of this blossom reminds me of my third wife."

"You must have been very fond of her."

"Yes. She is now locked up in a lunatic asylum in Dieppe. It seems my brand of fondness drove her insane," the count chuckled. "She spends the entire day scrubbing her body with detergent, claiming that it is stained with filth."

"An obsessive monomaniac."

"It is my theory that everyone is a monomaniac, but some manage to hide it better than others."

"An interesting theory. And what is your mania?"

"My dear young man, as I said, some of us manage to hide it better than others. Pretending to be sane is a fine art."

"So you are a sort of Picasso . . . "

"Oh no! My mania is far from abstract."

The count's eyes were riveted. As became those of the doctor.

It was Tandy. She wore a pistachio-coloured dress and floated by like an apparition; from a point A, to a point B, where the Australian was with sharp eyes awaiting her.

"A charming young woman."

"Yes."

"She must be delightful company."

"Yes."

"Only monosyllables?"

"What would you have me say?"

"Nothing more, for your very reserve tells me, a man of adequate experience, as much as I need to know. Monomanias indeed!"

"The male animal..." the doctor began in a somewhat embarrassed tone.

"Oh please, dear sir, let us stick to the female," the count said, taking out a De Reize and lighting it. "The beautiful sex is, after all, so very much more interesting."

"Yes, for those who find interest in perilous and exacting situations."

"That is the spice of life! I have been married numerous times; and all but my last ended in divorce."

"And your last?" the doctor ventured.

"I lost her."

"You have my condolences."

The count shrugged his shoulders. "It happened while we were staying near Oman, the guests of Prince Akhmar," he said. "The prince's family and my own go back a great distance, being tied together by interests financial and, occasionally, political.... It was summer. Olga (the name of the woman in question) was at the height of her beauty. Her long blonde hair shone like boiling gold in the desert sun and the mystical blue of the sky was reflected in her eyes. She was as charming as a poem by Gustave Kahn lisped out in a moment of ecstasy, as intoxicating as a five-day fast broken by a healthy and neat glass of Lemercier.

"During the day she would go off in the company of the prince's chief eunuch, whose name was Alek, while I would stay behind and play chess with the prince. At night we (Olga and I) would lie in each others arms enjoying the pleasures of paradise here on earth, a sort of symphony of dahlias punctuated by the brisk rhythm of lust.

"She was in the habit, after sating herself on my flesh, of taking a stroll about the grounds barefoot, with nothing to cover her person but the loosest of negligées, a semi-translucent frippery she could cast aside in an instant.... She would smoke fragrant cigarettes while gazing at the stars and, no doubt, congratulate herself on her good fortune.... One

Dr. Black in Monte Carlo

night, after certain zesty, extravagantly vibrant activities (les paons ont dressé la rampe ocellée), she wandered out the door of our apartment. I lay spread-eagle on the bed, my body floating on a flaming cloud of exquisite exhaustion, and was just about to drift off to sleep, to join the fairies of Neverland, when I heard a little cry of distress. Slowly I rolled off the bed (a huge emperor-sized affair) ... slipped into a bathrobe and sandals, and went to her. She was kneeling in the darkness on the sand. 'Something bit me,' she said, pointing to her ankle. I helped her inside, the poor girl limping like a wounded colt.

"Examining her ankle, I noticed two red dots on it and the commencement of swelling. I called out into the night and the faithful Alek instantly ran to our aid. 'It is the bite of the puff adder,' he said without hesitation, upon seeing the wound. And indeed, the poor girl was already beginning to grow delirious. Her eyes, shining balls of turquoise, were huge in her head. A croaking laughter wound out of her turgid lips. ... I was very distressed. ...

"... One would have to search through Dante's inferno to find a fitting simile for the following days. She lay in bed, suffering frightfully.

"... And the prince and I played chess.

"One evening we were sitting, on down-stuffed cushions and leopard skin rugs, puffing thoughtfully at hubbly-bubblies and drinking the sweetest of mint tea.

"I had seen Olga only a short while before and my mind was full of sadness. I firmly believed that she was going to perish and, in my own way, I really loved the girl.

"'You seem greatly troubled, Count,' Prince Akhmar said. 'May I ask the reason for your upset?'

"'Why, isn't it apparent?'

"'Is it because of your wife?'

"'Indeed it is. I don't think she will make it.'

"'No,' the prince replied, 'I bet she will live.'

"And he was right. Within a few days she recovered, and shortly thereafter became the prince's property, a lead member of his harem. It is just as well that I did not win though, as the only thing I would have gotten out of it would have been Alek the eunuch."

IV.

The sun departed, was replaced by the lights of the city, vaguely pink, hints of pale blue; the magic of a Monte Carlo evening.

The pale cream of his shirt contrasted suavely with the midnight of his jacket. His feet, in Capezio black jazz oxfords, ascended the steps of the casino. And he entered. Beneath the Bohemian glass chandeliers and rococo ceilings the gaming rooms were writhing with life; eyes slim with the vice of greed, lips clenched in inexplicable smiles. Many young men, who had lost their fortunes in a night, could be seen with panic-stricken expressions and undoubtedly some of these would end by hanging themselves, placing their heads upon train tracks or flinging themselves off one of the numerous cliffs of the region—seemingly put there by the hand of some omnipotent deity just for the purpose.

The place indeed had a decidedly tragic, carnal quality about it. The velvet carpet made the floor seem as if drenched in blood. The faces of the women were, for the most part, lewd masks—noses sniffing out fortunes, lips swollen with greed. Trente et quarante, chemin de fer, banque à deux tableaux, English and European roulette. There was an air of excitement peppered with an uneasy melancholy served on lower emotional platters; for here no one thought of God or spiritual experience, but of love and money—those demons which grip the world in their wiry arms, strangling the life out of it.

The doctor drifted through this strange jungle of vice, where gross materialism and lust were gilt with good manners. His eyes observed, his beard led him from table to table.

Presently, he came to a blackjack table.

"Yes," he thought, "I have always been good at cards."

He sat down, tucked his belly under the table, ordered an absinthe sour, lit a cigar and set himself to the task.

Dr. Black in Monte Carlo

At first he played with the utmost caution, never letting himself stake more than a thousand euros at a time, and always purposely losing one hand out of every three or four for good measure. But gradually the alcohol, thujone, and the much more potent drug of 'winning' began to affect his steady mind.

He felt himself surrounded by a whole range of bosoms, lips in every melody—he seemed to have become suddenly interesting to a number of very handsome women;—as well as one or two pale young men with languorous gazes. A Chinese woman eyed him hungrily. Obsequious men in oversized dinner jackets offered to kindle his cigars for him. The people gazed at him as if he were a celebrity. Before him was ranged an architecture of chips representing a small fortune.

At one moment, looking up, he saw Tandy there observing him. She neither smiled nor frowned, and he could not say whether she was pleased or otherwise to see him.

"Yet everyone likes a winner," he thought, with uncharacteristic naiveté, failing to take into account that pity is often a stronger stimulant than admiration.

In a high tide of excitement he won and won again, his appetite peaked, his mathematical mind pinched, stimulated to optimum performance / good stroking
tallow of riches + understanding / circles
genius /
man attracted by circles / hand whip dripping exunge
son with his net dripping exunge circles ball valves
love + an axle oleagine.

He puffed coolly on his cigar as they changed dealer, changed to a somewhat younger man with a very sharp face whose fingers were falcons prepared to plunge.

"The probability of any event = ratio between the value at which an expectation depending on the happening of the event ought to be computed," the doctor thought, taking a sip of his fourth drink.

"Deal," he said aloud, his subconscious instincts paying homage with ghee to the chance of the thing expected upon its happening subtracted the probability which is greater or less according to the number of chances by which it may happen compared with the whole number of chances by which it may either happen or fail one has of winning two or more remain the probability of winning which therefore will be found to be probability of an event a failure b probability being a.

"Faire sauter la banque," the sharp-faced man said, dramatically laying a shroud over the table.

A fresh stock of chips was sent for.

The count was there (stage left), grinning at someone, his eyes twinkling lasciviously under the glare of the electric chandeliers.

Ivan approached the doctor.

"The count asked me to give you this message," he said in a discreet voice, slipping a note into his hand.

The doctor unfolded the sheet of paper. A single word was written:

QUIT!

He stroked his beard momentarily and finally rose from his seat. In six hours of gaming he had won just over 900,000 euros.

V.

Back at the hotel:

The doctor puffed good-humouredly on the remnants of a Sancho Panza he had begun at the casino. His bed was covered with stacks of rainbow-coloured cash: green, yellow and blue 100s, yellow, gold and blue 200s, violet and blue 500s.

Out his window the night sky was just beginning to become tinted by the fingers of dawn.

A smile flowered his lips as he thought of the twinkling eyes of Tandy.

"The woman is fascinated by me," he thought.

There was a knock at the door and, upon opening it, the doctor was confronted by two men: one thin, with sunken cheeks and effeminate lips; the other of an enormous stature and extra-ordinarily low hair-line. The former, greatly the more refined of the two, spoke:

"Monsieur Black, I am Monsieur Gaborieou-Blanch, and this is my colleague Monsieur Beppo, sent by the proprietors of the Casino to discuss certain ... matters."

"Ah, please come in gentlemen."

The two men entered. Black offered them a drink, which they politely declined.

"You have won a great deal of currency," Gaborieou-Blanch said, nodding towards the bed.

"I have been lucky."

"Are you sure that you did not make your own luck?"

"My dear sir ... "

"Oh, I realise that it would be impossible to prove. But you must understand, that in gambling—there is no such thing as luck."

"Well, let us call it fate then."

"I am a strict compatibilist, Doctor."

"Yes, certainly one cannot deny a quantity of quantum randomness..."

"You won too much."

The doctor shrugged his shoulders. "I can understand that your casino does not find it amusing to lose so much money in an evening, but I don't really see——"

"We are not here to argue the matter with you," Gaborieou-Blanch interrupted. "On matters such as these our policies are very strict. You have twenty-four hours to evacuate Monaco. If you don't, or if we see you in the Casino again, things will become unpleasant for you. Very unpleasant. Isn't that right M. Beppo?"

A vague rumbling came from the throat of the latter.

"I see," the doctor murmured.

"Good. My job is to make people see and I always feel a certain personal satisfaction when I perform my job efficiently. Now, I believe we have intruded on your hospitality for long enough. Au-revoir Monsieur!"

The doctor, left alone, gazed at the pile of money. "Well," he thought, "it seems that I am going to have to expedite matters—push for a rapid denouement. I will deposit this sum in the hotel safe downstairs and set to work with vigour."

VII.

A SMILE FLOWERED HIS LIPS AS HE THOUGHT OF THE TWINKLING eyes of Tandy.

"The woman is fascinated by me," he thought.

There was a knock at the door.

"Monsieur Black, I am Monsieur Gaborieou-Blanch, and this is Monsieur Beppo."

"You have come to . . . "

"To kill you?"

"Yes."

"Well, how would you wish to die?"

"On some very far away planet, wearing a mask of beaten gold."

"Your beard braided?"

"Precisely."

"We will have to do a feasibility study."

"And in the meantime?"

"Please travel."

VIII.

THE SUN OPENED ITS VEINS AND THE AUSTRALIAN MILLIONAIRE HIS shades. Glancing below, he noticed a rotund form attired in evening clothes and caught the smell of a good cigar.

8:06 a.m. Breakfast room: coffee, croissant[1], and, stuffed behind a newspaper, him, right eye shooting a beam in Tandy's direction.

8:28 a.m. Glass-domed Jardin d'Hiver: Black seated on the leather sofa island. Rutter on the mezzanine above, leaning on the railing. Something, some metaphysical fluid, passed between the two men and the Australian remembered a dream he had had the night before: in a wilderness of aborted smiles and stillborn kisses, he was a tree (Brachychiton rupestris), and was being cut down.

Brock spent the morning sailing[2] and met Tandy later at the harbour. He attached his lips to hers, holding her waist tightly between his large hands. Then, talking in low intimate voices, they walked to the Louis XIV Restaurant; were quickly shown to a table near the window, with an ocean view—heart-shaped waves and a horizon made up of two copulating shades of blue.

He glanced over the menu, smiling stiffly.

Of a sudden, he felt inexplicably uneasy, as if something were about to fall on him. He looked up at the chandelier, which appeared to be well-fastened to the ceiling; then turned his head, and immediately discovered

1. Every morning Brock celebrated Jan III Sobieski, Grand Duke of Lithuania's victory at the Battle of Vienna.
2. 9:54 a.m. sightings of black dot skirting along the shore.

Dr. Black in Monte Carlo 143

the cause of this guillotine-like sensation. The doctor was placed a few tables over and was at that moment lifting a spoonful of soup to his mouth. Brock turned away with irritation.

"That man—everywhere we go he is there in the background."

"Does that bother you?"

"Naturally. I have the uneasy feeling that he is following us, or, more precisely, following you."

"Oh?"

"Yes. I think he is in love with you."

"How horrible."

"It is, isn't it? To have an ugly midget like that looking at my woman."

"Your woman?"

"Absolutely," he said haughtily.

"Still, I cannot help it if a man is attracted to me."

"No . . . but—" he paused significantly and took her hand in his. "Listen Tandy my dear, I know it might sound ridiculous, but—have you ever had relations with that man?"

"Relations?"

"Yes. Have you ever led him to believe . . . "

"I don't know what he believes."

"Have you ever been intimate with him?"

"Oh, Brock!"

Intimate axe of fingers run through monumental carbonised beard
palm condiment palm
/solar king/
prehistoric /solar king/
amours /solar king/
in marsupial
/solar king/
curve lusted ball valves tubing
roar poison machine
staple braided plastic hose
/solar king/
the sun is black plastic measured in inches of mercury
the sun is black suffering spitting twisting tails
sun is pudding

/solar king/ in intimate axe wrapped in sleepy blue coils and scarring emotions with nails stinging scorpions clouds are scorpions.

He frowned.

"Have you?" he repeated.

"Do you want me to give you a catalogue of my lovers?"

"Don't be a shameful bitch!"

"I don't see why I should be ashamed."

"Do you love me?"

"You know I do."

He stuck out his bold chin. The tendons on his neck vibrated like the strings of a violoncello.

"Then I am going to deal with this fat, black shrimp."

"I don't see how."

"You will."

The Australian ordered a steak, cooked 'as rare as humanly possible', and Tandy ordered a salad. He drank unsparingly of wine, she modestly of water. Three-quarters of an hour later, bill paid, they made their way out of the restaurant.

"Shall we go back to the hotel?" Tandy asked.

"No, wait here."

A moment later Dr. Black came issuing out.

"Hello," he said, with innocence.

Brock growled.

"I hope that you are not going to create a scene," Tandy remarked with annoyance.

"I'll create whatever the hell I want!"

"Well—then I will leave it to you gentlemen to work out your differences between you."

She turned and walked away and the Australian turned his gaze to the polymath.

"Do you know that you are becoming somewhat annoying?"

"A state of being you yourself should be quite familiar with by now."

"I do not like you."

"Nor I you."

"I would hit you, but I don't wrestle with dwarves."

"I would strike you, but it would be like striking a child."

"Bastard."
"A very crude way of..."
"Satisfaction."
"???"
"I demand satisfaction."
"I am not sure I quite follow you."
"I am a gentleman, a sportsman, and I hope that you have enough self-respect to accommodate me...."
"Are you proposing...?"
"A duel."
"Duorum bellum.... A duel? Don't you think the idea is rather barbaric for the 20th century!"
"Not at all. I believe it is a sporting way for gentlemen to decide such a delicate matter. And, even though I am the offended party, I will allow you to choose the weapon."
"A chess board would be appropriate."
"Sabres or pistols?"

Black's eyes took in the man's enormous arms [muscle] and imagined them driving a sword through him.

"Pistols."

The voice had come from his mouth, but he felt as if it were not his own.

Brock bowed stiffly. "Since you have decided on the weapons, I will supply them. Tomorrow at dawn, in the gardens by the Casino."

"As you wish," the doctor murmured, and watched his opponent-to-be stride away.

VI.

An hour later the doctor was back at his hotel. He went to the bar and there encountered Buxhoeveden.

"Ah, Doctor! I was just taking an afternoon whisky and water[1], if you would care to join me."

"With the greatest pleasure."

While partaking of his dram, Black explained the situation to the count.

"And who is your second going to be?"

"Second?"

"Why, naturally my dear man. You need someone to uphold your honour!"

"Though I am uncertain how high the integrity of my actions can be held, I do see your point, a duellist generally requiring one or more representatives. And who might you suggest?"

"Ah—I would do it myself, but I am getting a bit old for that sort of thing."

"Yes," the doctor agreed, as he surveyed the frail and wrinkled form before him.

"But if you were willing to entrust my man Ivan..."

"As well him as anyone, I suppose."

The count subsequently summoned the fellow and apprised him of the situation.

"I am most ready to assist the doctor in whatever way possible, the valet said, bowing. "I did, after all, serve nine days in the 138th Motor Rifle Brigade before being discharged for moonlighting as a waiter at

---

1. Hydrogen carbonate 190 anions mg/l.

Dr. Black in Monte Carlo 147

one of the finest restaurants in Kamenka, according to regulation 669-K of the Disciplinary Regulations of the Russian Armed Forces."

"My rendezvous is set for tomorrow morning at dawn, in the gardens by the Casino," the doctor said without enthusiasm.

"Then I will meet you in the lobby at half past five."

"Very well."

"Good man, Ivan," cried the count. "And, as soon as you help me to my room, you may have the rest of the evening off."

"Ah, you are———"

"Indeed I am," cried the count, interrupting his gentleman's gentleman and casting on him a rapid glance of intelligence.

Ivan took the wheelchair to take the count away and the latter, before parting, offered his hand to Black.

"Good fortune to you," he said, looking him directly in the eyes.

The doctor remained; ordered another drink, this time full-bore, determined to paralyze his taste buds.

An old woman in a black silk dress approached the piano, sat down, gave an anisodont smile, and began playing Franco Casavola's *Cabaret Epilettico*.

His mind mounted the notes, was gradually lifted to the ceiling where it skated along the gold trim before plunging dramatically to the bottom of his glass.

A slight and gentle pressure on his shoulder. He turned. It was Tandy.

"I heard," she said, sitting next to him. "Brock told me all about it."

"And what do you think?"

"It is awful. . . . Yet I can't help but be flattered."

"I am going to engage in single combat,   as the Koreans say . . . for you," the doctor pronounced in a quivering voice.

"I know it."

"And if I win?"

[See 1 Sam.18:20 for her approximate response.]

VII.

(To be read aloud in a vast meadow)

SOMEWHAT LATER: IVAN WAS SMOKING A CIGARETTE IN THE garden. The sound of the bar pianist reached his ears as did a cough.

The valet de chambre looked up. A man in evening clothes was standing not far distant, smoking as well.

"A nice night, isn't it," this other said.

"The temperature is good."

"Staying at the hotel, are you?"

"It would seem so."

"Fine, fine." He approached; was a nervous-looking fellow, of frail stature, large nose and small lively eyes. "So, are you in Monte Carlo to try your luck?"

"I should say not. I am merely here in the capacity of servant."

The other was silent and then silently trod away and years later would marry a Swedish woman twice his age and on many a cold winter night find himself eating very tough reindeer and drinking heavily of spirits.

VIII.

(To be read to one's children while looking at a lake)

SOMEWHAT LATER: IVAN WAS SMOKING A CIGARETTE IN THE garden. The sound of the bar pianist reached his ears between which a few repetitive thoughts were lodged:
nightsoundsaresofter
maintainwar drobeandcloth inginventoryandcloth ingstorageforgentleman
crickets soundsare followthroughpers onaltaskson be half of gentleman forgentleman nightsoundsaresofter mustproperprotocol
mustproperprotocol nightsounds crickets
handwrite thank you letters and notes and certain letters
d'amour
on
behalf of gentleman

A cough.

The valet de chambre looked up. A man in evening clothes was standing not far distant, smoking as well.

"A nice night, isn't it," he said with a rather overly brisk nod.

"The temperature is good."

"Staying at the hotel, are you?"

"It would seem so."

"Fine, fine." He approached; was a nervous looking fellow, of frail stature, large nose and small lively eyes. "World class hotel and all that."

"When abroad, one can at least try to meet the style one's accustomed to," Ivan replied pompously.

"So," the man asked, "are you in Monte Carlo to try your luck?"

Ivan shrugged his shoulders. He didn't feel like telling this fellow that he was there simply in the capacity of servant.

"I take my luck as it comes," he said evasively.
"The best way to take it! But, let me introduce myself: McEwen. Todd McEwen. Profligate son of a Scottish pharmaceuticals baron."
"Ivan Edzhubov. Um. Gentleman."
"You are Russian!"
"You are not."
"There is another Russian here I believe, a Count von Buxhoeveden. I suppose you know him?"
"Yes, I know the count quite well," Ivan replied modestly.
"Ah!"
"And you? You are here for the gambling?"
"Indeed I am, but the casinos do not attract me."
"Then you play privately?"
"Yes. I enjoy certain *thrills* that cannot be had in public," he said, winking at the Russian.
"It sounds interesting."
"It is. But, you seem like a good fellow. If you wanted . . . "
"Yes?"
"I might introduce you to tonight's circle. For our little game begins quite shortly, and to be truthful, we still need one more body for the second partita."
"It could be interesting," Ivan said with uncertainty.
"Of course you need one hundred cash to simply enter the game."
"I have one hundred and then some," Ivan replied, thinking of the 160 euros then sleeping in his wallet.
"On your person???"
"Naturally."
"Brilliant! And you being Russian will fit in perfectly."
"And why shouldn't I have a little fun," Ivan thought, as he followed his new acquaintance to the front of the hotel where a parking valet soon presented them with a sports car of exotic make.

A few moments later they were sweeping around sharp curves. Ivan's comrade babbled on incessantly as he shifted gears, went at great speed with two fingers on the steering wheel and his gaze everywhere but on the road.

The vehicle sped down a secluded lane at the end of which was a gate grinning out of a high white wall. McEwen honked, it swung open, and then down a gravel drive they went and pulled up in front of a grandiose mansion.

They were met at the door by a large, formidable looking man in evening dress.

"We are here to play," McEwen said.

"If you would be kind enough to provide me with the password for the evening."

"Our bodies will return to earth, our blood to water."

"Welcome gentlemen. Please follow me . . . "

They were led through a large antechamber, then down a long hallway decorated with impressionist paintings of tertiary importance and into a fair-sized salon made unusual by an apparently live python curled around a marble pillar. A balding man with a prominent chin and a small moustache came forward to greet them.

"Mr. McEwen, we have been expecting you. The other guests have already arrived. . . . And I see you have brought a friend."

"Yes. This is Mr. Edzhubov, who I have known for ages and who is an intimate acquaintance of Count von Buxhoeveden."

"How do you do? I am Monsieur Pietro D'Ennery and am very pleased that you could make it, as we were one man short." Then turning to the Scot: "You have come equipped with the proper funds I suppose?"

"Naturally my dear fellow, naturally."

"With Mr. Edzhubov, the players are now twelve—six for the first round, six for the second. If you are agreeable, Mr. McEwen, you will take part in the first, Mr. Edzhubov, in the second."

"Perfect!"

The gentleman led them through a large oak door.

"Now," McEwen whispered to the Russian as they entered, "this whole thing is hush-hush you understand?"

"Of course."

The room was poorly lit. In the centre was a large, round table, such as those used in poker. Around its edges a number of men sat. Others were positioned off to right and left—a few on a sofa, others in armchairs. The air was suffused with tobacco smoke and most present were sucking on whiskies.

Only one of the gentlemen did Ivan recognise, and that was Brock Rutter, who was one of the five at the table.

"What exactly is the game anyhow?" Ivan murmured to McEwen.

"Roulette my dear fellow, roulette—just as you Russians like to play.... Anyhow, I'm going to sit here with these other fellows for the first round and you're up for the second!"

D'Ennery now spoke, in a loud, clear voice:

"The rules are clear. The contestants will draw straws to determine the order of play. The man with the shortest straw goes first, the longest last. A single bullet will be placed in one of the six chambers of the revolver and the cartridge spun. The players will, in turn place the barrel of the weapon to their temple—right or left, it makes no difference—and pull the trigger. If there is no detonation, the arm will be passed to the next in sequence. In the unfortunate event of a detonation, my man Constantine will remove you to the wine cellar. A fresh bullet will be placed in one of the six chambers of the gun, and the game will continue. This process will be repeated until there is only one contestant remaining, who will be the winner of the entire pot, minus fifteen percent for the upkeep of the house. Any contestant at any time can choose to leave the game, but in so doing they forfeit their stake—said stake being the sum of 100,000 euros cash to be placed on the table at the opening of the game."

He then extracted an object from his breast-coat pocket and laid it on the table. It was a hand-ejector style double-action revolver equipped with a special shield to prevent the contestants from seeing where the bullet might lie. He placed this on the table and then placed an open box of rounds next to it.

"Your stakes gentlemen."

Six individual stacks of bills were silently thrust forward to the centre of the table.

Tension.

D'Ennery held forward his clenched fist, from which six straw ends protruded. Each man took a straw.

"The order of play has been determined: Warmington, Arabella, McEwen, Rutter, Mirkel, Sakura."

The first up was Warmington, a very heavy Englishman in his forties,

Dr. Black in Monte Carlo

with blue eyes and thinning blond hair. He pointed the barrel down and spun the cylinder on its vertical axis, thus eliminating any odds gravity would give to the single bullet in the cartridge, put the barrel to his head in a suicidal manner and pulled the trigger.

There was a loud clap and the gentleman fell back in his chair, dead.

"Bad luck for being first up," someone remarked.

D'Ennery pried the revolver from the dead man's fingers and then the servant with difficulty dragged the corpse away.

"Mr. Arabella," Brock said calmly, "I believe it is your play."

Youthful Mr. Arabella, with trembling hand, picked up the revolver and placed a bullet in one of the chambers. He spun the chamber and placed the barrel to his temple. His eyes dashed around the room as if they wished to escape. He closed them tightly, clenched his teeth and pulled the trigger.

There was a click, but no detonation.

Breathing a sigh of the profoundest relief, his eyes sliding down his face, he handed the pistol to McEwen, who went about the business with a smile on his face.

Click!

No worries.

Brock did his play nonchalantly and survived.

Mirkel was a German with very shiny lips. He was not so lucky. His corpse was treated as the first.

"Mr. Sakura."

At this point, the Japanese gentleman was all nerves. His lips were inverted into an awful grimace and his eyes were the hearts of hens. He put the barrel of the pistol to his temple. Several tense moments passed.

"Be a good fellow and pull the trigger now, would you," Brock said with annoyance.

Mr. Sakura showed his teeth.

"Out!" he cried, slamming the revolver down on the table. And then he burst out laughing, his tensed nerves finding relief in abstract thoughts of flaming hair and phantom almonds. A tear sprang from his left eyeball.

The first round had been completed, with three withdrawn from competition.

Arabella was first in the second round, but declined to pull the trigger, preferring instead to forfeit the 100,000 euros he had embezzled from the photovoltaic panel firm he worked for back in Brighton.

There were now only two men left at the table. Brock Rutter and Todd McEwen.

It was the latter's turn. He rubbed his hands together eagerly.

"Here goes," he murmured, winking at Ivan.

Needless to say, it was not McEwen's lucky night.

"Where is that Russian fellow?"

"He seems to have disappeared."

At that moment Ivan was jogging swiftly along the naked streets of Monaco, towards his servant's bed at the Hôtel Hermitage.

IX.

D R. BLACK LAY DOWN BUT COULD NOT SLEEP. A VISION OF himself dead kept entering his mind—his body stretched out like that of Christ in Mantegna's painting in the Brera in Milan. It is placed upon a bier, slowly lifted up by a group of men in hoods who chant the requiem mass of Clemens non Papa as they walk along through pearl-grey clouds of incense.

He felt trickles of sweat running down his temples. A sense of suffocation.

Yes.

He had left his body to science.

"In a matter of hours," he murmured to himself, "they might be dissecting this thing I have been hauling about for all these years. Young men with acne poking it with scalpels in some school of anatomy or balding Germans sawing me in two with sharp instruments. Weighing my brain, transplanting my heart into a fish.... Articles written about it in the Journal of Science and slideshows shown at obscure conferences in Eastern capitols."

He rose from his bed, drank a glass of water and then, remembering that the mini-bar was well stocked with liquor, extracted a miniature of 12-year-old zivania and poured its contents into his empty glass. He swallowed the liquid rapidly and wiped his lips with the back of his hand. He felt its raisiny heat rise from his belly and enter his head, painting it with a new lightness. The deadly-sharp, over-defined edges of disaster seemed to grow dull seen through the mist of liquor.

He picked up a book and tried to read, but the words simply danced before his eyes. Then, by dint of concentration, he began to be involved in the content, fallacious citations of scriptural passages, neither grass nor fire, short nor long (Br. Up. 3. 8. 8.) superimposition and de-superimposition...

He lay down the thin volume.

He recalled reading somewhere that one in four duels had a fatal outcome and approximately two-thirds ended in some form of bloodshed.

"I suppose the odds could be worse," he thought. "And, after all, the chances are still somewhat against his bullet piercing one of my vital organs. In all probability I will simply be shot in the shoulder or leg."

But then to have his life depend on chance, on another man's inability to shoot straight! And Brock Rutter was after all a famed sportsman, a hunter—one who was well familiar with guns and how to use them.

The doctor poured himself another drink.

"What is the purpose of this life anyhow? Is it just some vile experiment that will soon come to an end? Am I really hebetudinous enough to put it at risk to satisfy some bizarre sense of honour—to win the deranged love of a female, a Homo sapiens, a hundred pounds of woman flesh; ... flesh of milk ... blood of strawberries ... with eyes of soft lavender and hair of embroidered amber."

He gave a short laugh, recalled Bosquett, and that fellow's warning against getting into situations such as these[1].

"Though it was possibly unwise of me to accept the man's proposition, it is now too late to turn back. And I do know how to fire a pistol. And I am in love with this woman and should not cower at performing such a deed for her sake—to win her love as decisively as I won at blackjack. And hopefully I will come out of it with a mere schmiss, a bragging scar, some mark to add to my dossier of virility."

At 4:30 he ordered room service: black coffee fortified with brandy. At 5 a.m. he looked in the mirror and was confronted by a pair of wild eyes staring at him from out of a two-toned patch. He bathed his face in water, put on a fresh white shirt and a black neck tie, which he knotted with the utmost care.

He clenched his fists and looked again: an extraordinarily serious middle-aged man with a ferocious black beard. And then, with firm steps,

---

1. *The Young Man of Honour's Vade Mecum, being a salutary treatise on duelling, together with the annals of chivalry, the ordeal trial, and judicial combat, from the earliest times*, London, 1817.

Dr. Black in Monte Carlo 157

he left his room, made his way down to the lobby, where Ivan was reading a newspaper and waiting for him.

The Russian gripped him by the hand. "Good morning Doctor."

"Good morning.... An ugly business."

"Think of it as a little morning walk to wet the appetite," Ivan said grinning.

They went outside, inhaled the perfume of dawn, walked along, the doctor taking long strides despite the fact that he had little desire to arrive at the destination. Both men were silent. The doctor noticed the dew on the grass, the crunch of gravel beneath his feet—everything was defined with enormous clarity.

Ivan every now and again stole a glance at his companion.

"He is a dead man," he thought, recalling the game of roulette he had seen Rutter win the night before.

Soon they turned off the main road, down a small path veiled by trees. Then out, into a clearing. The spot was ideal, with sunlight, shadow and wind evenly proportioned.

Brock Rutter was sitting on the trunk of a large pine. He wore a pair of tan slacks tucked into leather riding boots and a white shirt buttoned up all the way to the collar. He appeared to be quite calm. By his side was D'Ennery, smoking a cigarette.

The doctor began to make his way towards the two men, but Ivan grabbed him by the arm.

"No, wait here. This is my duty."

He and D'Ennery met in the middle of the field. They shook hands cordially and talked for several minutes in low voices. The principals were then informed as to how the duel would proceed.

D'Ennery took out a rosewood box and, holding it between the two men, raised the lid. Two pistols and apparatus (bullet mould, powder flask, mallet, cleaning and loading rod, patent nipple wrench, correct key, etc.) sat encased in green baize. The pistols had 9" octagonal Damascus barrels with multi-groove rifling in calibre .54 percussion. The tops were flat and inlaid with the name *LORENZ BÖSSEL IN SUHL* framed with arrows. The stocks were of fine walnut.

The pistols were loaded.

"Choose," Rutter said.

Black slipped his fingers around the grip of one and weighed it in his hand.

"This will do," he murmured.

The two men nodded coldly to each other. Rutter behaved with complete aplomb, appeared to be absolute master of himself. The doctor felt a bizarre quaking in his spine.

"Now don't be a coward," he told himself.

The rivals each took twenty paces, one from the other, making the space between them forty, and then turned.

Black did not know how to stand, as his body was proportioned almost exactly the same from every angle—he made a perfect target from every point of view. He covered as much of his chest as he could with his right arm, drew in his stomach as much as he was able, which was very little indeed.

Then, while awaiting the signal, the two men measured each other with their gazes.

Ivan clapped his hands three times.

The doctor saw Brock raise his pistol. Then there was a small crack and a puff of smoke. He felt the bullet whiz through his beard.

"Now my turn . . ."

Without even taking aim, he pressed his finger against the trigger and heard the crack of his shot.

Brock raised his hand to his throat and fell back theatrically, in the manner of a bad actor playing a part. The doctor dropped his pistol and approached. He knelt beside his opponent, gazed at the distorted features of his face. The latter was dead. The bullet had entered his Adam's apple and severed the back of his spine. A thin stream of blood oozed out of the wound.

A bitter smile coursed over the doctor's lips. "Stupid young man," he remarked. "But I suppose there was not enough room on this ball of clay for the two of us."

"I will take care of matters," Ivan said. "Leave it to me."

Dr. Black gave him a look of gratitude.

"Now, back to the hotel," he thought. "Pack my bags . . . pick up Tandy, and go!"

Dr. Black in Monte Carlo

He turned and walked away as quickly as his legs would carry him. The trees of the park seemed to fly past; only if he had had wings could he have travelled with greater speed. The song of the birds urged him on, thoughts romantic filling his mind love caress feel beauty life, his person filled with a sudden sense of strength, manly qualities.

At the hotel he climbed the steps three at a time, arrived at her door like an arrow and knocked.

A vague, sleepy voice came from within.

"Come in."

The doctor turned the door handle and entered.

Scent of rotten jasmine. A scarlet wound, that deflowered smile. She looked at him from a tangle of sheets.

"It is not the morning champagne."

The count's frail body was wrapped in a red satin robe. He approached the doctor, linked his arm in his and led him out of the room. "Come," he said, "this is no place for you."

The doctor was stunned. "But," he said, "this is madness!"

"Do not be so naïve."

"Oh!"

"My dear young man," the count said, "can't you understand that a woman like that is not only repulsed by your admiration, but not even impressed by your manly virtues, limited though they may be. Only the most refined of libertines can understand such creatures, for they can only be subdued by acts whose very nature is as unpronounceable as certain Scottish lochs, as the Hebrew deity himself.... She tried you, as she certainly has a thousand other men, and became bored. She finds my own person, quite understandably, fascinating. We will be married this autumn, just as the leaves begin to yellow and drop from the trees.... And I will take her to my castle in Moravia, where her flesh, for the very application I will make of it, will soon become as flaccid and useless as leaves of rotting lettuce. But such is the way of nature. We pick flowers to smell them, not worrying ourselves that we thereby rush on the end to their beauty."

"But this is beastly!"

"Even beasts have craniums. The poetry of our minds is only there to garnish our hunger."

"I cannot..."

"You do not need to. I wish you a good day doctor," the count said, somewhat coldly, bowing slightly.

He turned and walked away, re-entered the bed chamber.

The doctor thought he heard a giggle.

With slow steps he made his way back to his room. His bag was already packed. He slipped his hand over the handle. Though it only contained a few items of clothing and toiletries, it felt lead-heavy—another burden to carry across the earth.

Down the richly-carpeted staircase he went; with difficulty supporting his torso. He leaned against the railing.

Two figures were in the lobby. Mssrs. Gaborieou-Blanch and Beppo. The former, smoking a cigarette, one hand buried in his trouser pocket, nodded at him. Black saluted him with a vague gesture and moved on, to the desk, deposited his key, turned, towards the door, walked...

"Excuse me Monsieur!"

He turned. It was the desk clerk.

"Yes?"

"Didn't you deposit some goods in our safe?"

"Yes... I did."

He filled his coat pockets with bills—thick wads of brightly coloured cash—and then stepped into the morning—not the morning of bloodshed, of pistol shots and lubricious Russian counts—but of butterflies and sunshine (the rays fell upon him, bathed him in a moment of strange glory)... the world
some Ducal park
where shoes are teeth
nailed to dreams
serene tangle of myrrh slips itself around his hand
the dunes of her hair
blown away
reveal
some Ducal park
where the birds are smelted to the trees
beaks bleeding songs shockingly green
sitting eating dates which are actually his own sorrows.

The doctor looked out over the blue sea—a great sheet of profundity—and felt as if the mirror of his sentiments, once covered with dust, had been wiped clean.

Red-Haired Man in a Sweater

From the Private Papers of Dr. Black

(The following case was related by Professor Kaltenbach, of Bonn, Germany)

*M*R. X. EYES NEUROPATHIC. SKIN CREAMY, GREY, MARKED WITH *purple blotches. Patient highly intellectual, of refined manners, though clearly afflicted with moral degeneracy. He believes himself to have been painted by Lucian Freud. When questioned about the logical ramifications of this absurd theory he becomes surly, stubbornly obstinate, revealing a lack of proper breeding in the process. He claims to be worth 1.2 million pounds sterling. Though Dr. Heuzé (Archives de l'Anthropologie bizarre, 1894, vol viii) mentions the case of a man who believed himself to be made of porcelain, I do not believe another case quite like that which I am presenting you with has yet been recorded. The following interesting document is a statement from the patient himself:*

I have never been a fool and that might very well be the reason why I have always suffered so much. A fool accepts his position with a shrug of the shoulders and manages to enjoy his life all the same. A philosopher—I am not ashamed to call myself one—has no choice but to plumb the depths of his being, to dissect it like some ambitious anatomist would a corpse. How frightening then to find that the great ocean before you is nothing more than a teacup, and realise that your own personality is canvas-thin.

But is not personality something developed in childhood? A man without uncle or aunt, father or mother, brother or sister—whose past is nothing more than a palette;—where could such a man have gained a personality? A painted man, unlike one issued from a womb, is born completely matured—a maturity both stunted and pure, narrow and as disappointingly profound as some cosmic syllable muttered between yawns.

The odd thing about being a painting is this: one has only one unalterable mood. A normal man is sometimes happy, sometimes sad. One day he opens his mouth like a horse and neighs in delight at some silly joke; the next his lips droop and copious liquid flows from his eyes. I, on the other hand, am always the same. The blasé expression you see today was there yesterday and, no matter what might happen, will be there tomorrow. I have a single emotion: melancholy boredom. Yes, this weariness you see is a constant and to calculate its numerical value would be as complicated and fruitless as calculating the atomic depth of a glass of schnapps.

I have had women fall in love with me. I don't know why, as I am certainly not handsome. But I have never fallen in love with a woman. You can love a painting, but do not expect it to return the emotion. Whether others are in possession of a soul, I cannot say. But I am certain that I myself do not have one. A sickly ego: yes. Masterpieces after all are nothing more than an ego dressed in paints or plaster or sometimes paper—the meagre glorification of the artist's will. Women have loved me, I suppose, in the mad hope of gaining some self-esteem. Nothing doing. I am symbolic of hopelessness and there is nothing jolly about me.

When Freud painted me, he used his brush like a weapon. The impasto was not terribly thick, but I believe if one looks closely the brush strokes can still be seen.

He gave me a distinctive physiognomy. My nose is small, somewhat snub, not altogether unlike that of a suckling pig. I have a thick neck. My chin is cleft. My lower lip is thin, my upper fat, making me appear almost beaked. And yet I am not ugly, almost handsome, in a way that only sentimentalists and libertines could understand. I am clothed drably in a grey sweater and a pair of loose, dark green corduroy trousers; but am thankful for these garments, for they protect me from being the lemon-fleshed nude I would otherwise have been.

I am not a portrait, but rather a conglomeration of many people—a sort of patched together puzzle—a real product of the studio. My eyes are those of Erasmus, my hands Pope Paul III. My body parts are lifted from great paintings of the past, and studies of obtuse modern day models—a baker, a financier, then a youth paid to strip naked and show his skin to my maker.

Red-Haired Man in a Sweater

I don't like to refer to myself as a work of modern art, for the only thing abstract about me is my mentality, the only thing conceptual my grim absurdity.

The incidents in my life are numerous, and probably not uninteresting from a scientific or sadistic point of view.

My first owner was an English gentleman whose name I can no longer remember. His flat stank horribly of cats, of which he had two—lounging balls of fur which for him I imagine took the place of wife, children, prostitute and lover.

I told the fellow that I found the animals vile, but he did not listen. He repulsed me, treated me like an insensible object and I sacrificed the warm comfort of his filth for the sidewalk, which my feet sought out instinctively as two orphans would a tureen of motherly love.

This trillion-faceted world will always provide a corner for a man willing to play the part of a machine. I worked as a factory hand, living in obscurity, earning just enough to pay for shelter, a few crusts of bread and an occasional piece of meat. The truth is that such occupations are the last refuge of genius—a quality which has long since fled the haunts of the rich who, in their sleek luxury, have become too lazy to form an original thought or emotion. Was not a Van Gogh once found in a chicken coop?

That manufactory in North London, that landmark of the city's industrial heritage whose high brick walls were decorated with broken glass, had colouring as sombre as a piece by Millet. A huge chimney poured out black smoke. Workmen, mostly foreigners, Asians and Eastern Europeans, moved about with sluggish fortitude, their brows contracted, twisted in resignation—these men impaling themselves on their meaningless fates like ancient Roman soldiers on the cold spears of the Alamanni. Occasionally one of these nameless men, one of these heroes of the age of petroleum, would get sucked in by a machine, turned into a great lump of ground flesh—spat out in bloody gobs that a bow-legged janitor would collect while grumbling.

I lived according to the clock. Lunch break at twelve on the dot. Visit to the pub at exactly a quarter to seven. A jacket potato beneath a coagulation of melted cheese. The squeak of female voices. Stagger back to my little flat.

One Saturday, after letting my lips extract a pint of Old Familiar from the depths of a chilly pub, I wandered, from Regent's Park to St. James's, kicking a can and then a pebble and then a stick that lay in my path. I crossed over Westminster Bridge and let my feet make their way along the embankment. I gazed about me with suitable abstraction, soon however finding myself called back from reverie by the unpleasant yelping of a quite young water spaniel which my feet had decided to kick along in the same way they had the objects previously mentioned.

I scrutinized my feet and the dog, finding in their mutual revolutions a vague sense of oneness with the universe around me. The wind did not stir. The world only quivered. I knelt down, examined the animal more closely and found that it was something like a piece by George Stubbs. I put out my hand and it treated it with affection, massaging my fingertips with a tiny little pink tongue, wet and soft as the tail of a goldfish.

It was without a collar; undoubtedly without an owner. I put it in the crook of my arm and took it home with me.

Though I do not dislike dogs, I cannot stand their barking—an unpleasant form of assertiveness, an inappropriate reaction to the frustration of their primary needs—and I much prefer the singing of birds. I considered having the animal de-barked, having its laryngeal tissue extracted from its throat. But what a lot of trouble, that cruel surgery of convenience! And then I recalled the words of Kant when he stated that birds do not instinctively know how to sing but learn to do so. I went to the British Library and took out the works of Conradi and Portmann as well as Witchell's *The Evolution of Bird Song, with Observations on the Influence of Heredity and Imitation.*

I saw clearly the path that lay before me. I purchased recordings and visited aviaries.

First I taught Tikvah (so I named the spaniel) the one-note songs, those of the laughing gull, red-breasted nuthatch and ruffled grouse. The creature adapted himself to these so well that it was but a short time before we had advanced to the two-note calls of the prothonotary warbler, soft as the stroke of a sable brush, and then the delightful call of the whiskered tern. Finally we arrived at the three-note songs: the eastern wood pee-wee, the ruby-crowned kinglet and the post-copulatory call of the winter wren, all of which Tikvah gained a remarkable proficiency in imitating.

My concern with the animal's education however distracted me from my work and it was not long before I found myself terminated. After lavishing my supervisor with epithets in fleshy ochre and azo yellow, as offensive as they were colourful, I returned to my humble flat, my spirits, naturally low, untainted by the occurrence. But fate, like a skilled boxer, often strikes with double fists. My flat had been broken into and I had been robbed of my few meaningless possessions. The dog, Tikvah, was also missing. I celebrated the disaster with three too many aperitifs, slept poorly that night and was roused from my bed late the next morning by the pale disk of the sun groaning at my window.

Days succeeded each other, marked by threats of eviction, meals of potatoes and peas and general unpleasantness.

On one of these day I was at the Bow Street tube station, waiting for a train.

There were very few people there, not more than half a dozen, and one of these was a chubby little man, immaculately dressed and fondling the handle of a black umbrella. It was clear that I interested him, for he passed me and repassed me several times, casting on me a look at once embarrassed and keen, like certain dogs who wish for attention, but are afraid of being beaten.

The man continued to eye me with curiosity, and then, flourishing his umbrella like some agitated, out of practice D'Artagnan, finally approached. "Excuse me, but do you mind if I——"

"Yes?"

"Are you by any chance an, um, Lucian Freud?"

I shrugged my shoulders. "And if I were?"

"Oh, don't think this is the curiosity of a nosey-parker. I am a professional."

He handed me his card.

> ## LEO KRAYL
> DEALER IN FINE PICTURES
>
> *consultations and evaluations*
>
> 23 Chapel Pl   London   W1S1AW

"So are you evaluating me then?" I asked, lacing my words with the appropriate hint of bitterness.

"Why my friend," he murmured, "I only wished to ascertain..."

"Oh yes," I broke in. "I am a Freud. Does the fact amuse you? Do I inspire you? Do you wish to look for meaning for your undoubtedly insipid life in the dreary shades of my face?"

The man seemed to enjoy this insult, for his face brightened. He obviously considered it as a sign of intimacy and it became instantly clear to me that he was one of those types who become deeply attached to their tormentors.

"It seems rather astounding to find you here in this filthy place," he continued. "Surely I might be able to help you."

"Maybe I don't want help."

"But it is not merely about what you want," he said eagerly. "You are a masterpiece, and as such have certain obligations. It is an injustice to have your presence hidden away, without anyone being able to appreciate you. Is it a buyer you lack? Well, I could find a hundred.—Your facial expression is delightfully underplayed!" he suddenly broke out. "Delightfully underplayed—yet mysteriously suggestive."

"You professionals," I sneered, "always manage to sugar-coat misery."

He looked distraught. "I certainly have no desire to misrepresent you—but after all, you must see for yourself that art is subject to various interpretations. Sometimes the viewer has a deeper insight into the work than the artist himself, how much more so the picture. And——"

I let him distribute his words in the air as a magnolia tree might its flower petals in the month of June, indirectly aware that the former were cosmically purposeless. If I had been created a man of vigour, I might have struck him; if a man of ignorance I might have lapped up his words like a starving cat at a dish of milk. As it was I hung in the void, like an icicle, fragily cold, hangs from the eave of a lonely house in Siberia.

I had already missed my train twice. I decided not to miss it a third time.

"I must go," I said.

"I feel nervous about leaving you here like this. I feel that I might not ever see you again."

"I don't guarantee that you will."

"I have a mind to drag you home with me."

"Don't do that. One of us might get damaged."

He pursed his lips together. "Yes. There is always a risk of damage. But I will not say goodbye, but simply see you again!"

A few days passed during which I drank a good deal more than usual, letting myself drift from disreputable pub to pub like a ghost from room to room in some great crumbling mansion on a hill. I swallowed little absinthes the colour of pond scum, strong glossy ales, and martinis as clear as the water of a Norwegian brook. I let myself be lashed by the laughter of young harlots. I made merry. And soon my wallet was empty of everything but that thin rectangle of card-stock paper.

I decided to call on him. After all, from a strictly physical point of view, my situation was miserable. Happiness was never an option. But the possibility of having physical comfort appealed to me.

The little man was quite delighted to see me, and rubbed his hands together with such avidity that it would not have surprised me if flames had burst forth from them. He guided me through an incongruous forest of antiques, poured me the stiffest of drinks and stuffed an enormous V-shaped cigar between my teeth, murmuring the platitudes of his profession.

His place was full of quadros, for the most part inferior stuff, though there were a few pieces of slight interest: an Emil Nolde which kept making the most awful faces; a Nitsch, a great emasculating splash of blood; an Ernst Ludwig Kirchner, a woman whose face was the most repulsive shade of green and whose whispered innuendoes could not fail but to entice.

Krayl grabbed me by the sleeve and placed me in a Henry IV chair.

"Ah, you will not regret having come to see me," he murmured. "I have clients—clients—clients who would be delighted to have an opportunity of doing you a good turn. Yes, it will be easy to find a buyer for a painting like you, one that can be smelt, touched, tasted—for people like that sort of thing you know."

I nodded my head and told him to do as he pleased, my only stipulation being that I wanted a private situation. I did not want to be in some museum, on public exhibition, having to watch day in and day out children picking their noses in front of me and men dressed in visors and shorts shoving their near-sighted eyes against my chest.

"Ah, of course," he said. "I would not dream of doing you such a disservice.... But wait;—I know just the people for you! Only last month they were asking about a Freud.... A very prestigious—a very comfortable collection."

Krayl found a place for me in the collection of one Hanspeter Liniger, of Berlin, at what advantage to himself I never learned.

The Linigers lived in a house designed by Richard Neutra, a blend of art, landscape and practical comfort decorated with a small collection of paintings of only slightly less importance than myself. There were a few pieces by Motherwell and a rather interesting, though diminutive, piece by Mr. Richard Tuttle. He had a nice assortment of lunette-shaped pen and inks by Francesco Salviati, all done with a brown wash and heightened with white. In the library there was a Monet—a pond on which a few water lilies rested rather sadly.

I was treated with the utmost respect—more respect than I desired—and was allowed to dine *en famille*. When they had guests over, I was shown off, and became the subject of a thousand opaque remarks;—such remarks as are designed to make the speaker sound intelligent without actually having to make use of that latter resource: the theoretical frill which they haul out by the yard and throw around like confetti.

"A real comment on the fate of man in an age of social disintegration," said one man.

"Absolutely chthonic."

"The eerie lack of depth in the volumetrical treatment leaves one..."

"Dazzled."

"Almost seasick."

"But there are several independent themes at work at once here..."

I believe they found my acrid solemnity charming—just as certain geographical locations, Death Valley, the Sahara and such, are, for their very bareness and lack of vegetation, considered beautiful. And the rich love nothing better than to contemplate life's ugliness from the comfortable depths of their cushions, just as ancient Egyptian pharaohs would, while eating pickled pearls and listening to the strains of the harp, watch their slaves flogged and their impertinent toadies beheaded.

But this sort of bigoted laziness appealed to me.

I lounged around the place, yawned a great deal, slithered about the liquor cabinet, emptying bottles of old Scotch and sampling odd liqueurs. I was a sort of mascot—a slab of dreary colour to be dragged out in front of dinner guests and pondered over in one's leisure moments. Unfortunately the rich have many of those—leisure moments.

Mr. Liniger would often fling himself down on the couch and gaze at me from behind the huge knot of his necktie with the weary eyes of a pampered imbecile. It is amazing how many unhappy millionaires there are in the world and, if it were not for the fact that the rich deserved to be despised, I might very well have felt some slight measure of pity for them. As it was, I supplied the man with an abundance of poisonous council, sought to show him the nakedness of his soul, which was like a soft, white-skinned gobbet of flesh cast in a whirlwind of glistening black thorns, twice as sharp as hypodermic needles.

He gurgled under my care, like a baby being fed pabulum.

"I always used to consider myself a happy man," he said.

"It is always better to know the truth."

"I suppose so . . . "

"You first have to realise how wretched you are in order to be able to weigh life's options intelligently."

"Life's options? But—and—will I ever find . . . true happiness?"

"It is doubtful. You are far too dishonest with yourself. And happiness, truly speaking, is one of those things which neither exists nor does not exist, nor both exists and does not exist."

And off he would go, to get lost in crowds of suited men, like a drop of water cast in the sea.

The wife, Sigrid was her name, would often come milling around me, with thermodynamic inference, her robust hips grazing me, her lips, like great wads of raw beef, twisting themselves into an obscene mockery of a smile. She was a dog-eared maiden addicted to Veronal, one of those women who, though they are as carnal as veal, make a pretence of being mystical. She dressed herself in loose, light-materialed pastel dresses, such as are worn at séances and intimate outdoor August grills, and glanced through books on theosophy, murmuring corrupted phrases of ancient wisdom with the same complacency that politicians speak of freedom and democracy while flagellating cities with million-dollar bombs and drowning third-world nations beneath the thick brown gel of poverty.

Sigrid would parade herself naked before me and, when her husband was not at home, you can be sure her advances were anything but subtle. On occasion, from sheer boredom, I complied with her wishes, making myself ill with the over-ripe, let us say rotten, fruit of her passion which combined, farcically, the pungent aroma of the sewer with the music of a thick-tongued heathen being flayed alive.

Somewhere in that tangle of limbs which resembled the capering of some eight-legged insect crushed by a boot heel, a flower was born. Its stem curved dizzyingly upward, its petals, the colour of lamp black, gave out a stench like rotting flesh. Its pistils, uncompromisingly sharp, were as ready to strike as the fangs of an agitated viper.

"I want to have your child," she murmured in the depths of the night.

"But you have had one... with your legitimate spouse."

"Oh... oh...!"

Indeed, some nineteen years previous, a wriggler had already crawled out of the Pandora's box of her womb.

Their son was an anaemic-looking individual with shoulder-length black hair which he kept parted in the middle and an outstretched, extremely thin nose which barely seemed to suffice to supply his meagre brain with oxygen. One could have eaten soup from the hollows of his cheeks and, when he opened his mouth, his long front teeth, attached to purplish gums, reminded one unpleasantly of the bits of fat around a piece of raw sirloin. That he had no friends was not surprising, for he was a thoroughly repulsive creature who did nothing all day but warm the couch with his meagre bottom, occasionally float to the piano to let his wiredrawn fingers slither over the keys like so many blind earthworms.

He would often come and moon around me, the lonely disks of his eyes suffused with petrified amberish tears.

"While other lads are off sniffing glue, gambling away their father's money, and visiting hookers, what are you doing? You seem, like a clam, to be incapable of both good and evil. I would call you a vegetable, but even carrots grow."

Red-Haired Man in a Sweater 175

"I play the piano."

"My dear boy, you do it with such utter passivity that it would be more apt to say the piano plays you. Your music manages to be both radically annoying and infinitely boring,—a rare accomplishment indeed!"

"But what should I do?"

"Get drunk," I said, stirring the whisky in my glass with my little finger.

"But alcohol usually makes me vomit."

"Another irony."

"If I could fall in love," he said shyly.

"As you are clearly incapable of feeling lust, the ability to love is as far away from you as the planet Neptune."

"Oh!"

I lighted a cigarette.

"Yes, you might tour the entire solar system and still not find a woman unambitious enough to fall in love with you—the most misshaped of human satellites—a mere lump of coal floating in space. Essentially you are the equivalent of a mould. As far as human beings go, you are a nullity. If there was a war in progress, I would suggest you go and become cannon fodder. As it is . . . " I paused significantly.

"As it is?" the young man gurgled.

"As it is, you might as well just go and kill yourself," I said, picking a bit of tobacco from my tongue. "You can be quite sure the world will go on just the same without you. After all, you have no friends and your parents are certainly not fond of you. For my part, I can honestly say it would cause me no other emotion than the slightest tinge of relief;—for truly these little philosophical conversations of ours are on the tedious side!"

"But what if I want to live?" he murmured. I saw an amberish globule lodged on the tip of his lower left eyelid.

"Want to live? Why you know very well that you don't want to live! If you wanted to live, you would be living right now instead of clinging to the rug like a mollusc. If you want to come bumbling in here begging for advice, the least you could do is be courteous enough to take it!"

His bottom lip quivered pitifully, like a half crushed caterpillar, and then he began to gnaw on it as if he wanted to put it out of its misery.

With spasmodic movements, idiot inspiration, he bounced towards the liquor cabinet, a few words dripping from his mouth like slobber:

"Drink ... man ... hopefully ... "

His fingers, wilted weeds, wrapped themselves around a bottle of Château Lascombes—vintage of '34 I believe. He discovered the corkscrew and tried to open it, but managed in doing so to drive the majority of the cork inside the bottle.

"We ... drink ... "

"No thank you. That wine-soaked cork is all yours."

I went to the liquor cabinet and refreshed my whisky. When I turned around he was gone, as was the wine bottle.

Later that evening he was discovered floating in the Monet, as green as the water-lilies around him. We fished him out and he threw up on a 16th century Armenian Kazak rug.

"I tried to ... drown myself. ... But ... wouldn't sink."

"The cork," I murmured, gazing meditatively at his pale face in its pool of vomit, the latter studded with a few undigested Veronal tablets.

This incident naturally livened things up a bit, and I believe that young man did well to follow my advice—though the results, due to the weakness of his mental facilities, were nothing more than a rather absurd fiasco. His inept attempt at suicide impressed his parents far more than it did myself; and their offspring, their coward, threw all the blame for his action on myself.

Liniger stormed through the house, howling out invectives to his concubine.

"This painting is cruel! We must get rid of it!"

"But you can't Hans!"

"Can't be damned! It has made a cuckold of me, almost killed my son. Under the auction hammer it goes!"

"I don't know what you are talking about."

"Come now my dear lady, do you think I am so blind as not to see the paint chips between the sheets? Do you think that I am not aware of the aroma you take on—like that of a dirty sheep—whenever you are in its presence?"

Red-Haired Man in a Sweater

The man's fire was impressive. I was on the verge of admiring his spirit; and if it were not for the fact that he was an utter fool, I might have applauded.

Singrid of course saw where her interest lay. Whatever prohibited sympathies she might have entertained for me, she was not about to stick her neck out for a lost cause, to sacrifice the security of her matrimony for the grudging caresses of a scrap of paint-clotted canvas.

And so, with rather remarkable haste, I was removed, sent back to England. I lounged about a warehouse for a while and then, at precisely eleven o'clock in the morning of a particularly hot day in July, was put to auction by Messrs. Sotheby & Co. at their large galleries, 34 & 35, New Bond Street, W.1.

I felt like something of a celebrity on the auctioneer's platform as I gazed over the lake of silent craniums before me. The bidding, at first slow, picked up its pace. The sobriety of the conductor of this public sale's Oxford accent began to show hints of agitation, which soon enough he crushed with his mallet. I was purchased by a consortium of Japanese businessmen for a large sum and crated off to Tokyo, where I was managed with the most delicate attention. Small, subtle hands sheathed in white cotton gloves escorted me, placed me in the board room of an office building—the apex of a mountain of glass amongst a bizarre menagerie of similar constructions.

My patrons would come in, bowing stiffly to each other, wearing identical dark-grey suits and commence fencing with words whose meaning I did not understand, but whose deadly sharpness was obvious. They treated me with rigorous cordiality, but more with that which befitted a large investment than a great work of art. Though on occasion these gentlemen went out, enjoyed nights on the town compounded of steakhouse suppers, karaoke bars and upper-class brothels, never once did they invite me to join them. They were obviously afraid that I would be damaged.

I spent my time looking out over the Tokyo landscape, the cliff-like buildings rising up on all sides, in the distance the harbour with ferries slowly gliding over its glassy surface. The melancholy and stiff luxury of my surroundings made me feel like a grey cloud hanging over an orchard in heavy bloom.

The office secretary, a Miss Kiyonaga, would sometimes come in and dust me. Her neck was the brilliant white of freshly fallen snow and her hair fell against its nape like the wing of a raven. In a soft voice reminiscent of an October wind stripping the last leaves off a cherry tree she would speak of her sorrows. She was the mistress of one of the chairmen who was married with five children. She loved him desperately, but the fragrant blossom of her emotion was always kept in check by his vigorous loyalty to social mores and his spite for the very looseness in her which he enjoyed.

"You should break with him," I said.

"I can't, no more than you can change the colour of your face."

"So our situations are similar."

"Yes. We could run away together."

"And what would we do?"

"I would work for you—try very hard to make you happy."

"That is impossible."

"Yes, in this floating world..."

One day I was taken and put, with a few other paintings in the company's collection, in a small museum in Sekino. Though, as I have previously stated, I despise that sort of thing, it was better that it was done in Japan than elsewhere, for in that country the people stood humbly before me, whispering to one another in the most reverential undertones as if they stood before the image of some dragon god, bringer of wind and rain.

I fed off their whispers, their muffled speech, as an overly pampered dog might goose liver.

Human beings have a tendency to offer up their admiration to the most unfitting subjects. That I inspired these people with sadness, disgust and fear, I have no doubt—but they cherished these emotions, inhaling the misery that pervaded my person as if it were some exquisite perfume, scenting their sleeves with it like apricot blossoms. And yet their admiration was not folly, for I fully comprehend it, and consider myself one of the finest paintings ever painted in England—which is understandably a bit of an odd statement, something akin to saying 'the largest lake in the Sahara' or something of the sort, considering that the entire history of

Red-Haired Man in a Sweater

England has only produced two great painters: Francis Bacon and Lucian Freud—and the latter, my creator, was after all born in Germany.

In any case, the inhabitants of the city, as well as others who travelled from distances, admired the chill of my incongruity for several weeks. And then, during the night, I was stolen, rolled into a sheaf and tucked under the arm of an able thief. When I awoke the next morning, I found myself surrounded by a group of shirtless men, their arms and chests heavily tattooed. Later I found out that they were the Black Flowers, a sub-gang of the notorious Kabuki-mono.

"You will stay under our protection until you are told otherwise," a man with a great U-shaped mouth told me. "If you disobey this injunction, I will be obliged to cut you to bits."

There was a certain charm in being abducted by the yakuza and, as I afterwards found out, the whole scheme had been instigated by the very businessmen who bought me in the first place. For, realising that they could never resell me for the exorbitant sum which they had paid, and finding themselves in financial difficulties, they had decided to have me stolen and thereby collect on the insurance.

For a number of weeks I was kept locked up in a room decorated with nothing but tatami mats, my chief amusement being to play *cho ka han ka* with my jailors while drinking a steady stream of saké. The life however was not unpleasant. I ate *ayu*, caught in the traditional manner by trained cormorants, and composed allusive verses with a ballpoint pen on the walls of my chamber. This is called adapting oneself to circumstances. One steps slowly when there is no place to arrive. One needs leisure to properly appreciate the tedium of being.

The hours passed like a mountain stream in springtime.

Days disappeared like dust before the wind.

And it was with some regret that, after several weeks of this existence, I received the news that I was to be set at liberty. I was slapped on the back, joked with, blindfolded, and taken for a ride in a comfortable vehicle.

After driving around for several hours, the car stopped. I was gently pushed out the door. I felt my hand grasped. The blindfold was removed. A large black car sped away into the night, leaving me standing, a solitary figure against a backdrop of deserted docklands. I pushed my hands in my pockets and felt a wad of yen—money I had won at dice. I looked over the water, which expanded before me like the endless pulsating skin of some universal deity. Somewhere out there, over oceans, on the other side of Asia, was Europe, the land of spiritless vice and jagged etiquette where a population sedated by faux democracy and cheap manufactured goods, babbling about history while treating that watchword as a toilet, chain themselves together in that self-imposed slavery called capitalism. That was where I belonged; just as a maggot belongs in a dog's corpse.

I was in no way tempted to throw myself at the feet of the authorities. I had had enough of living off the crumbs of the rich. I purchased an airline ticket and went back—to England. The small stock of money I had was soon dissipated in dissolute behaviour and I was once again forced to live by my wits—a commodity which the going rate is far less than that of any precious metal and can, in truth, often be bought for less than petrol.

I rented a room from an elderly French woman with an unpleasant relish for sentimental conversation and a large orange cat. The room was extraordinarily narrow; the cat monstrously fat. I seem to have come full circle, for the aroma of earlier times found me again and the creature clawed at my trousers with as little respect for art as an aborigine for the flavour of a white truffle.

At night Miss Baisieux (such was the woman's name) would cook over-sauced meats and open inexpensive bottles of Beaujolais, treating me with a motherly care that bordered on the incestuous. She told me about her numerous love affairs—with Sardinian fishermen, disconsolate priests, fetishists and Middle-Eastern royalty. In the réchauffé atmosphere of her confessions the heavy French cooking churned in my stomach; the cat rubbed against my leg; I felt like vomiting—but washed down the sensation with another glass of wine. Then I would make my way to my room, lay down on the child-sized mattress provided for me and let my thoughts stumble over the vanity of human existence, nations sinking, festal bacchanal blazes red like quinacridone rose, as my mind soon became invaded by dreams of black paintings, like those of Francisco Goya y Lucientes. From the depths of my subconscious poured visions of strange Sabbaths, in Vandyke brown, done in broad, surreal strokes; cackling music flowed over me like a cold, rippling stream, as I merged with the void.

It was late one morning at Primrose Hill. I stood and looked over the city, which lay smoking before me like some infernal battleground—a place where the conquered outnumber the conquerors by more than a thousand to one. A child came up and began to play in front of me with his mum. I turned and walked down.... There was a bench. I sat and lighted a cigarette.

I could hear a ruby-crowned kinglet call nearby—a series of whistles, short clear notes, and a rapid warbling of agitated mixed notes. At first I thought nothing of it, but then it occurred to me that London was hardly the habitat of that little bird whose range is confined almost exclusively to the pine forests of the Americas.

I looked up, expecting to catch sight of a fugitive from some nearby aviary, but was amazed to see a dog perched in the branch of a tree. It was Tikvah. I called his name. He leaped down and licked my hand and I, a being without mother, father or family, welcomed him with what tepid warmth was at my disposal.

I took him home with me. Miss Baisieux was hardly pleased with the new housemate.

"The room is for a single man," she said.

"I am a single man."

"No pets my friend."

"But you have a cat."

"Precisely. This dog of yours puts him in jeopardy.... Come, dinner is served."

I walked into the dining room and was met by a plate of pâté de lapin with cornichons. Morbidly I went about my task as a soldier shoulders his rifle and advances into the hail of enemy fire. She prattled away, her foot occasionally, in all innocence, drifting over to mine. My eyes examined, beneath the thick layer of iridescent make-up spread over her face, trembling folds of skin reminiscent of the rugged untamed scenery of Australia or North America—vast canyons and desolate wastes.

A faint but pleasant piping came from the other room where Tikvah rested.

"Un oiseau!"

"A dog, Madame, a dog."

By the time the cheese was served I felt thoroughly nauseous.... Miss Baisieux chattered away. Tikvah no longer whistled.... The cat came in and rubbed against my leg. I pushed it away; looked down. It had a bloody bit of fur in its mouth.

I rose from table... stalked solemnly into the living room.

The dog's bones, to which red flesh still clung, lay scattered on the floor. My lips pressed tightly together, I pondered the scene, then, with a shrug of my shoulders went to bed. Undoubtedly the cat had had a better supper than I.

In this bizarre serial of past, present and future I have haunted all the most depressing corners of Europe: small German towns where people's lips hang down to their knees, the industrial quarters of Northern Italian cities where the sky is blotted out by atrocious architecture and spirals of grey smoke. I am attracted by dark alleys where the smell of urine is so strong that it can be seen and neighbourhoods where the women's voices sound like the shrieks of the damned.

A few crumpled up bills, filthy as used hygienic paper, suffice for my maintenance—and such documents can be earned easily, in a hundred different clandestine or perceptible ways. How many odd jobs I have had! A taxidermist's assistant, a part-time procurer, a waiter at a Hungarian restaurant, a vendor of smut! Currently I am employed part-time by the post office. It is a night job. From 11 p.m. until 3 in the morning I sort mail.

I am what you would call a forgotten masterpiece. People pass me by without realising my true worth—and if I allude to it myself they think me bombastic, crazy. I am perfectly aware that I drink far too much and a cigarette, like a smoking icicle, eternally hangs from my mouth. I am a man with a canvas heart—a man painted with a certain amount of impatience, cast on the world by the brutal hand of genius and now doomed to wander its dirty boulevards like a rather blasé ghost. But so be it. It is depressing, but the world after all is nothing more than a voluminous void, smeared on with a palette knife—a strange, grey, voluminous void. Others, as they grow old, find their skin gradually begin to web with wrinkles. I on the other hand find some of my paint cracking. I am gradually becoming endowed with a slight patina—a slight changing of hue—a patina of nausea and profound ennui.

Fragment

Group

C

I.

THEY HAD DINED WELL. OUTSIDE THE LAWNS WERE COVERED WITH a thick white sheet; huge flakes of snow drifted slowly down from the sky;—this frigid exterior, viewable through window panes, accentuating the comfort of the interior, of the doctor's study, lined with leather-bound volumes, the parquet floor rugged with an enormous tiger skin, the mouth of the fireplace yawning with logs which could be sugarcane
immersed in divine experience
pike
snake
rosary.

The doctor revealed a bottle of 1949 Ferté de Partenay Armagnac, filled two glasses with 3 cl each, and handed one to Jack Brown. The latter admired the shiny eau de vie with its golden-amber colour, reminiscent of the patina of a piece of the best quality pre-Revolutionary American Colonial Chippendale furniture. The doctor shook his gently, with a circular motion, so as to wet the walls of his glass, then set it beneath his nose and inhaled its forceful, extremely intricate woody aroma, a sign of its maderisation. The two men, like shadows in a dream, sipped at the drink, letting it attack their tastebuds, subtly, somewhat unctuously, with a delicious warmth.

"Ah," Jack said, "civilization is an incredible thing. It is hard to believe, sitting here like this in front of the fire, drinking this delightful beverage, that only a few weeks ago I was encamped in one of the most remote areas of the world!"

Beating the drums beating the drums footprints of giraffes drink of majestic river of dirty milk predatory beasts predatory beasts
beating the drums beating the drums   loathsome insects beating the

drums
milk
milk
ethereal revolver reports beating on the drums with an oar predatory beasts ate the boat   besmeared   but not the oar drums footprints of giraffes a big white tusk the dwarf concealed itself in the mountains.

The doctor rolled out two cigars, and, with a guillotine-like instrument, clipped the end of one and lit it. Jack followed suit.

He had a sunburnt face. Though he was somewhat thin, his bone structure was that of a large man.

He walked to the window and looked out at the winter night phenomenal world legendary associations
   eating tears out of date leaves.

II.

He was obliged to rise in the dark of night, at 2 a.m., for the Sacrifice of the Lips. At 4 a.m. the Angelus bell. Prayer and first meditation until 5:15 Mass.

The days passed. He played his part well—the part of a sober sister bent on devoting herself to her God, voluntarily shouldering the yoke of Christ. With exterior humility, he devoted himself to the *Divine Scriptures* and the *Lives of the Fathers*. Repression of self-will. Though he was so hungry that he could have devoured iron, he restrained himself and ate but little and often let himself be seen in spiritual inebriation. Still however, he saw little evidence of the practices of the sisters or of the famous image by Bramantino.

"I have heard that there is a picture by Bramantino here," he one day ventured to a sister. "But I see that it is not in the chapel..."

"*Christ of the Frogs*," the woman sighed. "It is not my place to gossip over such matters."

III.

PUT THE WORDS IN THE CORRECT ORDER

1. looked / Black / stone / exactly / rust / peduncle / it

2. indifferent / to / nailed / squirting / fugitive / left / the / a / into / chalice / red

3. stringendo / it / yirr / the / of / humiliating / beasts

Dr. Black and the Village of Stones

Blank is the book of his bounty beholden of old, and its binding is blacker than bluer:

Out of the blue into black is the scheme of the skies, and their dews are the wine of the bloodshed of things.

Charles Algernon Swinburne, *Nephelidia*

I.

"QUAI D'ORSAY. GRAN CORONA. A BOX OF TWENTY-FIVE."

His German was perfect—far too perfect, too true for him to be Swiss. The shopkeeper nodded, fetched the box of cigars and returned.

"That will be 310 francs," he said, looking down at the man before him, a strange and gruff deformity who, far from inviting laughter, inspired him with the utmost respect.

The money paid and the shop exited, Dr. Black stuffed a cigar between his lips, lit it and proceeded down the cobbled lane, his thin legs gingerly carrying the main portion, that massive torso and head, those distinct and notorious pieces of matter. His reputation had been made, years before, in more than one branch of learning, in multiple applications of science. The general run of human ambitions he could not help but consider petty things: knaves running after base metals and goring themselves on the illusions of prosperity; pleasure seekers letting their organs of speech hang limp from fluted mouths at the prospect of a few moments carnal interaction.—Oh, he had, upon occasion, been seduced by certain chains of events—but this made him all the more impenetrable to future discomfiture. Dr. Black was a man who knew how to pass fair judgement on the fractured parts of his experience.

He sauntered easily along Stadhausquai, past the Fraumünster (which read 2:00), and on to a café, where he secured himself an outdoor seat, ordered a glass of beer, a plate of rösti and a sausage. The beer arrived, a pale golden, frothing spire, and he attached his lips thereon and drank. A shadow, not thick by any means, lingered over him.

"Doctor—Dr. Black?"

A quivering, pale young man of neat, straw-coloured hair leaned forward.

The doctor licked the white deposit, the yeasty mass of small air bubbles from his upper lip and moustache, set the glass down upon its coaster, and rose to his feet.

"Wilhelm Künzler?" he asked, stretching forth his hand.

The other grabbed it eagerly. "Yes, Sir. Yes, this is Wilhelm. Such a pleasure—such a pleasure!"

"Please sit down. I have already ordered, I hope you don't mind."

"Eat!—Oh no, I could not eat right now!" Wilhelm sat down and adjusted his glasses. "I am so eager to carry out these studies with you."

"Investigations," Black corrected as he watched the waiter advance through the door, a great steaming plate poised in one hand.

"Yes, I am so very eager to carry out these investigations. In this country, for a student, such opportunities are quite rare."

Dr. Black, with knife and fork, manipulated his sausage away from the stack of potato cake. "Such opportunities are rare in all countries," he said, letting his knife pierce the skin of the tube and descend into its flavourful substance. "Have you brought the samples?"

"Yes, Sir—a few.—The rest are still in refrigeration back at the University."

The young man took several small plastic vials from his jacket pocket and placed them on the table. The doctor, while chewing a mouthful of sausage, glanced at them, opened one, knocked its contents, a few small red lumps, onto the palm of his hand and examined them closely.

"It is, I believe, swine," Wilhelm ventured.

"Sus indicus."

"Yes, Sus indicus—but in the other vials: it is certainly some kind of vascular fluid, one would guess from a vertebrate, but I cannot place it. Certainly nothing like this has occurred before!"

"Wrong. A similar incident is mentioned in *L'Astronomie*, in the November 1889 edition."

He placed the small gobbets back in their phial, produced a notebook from his own jacket pocket and, opening it, handed Wilhelm a very old bit of magazine clipping that he had therein. The doctor took a sip of beer and, navigating his fork to the pile of potatoes, listened as the young man read aloud.

Dr. Black and the Village of Stones

"'A perplexing phenomenon has been observed recently in the Entlebuch district of Switzerland. The surface of the earth has been covered above three times by a very fetid, thick, and tacky residue, distinctly plasmatic, falling in nut-sized lumps of irregular shape and particles thought to be as small as 1/5,000th of a centimetre. Specimens identified as masses of cartilage or muscular fibres. The origin of the substance is indiscernible.'

"So this *has* happened before?"

"If we are to believe the article."

"Quite exciting!"

"I will need to further examine this fluid. I am concerned that it might be a false alarm—some deceptive mixture of silex, chrome, alumina and carbonic acid. If it is of volcanic origin, then the presence of chrome will assimilate it with meteoric stones."

"But it is surely blood."

"I will need to go to the location of the current phenomenon in order to investigate."

"Yes, we must go!"

"You have a car at your disposal, I presume?"

"Of course. We can leave tonight if you wish."

"No, I do not wish. I want you to pick me up at my hotel at half past eight tomorrow morning."

"And tonight—would you like me to show you the lights of Zürich?"

"Absolutely not. A quiet evening with books, rooks and papers is what I presently care for. I have been invited to a chess match in Milan next week with Maurizio Ferrantes, and, if I am to come off unembarrassed, my strategies must be honed."

The Babylonian firmament in 12 x 3 celestial houses:

As a boy he became an expert at checkers   age of 12   notebooks. diagrams played an informal chess match with Alabama state champion Jim Lester and won, scoring four wins, six draws, and three losses and then Columbia University (first studying chemical engineering before moving on, grazing off sundry fields of knowledge); spending much time at the Manhattan Chess Club   New York state championship. Six wins. One draw. Later: Havana (*night clubs, acquiring visibly vaporous, carbonic habits*): *defeated champions of Spain and Mexico. Fulfilling the astronomical omina of Enuma Anu Enlil. Current condition: Ranked #49 on the earth, amongst its countries and people.*

II.

THE CAR SPED OVER THE WINDING HIGHWAY, LUSH GREEN PASTURES off to each side, staggering mountains towering in the near distance. Cows grazed and farmers strode around the precincts of their wooden lodges, toting buckets and large canisters of milk. It was beautiful scenery in a light-green sort of way—bucolic, hemmed in and alpine. They drove through the long, strange tunnel of the Gottard (sinister, toxic) and into the southern canton of Ticino. They turned off onto the Val Bedretto, past Ossasco, and Ronco and then over the Nufenenpass, toward the Brudelhorn; descending along tiers of winding, treacherous roadway and then gliding through the shadows of the sharply-peaked highland. Presently Wilhelm gyrated the steering wheel to the right and the car veered off the highway, onto a smaller road that snuck in between the vertical mountains, a shallow, rushing river off to one side, a narrow strip of ill-tended pastureland to the other.

Dr. Black, his torso easily filling out the seat of the small, European car, struck a match and applied the flame to a D'Orsay.

"You see the beautiful country?" Wilhelm asked, making an expansive gesture with his right hand.

"Yes. By all evidence my power of sight is perfectly intact."

"In this part of the country, in the remote villages here, the people are very backward."

"That is one of the drawbacks of a rural existence, but we must admit its calm to be highly pleasing."

The car rolled on along the road, into the cleft of the valley and along the side of a moraine. Presently the stretch of land widened out slightly and Wilhelm pulled off onto a patch of gravel. There were a few old cars and lorries and then a wooden footbridge which led toward the base of a rugged col, well-littered with boulders amidst which were stationed two or three huts and out of which jutted a stone church tower.

"Is that the village?" The doctor asked. "I expected it to be small, but..."

"This is the village. The people, for the most part, live within the boulders. Their houses are carved in the rocks. As I said, the people are very backward here."

The car doors slammed shut, the bridge echoed under their feet, and the doctor's cigar, still only partially smoked, perfumed the pure air around them with its stink. His well-polished, patent leather shoes trod gingerly along the rock paths; within the village, his eyes steadily surveyed the solid mineral matter. It was now obvious that they were habitable. Many of them had doors, some steps leading beneath, most openings that functioned to admit light and air to the enclosures and often framed and spanned with glass mounted to permit opening and closing.

"Quite an array of pyrogenous ultramafic affinities," Dr. Black grinned, running his hand along the side of one of the cottages. "It is like Cappadocia."

"We must secure lodging."

"If we can. Otherwise it is the pup-tent for us.—Where did you stay when you were here previously?"

"I was not able to stay, Doctor; I had an exam the next morning on the practical uses of ultrasound in cattle reproduction."

"Did you do well?"

"Yes, thank you. Most satisfactory."

The two men wound their way amongst the quasi-troglodyte dwellings, which were laid out at random. Often stone steps led up narrow inclines or the way led through a passage carved in the rock and supported with resinous old timber. The place at first seemed almost deserted, many of the doors were boarded up, the only person they crossed was a fleshy woman bustling around a corner with a cabbage in her arms.

Presently they came in sight of one of the few wooden structures, a small building with a sign which read: RIEMENSCHNEIDER, FLEISCH & KAFFEE PRODUKT.

"Let us make inquiries here," the doctor said, wagging his beard, the curling black axe, in the direction of the shop.

Inside there were two small tables near the door, and at the other end

Dr. Black and the Village of Stones

a butcher's counter, rife with price signs, behind which sat an iron-haired woman with penetrating eyes and a severe, small-jowled face. Dr. Black expressed his desire for refreshment, and the woman asked him and Wilhelm to be seated. Soon a young lady came out to serve them. With long black hair, a lively oval face, and eyes that sparkled, she was remarkably attractive. The doctor, with all the gravity of a man expressing the most profound truths, ordered a tongue sandwich and coffee. Wilhelm requested cheese and wine.

"And where do you boys come from?" the young woman asked.

"Do we not look like locals?" the doctor said smoothly.

"I should think not! I know everyone in the village by name."

The doctor introduced himself and his apprentice as 'researchers.'

"Researchers—as in scientists?" she asked turning to Wilhelm.

"I am just—just a student," he faltered. "At the University of Zürich."

"And what do you do there?"

"Currently at the University I am mostly studying cows—pullulation—their reproduction—artificially inseminating them—I have been inseminating cows."

"And is it just cows you inseminate?"

Wilhelm blushed. "No, not just."

She laughed a pile of marigolds.

"Oh, well my name is Piera, and it's very nice to make your acquaintance!"

The doctor, with the utmost appetite, set his jaws to the sandwich, cleaving out a half moon; the article of food, the ox's tongue, veritably evaporating under his dentine pressure. Wilhelm nibbled at cheese and sipped red wine. He watched the great torso opposite, the formidable cranium, the beard as couthly cut as that of an Assyrian king: the kymation, the rising cornice of that monument, Erechtheion of thread-like growths.

The door opened, both men turned. A stocky, moustached man came in, taking off a chequered wool cap as he entered. He walked up to the counter with heavy strides, nodding to the doctor and Wilhelm as he passed. The iron-haired woman rose from her seat.

"What can I do for you today Waldmüller?" she said, her mouth showing a set of fine, sharp, piranha-like teeth.

"Frau Riemenschneider," the man replied gruffly, "I have come again to ask for your daughter's hand."

"Apparently we are witnessing a local courtship," Black said in an undertone to Wilhelm.

"My apologies Waldmüller, but, as I have said before, I cannot accommodate you there."

"How much for your daughter's hand?"

"More than you can afford."

"Come now, what price for your daughter's hand?"

"Forget it, it is not for sale to you. Why not try the lips of Fräulein Baargeld or the eyes of little Nuzzi instead?"

Black. What strange custom is this?

[*Aside*.

Wald. The lips of Fräulein Baargeld are like chicken gizzards and the eyes of little Nuzzi no more attractive than a minnow's!

Riem. Well, then I suggest you take your opinions and the few filthy francs you have in your pocket over to the Grotto Wüste. Buy yourself a beer, because there is nothing for you to purchase here!

There were oaths, guttural, hoarse, and the man stormed out. Wilhelm explained to the doctor, in a well regulated whisper, that this was indeed the custom of the village. He himself had heard of it, but never until now witnessed it first hand: To a specified person, the subservience of a young woman's numbers of things, but always less than the whole; the exchange of ladies' living portions for coin of the realm.

The doctor raised his eyebrows in interest. In his life, he had seen, experienced many things. Very little shocked him; seldom was he surprised; but he certainly experienced satisfaction when his frontal lobe was peaked into a condition of wanting to know or learn about something. When his food had been consumed, he rose to meet the bill, taking note of the scrawled signs on the counter as he did so:

Eva Vögeli, Hand—Fr. 510

Patricia Ris, Waist—Fr. 700

Viola Hälg, Ears (set)—Fr. 420

Sibylle Gmür, Tongue—Fr. 980

Pocketing the change from the meal, he asked Frau Riemenschneider where he and his assistant might find lodging. The good woman suggested that they try a man on the edge of town by the name of Wolf Knellwolf, who had a spare room he sometimes rented out to summer hikers passing through the valley. Following her advice, they secured a room at the aforementioned location. It was small and dark (having only one minute window carved in the granite wall), but it would do for a short period. Knellwolf, who grazed a party of cattle nearby, gave them the run of the place and included coffee, bread and as much milk as they wished to drink for the board.

III.

May 14, Sun.—Weather too fair. The visible spectrum of the sky lying between green & indigo; radiant energy with wavelengths of approximately 420 to 490 nanometres. Awoken by yawning peals; vibrating object hanging from church tower. Burned D'Orsay & informed myself of vicinity: Rocks tremendous, vastly appealing: Highly deformed diorite xenoliths in granite misshapen by a right-lateral ductile shear zone.

May 15, Mon.—Improvement. Sky achromatic. Talked w/Knellwolf. Stories of viscous, pulpy substance descending w/brilliant light (check annual registers). Künzler & I drank coffee in front of shelter; gathered dirt samples. He deports himself in some degree clandestinely. Walking through village without apparent company.

May 16, Tues.—Weather ditto. Lunch w/Künzler; applied him to classifying samples. Keep youthful blood in check. To parochial house without luck, no discovering priest. Further examination of the igneous masses, foreign fragments. Conjugate normal faults cutting banded granite gneiss. Right-dipping fault is cut & displaced by left. Read from Anderssen's *Aufgaben für Schachspieler*.

May 17, Wed.—Drama from sunrise to set. Künzler woke early; gone when I dressed. Sky achromatic in ante meridiem. Relatively strong upcurrent. Coffee and brioche w/Künzler. Alone to parochial house. Saw Father Tito (not far advanced in life, behaviour unnatural, rude, gestures effeminate). Request for annual registers flustered lit/beast. Produced thin volume of recent production: claims of fire: scarcely acceptable as genuine. Returned to shelter

Dr. Black and the Village of Stones 203

amidst atmospheric condensed moisture build up, weakened up-current. Primo: a few small fine drops, cinnamon-coloured. Secondo: they grow ($B = \mu H$!) Terzo: descent!

It was late in the afternoon when the wind began to blow and the pine trees which grew along the creek's edge bend like fishing poles. A string of black clouds appeared on the horizon, lurching over the ridge of the mountains and light escaped from the land's surface; Black's mouth twisted to a half grin; he (*weight on slender left leg, right advanced taking but a part of the burden*); the fumes of his D'Orsay danced wildly from their cherry.

At first they appeared, just a few, like spots of red wax on the lanes. Farmers' heads tilted back and village eyes turned upward. A sound, a slight drumming, filled the air and then the shower swept across the village. Black sprang towards the house of Knellwolf, his short legs working nimbly, his cigar poised protectively before him. He dashed through the doorway of the stone lodge just as the crimson deluge came sweeping behind him, a mad rush of scarlet mayhem which flushed from the skies like some supraglobal surgical operation gone awry.

The doctor chuckled merrily and Wilhelm looked up from the table, where he was busy with pen and paper.

"What is it, Sir?" he asked, rising in astonishment.

"Come see for yourself my boy—The blitz of rain has come!"

A moment later, at the door, Wilhelm Künzler stood
with mouth open wide
to facilitate a
pervading cinnamon condition:
hued,
by the long-wave end
of the visible, dimpling
spectrum, plashes, puddles,
ground a network of veins

and then night fell and the doctor stood smoking on the doorstep, the aroma of his D'Orsay mixing with the rich heat of countless corpuscles; and he thought of the meal of the Israelites after the battle of Gilboa; and further of the sacrifices, it caught in a basin, and then sprinkled seven times on the altar (consecrating the people to that being worshipped as having power over human affairs), and what issued from the Saviour's side when it was pierced by the Roman soldier.... And through the cleared sky the stars were cast overhead.

IV.

For one even mildly dedicated to anthropology, the place held interest. The custom of the village, at least that promoted by the establishment of Riemenschneider, was odd indeed. Men could be seen walking through the lanes, hand in hand with a young woman—not because the latter was in any way fond of the fellow, but simply due to the fact that he owned her left hand. Another might be possessed of a lady's eyes. He would call on her after his day's labour, gaze into the other's organs of vision for thirty minutes, and then depart, fully satisfied.

On occasion there was a conflict of interest. The doctor observed two men quarrelling in the street one day, a plump young woman between them.

"What is the cause of this bad tempered differing of views?" he asked a wiry old man with a large, aquiline nose by the name of Viktor who stood near at hand.

"Oh, it is the usual," the fellow answered nonchalantly, spitting off to one side. "Fräulein Hänggi has been split too many ways. Georg there owns her right hand and arm; he desires to take his property over to the chestnut grove. But her lips are possessed by Werner, who insists, that if the two go so far, he be part of the company so he might use his goods as he will."

"This custom must make it terribly difficult for the men of the village."

Old Viktor let out a short chuckle. "Oh, you can be sure it does," he said. "But it is not much of a custom. It was not around when I was a young man. Certainly I never let go of a franc for any of the lips I joined to under the chestnuts."

"Not a custom? Then who introduced this bit of now generally accepted behaviour amongst the social group?"

"Oh, Frau Riemenschneider; she was not making enough off her cutlets.... Joined by the other old widows of the area.... I suppose they fancied the men needed the fräuleins and would pay for the privilege of their glances if they must."

May 18, Thurs.—Woke early, scoured lanes w/Künzler. Much blood. Some bits of flesh, particularly around the vicinity of Riemenschneider's. Curious inconsistency in pattern. Dismay and some anger in village. Father Tito stirring trouble, directed at Riemenschneider. Watched feathered creatures circumnavigate shoulder of mountain: Passeridae or Emberizidae; possibly swallows gathering at some seed-rich niche. The forest is thick with the sound of the Cuculus canorus.

He watched the priest descend along the trail, now disappearing behind a mass of chestnut trees, now reappearing, walking stick in hand. The man was apparently coming down from somewhere on the face of the mountain; or higher: its shoulder or some unseen pass.... Presently the two met near the scree-strewn base; one short, with outcrop of hair the colour of printing ink, the other a scowling, narrow-limbed ecclesiastic streak. The doctor spoke first, and then the priest, in a jointly discourteous and beseeching tone, his voice thin, nasally: He had gone for a hike; he hiked often; it was all there was to do in the vicinity of that dreadful little village.... Would the doctor like a refreshment?

Dr. Black stood admiring the Papilionoidea mounted and hung on the wall, and then, on the mantle, a fine piece of Lebanese amber, undoubtedly a good one hundred million years old, containing a splendid example of Heterocera. His host came up from the cantina, his hand gripped white around the neck of a bottle. The doctor sat down and hooked one leg over the next. The young priest set two small glasses on the table, filled them with French white wine, and took a seat opposite. Health was proposed and the two men drank. The doctor, in measured tones, somewhat mellowed by the fermented juice of grape, asked the priest what his view of the situation was.

"My view? My view is that it is the Devil's play."

"Then you are proposing it to be a supernatural occurrence?"

"Yes, I am saying it is unnatural—that is clear enough. Blood showers and such things are obviously manifestations of evil; and you can be sure that to be the priest in such an ungodly place is no great fortune."

Dr. Black drank of his wine.

"So your theory is?" he asked, slightly raising his eyebrows.

"Witches."

"Where?"

"Here—the fleisch shop and other places!"

"Explain."

"Explain—The old women of this valley worship the Devil. See how they sell off the lips of one young woman, the thighs of the next? They are casting spells and bringing demons down to scatter us with their red gore!"

"Surely you exaggerate."

"I tell you, it is all the work of Frau Riemenschneider and her cronies! They are witches, every one of them. In league with nefarious forces."

"Though their practices regarding the young women of the town I cannot pass over without condemnation, they seem otherwise to live within the confines of proper conduct. To adhere all unexplainable phenomena to their persons, without adequate proof, seems to me to be an extremely unwise course,—particularly for a man in your position."

"Ah, it is easy for you to say such things. You are an outsider."

"My dear Sir, I am an outsider to nothing. The world is my studio. I suggest you refrain from overly pungent comments."

The doctor did not like Father Tito's manner. He spoke without respect, with more emphasis than the occasion required. His wine was decent, but it was white. Black preferred red, and would rather have been alone with a smoking cigar than together with a fuming priest.

Father Tito slapped the table. "My house!" he exclaimed, and the glasses rattled.

Dr. Black rose from his seat. "So it is, Sir," he said coolly, "and I do not believe that I desire the further advantage of its hospitality."

A minute later he was outside, carefully pursuing his way along the side of a pasture. As a man of logic he did not put much store in the priest's bitter paranoia, but at the same time he had to admit that the phenomena of the blood rains he could not as yet explain. Frau Riemenschneider and her fleisch shop were certainly bizarre; but that the woman was a practitioner of black magic!?!

Dr. Black extracted a cigar from his jacket pocket, bit off the end as if it were the head of a snake, and was soon industriously puffing away.

V.

WITCHES LIKE MOUNTAINS LIKE FLOWERS THE SUN LIKE FLOWERS the sun some souls without bodies maybe never had bodies and the devil has slaves little ants. Witches like mountains like flowers watch out they fly out the window fly out on pitchforks and go to kiss gnomes. Witches like mountains like roses what bodies of butterflies of gnomes wrapping themselves together with attenuated ropes ride on a reed and stealing the sperm from dead bodies ride on reeds. Witches like mountains like roses like mountains and tempests in bottles souls without bodies maybe never had bodies and the devil has slaves and the slaves are little ants which play flutes made from hollowed-out human hairs. Witches like hills like roses wringing hands out comes hail and whispering phasmata and the devil has slaves trimming three hairs from the udder of a cow.

VI.

"OH, HE'S GOT HIMSELF BURIED BETWEEN HER SHEETS!"

"It's these Northerners, these blond boys—the women always throw themselves away over such trash."

Old Viktor laughed. "From what I hear," he said, drawing at his pipe. "From what I hear, it was a deal made out on the instalment plan; for her left ear. A pretty price it is said he's paying too!"

"You are right enough about the instalment plan," a stout farmer put in, licking yeasty froth from his moustache. "But it has nothing to do with her little ear—it is her right hand he's got."

"Her right hand! Hear that Waldmüller? How much was it you offered Frau Riemenschneider for that item, and she refused to part with it?"

"Oh, it's the usual thing," Old Viktor added. "A northern franc is worth two of a local fellow's."

Waldmüller, who had been morosely silent during this dialogue, pushed away the mastodontic beer jug he had been sweating over for the previous thirty minutes and rose from his seat. There was the glistering night sky and his swinging steps; then circling, noctivagation, tracking around the fleisch shop, lurking in the shadows (he had always been laughed at, somewhat derided for remaining womanless, with some hinting, winks and half grins, at trips to Lugano brothels).

He had watched her grow, skipping around the village, braid swinging; then older, while he sat with his goats on the hillside, she passed, with friends, expressing certain emotions, mirth or delight, a series of spontaneous, unarticulated sounds accompanied by corresponding facial and bodily movements; he watched them graze and dreamed of her in an emerald cloud and then the saving: he had saved his silver and had a jar of it (five franc pieces) buried near the roots of a chestnut tree on the

Dr. Black and the Village of Stones

hillside. He watched as the two figures emerged, and then pressed together, soft words spoken and then a clasping goodbye. The figure walked off, wound through the lanes and Waldmüller followed, stalking, slowly gaining ground and then hurling himself forward.

"You stranger boy!"

(A slap to the face.)

Wilhelm staggered back. Waldmüller advanced, both fists clenched, an ominous dark mass. He reached out and grabbed the young man by the shoulder.

"I am going to show you how we deal with outsiders prying into our women," the goatherd growled.

He raised a fist and then felt the wrist grasped and, simultaneous with the arm being twisted behind his back, a voice:

"Hands off!"

A moment later the big man was sprawled on the ground, a small knee in his spine and his head pressed against the dirt.

"Let me up!" he cried (he felt his shoulder blade strained out of place).

"You will be pacific?"

"Let me up I say!"

"Get up, but if you attempt violence again it will go badly for you."

Waldmüller was released and quickly sprang to his feet. He briefly stared, with angry, frightened eyes and then, murmuring discontented phrases, turned and lurched off into the darkness.

"It seems you know how to fight!" Wilhelm said gratefully.

"Aside from being not unskilled in Western pugilism," the doctor replied, taking him by the elbow and guiding him homeward, "I am also a brown belt in the Japanese art of 柔術. But let this be a lesson to you: Tomcatting in rural villages is never advisable for a young man without adequate means of self-defence."

Through the minute blackened lanes, toward the edge of town and Knellwolf's; passing one outlying mass of rock lying partially embedded in the soil and well rounded by weather; through a lit aperture a moment's sight of Frau Riemenschneider and two other old dames of the village, their fractured voices scratching out into the night—the mewing

of thrice brindled cats mind ordering quasi suppositions: *compacts.*
mekhashshepheh wicche.   Ex. 22:18 (remembering—boyhood tales—decollated men wandering through the marshes on mule back—the pursuit of lights through woods, thickets, briar, footlogs across sloughs) the simple fact away from electric device lines telemicrowaves information on discs and magnetapes data midst mountains forces stronger abnormally misshapen things (him too) of
extraordinary woollen qualities
coverings elastic substance
of the animal body loose nervous
system relaxed.

VII.

The Grotto Wüste was lively that night, old timers sitting square before drinks, pipes and cigarettes hanging from their mouths. Dr. Black sat at the end of a bench, enjoying a cigar and a ratafià, a walnut liqueur, while listening to the talk, letting his ears savour the flavour of the local dialect, which was not without a ragged sort of charm. There were conjectures, insinuations (maybe it was the work of Riemenschneider and her ilk after all—the wrath of heaven and all that sort of thing. . . . Or so said Father Tito).

"Oh this! Why this is nothing my friend!" Old Viktor cried, setting his half consumed beer down on the table. "When I was younger a rain of flesh fell so heavy that you could barely walk through the lanes. It came down in bowl-shaped disks about twenty centimetres around, and three or four thick. They were a dull yellow colour and had on them fine layer of short hairs which were smoothed and brushed up. When we stripped away this skin, we found a pink, pulpy substance like soft-soap inside. . . . Which was offensive! The smell suffocated! My family was poor and we were all hungry for protein, but we could not eat those meats, because in the oven they liquefied straight to blood!"

And then the stories went the round:
ludicrous boasting
churning haze of carbonic vapour
creamy accumulations and little shots of liquor:
beef-flakes fell from the clear sky; a thick shower, on the ground, draped in trees, hanging on fences   mutton or venison   lung-tissue   shower of frogs darkened the sky and covered the earth very young minnows, fishes, falling in a straight line, in a space not more than a metre square   or grain which the goats ate and women ground into flour, made burebrot, decent, but not of the highest quality dried spawn of some reptile, doubtless

the frog   each drop was made up of many thin red blood river worms with transparent bodies   stones from the clouds   caterpillars, over beyond the shoulder of the mountain   more extreme: eggs; barrels of sugar; falls of salt; butter; ham; a typewriter
nectarischnapps
　concealed wonder
preternatural (intramural shouts)
　and the doctor wandered with steady intoxication into the night, curiosity: migration of larval life forms aside from their lies there is certainly evidence shower of perch, fish-rain at Soulac-sur-Mer   France shower of shells (torrential downpour with rattling sound) pavement covered with muscles   special local whirls or gusts with high pressure gradient carried heavy objects from earth's surface to the troposphere possible explanation that a body of water in the area was imbibed (suction established through a partial vacuum) by a passing tornado, and afterwards deposited its live cargo   spiders;   snakes reptiles in the road, gutters and yards, on roofs, a very dark brown, almost black, thick in some places, tangled together like a mass of wire or yarn   black worms   sweet. nasally
　figures he saw, convened
by the fleisch shop:
　"My mother already told you no; why do you bother me when she is not here?"
　"You can influence her."
　"I won't—not for you!"
　"Come now..."
　"Disgusting—don't touch me!"
　"Come now; otherwise it will go hard...for both of you."
　And then one shape pulled away and the other cursed, was gone, the doctor continuing his intoxicated course towards bed.

VIII.

THE NEXT MORNING DR. BLACK AWOKE EARLY, ACCORDING TO habit, splashed water on his face, dressed and stepped into the kitchen. Wilhelm was there, just completing the process of making espresso over the wood stove. He greeted the doctor and handed him a cup, and the latter, after admixing two spoonfuls of sugar in the black sap, stepped outside, the petite porcelain vessel poised between his right thumb and index finger. He took a sip, smacked his lips and blinked his grave eyes. Presently Wilhelm joined him.

Künz. (Hypothesis) A whirlwind takes up cows and pigs from some near distant farm, decimates them and disperses their remains.

Black. An interesting proposal, or starting point of reasoning, but utterly fallacious. Examine: A whirlwind picks up objects of the weight of cows and pigs, but refrains from picking up objects of equal or lesser weight, such as plant life, timber, small stones and fence posts. Thus, for your hypotheses to work, a whirlwind would need to segregate the cows and pigs from other matter. And the laws of nature, the laws of science, state that a whirlwind can do no such thing. And what of the flesh?

Künz. The flesh, Doctor?

Black. Yes, the flesh Wilhelm.—The flesh, unlike the vascular fluid, was not dispersed evenly, but primarily in the vicinity of Frau Riemenschneider's.

Künz. But when it rains, it often rains more in one spot than another.

Black. But when it rains, it generally does not rain both flesh and blood.

IX.

peeping
demons flourish forshortened
in pouches carrying tongues
which taste wet fur marlaceous some creatures who live on
juice of lichens
muttering effigies marble pushed the day
the skin of a bison
is called a robe
immortal calf ate the moon leaping
titubating before
footsteps on the air and water of singing splendid worms in skeins
sun never old such things such things
choreographed planets learned from the lesser bear
amber fruits hooking leg such things things

X.

WHEN THE NEXT RAIN COMMENCED, WILHELM WAS HAVING A rendezvous with Piera in the chestnut grove; the emerald, primary light, echoing off luxuriant black hair, the pink crease on her oval face; and then a blast of wind made the branches quiver. Crowding together; osculation.

"The sky is growing dark," Wilhelm murmured.

"I hope it is not another one of those awful storms."

"They must be terrible for you."

"Oh, I don't mind the storms themselves. It is just that people seem to blame mamma."

"It is the priest. He stirs up trouble."

Her, blushing: "I . . . I know."

As conciliation, there was further contact of curved surfaces; caressing of the fleshy edges of the mouth. The dark cloud moved through the valley, a crimson tail dipping behind it.

Wilhelm pulled himself away from the young woman. "I must go," he said, adjusting his glasses. "The Doctor will be expecting me."

They touched hands and he departed, the shower, a deep and vivid purplish red, dashing at his heels. Past the fleisch shop he went, Frau Riemenschneider at her doorstep, giving him the evil eye, the cloud beating overhead. The doctor was standing in the lane, legs apart, arms akimbo, his beard bristling fiercely from his face.

"Where have you been?" he growled.

"I am here, Doctor."

"Come; inside; under cover; the cloud is emptying itself!"

An incarnate mist began to fall, succeeded by the bloody drops. The blast swept over the village; rivulets formed, red as if fire ran along the ground. The substance seemed to almost cry out as it shed from the sky;

and it stank and the pigs in their pens wallowed in it; and the children stood dazed staring at their doorsteps and then hid within.

"It is too awful!" Wilhelm said.

Then there was a flicker of sunlight and the black cloud was past.

"Come," the doctor demanded.

"Where to?"

"Into the car. We have things to learn; we must chase that cloud."

Minutes later the two men were pulling onto the road, the gravel bursting from beneath the tires with the car's impulsive movement. The motor revving; gears switching; and away.

"Drive, Wilhelm; drive!"

"I feel like a tornado hunter!"

"The accelerator pedal; use the accelerator pedal!"

The car flew through the narrow valley, trailing after the dark, airborne mass. The doctor aggressively stroked his beard, peering through the windscreen with furrowed brow and intent eyes. Wilhelm bent over the steering wheel. The ball of his foot applied the maximum pressure to the gas pedal and the needle of speedometer crawled into high numerals.

"It looks like it is heading over the mountain Doctor," he cried in exasperation.

"No, it is settling up against the saddle. It is alighting Wilhelm!"

"A strange cloud . . . "

"We will get it yet."

"But it is so high up."

"No, drive further on. I see lines descending from the mountain. There is a funicular leading up by yonder arête."

Ten minutes later they were gliding up the side of the mountain on a seldom used funicular line, the pines spiring up beneath them and the road shrinking behind. The vehicle pulled into its station on the saddle of the mountain and the two men leapt out and began pursuing their way along the descending foot path. The doctor's svelte legs worked well, guiding his torso and crown of cranium down the steep trail with rapid ease. Wilhelm followed in his wake, every now and again adjusting the glasses which sat unsteadily upon the bridge of his nose. Presently the

Dr. Black and the Village of Stones

doctor veered off the trail, to his right, through the alpine woods, and on through shelves of blueberry bushes.

"You hear them," he said in an undertone.

"I hear something, Sir."

"Ahh!"

"Yes?"

"We are coming into their vicinity."

"What is it Doctor?"

"Lepidopterans, Wilhelm. Lepidopterans."

"Doctor..."

"Come, let us advance."

The two men entered their midst, the delicate wings brushing against their faces, clinging to the doctor's beard and adhering themselves to the frames of Wilhelm's glasses.

"Note their ommatidia, Wilhelm; they are watching us!"

"Doctor, they are strangely beautiful! What variety are they?"

"I cannot be certain. They have obviously been pulpating on the opposite ridge and, while migrating across the valley, ejecting their meconial fluid!"

"The blood, Doctor!"

"Exactly!"

"So this explains it," the young man said, gazing at a butterfly that had mounted his forefinger.

"Almost."

"Almost?"

"There is still the little matter of the flesh, Wilhelm. We can certainly not regard that as meconial fluid."

There was a moment's silence. The small, murky-winged insects filled the surrounding woods and began to slowly clothe the two men, alighting on their faces, heads and vestments. Thousands of wagging and knobbed antennae, slender bodies, curling proboscises; as the daylight waned the insects descended, perched mellowly, and observed.

"Then what is the answer to the mystery?" Wilhelm asked, almost in a whisper.

Dr. Black grinned. "Come," he said, "it is getting dark. Let us see."

The doctor and his assistant stood, backs against the outer wall of a stone dwelling, feet resting in a few centimetres of relatively fresh gore. He, Black, felt sorely like igniting a D'Orsay, but refrained;—it was, in any case, his last.

"Piera and her mother are asleep," Wilhelm murmured. "Why do we watch their house?"

"Shhh!"

They waited; the moon swung over the peaks, its dim light slashing across the valley, filtering through the village. Wilhelm yawned and leaned his head against the wall. The doctor stood alert, eyes scanning the zone before him. Presently there was a sound, footsteps trodding through butterfly slurry. A hulking silhouette appeared at the end of the lane. It stepped cautiously, one arm occasionally flying off to the side: as Millet's *Sower*, prowled the vicinity, with lumbering care, and was soon around the corner of the fleisch house.

"Who is it?" Wilhelm whispered.

"Come," growled the doctor. "We will see.... Around this way.... Here. We will wait at this corner."

A few moments later the lurking figure rounded the way. Dr. Black, producing his all powerful cigar-shaped Varta 645 pen light from his pocket, flashed the blinding ray in the creature's face.

"Halt!" he cried. "We have you!"

"Damn you; put that light out of my face!"

"It is Waldmüller!" exclaimed Wilhelm.

The stocky man stood before them; a satchel over one shoulder; a hand raised, shielding the light from his eyes; a robust claw before his face gripping dripping guts.

"Look what he holds, Wilhelm."

"Flesh!"

"Check his bag."

"I was on my way home," the goatherd protested. "It is my supper."

Wilhelm had the satchel on the ground and was examining it. "It is full of raw meat," he said coolly.

Dr. Black extinguished his light and the three men stood silent in the dark. "It is long past supper time," he said presently. "Waldmüller will come and join us for a glass of wine at headquarters. This is not the place for explanations."

Waldmüller hung his head and let out a consenting grunt.

VIII.

What peace,
so long as the whoredoms of thy mother and her
witchcrafts are so many, scrivening through
hours of night due to the multitude of the whoredoms, at
fingertips' end a glass of pale wine of the well-favoured harlot: and I will cut off witchcrafts out of thine hand; the mistress of witchcrafts, that selleth villages through her whoredoms, and families through her witchcrafts (his mind quivering in the vocabulary of the sacred writings, snorkelling in that of the latrine) whom thou hatedst for doing most odious works of witchcrafts, hatred, variance, emulations, wrath, strife, seditions, heresies there shall not be found among you any one that maketh his son or his daughter to pass through the fire, or an enchantress, or a witch and they shall no more offer their sacrifices unto devils
after whom they have gone a whoring.

 Ears stuffed with cotton, he hung from the ropes and the bells tolled, vigorously, impetuously, echoing over the village. Then, unplugging his organs of hearing; he climbed down the precarious tower ladder and made his way around to the front of the old church; stopping his progression, he stood and waited for the flock. It was however not a lamb or sheep that first appeared to his sight, but a top-heavy black being walking easily towards him in the morning light.

 "Good morning," Father Tito said in his thin, nasally voice. "I am glad to see that you have come for our Sunday gathering. I flatter myself that my sermon will be of interest to you—Though unquestionably it will not be much to the liking of our local sorceresses."

 "It is not to enter your building of public worship that I have come, but to see you about these... sorceresses—I intercepted one of them last night."

Dr. Black and the Village of Stones 223

"Oh... indeed!"

"Yes, I caught one red-handed. He was of but small intelligence, with a rather large moustache and a satchel of meat stuffs."

The priest paled slightly. "How—How very odd."

"Come now. Not so odd. From the décor of your home, it is apparent that you are an amateur lepidopterist, of a high order. Your interest obviously led you to the discovery of the migratory habits of this butterfly—these butterflies which have been pulpating on the shoulder of the mountain; attracting hungry birds and then, in a cloud, crossing the valley.... Producing rains of meconial fluid.... The other night, in the darkness, at Frau Riemenschneider's, it was you I heard making importunities to young Piera. For neither lust nor money could you ascertain her lips, so you stooped to drumming up hatred against her mother—hiring Waldmüller to dump gristly bits of flesh around the shop's vicinity and then denouncing her publicly as a witch."

The priest was agitated, silent. He bit his bottom lip and turned away.

"So then, you will indict me," he said.

"Nothing of the sort.... If you obey my directives.... First, you must say publicly, today on the pulpit, that the cause of the blood shower has been determined, and it is *au naturel*. Secondly, you will remark that the flesh was not actually part of the showers, but was strewn about by some village boys, as a prank. As the latter piece of information was told to you in priestly confidence, you are unable to name the culprits, but are assured that they will refrain from further tricks.... Thirdly, you yourself must give up all hostile behaviour towards Frau Riemenschneider, and all designs on her daughter.—If you obey these commands, then you will be fine, but if you hesitate, if you prove a recidivist, then you will be exposed."

The priest shrugged his shoulders, as if to say 'What choice do I have?' It was apparent that the man opposite him, the man regarding him with the eyes of a judge, was a higher order of being. He was a man whose friendship it was wise to tender, but Father Tito had acted the churl.

The doctor retraced his steps, wagging a freshly lit cigar in his lips as he went. Approaching headquarters, he saw Wilhelm, seated on the doorstep, a coffee balanced in his fingertips.

"It is all settled?" the latter asked.

"I believe so," answered Dr. Black, exhaling a jet of smoke. "If not, you have the evidence and know what to do."

"So what next?"

"What next! Why, you load up the car and away we go. I have a train to catch."

"Ah, of course, your chess match."

"Not to mention the fact that I am currently in the process of smoking my last D'Orsay."

IX.

"So you will spend long in Italy?"

"Only a few days as things currently stand, and then back to the United States."

There was a moment's silence. Wilhelm stared at the ground. Passengers bustled onto the train.

"The girl?" Black asked.

"We get on well together," Wilhelm replied, lifting his head.

"Good. But I hope you did not pay too much for the pleasure. Or am I to understand that you have been granted a scholarship to the University of Love?"

The young man blushed.

The doctor offered him his hand. "I must go; the train will soon depart."

"It has been wonderful working with you."

"It has been my pleasure."

Dr. Black took up his valise and climbed onto the train. Wilhelm stood, looking after him with sad eyes. The leaving bell rang.

"Wilhelm," the doctor said turning. "Apply yourself, and you will go beyond the limits of the average."

The door closed and a moment later the train slid easily, almost silently out of the station. It moved out, wrapped itself around a curvature in the mountain and, reappearing just beyond, entered and then disappeared in a tunnel cut through the rock; aboard it the man thought of sixteen pieces, sixty-four squares, the firmament, and its division into twelve sectors and three celestial planes.

*Dr. Black,
Thoughts
&
Patents*

I.

2 P.M. SUMMER SOLSTICE. THE DOCTOR'S LONG ISLAND STUDIO[1].

The large front hall, with its 30-foot high ceiling and two tiers of surrounding galleries. This extraordinary space stored more than 10,000 of the doctor's books, displayed many of his initial inventions and several of the numerous awards presented to him for his achievements. In the centre of the hall he sat at an extremely handsome Edward and Roberts inlaid desk on which were scattered diverse papers, a press and pic paperclip dispenser, a variety of pens and an ashtray, in which sat two cigar butts. He was dressed in a white smock.

In his hands, before his eyes, was the following letter:

> *Dear Dr. Black,*
>
> *I hope that this letter finds you in good health.*
> *Not long ago my husband, Alberto[2], returned from Milan with a significant box of books which he had bought at the flea market. I scolded him—as we have far too much literature in the house already—but he brushed my complaints aside, saying that he had had no choice but to buy them, as they were quite rare and had cost him very little (48 euros). He began to show me his purchases, in rapid fire, putting before me four different items:*

1. Near the doctor's house (a large, brick structure, American descendent of Indus Valley Civilization), on the other side of the Japanese-style tea garden, at the end of a statue-flanked path (broken bits of torso, marble heads of griffins and bulls) that leads through a stretch of lawn (a melange of nine species of diploid Poaceae grass).
2. Author of *Blu cobalto con cenere*, Bellinzona: Casagrande

1. Eça de Queiroz. Echos de Paris. *[Porto]: Livraria Chardron, 1927*
2. Paul Adam. Les tentatives passionnées. *[Paris]: P. Ollendorff, 1898*
3. Francesco Mastriani. Valentina: dramma in un prologo e quattro atti. *[Napoli]: S. De Angelis, 1878*
4. Camillo Boito. Sull'avviamento delle arti belle in Italia. *[Milano]: Pirola, 1864*

He then pulled out a fifth, younger but more tattered than the rest, a large volume which consisted of five works bound together as one:

1. Paul Féval. Il cavaliere di Lagardère (Il Gobbo Misterioso di Parigi). *[Firenze]: G. Nerbini, 19..?*
2. Michele Zévaco. I Borgia. *[Milano]: Casa Ed. Ital. Gloriosa, 19..?*
3. Michele Zévaco. Il capitano. *[Milano]: Casa Ed. Ital. Gloriosa, 1925*
4. Michele Zévaco. Il buffone del re. *[Milano]: Casa Ed. Ital. Gloriosa, 1924*
5. Michele Zévaco. La corte dei miracoli. *[Milano]: Casa Ed. Ital. Gloriosa, 19..?*

Examining the last said volume with little enthusiasm, I noticed that the spine was dangling freely, thereby revealing the inside material used in the binding process, which was covered with writing. The characters of it seeming unusual, I looked closer and was surprised to find that they were in the ancient Greek language and that the material was a very thin, very old vellum.

With my husband's eager consent, I took apart the binding and found it to be composed of a number of tattered manuscript fragments adhered together. Later that evening, after a light supper of cream of finocchio soup[1] and salmon, I went to the living room and, a cup of

---

1. 5 finocchi, 50 gr. of extra-virgin olive oil, 2 garlic cloves sliced finely, parsley sprigs, salt and white pepper. Wash the finocchi and then cut into slices. Put these in a saucepan and mix in chopped garlic, chopped parsley and oil and sauté for a few minutes at a low heat. Add 1 litre of water, two glasses of

chamomile tea steaming at my side, studied them, carefully removing one from the next and laying them before me.

Though the writing was by a single hand, it soon became clear to me that these fragments were of two different manuscripts. One of these I was very excited over, as it appeared to be an original and yet previously unknown work of Archimedes. The other fragments were from Elex of Dalmatia's lost work Guide to the Poetic Eccentricities of Sybaris, *which held no interest for me. Some fragments clearly belonged to one text, some to the other, some I could not with certainty determine to which of the two they belonged. I divided the fragments into three groups, designating them as follows:*

A) Those fragments which were clearly from Archimedes' text.
B) Those fragments which were clearly from Elix's text.
C) Those fragments which were indeterminate, and could belong to one or the other.

The C category I then subdivided as follows:

1) Those fragments which I believed to be part of the Archimedes text.
2) Those fragments which I believed to belong to Elix's text.

I then took categories A and 1 and went about trying to piece them together, as best I could, and now submit to you a facsimiled copy of the results, together with my own translation thereof for your opinion, which I value highly, having long been a fan of your commentary on Eutocius' commentary on Archimedes which I keep by my bedside.

Undoubtedly some would find the account given below to be fantastic. But we know, with the discovery of the Antikythera mechanism, that the ancient's knowledge of mechanics was profound, a fact

Riesling and salt and raise the flame to medium. When the water begins to boil, reduce the heat and cook slowly until the finocchi begin to break down. Using a blender, process until smooth. Season to taste with salt and white pepper. Return to pan and simmer at low heat until thoroughly warm and then serve with a sprinkling of freshly chopped parsley.

which is further confirmed by the battery in the Baghdad Museum. Then there is also the account of Archytas of Taretum, the friend of Plato, who built a wooden pigeon moved by steam, not to mention the other similar contraptions mentioned by Heron in his Spiritalia.

Whether what we have is simply the single letter it appears to be, or a part of some greater work, such as the biography that Heracleides wrote of the great mathematician, I do not know. Many passages are unreadable, and the deciphering of many words requires a certain amount of guesswork.

The "appended pages" he mentions in the letter are, of course, not in my possession.

I leave you to your reading and look forward to hearing from you.

Cordialmente,
Raffaella Nessi

The doctor lay down the letter, ignited a cigar and proceeded to read the following document:

Archimedes to Dositheus greetings,

You will excuse me for not responding to your last letter earlier, but I have been....... It has been almost a year since I received it, and over an Olympiad since I last saw you........... and thanks so much for the manuscripts.......

...that the entire universe is made of circles, a variety of circles...

......because man himself is nothing more than a complex series of interlocking spheres—a machine which can be calculated with mathematical precision.

As you know, I have always been fond of proving my theories by means of mechanical experiments. And so I determined, through systematic calculations of magnitude, quantities and forms, to make a creature having the nature of womankind. But save your smile for the flute girls Dositheus, and read what I have to tell you.

Suppose a lever AOB be placed horizontally and supported....

Let EF meet BO in H
TG > GA
> GH
.... $\pi = 3\,{}^{17}\!/_{120} = 3.14166$ .... because that was clear... oblong number...
...... Eudoxus of Cnidus said of magnitudes.
...... If a straight line of which one extremity remains fixed be made to revolve at a uniform rate in a plane until it returns to the position from which it started........
[here follows a long patch of indecipherable material]
...... optical...... oral gears.....
... each of the aforesaid theorems has been accepted...... so it is only a matter of course that life itself can be summed up in terms of......

But if you look at the pages I have appended, you will see clearly enough how I went about the business.

As you know, I never do things by half measures. I hired Boethos of Chalcedon to make me the shell of the machine, and this he did with unparalleled skill in silver... with moveable joints. Her proportions were almost perfect, with an ample bust and hips and a slim waist;—though, as is the fashion with artists, the feet were made somewhat larger than normal, for purposes of balance, and also fitted with soles of soft pig skin.

Meticulously I drew my designs on sheets of low-tin bronze and had my assistant Hypenos, a most ingenious fellow, cut them out for me, which he did with infinite care, knowing full well that the slightest divergence in the lines could shroud success with failure.

"Trust in me," he said, "for my fingers are as nimble as ants."

Soon my studio was filled with numerous minute springs, levers and gears and I was at work assembling them—attaching them to their axles, fitting them in place. I worked tirelessly, as I always do when touched by the fire of invention, forfeiting sleep and bread for the pleasures of science.

Hypenos guarded the door of my studio with the utmost care, turning callers away, for nothing is worse for genius than to be meddled with when at the peak of concentration—a time when man resembles most the gods we worship, thought being as impalpable as the heavens and, at its best, soaring to greater heights than the blazing sun.

Indeed, I felt like an immortal during those days and nights when, with the fingers of my own two hands, I swept up thought and moulded it into mechanism, bringing mechanism in its profundity to a place to rival the natural world.

Not of course that there were not certain problems, such as the......People often make simple things complex and many indeed are like the inhabitants of some strange land where the only number they know is 4 and thus are forced to express simple concepts, such as 18, by complex formulas, like $44 \times .4 + .4 = 4 \times 4 + 4/\text{sqrt}(4)$.....But, give me a good place to stand, and I will move the earth.......Drinking shade from tall trees and dining on the song of small birds...

........a parade helmet...

Finally, the work was done, risen out of raw metal and ideas, incarnate.

"And now?" Hypenos murmured, his voice faintly perfumed with scepticism.

Inserting my pinkie-finger into her left ear, I released the spring of activation. A faint whirring, that of my eternal wheel, came from her breast. She raised her right arm and then, a moment later, stepped forward.

Hypenos, after picking his jaw up off the floor, danced around the room like a fool. He sang and moved his limbs in such a ridiculous way that I almost thought he had lost his reason.

"Come my dear fellow," I said, "calm yourself."

"It is a woman!"

"It is a machine—it is order given to chaos."

....to name it...

...48 is an interesting number, since if you add 1 to it, it becomes a square number, and the same occurs if you divide it by 2 and add 1.....

"Why yes—because now that pile of screws is like a sister, daughter or mistress!"

...while outside flecks of wool passed before the blooming gold......

...it Cleobuline...

II.

IT WAS THEN THAT THE DOCTOR'S READING WAS INTERRUPTED BY A knock on the door and then the door itself opening and Mr. Clovis, male servant of the household, appearing.

"The committee is here," he said and, receiving a signal from the doctor, showed three entities into the room:

A) Mrs. Joan de Merlin, a stoutish woman with a sharp nose, dazzling red hair and 46 years to her name who wore a violet dress (45% cotton, 52% polyester and 3% lycra) with a Peter Pan collar, two front pockets and faux black buttons and, on her feet, a pair of black and white Oxford heels.

B) Leon Claudel was a young man of somewhat delicate appearance. His upper lip was stained with a faint growth of chestnut-coloured moustache, his nose, decidedly petite, was upturned and his eyes were sleepy.

C) Mr. David Naphtali, a gentleman with a rather thin beard and a thick neck, the eyes of Zero Mostel and the voice of Martin Balsam. He wore a blue, short-sleeve button up shirt with a green tie with a red and yellow helium atom pattern.

The doctor stood up, stepped around the desk and came forward, his right hand extended like the thick blade of a Magyar sabre. The visitors, though feeling more inclined to retreat than otherwise, put on as brave a face as cowards can and relinquished their fingers to the grip of Black.
Formalities of speech were exchanged.
"I hope we are not disturbing you?" Mrs. de Merlin said.
"You made an appointment. I was expecting you."

"We are the committee for the McRivers Foundation."

"I am aware of this fact."

"You are on a short list."

"Well, it is true that I am not a man of more than average stature, am indeed below the standard in physical extent."

"A short list," Mr. Naphtali continued, "of candidates for our annual Advanced Genius Award."

The doctor bowed his head in false modesty.

Claudel, gazing about the room: "An incredible book collection you have here!"

"I am an avid reader. I read anything and everything, from light pornography to Uighur block prints. There are very few books from which one cannot glean some piece of useful information."

"Fascinating."

"But let us pass into the laboratory . . . "

III.

Put the words in the correct order to make post-symbolist idioms

1. elastic / herd / whores / flames / bulges

2. painful / fruit / is / capital / a / enormous

3. spongy / flesh / dulocracy / the / Primo de Rivera

4. macerated / ate / lunacy

IV.

THE DÉCOR WAS MARVELLOUS; A VERITABLE FOREST OF SCIENTIFIC instruments. Beakers. Glass tubes. Odd machinery. Hygrometers and hydrostatical glass bubbles. Saccharometer. A large, French, grain testing balance. A hand-driven ciphering machine. Capillary tubes. Optical goniometer. An enormous worm floated in formaldehyde.

"In this place I can make anything I want. Tools to both help and hinder mankind, as my fancy dictates. Delicate poisons—marvellous cures—machines to perform sundry bizarre tasks both practical and useless. With my compounds," he waved his hand towards a wall completely covered with racks containing jars of chemicals, a dazzling rainbow of colours: sulphurous yellows, violent greens, dazzling sun-set oranges, "I have all nature at my disposal. I can synthesize anything, from a simple mammalian protein, to a flower."

They came to the famous chicken heart, which sat pulsating under a small glass bell, and next to it, under a similar glass bell, sat a small black, furry object, about an inch long, and a third of an inch thick.

"What is it?" Mr. David Naphtali asked.

"Watch this."

The doctor lifted up the bell, removed the item and placed it on the palm of one hand, where, after a moment's hesitation, it began to inch its way across, and then up his arm.

"Is it some sort of caterpillar?"

"No my friend. It is an electronic eyebrow."

"An eyebrow?"

"Surgically removed from a dead man—an ex-colleague of mine as a matter of fact—who dedicated his body to science.... Surgically removed... and... electrically charged, energetic neutral beams being injected and trapped by interaction... "

"And?"

"And I am not keen on revealing my professional secrets."

The doctor delicately replaced the eyebrow back under glass where it quivered momentarily before relapsing into a dormant state.

V.

A Patent

Standardised pocket mind controller
The mind controller can induce brain waves into an alpha wave state or a theta wave state by sensing and analysing human brain waves and then transmitting a mind control message suitable for the said analyzed waves. The mind controller includes: an EEG (Electroencephalogram) sensor for sensing a frequency band corresponding to alpha waves and theta waves; an MCU (Memory Control Unit) for analysing whether the brain waves sensed by the EEG sensor are alpha waves or theta waves through a built-in program of a brain wave analysis program pack and controlling output of a message, which corresponds to the alpha waves or theta waves.

A Patent

Thunderstorm fear-reducing cape for Orthodox Shakers
Orthodox Shakers often sense an oncoming thunderstorm before other humans do as they sense and respond to a build up of static electricity prior to and during a thunderstorm, some showing a fear of said storms that borders on terror. These Orthodox Shakers exhibit signs of anxiety upon the approach of a storm, such as pacing, panting, hiding or getting under things. They seek shelter in bathrooms or around pipes. Their behaviour resembles that of a phobia. Doctors sometime prescribe tranquilizer-type medications for Orthodox Shakers who respond this way to thunderstorms. Behaviour modification therapy, counterconditioning or desensitisation style treatment has often been recommended, but these treatments are extensive and minimally effective. Accordingly,

there is a need to provide a means to reduce the stress and soothe these beings during that period surrounding thunderstorms, to whit the current invention: A thunderstorm fear-reducing garment for Orthodox Shakers, which comprises: (a) A flexible cape that is comfortable to wear and covers most of the torso, said cape having an inner lining; (b) said inner lining being comprised of material which is electrically conductive; and (c) fastening means to hold the cape next to the skin.

A few other interesting patents

1) *Carnous vegetables*, being herbaceous plants (carrots, broccoli, etc.) made from processed meat; for those who enjoy the flavour of vegetables, but wish to avoid their healthful benefits.

2) *Method for synthesising diamonds from roses*, isolation is achieved through use and adaptation of a 2-butoxyethanol precipitation technique using large amount of initial tissue in order to achieve critical mass for precipitation.

3) *Method and apparatus for extracting meaning from life*, a prefabricated adaptable lightweight hollow core; when consciousness is active appearances do not come from elsewhere; when inactive they do not go elsewhere.

4) *Artificial sheep dung*, made from ammonia, ink and guar gum, looks and smells like the real thing.

5) *Method of pan-frying small game*, small game are pan-fried by a method which provides a thoroughly cooked food article.

VI.

"And this," the doctor said, "is a Patented Method for Metaphysical Experience."

The device was composed of a small burlap sack, a very large syringe, and a chair adorned with acanthus leaves and having a padded seat covered with brown vinyl and a pediment featuring a pair of baluster front legs joined to the back legs by an H-shaped stretcher.

"It looks very . . . inquisitorial," Mrs. de Merlin commented.

"If any of you would care for a demonstration . . . "

"Is that your recommendation?"

"Empirical experience is a fine tool for education."

"Leon will put himself at your disposal," de Merlin said.

"Yes," Mr. Naphtali confirmed, "Leon would be glad to put himself in the role of a guinea pig."

The young man looked uneasy as he was hustled into the chair, his features however soon swallowed by the burlap sack (rot-resistant jute and allied vegetable fibres meeting Class A Requirements of U.S. Military Specification CID A-A-52141 (formerly MILB-12233E)—14" x 26"). The doctor then took up the syringe, a large, plastic descendent of Iraqi ophthalmologist Ali al-Mawsili's original invention, and injected the young man with 15 ccs of 64-beta-betrosachrinal admixed with just a hint of melon seed extract.

Mr. David Naphtali stroked his meagre beard and looked on with interest.

Mrs. de Merlin smiled innocuously as she watched the doctor at work.

Claudel felt a strange sensation, as if the inside of his skull were being turned to ice.

"I feel a little——" the words died on the tip of his frozen tongue, a vague thrill of horror taking the place of articulation.

It was at this point that the consciousness-components-bundle of Leon's being was transported, almost instantaneously, to the Club for Advanced Gentleman Tailors (London, SW1X7RL, Tel: +44 871 7398572); to be precise, said consciousness being temporarily lodged in a philodendron (P. calophyllum, leaves pointed, heart-shaped, bright, glossy green) by the window and he was privy to the following conversation:

"Personally, I always leave a half an inch of shirt collar showing at the back of the jacket."

"But, my good fellow, it should really depend on the amount of cuff shown around the wrist, as the length of these two should be equal."

"I am not sure that I follow your logic, for if the Euclidean distance of the cuff were to be to some degree exaggerated, it hardly seems right to then burden a man's collar with the same drama."

"Well, as far as I am concerned, congruence is one of the most important principles of tailoring."

At this point Donald Sapphire, a 39-year-old man with a cleft chin and a fine, silken moustache, like two wings of spun gold, felt it incumbent on himself to intervene.

"But," he said, removing a silver cigarette case from his jacket pocket, "are we not to take the man wearing the shirt into consideration? A man with a long neck obviously deserves a little more collar while, for those poor fellows who are lacking in that department, an extra centimetre is nothing less than ignominious. And then," he continued, lighting a cigarette and blowing a jet of smoke towards the ceiling, "in the end, isn't harmony the point after all? The collar of the suit and the shirt should work together like a violin and its bow, of course never losing sight of such grave considerations as whether the collar is cutaway or straight and so forth. These matters, truth be told, are exquisitely subtle and must be deliberated on in the same manner some Medieval alchemist would the Philosopher's Stone."

The men sat around on Barcelona chairs in a large room, the walls of which were painted a delicate shade between amber and apricot, the trimming done in a dark Bordeaux. An extremely large, faded Persian carpet covered the floor and the overlapping geometric patterns of this masterpiece of knotted wool added a vaguely mystical aura to the scene.

"Speaking of collars," said a very lean gentleman wearing a bamboo sports coat, "is anyone familiar with the Earl of Ionia?"

"Immensely wealthy, isn't he?"

"Rather."

"I have heard that he is quite original."

"As sin."

"But these days, there is nothing more mundane than sin."

"I couldn't agree more. Only in the wrinkles of aged virgins can true originality be found."

"In any case," said the man in the bamboo sports coat, Jeremy Lions, a former monk who decided that his true higher calling was tailoring, "original or not, he is one of my newer clients."

"Congratulations," was heard flatly from all sides.

"Oh, there is nothing very pleasant about it, I assure you. I received him on the recommendation of another client of rank, whom I will not mention, as I don't wish to be the object of jealousy. But, anyhow... he came to see me in a frightful state, his very eyebrows screaming for help.

"'My old tailor has made a fool of me,' he said.

"I nodded my head in agreement.

"'Be frank, what do you think of my collar?'

"'I think it horrid.'

"His lips, which were thin and colourless, frowned before parting, letting a few naked words roll out from the gaps in his teeth.

"'Can you fix it?'

"'Well, your neck is rather long.'

"'Yes, it has grown 3 inches in the last year. My physician, who is a native of Brussels, says it is due to the angle at which I wear my nose.'

"I gazed up into the cavities of his organ of smell and felt like a man standing on the edge of an abyss.

"'If I might suggest...'

"'I think not. My analyst, who was born in the seaside village of Stintino, has informed me that it is a perfectly healthy defence mechanism.'

"Now, naturally, I was somewhat perplexed. Before me stood a gentleman with an eight inch neck, a small head upon which grew a few scraps of straw-coloured hair, and broad shoulders. In short, he was a human riddle that I was not sure I was Odin enough to decipher.

"I spent the evening drinking Campari and soda, pouring over resources, consulting the *Necklothitania* and Cesare Vecellio's *Degli habiti antichi et moderni di diverse parti del mondo*. I wrapped my mind around patterns, convened with the Gods of the Ten Thousand Stitches and burned incense before a statuette of St. Homobonus of Cremona. It was only as a grey dawn was breaking outside my windows that a solution came to me, a satori worthy of Jôshû himself.

"That afternoon I met with my client.

"I offered him a stiff bow and served him a cup of green tea flavoured with attar of roses.

"'Would you,' I said, 'be willing to make an adjustment in neckwear?'

"'I am willing to do whatever is necessary.'

"'Very well. First, your shirt will be made of poplin, with an attachable upturned, pointless collar made of pure silk. Around this you will tie a band of lightly starched cloth of the most brilliant *blanc d'innocence virginale* in a knot, admittedly long forgotten, called the *ronéoter d'amour*. Your neck will then appear as noble as one of the columns of the Temple of Hera in Paestum.'"

"Paestum, yes—I was there the summer before last," Donald Sapphire could not refrain from interrupting. "Nothing noble about the place as far as I could see. A pile of stones to be looked at through the gurgling rivulets of sweat flowing from my brow."

"One should never visit Italy in the summer," another present, Henri Pierce, said sententiously, "for in the south, the most telling experiences are found under grey skies."

He was a man of around 50 years of age, known as a bit of an in-crowd tailor, with a stout belly and rather weak legs, the knees of which often grazed against each other when he walked. Of course he was sitting now, one leg hooked over the next, a glass of Madeira in his hand.

"And what exactly is a 'telling experience'?"

"That which I will tell."

"Please do!" most present said, not because they found Pierce's stories to be interesting (quite the opposite), but because the majority of them suffered from acute sedatephobia (a disease common amongst those top-

Dr. Black, Thoughts and Patents 247

drawer tailors who practice their profession on Savile Row) and would sooner have heard the sound of his voice than that of silence.

"Well, have you ever heard of the Monster of Milan?" said Pierce, fondling his drink.

"I recall hearing something about him. A murderer of some sort, wasn't he?"

"Yes, he strangled his victims to death with their own innards which he would extract from their bellies by means of a sharp instrument."

"How gruesome!"

"Yes, it sounds almost as unpleasant as a navy jacket with a green tie."

"Very vulgar."

"In any case," Henri continued, "let me tell you about what happened..."

VII.

Henri Pierce's Narrative

I HAVE ALWAYS CONSIDERED THE WINTER TO BE THE BEST TIME TO visit Florence, or any of the major attractions in Europe for that matter. It is not that I am a misanthrope, it is just that I don't like people. Hoards of them especially. For in a hundred, one will be lucky to find two or three worth looking at.

As is apparent from the spray of grey along my temples, I am no longer young and the noise and tumult of crowds affects my nerves, my digestion, which is as delicate as a veil made of tulle. I strive for tranquillity, a stress-free existence where wines correspond to entrées and the tenor of an evening is punctuated by nothing more violent than a Clementi sonatina played at a reasonable distance by a young man with sparking blue eyes wearing suede gloves. And, as can be attested by all present, in the cooler seasons, people tend to dress more chic. My gaze is less likely to be injured by the sight of shorts and sandals. There is the likelihood of seeing the slender necks of women encased in languid fur.

It was in November. I had been exploring that city for several days, studying the masterpieces at the museums and passing through the boutiques. I had bought a pair of handmade shoes of a beautiful brown leather, deliciously soft, as well as several nice cravats—heavy silks, nice interlinings, back tipping and bar-tack stitching—and a few delicious seven-fold ties...

Anyhow, on a certain forenoon, I decided to drop into the Basilica di San Lorenzo, that creation of Brunelleschi's, which my guidebook, a 126-page affair in glossy covers, said was exceptionally impressive.

I mounted the steps, filthy with the residue of pigeons, entered the building, left my maple solid shaft umbrella by the door and stalked

Dr. Black, Thoughts and Patents

forward. The heels of my shoes echoed through the vast space pleasantly.

I spent some time admiring Donatello's bronze pulpits, works of great spiritual depth and remarkable detail, and then turned towards the Old Sacristy. The tomb of Giovanni and Piero de Medici by Verrocchio was remarkable, and indeed I thought the designs on it would make a lovely pattern for a scarf—the sort of thing one might wear to a June tea party, a silken accompaniment to thin sandwiches and sliced cakes.

My mind working in this manner, I left that room and seated myself, so as to meditate on those weighty matters, before the high altar of the great chamber. I felt a marvellous sense of tranquillity and, in a relaxed manner, proceeded to caress my naked chin,

enjoying the dangerous delights of reclusion and misanthropy,

to quote rather broadly O.V. de L. Milosz.

It was then that a man came and stood not far from me, coughed, breaking the tranquillity of the moment like an undercutter entering his shop after dining too well at Mulligan's Pub.

He, a stooping, thin fellow with a watery gaze, was alone, undoubtedly a bachelor like myself. But, looking at him with pitying eyes, I noticed the critical difference between he and I.

He wore a black overcoat and his pants, beige, apparently made of some kind of moleskin type cotton, more suitable for the sail of a ship than a garment for a human person, were entirely without a break. Now, I am not saying that one should have such a break as to leave the cuff puddling. But a gentleman *always* wears his pants with a full break, and anything less than a half break should be viewed as a variety of self flagellation.... Of course it is true that there are exceptions, such as in the case of the Duke of Windsor, who lets his cuff just shiver above the shoe, denying the two any sort of intimacy.... But the eccentricity of a king is the madness of a fool.

Thus was the pattern of my thoughts, when I noticed a fat old priest approaching me.

"It is time for you to leave," he said rather roughly.

"Leave? But the hours posted on the door——"

"Hey, I said you have to leave. We are closing for a while *caro mio*, so move it."

He had me by the shoulder and was ushering me towards the door and, a moment later, I found myself in the piazza with an ego chipped like glass and my shirt front feeling rather less stiff than it had a few moments before.

"Excuse me sir, but I believe you forgot something."

I turned. It was he of the breakless pants, in his right hand my maple solid shaft umbrella.

"Ah! But how kind of you to come chasing after me."

"Think nothing of it. I was ejected from the church just like yourself. Italians are without manners."

"And by your accent," (it was surprisingly refined), "I take it you are English."

"Rather."

"Then allow me to offer a fellow countryman a drink."

"I will allow nothing of the sort. It is lunchtime and I therefore insist on offering you a meal."

"But really ... "

"I insist!"

I bowed my head in assent. I was hungry and the pleasant-looking trattoria across the way was soon ushering my companion and I in.

He took off his overcoat and arranged it over the back of his chair and I could now see his pants in full. He was wearing flat-front trousers. His hips were narrow and his behind somewhat flat, and I could not help but think that he would have benefited by a few pleats and it is also possible that thereby the lack of break might not have appeared quite as acute.

Our waiter was a grave-faced gentleman with proud lips and a nose that looked as if it had been chiselled from Carrara marble. He had an air of respectability about him that I found quite pleasant.

"Is your rabbit good?"

"Everything here is good signore," he replied with an offended air.

"Then I will have the pappardelle with hare sauce, and to start a rocket salad."

My companion, less restrained than myself, ordered fried baby eels, gnocchetti di spinaci, and cibreo[1] and then: "What do you say to a bottle of wine?"

I expressed my approval and he ordered a '97 La Mandria.

The food was good and the wine excellent, a pretty garnet-coloured liquid letting off a slight scent of violets. It was balanced, dry, sapid and slightly tannic, running over the tongue with exquisite softness—the same softness one might find in a finely-made velvet jacket;—a little rush of luxury.

I was surprised in no small degree by the tastes of my host. I have always equated, quite rightly, slovenliness of dress with lack of breeding. This man, like a fast-moving snail, seemed to be an exception to the rule. He knew his wines and how to use his silverware.

"So," I said, as I inserted my fork into the squirming pile of noodles before me, "are you in town, like myself, in the capacity of a tourist?"

"No, unfortunately not, I am here to visit the churches."

"I see. . . . You have some sort of business with them?"

"Not in the least," he said, moistening his tongue with wine. "But I have, I think, visited every church in Europe. I know the undercroft of St. Peter's in Rome better than most people know their own homes, and can tell you the number of stained glass windows and pillars there are in the great Duomo of Milan. The cold solemnity, the smell of propolis incense, these have become as familiar to me as my own heartbeat. I have gazed at enough incorrupt saints to fill a football stadium. I have seen them all, from the most humble churches, little niches where there is hardly space to turn around, to the grandest cathedrals, those of Chartes, Cologne and Reims."

He was eating his eels, golden in colour, with a remarkable appetite.

"You must be a very religious man."

"Religious? No, I am not. The truth is that . . . " He paused significantly. "The truth is that I am an atheist."

"Ah!" I exhaled, raising my eyebrows about a centimetre above their usual orbit.

---

1. A favourite of Catherine de Medici, this is a simple chicken soup that includes giblets, embryonic eggs and cockscombs.

"Yes, I believe that, upon the termination of this life I will not go either to heaven or hell, but simply enter into a state of oblivion, non-existence. There is no homogeneous mass of eternal consciousness and I believe that one is never redressed for one's sins unless they be against the actual written law of the land."

"Personally, I believe in reincarnation."

"Oh, and what were you in your past life?"

"I am not quite sure, but probably something in lace."

"Well, each to their own. The important thing is to enjoy lunch."

"Indeed. I must say though, that I find the idea of an atheist who loves churches to be somewhat like fake buttonholes on the sleeves of a coat—not only meaningless, but common."

"I am not asking you to appreciate me, but rather the rabbit sauce on your plate."

There was a hint of violence in his voice. I fumbled with my napkin and tried to look like a man trying not to look embarrassed.

"But," he continued a moment later, as he gazed mournfully down at his empty wine glass, "I suppose you are entitled to an explanation."

"Well, I don't want to pry..."

"Oh, come now, we are friends. We have drunk wine together and broken bread."

"So, if you hate churches, then why..."

"Let me explain," he said, replenishing his glass, beginning on his gnocchetti. "As a child nothing frightened me more than those dark temples only fit for skeletons and ghosts. I would not even pass under the shadow of one, which seemed to carry with it the icy coldness of the tomb. I grew older and so did my fear. Every time I saw the spires of a cathedral in the distance, I would have an anxiety attack. I went to a psychiatrist, was diagnosed with ecclesiophobia, and given a prescription for a mild tranquiliser. The drugs somewhat deadened my nerves, but in no way cured me.—Most men live their entire lives with one phobia or another, managing to bury their anxieties under the swift sands of activity—work, sports, ambition.... But with a fear such as mine..."

"It was very difficult?" I ventured.

"Well, you see, I fell in love... with a very beautiful woman. She had long, curly, chestnut-coloured hair and a very small white face. Her body was a marvel of perfection—a dazzling flame—a sculpture of flesh crying out to be introduced into the mysteries of procreation.... But there was a slight problem. She was as religious as a nun, a chalice in which the profane could not dip their fingers. She would not... consummate our relations... without them being sanctified by the Church. I was full ready to marry her, to sprinkle my temples with her fragrant dew, but dreaded having to enter an edifice of Christian worship. I suggested a simple public ceremony, but she wouldn't hear of it. The situation was critical."

I looked at his naked fingers, unbound by any circlet of gold, as he poured the last of the bottle into his glass.

"Do you think we should get another bottle, maybe something special?" he said turning to me.

"I am actually quite fine, I assure you."

"No, I insist you share another bottle with me. A Sassicaia," he told the waiter. "And make sure it is not a '92 vintage, or I will send it back. A '90 or '91 would be best."

The waiter inclined his head with the solemnity of a topaz idol being brought to life by the wand of a magician, then turned and I watched his sweeping lapels retreat towards the door that led to the wine cellar. Around two minutes later he was uncorking the bottle, letting our glasses drink from its neck...

"True love," the other continued, "so the poets assure us, only comes along once in a lifetime. I did not want to let this bird escape me. Bravely I went about the business, determined to conquer my enemy, my fear. At first I made myself enter All Hallows-on-the-Wall associated with the Worshipful Company of Carpenters. I stayed for not more than two minutes. The experience was absurdly painful and, upon gaining the street, I gasped for air like a man half drowned."

"You are brave," I said, taking a sip of the latest vintage.

"No, I am a coward," he replied, "but it is cowards who commit the most daring deeds. And so it was that the very next day I entered St. Bartholomew-the-Less, thrusting myself into its octagonal interior with the hardihood of a Kalahari Bushman stalking across a bed of burning coals, my skin prickling all over, my temples impearled with sweat. After that it was a mad race through all the churches of London—from St.

Sepulchre-without-Newgate to St. Andrew-by-the-Wardrobe. One day I crucified my nerves in St. Martin-in-the-Fields, the next, let my bravado be crushed beneath the weight of St. Magnus-the-Martyr.

"Just as long sustained pain, in certain individuals, can begin to resemble pleasure, so it was that this self-inflicted torture began to become an actual necessity. I would stay seated there until I began to feel actually physically ill, enduring the tortures of a martyr. Indeed, that Jesus I saw nailed to the cross could not have suffered more than I!

"The church began to resemble some fateful mistress—like Wanda in *Venus im Pelz*. The coldness of her skin, the cruelty of her womb..."

Lazily he took a swallow of his wine.

"And your fiancée?" I asked.

"What can I say? I frightened her... and the sight of her became nothing to me."

"Tragic."

"Yes. Now I cannot go a day without visiting a church, and if possible like to visit two or three. If I don't spend at least half a dozen hours wandering through the nave, gazing at the doorways of Christ in majesty, I find it difficult to sleep at night, and my mind becomes haunted by belfry-like nightmares.... And so I go from city to city, always preferring those old towns where there are an abundance of those awful buildings that I am addicted to. One day Paris, another Rome. Sometimes sadness, loneliness overtakes me, and I weep. In Lithuania there is the Vilnius. In Norway, the Nidarosdomen. I could describe to you in the most intimate detail the Cathedral of Santa Eulàlia in Madrid and, my tongue greased with good grape, paint the most hallucinatory word paintings to do with St. Barbara's in Kutná Hora."

It was at this point that he abruptly quit talking, speech seeming to be sundered from his mouth by the bells which at that moment reached our ears.

He rose brusquely from his seat. "Ah," he said, "but I must hurry. I am missing the opening of the doors of Ognisanto!"

A quick handshake. A few murmured words on my part. And then his back, the sight of his unbroken pants making their way out the door.

I saw him walk off across the piazza, a mournful figure.

"Excuse me signore, but the bill..."

And large quantities of prettily hued currency fluttered out of my wallet like butterflies in springtime.

"Is Ognisanto very near here?" I asked the waiter as I was leaving.

"Yes," he replied, "it is just up the road. But there is no use going there now. It is only two and the cathedral does not open until four."

A few days later I took the train north, through the lovely hill-country of Tuscany and then the rich farmland of Lombardy, to finally ascend into that immense heap of buildings called Milan. I spent a good deal of time walking around the Triangle, my eyes drinking of the champagne served in those shop windows. I observed the pretty young women and prettier young men, tried on a pair of pineapple fibre trousers and bought a scarf with a Penrose tiling pattern.

The city was at that time in a state of fear. Few would walk about at night alone. Suspicious glances were exchanged without cause. Policemen stood on street corners fingering sub-machine guns. The Monster of Milan, as I am sure you all know, was the terror of the place, creeping up on unsuspecting pedestrians and, after slitting open their bellies, strangling them with their own intestines. The beast was reportedly around 3 feet tall and wore a red poncho and a Lurex cap. Whether male or female was a mystery and the horror was profound.

Anyhow, on a certain afternoon I went into a bar and drank a cappuccino which the bartender had kindly sprinkled with cocoa powder. After swallowing the last drops of that liquid, I went up to the cashier, a rather large unshaven fellow with dreamy eyes, paid for my drink and left. As I walked down the street I counted my change and, glancing at the receipt, noticed the following sentiments written in a fine hand:

> *I awoke this morning wrapped in tentacles, bathed beneath a shower of lead, felt my blood tumble through my veins and laughter mingled with the scent of flowers. All things in this world are the colour of d'Anjou pears and that is why only very young and very old men are capable of love. When you close your eyes, look to your left and you will find me buried in the inner folds.*

I tossed this into the gutter and continued my way along the Via Santa Margherita, past La Scala. I rounded the corner on the Via Tommaso and found myself at the entrance to the Galleria Vittorio Emanuele II, confronted by an amassed group of people, a twisted splash of colour in their midst, and police gravely present.

"What seems to be the trouble?" I asked a gentleman in a malt-coloured overcoat whose upper lip was suppressed by a wad of grey moustache.

"It is the Monster—it has struck again."

"Ah! And the victim?"

"I don't know. A young man. An unlucky bastard."

My morbid interest peaked, I worked my way through the people to get a glimpse of the corpse which was lying there in a puddle of blood. It was a male. As soon as my eyes became accustomed to the sanguineous glare, I noticed the trousers—a pair of beige things, clearly cut too high, so that if the fellow had had the good fortune to still be standing, there is no question but that they would have been—without a break."

VIII.

Jeremy Lions lit a Pêche brand peach-flavoured Japanese cigarette.

"And, naturally, it was the man you had met in Florence," he said.

"No, not at all. It was a completely different fellow."

"Your story reminds me of another."

"Oh?"

"Yes. My cousin once-removed, an olive merchant from Tuffley, discovered that his wife was having an affair with another man."

"And?"

"It turned out that the woman was not his wife at all but that he himself was the man."

It was at this point that young Leon's ganglion of intellectual and perceptual comprehension was, in the duration of 9,192,631,770 periods of the radiation corresponding to the transition between the two hyperfine levels of the ground state of the caesium-133 atom, transported back to Long Island and re-deposited in his physical being. He moved his limbs, removed the burlap sack from his head, and stood up.

The room was empty, but he could hear sounds coming from an adjoining chamber which, with unsteady steps, he entered.

On one wall was a monotonal painting by the famous San Corradan minimalist Ignacio Valdez titled *Escaped Convicts Running Through a Pumpkin Field at Harvest Time*. Mrs. de Merlin, Mr. David Naphtali and the doctor were seated on leather lounge chairs around a glass-topped coffee table.

"Ah, there you are Leon! The good doctor was just giving the most marvellous scientific dissertation on vodka martini preparation!"

"Yes," the doctor pursued, "the big brother of this drink, invented at the Occidental Hotel on Montgomery Street, San Francisco, and not, as some would think on the corner of Alhambra and Masonic in Martinez or for that matter by Signor Martini di Arma di Taggia, principal barman the Knickerbocker Hotel in New York, is indeed pleasant. But I am something of a modernist, and have allowed my bottles of gin to gather dust.... So," he continued, giving a physical demonstration as he spoke, "for a martini as perfect as any sonnet, only ice-cold Grasovka Bison Brand vodka, each bottle flavoured with a single blade of bison grass, that plant which grows in bunches in the clearings of the national park of Bialowieza on the border between Poland and White Russia, should be used. I take a 28 oz stainless steel cocktail shaker direct from the freezer and, holding it between my two hands, quickly bow à la Winston Churchill in the direction of France, thereby paying adequate respects to vermouth. I now fill the shaker one-third of the way full of ice made from good water from the Pirene Fountain in Corinth and add eleven jiggers of vodka. Swish thrice, ever so gently, so as not to bruise the liquid, so as not to overly excite the molecules. And now I strain the contents into four 4 oz chilled delta-shaped cocktail glasses and, after fetishistically waving a 1.5 x .75 inch rind of lemon over the glasses, while being careful not to let it so much as touch their rims, serve."

Hands extended themselves. Fingers wrapped around delicate stems.

"Well," Mrs. de Merlin said, "judging by your drink-mixing skills, I would certainly say you are a genius."

"Indeed he is," young Leon confirmed. "My metaphysical experience was exemplary."

"But, according to the strict rules of the McRivers Foundation, before your election for the award can be approved, you must answer a few questions."

"You ask, I answer," the doctor said tersely.

"Do you know the game of evolution?"

"I do. One transforms one word into another by changing one letter at a time. Thus, if one wants to turn a cat into a rug: cat, rat, rag, rug."

"Precisely.... And so your task is to turn a lion into a lamb."

"Lion, limn, limb, lamb."

"Bravo!"

"And," Leon Claudel said with a sly look in his eyes, "a lily into a rose."

"Lily, lilt, list, lost, lose, rose."

"But the most difficult of all Mr. Naphtali added, is for you to turn milk into grog."

The doctor pondered for a few brief instants before giving his reply.

IX.

A Patent

Therapeutic doll for storing emotions

A rag-type doll has built-in cavities for receiving human feelings and other attributes. The cavities are located on the doll to show where on the body such feelings are experienced by inserting the appropriate form into the cavity. The doll is composed of: a body having a head, torso, arms and legs; at least one of said head, torso, arms and legs having at least one cavity with a corresponding opening allowing access to said cavity and means for closing said opening; means, insertable into said cavities, for expressing human emotions, said means comprising a plurality of forms, each form having an emotional connotation.

X.

[1]"WELL," MRS. DE MERLIN DAIS WITH PHAEMSIS, "TI SMEES clear atth you rea more than geliible rof the waard."

"Your negius is arkmed", Mr. Naphtali edadd.

The ordoct elowed eth exa of ish brdea as na ecexutinero ighmt his eax ot measure the enck of the signatedde timciv forbee prelying: "Genius edos ont xeist, noly dieas and eth nem who drive ethm."

And ethn, iwth those owrsd lloring tweeebn ethir ears, with aguev smesil layping puon their spli, thwi armtini cingdan ni their ellbies, the reeth voyens of the McRivers Foundation ftle eth awy they adh mceo.

---

1. The typographer, while working on the following chapter, was unfortunately under the effects of a psychotropic brainwashing agent. As there was not enough time to make the necessary changes before sending this book to the printers (original manuscript misplaced), we will leave it up to you, the reader, to make the necessary anagrammatic corrections.

XI.

THE DOCTOR, NOW LEFT TO HIMSELF, SET FIRE TO THE TIP OF A lens-shaped figuardo rolled by world renowned torcedor Carlos Valdez Gonzales[1], took up the manuscript he had been reading, and continued:

> For a period, due to the very novelty of the adventure, Cleobuline took up all of my attention. When people saw me walking with this bronze maiden through the streets, they would stare in wonder. Some thought she was a goddess—others that I was a magician who could cause statues to perambulate. Such is the ignorance of the unscientific mind. There are things which seem incredible to most men who have not studied mathematics, while nothing is impossible to us who realise that the entire universe moves on hinges.
>
> As for Cleobuline, she behaved not dissimilar to a new born human infant. She looked about her with curiosity, taking apparent, though subdued, delight in all the simple things that make up this world: a buzzing bee, a horse, a few white clouds rolling across the heavens.

1. As a youth he worked making fake pre-Columbian masks in the Nicaraguan town of San Ramón. At the age of 15 he was arrested and falsely accused of murdering the Marquis de Alameda. In prison, among the stink of rats and the rough-pitched voices of impenitent crime, he was mentored by Señor Augusto Somoza Fonsesca, who taught him the ancient art of the torcedor, most especially many secret rolls, such as the goose egg, the mandorla, the obtuse triangle, the enneagono, etc. At 19, during the famous riots of Muy Muy, he escaped bondage and fled to Cuba, where his fame as a cigar roller was assured.

It was springtime and I took her on short expeditions outside the walls of the town. The meadows were bursting with flowers, each one a perfect expression of geometric calculation. I picked a bunch and, in play, handed them to the maiden, who was apparently attracted by their bright and beautiful shades;—but her touch was not delicate, and before I could stop her she had ground the petals between her metallic fingers.

I took my mechanism by the hand, and caressed it gently.

"Be careful with organic things," I said, "for, against your hard skin, they will easily damage and be no more."

She then stretched forth her hand and touched my beard, in a manner which won my admiration—in a manner indeed as sweet as that of Odatis, who my thoughts strayed to even then.

Ah, Odatis! I have not yet mentioned her.

But now let me go back a little.

During this time I had begun to frequent the house of a certain woman by the name of Odatis. Wipe that look of surprise off your face Dositheus, for I have no doubt that you yourself, when you are not engaged in making calendars, are gazing at the sky and finding new constellations to name after the local flute girls—and, if you are not careful, you might meet the fate of Thales who, while walking in amorous conversation with his maid servant, his eyes turned towards the stars, fell over the edge of a cliff and was broken to pieces. No, you cannot tell me that the men of Alexandria are any less subject to romantic follies than those of other parts of the world—for men, like cones, follow certain set principles, regardless of their focus directrix.

If you had met Odatis, you might have been astounded that I found such a woman attractive. There is nothing remarkable in the fact that she was my intellectual inferior, as that is to be expected. What is remarkable however is that she was *intellectually inferior*—not only to me, but to the average Syracusean of her sex—and yet I still loved her. She took delight in gossip, talked rather than listened, treated her make-up box as her most intimate friend, giggled at serious things and became serious at a good jest. And yet all these things, which should have filled me with disgust, I viewed as charms, little traits and features put there for my own individual pleasure.

As a wise man, I should have followed the advice of Pittacus, if we can trust the story as given out by Callimachus, and kept to my own sphere, but even the gods sometimes commit acts of folly, so what mortal can expect to never be caught in its snares? And so it was with me. I do not believe the depths of the intellect have anything to do with the depths of the heart. Often it is that we find highly refined men and women to be incapable of love—and it is frankly a surprise to me that I am not among their number. But neither was Socrates, for he, wise as he was, is said to have married a less than ideal woman; and men whose intellects soar to Olympus often allow their hearts to skip in the mud. I was in love with this woman, whose mind was certainly far from ideal, but whose physical lines were as perfect as those of the sun—for let it be understood that, geometrically, she was a masterpiece, her breasts fully satisfying the equation $y = x^2$ and the hyperbola of her hips $ax^2 - by^2 = 1$; and when she smiled, her gums, which were the appetizing red of cherries and bore in them clusters of shiny white rectangles, attracted me greatly. So obsessed is the mathematician by shape that, while a sword is being driven into his breast, he will admire the purity of its lines.

Sometimes we would lie, bare of any covering, and with my fingers I would trace geometrical figures on her body. I composed a poem for her in logaoedic metre. Together we would laugh and play in her apartments and, truth be told, from time to time she made me forget about math, bathing me in the cascades of her rich black hair.

As for my bronze maiden, I must in truth say that I began to ignore her. My interest it seems had been in creating, not the creation, and I spoke to Hypenos of giving her to King Hiero as a gift.

"You would give the moon away as a gift," he said with a shrug of the shoulders, "if you could catch hold of it."

The next day, with the intention previously mentioned, I went to King Hiero's palace accompanied by Cleobuline.

Needless to say he was astonished at that invention, for it made the trick I did with the golden crown truly appear as mere child's play.

"Archimedes," the king said, "give me this thing and I will make you a rich man."

"Good King," I replied, "I am already as rich as any mortal could dream to be, for I have at my command every number in the universe. But you have forestalled me with your request, as I came here with the specific intention of giving you this metal maiden as a gift."

Just then his wife, Philistis, that stern but beautiful woman, came in and was soon apprised of the situation.

"I will not have it in my house," she cried, "for such a thing is a corruptor of morals."

"Morals?" Heiro said in astonishment. "Whose morals?"

"When Gelo, our son, sees this maiden about the house, this woman with her metal womb, he will compare her with his wife Nereis, daughter of Pyrrhos,—and the latter will come off unfavourably, for she is far from being a beauty, while this silvery creature here is certainly comely. I see danger in this monstrous machine, which has the beauty of a woman without a woman's flexibility—that quality that allows us to live together without eating each other like spiders."

I left the palace as I had come, with Cleobuline by my side, making my way through the market and to the house of Odatis, thinking that it would be pleasant to lunch with her and, indeed, the woman greeted me in a most sympathetic matter.

Over wine and cheesecake, I told her of my visit to the king.

"But why give her away when she can be a wonderful servant to you?" was the woman's remark.

I laughed and caressed her chin as one would that of a child. "A servant my dear? Well then, why not have her for yourself if the idea amuses you."

Odatis clapped her hands in delight.

I turned to the bronze maiden.

"Cleobuline," I said, "from this time forth, you will belong to this young lady. She is your mistress, and you will obey her every command."

The mechanism bowed and, though her metallic features were inflexible, I could not help but imagine there was a note of disappointment in her attitude.

Odatis for her part however was overjoyed. To have such an unusual slave seemed to her the height of luxury........... Like shade with a retrospective manner...

...... perhaps conic sections... trochoid......

.... conchoid......

...... since *A*, *B*, and *C* are commensurable............ like lilies of flaming oil......... my home... maiden late that night, I felt a slight hint of regret—almost, I imagine, as a man might feel after selling his only child to a procuress. But the greatness of the human mind can only be measured due to its baseness, for without comparatives, superlatives cannot exist.

As for Odatis, she showed full proof of her low mentality, for it has been justly said that a man (though in this case we speak of a woman) can best be judged by how he treats his slaves. By treating those below us without dignity, we rob ourselves of that very quality.

She made the woman clean her apartments and do all sorts of menial tasks, while she lounged about, eating honeyed wheat cakes. Once, when Cleobuline was going about her work at a pace not to Odatis' liking, the latter struck her with a sandal and said that she would have her made into plate for her table if she did not perform her duties with greater punctiliousness. Another time, to amuse some dinner guests, she had Cleobuline crawl about the apartment on all fours, while those present took turns riding her like a horse, their squeals of laughter...... an embroidered water of rough nightmares and virgin lilies play their lutes, pouring suave philtres from target-like lips......... rusty scabs, like jewels...

... For the first time the flanged mouth of Odatis struck me as being unpleasant.

"Don't you think you are treating Cleobuline a little roughly?" I asked.

"Roughly? But she is only an object—like a lamp or jug, the owner of which can treat them howsoever they want. And, in any case, my love," she continued, running her fingers enticingly through my hair, "why should you ask me to forgo my pleasures, when I am so ready to accommodate you in yours."

Her lips then sought out mine, our limbs became entangled and I was refuted by the most carnal of arguments.... The lilacs were on fire, naked and white, navels exposed, waving before the Satyr as honeycombs flew through the air and earth was heard in a semi-voice....

[here follows a number of lines which are indecipherable]

Upon rising from this delightful little comedy, I noticed Cleobuline standing in the doorway. She had apparently witnessed all.... bit...... and do in earnestly believe I blushed........... peacocks dressed in dahlias, the lassitude of their foliage pure lunar rosettes, pale faces and pure music, bodies ... rocked by boredom, moved to the odorous rate of carpets being unrolled before the ornamented body of falling petals ...

... That day I spent wandering about the docks, watching the seagulls soar through the air and listening to the hoarse cries of the seamen. My spirits were heavy and mis-shapen; my thoughts dull.

... ponds of eyes...... the language of the axle ...

...... magnitudes ... rots of green gold ...

I entered. The room was decorated in red.... I stood for a moment transfixed, vaguely calculating the diameter of my surprise....... lost in an aromatic undergrowth...... But it must be said that all living beings have seen yesterday, but will never see it again ... salty globules rolled from my eyes..... violent......

I heard a metallic sound behind me and, turning......... stained...... draped with fragments.........

...... hard rims of her lips.

Unappeased centres ...

.... springs, levers, wheels and gears ... thousand spirals of thought ...

.... phalange...

.... together we cast her into the ocean, watching with solemnity as she was swallowed by rhythmic azure............ algae and wind...

XII.

THE DOCTOR, AFTER COGITATING FOR THE BRIEFEST OF MOMENTS, set down the manuscript, took up his pen and proceeded to scribble away furiously:

Dear Signora Nessi,

Thank you very much for your letter and the documents which accompanied it.

That which claims to have been written by Archimedes I cannot outright refute. If it is a forgery it is a very clever one indeed; if it is genuine, its value is inestimable. I mean of course from an intellectual standpoint. But if you care to reference finances, you only need to look at how much the Heiberg manuscript fetched at auction.

But, to business:

I believe that it might well have been possible to create such an automaton at such an antiquated period of history. The Shai Shih t'u Ching, *or* Book of Hydraulic Excellencies, *enumerates many such devices. And I see no reason to why, if De Vaucanson was able to create a mechanical duck in every specific like a real duck, Archimedes, one of the greatest thinkers the world has ever known, would not have been able to create a woman such as described in the manuscript. It is extremely unfortunate that most of the technical details are lacking—most particularly those regarding the apparatus which must have driven the machine. I suspect it was something along the lines of those put forward by* Pierre de Maricourt *and* Johanes Taisnerius—*or then again it could have been something such as the self-operating mills of George Andreas Bockler—which in any case were simply variations of Archimedes' screws. Some would view such a thing as a perpetual motion device, but naturally, as a man of science, I cannot help but be a sceptic for this variety of absolute term, for the laws of thermodynamics forbid such a possibility. But it must be said that, though perpetual motion is an impossibility, it would be theoretically possible for man to produce near-perpetual motion—a motion that could last many billions of years. This being the case, we cannot rule out the prospect that the manuscript is indeed genuine.*

All this being said, I am sure that you yourself are aware of certain grammatical inconsistencies in the manuscript which make a dating of it somewhat uncertain. But of course a thorough study of the text needs to be done before we can say conclusively one way or another if it is truly Archemedian. I will not go into the glaring errors regarding certain small passages of the Guide to Poetic Indisciplines *getting accidentally mixed in the body of the work, for were you to re-peruse the document between 2 and 4 p.m., when the circadian rhythm is at its optimum point (the neuronal and hormonal activities of the suprachiasmatic nucleus being then especially keen on intellectual activity), you would discover them soon enough.*

I hope that my present comments are in some small way useful to you and I would be happy to shed more precise rays of light if you care to propose specific questions.

*Yours most respectfully,
Dr. A.T. Black*

The doctor finished the proceeding letter at precisely 6:27 p.m. At precisely 6:28, six thoughts simultaneously collided in his brain:

1) A French nude photo taken in 1890 showing a large-hipped woman with a palm frond in her right hand (135 x 95 mm).
2) A night in San Luis Obisbo when he had drunk one too many Cerveza Sagres at a Portuguese restaurant and stumbled back to his hotel room singing an air from Vejvanovsky.
3) The centred triangular numbers 409, 235 and 2584.
4) A slice of an orange posed against a cerulean blue sky.
5) Image of bizarre cannibal rituals young men wiggling their slim

shanks over grilled ribcage (mystical protection); Emil Carthaus and Dr. Bruno Bernhard found 1,891 signs; pushing sharp pieces of wood through their cheeks.

6) For any positive integer N, any sufficiently large finite set of points in the plane in general position has a subset of N points that form the vertices of a convex polygon.

He set down his pen and, just at that moment, the Scottish grandfather clock which stood against the eastern wall, a piece by John Brown of Edinburgh, with a 13" brass arch dial, rolling moon phases, and subsidiary seconds dial and date aperture, chimed six.

"Ah, east I'm force upper," the doctor said, imitating the accent of a South American gentleman.

Fragment

UTUG UL A LA
pull out its heart
serpent
ghoul / hag / ghoul
AZAG AZAG AZAG AZAG AZAG
Dr. Black rode an ibex he rode   you are suffering from sea-sickness
ZAG AZAG   serpent Dr. Black threw the serpent   it was about 60 feet long   UTUG UL A LA an ibex UTUG   you are performing an incantation
AZAG AZAG AZAG
the word is eating him
Dr. Black rode an ibex   ZAG AZAG if he can just get from the canal to the marsh
UTUG UL send six rams quick
too much tablet R
AZAG AZAG
Dr. Black rode an ibex   he hit him on the shoulder and out of the bruise came an animal and it asked for food
AZAG UTUG UL

275

Dr. Black

in

Rome

I.

"POLIPO ... FROM POLYPUS, POLUPOUS."

"Cephalopod." (Thinking of the 650 living species and five orders of those dioecious creatures, their very habits of copulation, the male removing a spermatophore from his mantle cavity and placing it with imperative grace in the mantle cavity of the female, that fruit-bearing sex.) "As Apicius recommends, simply pipere, liquamine (we can assume he means fish sauce), lasere. Infreres."

"The polypus loves the olive tree, and, wonderfully, near the speckled leaves is caught."

"Oppian."

"They are also said to be found clasped to fig trees which grow near the sea."

"Says Clearchus."

"And it is born in the dark eddies of deepest ocean."

"Xeanarchus, *Butalion*."

"But as for the calamari," said Professor Galassio, "it will be cooked in boiling oil."

"You mean fried," said Dr. Black.

"I do," Professor Galassio replied.

"And never, properly, boiled."

"Exactly."

"Yet Alexis, in his *Wicked Woman*, mentions that it is best if first boiled in water, then diced, then rubbed with salt, and *then* fried—to be served hot toward the end of supper."

"It is a good food, mentioned by Aristophanes twice." The professor rolled a bread pellet between two pale and delicate fingers, nimble as a spider's legs.

"Is this a quiz?"

"Just fun Doctor." Galassio's small eyes glistened.

"Aristophanes, *Danaides*, 'And when I have the calamari and polypus...' Then, in his *Thesmophoriazusae*, there is the line, 'Has any fish or calamari been brought?'... You said twice?"

"Yes. Twice."

"Then you are obviously not especially familiar with the existent fragments of that play of Aristophanes called *Daedalus*, in which calamari, the squid is mentioned.... As it is in many classical writings.... Aristotle says that it has eight feet, and two proboscises, and two teeth.... And, according to Pliny, it is able to launch itself out of the water as if it were an arrow; then, that same author writes about the giant squid, or nautilos, or pompilos, which he tells us lays on its back, turns up its two foremost arms and then, between them stretches out a membrane of wonderful thinness which acts for it as a sail."

Dr. Black wet his lips and tongue with Pinot nero, velvety and dry of flavour, spicy of cadence and favourable of intensity. He had that afternoon concluded his celebrated series of lectures on canine sexual dimorphism in Egyptian Eocene anthropoid primates (Catopithecus and Proteopithecus) at the University of Rome. He now sat at a restaurant, La Meridiana, with his colleague and host, Professor Galassio, whose face was very much like that of Federico Gonzaga as painted by Andrea Mantegna in the Palazzo Ducale at Mantova, though our man was certainly much smaller, much leaner and more slight of frame, wearing a suit that appeared to be significantly larger than his actual measure required, two elusive and minute white hands emitting from the cuffs and the professor's body seeming to float, suspended within the spare vacuity of the jacket itself. Clelia, the professor's wife, a dignified woman possessed of an attractive figure, full lips and large inviting eyes, was there as well as a number of other personages, those exceptionally expert in all branches of learning, *id est* Dr. V.S.I. Subrahmanya Rai, holder of doctorates from no less than six of the world's top universities, beneath no man in his knowledge of obscure grammars and occult philosophies; Professor Lydia Perrin-Granger, L.H.D. M.A., F.R. Hist. Soc., an expounder of all things associated with past times, political, social, and economic, a woman who was no superficial student of everything classical; Edoardo Dalmasio, a fresh and wealthy genius who had published more hyperscientific and panhistorical works than any man alive or likely to ever live and who never let a day go by without jotting down seven or ten thousand words of the most profound meditations and intellectual posturings; and Karel Van Oost, bred up from infancy on books of all orders, a diagnosed bibliomaniac with an almost frightening collection of information, histrionic quotes and homiletic anecdotes at his well-worded disposal.

"But really I have no pity for these many-armed dwellers of the sea, these squids and octopods," Dr. Black continued, all eyes glued to him, his large cranium and upper torso. "After all, good old Diogenes, who I try to imitate as often as I am able, came to a premature end through an unpleasant karmic connection with the polypus."

"While distributing tentacles to his dogs," added Edoardo Dalmasio, in a mournful tone, "one of them bit through the tendon of his right foot."

There was a moment of grave silence.

"Personally," Professor Lydia Perrin-Granger said haughtily, "I find the story that Antisthenes tells us in his *Successions*, that Diogenes died by holding his breath, much more believable. And in the *Meliambics* of Cercidas we find verification for this in the lines, 'would not bear life a moment longer, so shut his teeth, and held his breath.'"

Dr. Black, rather annoyed by this uncouth refutation of his own view, was just parting his lips to apply a mortally wounding blow of the intellect to Lydia Perrin-Granger, a creature surely several rungs lower on the ladder of brains than he, when that fortunate woman was miraculously saved by the timely arrival of distracting food.

"Ah, our antipasti." Professor Gallasio pointed in the direction of three approaching waiters.

The doctor's head swivelled slightly to one side. The double majesty of his eyes now followed the plates, carried in those parts of the waiters' human bodies that extended beyond their wrists, that sat in the nimble crooks of their heavily burdened arms, upper limbs.

Antipasti:
Fried rose petals
Tartare di manzo con cipolla
Lampascioni in purgatorio
Anchovies marinated in wine
Cime di rapa
Crostini di fegato
Insalata di radicchio con prosciutto di Parma

"Rose petals," said Professor Lydia Perrin-Granger, observing the plate of Clelia Gallasio. "I should have ordered those."

"Yes," replied Clelia, "they are very light."

Dr. Subrahmanya Rai, touching his fork to the small mound of *cime di rapa* set before him, said: "I am a great lover of horticulture, and have roses, damasks, galacias and floribundas in my garden. But I never thought of eating them."

As all the other mouths were momentarily stopped with food, Professor Lydia Perrin-Granger saw her opportunity. The aggressive, ringing sound of her voice corresponded admirably with the acute angles of her features, both sharp; then that visible epidermal tissue, between the colour of the yolk of a hen's egg and a sheet of writing material prepared from the skin of a sheep or goat. "According to Nicander," she hastily said, "Midas was the first man to cultivate the rose; having brought them from Thrace, he transplanted them in Macedonia, in Emathian lands. Herodotus, visiting Macedonia, observed that the roses there had sixty petals and were the most fragrant in the world. Theophrastus of course mentions the flower as does Pausanius, telling us that it was sacred to Aphrodite, and later writing of an unguent made from rose petals in Chaeroneia which, when smeared on a wooden image, would prevent its decaying. And Apollonius of Herophia says that the best rose perfume came from Phaselis. Hicesius, who though probably somewhat of a libertine, was still obviously an educated man, wrote that perfume of roses is the best kind to use when attending a drinking party. And this is confirmed by Hippocrates who, in his *Against the Cnidian Theories*, mentions that anointing one's head with rose ointment helps ward off the effect of drink. Virgil, in his fourth *Georgic*, introduces, in gracefully measured verses, his old friend Corycius at work in the garden cultivating roses which bore their blossoms twice in a year. Cleopatra covered the floors of her palace in fresh rose-petals to a depth of half a metre and Nero actually even managed to kill a few of his dinner guests when he had the whole room flooded with rose-petals. And it was Sappho who first called it 'queen of the flowers'. And Pancrates speaks of 'the fragrant rose, whose petals open to the vernal zephyrs'. And 'lovely-flowered roses, splendid nurselings of the springtime' were the words used by Chaeremon." After vomiting out this torrent of information, Perrin-Granger sucked oxygen through her nostrils and then tri-umphantly stuffed an anchovy marinated in wine into her mouth.

By the time the primi piatti arrived all, except for Dr. Rai, who did not drink, were feeling to varying degrees the intoxicating effects of the wine. The talk was lively and relatively unconstrained. A few humorous remarks were made, and even the waiters bringing new dishes to the diners was a circumstance to cause amusement.

<u>Primi piatti:</u>
Fregula with mussels
Spaghetti alla Eros
Zuppa alla Valpellinese
Eliche ai fiori di zucca
Linguine with caviar
Risotto caviale e salmone
Trofiette allo zafferano

Dr. Black, looking down at the open and night-shaded-hinged double shells before him, spotting those bits of soft interior flesh, felt his tongue of its own accord run itself over the smooth cubes of his teeth. Deftly he transferred one of those creatures from its now useless shell to his fully functional mouth, his taste buds instantly apprehending not only the spirit of the sea, but also that of the vineyard, as well as the slight bite of Malabar pepper.

"Ah, you ordered mussels," Edoardo Dalmasio said. "A good choice, moderately nutritious and quite digestible, certainly one of my own favourite shell-fish.... And I do know a little something on the subject.... But... I don't suppose—I don't suppose that you have ever read my book, *A Brief History of Bivalves*?"

"I received a copy from you several years back," Dr. Black replied, "but, due to my heavy schedule, I, unfortunately, have not yet had time to give it more than a cursory look.... I do recall however that it contained a rather interesting quote from the *Locrians* of Posidippus regarding mussels—but, as I said, I have only had time to skim through it."

Even this rather flat comment of Dr. Black's greatly flattered the vanity of Dalmasio. "Oh," he said eagerly, "but there is a whole budget of information on the mussel in that little volume! Many things of the greatest importance are touched on: the famous passage of Xenophon's, in the fifth book of his *Anabasis*; and Macrobius, that delightful segment where we learn that Julius Caesar was an eater of mussel pasties; and then, of course, I go through a whole analysis of Diphilius, who recommended the female mussel as being far more sweet and juicy than the larger male."

"Plautus talks of 'mussels and fluted scallops.' "

"A pretty line."

"He was a poet."

"So is our chef," Clelia said. "This spaghetti is marvellous."

Van Oost. Spaghetti?

C. Spaghetti alla Eros.

Dalmasio. 'Eros, nurseling of wisdom,' wrote Euripides.

O. But when the word is applied to spaghetti?

Black. Then it translates to 'spaghetti with sea-urchins'.

Prof. Galassio. My wife is an epicure.

O. Looking at your wife I would say you were the epicure.

(*Laughter.*)

Dr. Black in Rome

Secondi piatti:
Pork cutlet with corn
Rabbit with prunes
Anatra alla salsa di mele
Braised carrots and finocchio with artichoke hearts
Roasted eel
Snail soup
Fried calamari

He picked up the salt shaker and salted his soup then placed the mass-produced piece of glass back down on the table, fully conscious of the development of its design *from the tree which Egyptians imitated in their proto-Doric columns—the archaic capitals of Corfu—Aeolic capitals of Neandra—to those of the Parthenon—imitated, turned into a fully bourgeois element by the Romans and afterwards revived in the Renaissance, mimicked in every way possible during the industrial revolution—symbolism raped of all meaning—a simulation kylix a receptacle for synthetic fruit; the relief decoration on the Ara Pacis used for the floral pattern of a polyester bedspread at a chain roadside motel; those magnificent arches perfected in the Theatre of Marcellus, the Flavian Amphitheatre, the arches of Severus and Constantine, metamorphosed into a representation for grim hamburgers—the Americanisation of antiquity—the ancient origins of everyday functionary implements—even the standard stainless steel cooking pot of modern mankind simply a debased descendant of that bronze vessel, the* patera, *or saucepan, discovered in a burial hoard at Hobby on the south coast of the Danish island of Laeland.*

Rai applied himself to his vegetarian brasato; he savoured the artichoke hearts, which he believed were of that variety called 'violetto', and imagined sowing them in spring with 4 gr./sq.m.

Then, speaking his thoughts:

"I have always been fascinated by the causal relationship between the seed and the sprout."

"In what sense?" Dr. Black asked as he lifted a spoonful of snail soup to his lips.

"In the sense that it is profound, being without beginning."

"Not so. The beginning of all antecedents must be admitted, as is the case with the consequents. As a sprout just produced from a seed is with beginning, so the seed is also, produced from another sprout, by the very succession implied in the act of production, is with beginning. Therefore all antecedent sprouts as well as seeds are with beginning.... It is profound.... But so are these Helix pomatias."

"Yet certainly," Dr. Rai ventured, severing a wedge of finocchio in two with his knife, "this sprout/seed sort of thing can go on ad infinutum, therefore..."

"Therefore, some arguments are true, and others are false; but can a true argument, one which deduces a conclusion from a true premise, ever be false?"

Edoardo Dalmasio, flourishing the index finger of his left hand in the air: "It is dark outside, therefore it is night, therefore, Lydia Perrin-Granger is not a cow."

"Thank you," she replied. "I like nothing better than to be made the butt of a syllogism." And then, envenoming her words: "Edoardo is drunk, therefore Edoardo talks nonsense."

Professor Galassio: "If anyone is here, then he is not in Rhodes!"

"But, to get back to Dr. Black, who seemed to be hinting at the existence of some sort of original seed..."

"You are missing the point entirely. It is not about an original seed that produces the very first sprout. The problem lies in how you view the seed and the sprout. You view them as two distinct things, when in fact they are not. To talk about a seed and its sprout is like talking about a rabbit and its horns—when, obviously, the horns of a rabbit are non-existent."

"That may be so," Van Oost commented, holding up a tiny humerus, "but I have first hand knowledge of the animal's legs, which are absolutely delicious."

" 'Many are the ways and many the recipes for dressing rabbit'," said Dalmasio, quoting Archestratus.

Galassio: "Not half as many as there are for dressing non-dualist views to make them look reasonable."

"Professor, an ignorant man, on seeing the reflection of the moon in many diverse vessels of water, would say that there are numerous moons, but an intelligent man knows there is only one."

Perrin-Granger: "There seems to be a whiff of nihilism in the air."

Objection: "No, it is just the eel, which is nearly encrusted with crushed bulbs of that onion-like plant called garlic."

"People always cry nihilism," said Dr. Black, "when they are confronted by a system of assessment that refutes conceptual thought that they can't quite grasp."

"All this philosophy," Clelia murmured in a supple and sexual voice, "certainly is interesting, but what good does it do you?"

Black: "When alone, it allows me to talk to myself intelligently."

<u>Contorni:</u>[1]
Asparagus and gorgonzola
Sformato di spinaci
Zucchine trifolate
Tomatoes cooked with knotgrass
Crab salad
Peperoni con mollica
Roasted egg plant

"What delicious asparagus!"

"Well, with gorgonzola;—you could hardly ask for a better combination than that."

"In my humble opinion," Professor Galassio said pompously, "gorgonzola is the best Italian cheese, especially that of Lombardia."

"I prefer caciocavallo of Sicilia."

"Puglia is the best place in Italy for cheese, having wonderful mozzarella, giuncata, pecorino, stracchino, caciotta, ricotta, and fagottino."

"But only Emilia Romagna has Parmigiano Reggiano, the king of cheeses."

"But gorgonzola is still the only cheese to dress asparagus with."

"I have tried to grow asparagus," Dr. Rai said, lifting a piece of roasted

---

1. Served, naturally, with the primi piatti, and seven-eyed stones are hot and sweet and make the body glow, and drink asparagus wine for 100 days to double your speed.

eggplant up to his mouth with his fork, "but have always had poor luck."

"My dear fellow, asparagus requires an incredible degree of patience..."

Van Oost, who had already breezed through his crab salad with astonishing speed, now set down his silverware and spoke, his fat grease-coated lips moving easily beneath his white moustache, like a pair of well oiled bevel gears; speaking of: Palladius' instructions to sow around the first of April in rich, wet soil spread over with a sheet of dung and weeded well. "Straw should be thrown over it until spring, when it may be taken off."

"Palladius is hardly an authority when it comes to asparagus," said Dalmasio with the philosophical seriousness of one who is drunk. Then rebutting with: Cato's prescribed sheep's dung (produces no weeds); Lucius Junius Moderatus Columella, Marcus Terentius Varro, with more interesting things about asparagus, "but Palladius—I don't consider him to be worth reading, let alone citing."

"And Diphilus?"

"Oh, well Diphilus..."

"Galen says that asparagus has many edifying medicinal properties.... And was it not Lucullus who first introduced them to Western Europe, after trying them in Asia Minor?"

"Antiphanes has a beautiful line: 'The asparagus was shining; the pale vetches had faded.'"

"According to Suetonius, the Emperor Augustus was very fond of using the expression 'Quicker than asparagus is cooked'."

"Marcus Valerius Martialis proscribed asparagus for 'young men suffering from impotency and not-so-young women suffering from lack of desire'."

"Well, the very shape of Asparagus officinalis, which belongs to the lily family, indicates its potential as an aphrodisiac."

"Of the asparagus, Asparagus gonocladus is the strongest aphrodisiac, particularly the roots."

"You talk as if you were speaking from experience, Doctor."

"A true man of science, Signora Gallasio, must consider all fields of knowledge within his spectrum."

Dolci:
Budino di pane e caffé (per tutti)

(Dr. Rai, just as dessert arrived, made his departure, saying that he had an early engagement the next morning and had still to write many letters that night.)

Clelia. How is your budino Doctor?

Black makes a motion of indifference.

Prof. Galassio. It is inferior stuff! The cook has suffused it with chocolate. Outrageous!

B. Yes, I have had better.

G. To be sure.... There are certain secrets... no man knows better than myself.

C. My husband prides himself on his budino.

G. Yes, I pride myself on it. The trick is the Marsala... and the correct quantity of orange peel. I will entrust you with my recipe Doctor.... Just as long as you don't publish it.

So saying, Professor Galassio removed a small notebook, and then fountain pen, a good 40 centimetres in length, and eight of circumference, from the vast confines of his sports jacket, balanced the latter item in the meagre breadth of his right hand, and proceeded to scribble on a sheet of the notepaper. He then placed the sheet before Dr. Black.

"My gift to you Doctor. Cherish it well, give it to your cook, and you will have many happy moments.... Now, if you will excuse me..." He rose from his seat and made his way to the restroom; Van Oost, a moment afterwards, followed suit; Lydia Perrin-Granger and Edoardo Dalmasio, sitting opposite each other at the far end of the table, were engaged in repartee concerning the pathological symptoms of obsession *come i cerimoniali relativi al tabù del toccare, o i riti superstiziosi, o l'eccessiva meticolosità, o il lavarsi le mani un numero esagerato di volte durante la stessa giornata ecc.*

"I also have a recipe," Clelia said in a quiet voice to the doctor, as she scribbled on a sheet of the notepaper. "Don't tell my husband, but in my opinion you will enjoy it somewhat more than his."

Black read:

*Come to my house tomorrow night at 24:00
or somewhat after and I will treat you well.
Husband away from the house throughout the night.*

II.

"PACE THIS WAY GENTLEMEN, PACE RIGHT THIS WAY GENTLEMEN and distinguished ladies and purchase a ticket to view the most spectacular scientific discovery of the millennium, the most amazing female specimen on the globe! For only twenty lire, a measlissimo twenty lire you too can see the Argiope Woman right here in the capital of the world arriving fresh from her South American tour, from the countries of Ecuador, Brazil, Colombia, Argentina and Chile! The most amazing female specimen on Earth ladies and gentlemen, the most amazing," the man cried through the long elastic trumpet of his lips, one hand waving a rattan cane, a straw hat sitting at an angle on his somewhat pointed head.

"One," the doctor said, fishing twenty lire out of his trouser pocket.

He joined the file of humans that were making their way into the mouth of the tent. A dark interior. Wooden benches. Laughter of green-tinted teenage girls. A corpulent man sat smoking a cigarette. A young couple, by his side, smooched while an old woman fondled a closed black umbrella. A pedant, aged, fragile, with a long ivory-hued beard stretching to his quivering knees slowly stalked onto the stage; raised his hand. Two handsomely buff Italianate individuals dressed in white slacks and tight white t-shirts sprang forward, wheeled out a great ingot-shaped mass covered by a plum-red satin cloth. The pedant began to speak with high-pitched imprecision regarding mites, ticks, scorpions and then, "found in those most savage fluvial jungles on the borders of Bangladesh and Hokkaido she comes to us... without backbone, invertebrate... a most curious and extraordinary creature... in the company of her vortical spinning-glands the most unusual of all the 40,000 species... taking note of her fused head and thorax and abdomen... eight... legs and... pretty... eyes..."

The cloth was removed. The crowd gasped. The creature cowered toward the back of her cage and gazed anxiously around. Her eyes were an icy blue-grey with lashes long and black and undoubtedly false. She had a mass of curly blonde hair, a small upturned nose, thin lips, a wide mouth and a beauty mark on her left cheek.

"Isn't she ugly!" a young woman said.

"Oh, I don't know..." her boyfriend replied, his eyes fastened on that healthy thorax.

The pedant offered a gnat and, scurrying rapidly forward, the octoped gobbled it up.

(*Applause.*)

An anopheles, a louse and an earwig each in turn were administered, then extinguished by the serrated rows of her teeth. The doctor watched in disgust, unaccountably attracted to this monstrosity, as in truth all the males of the audience were, their fancies bound by this horrible phenomena of the natural world.

"Now, I will need a volunteer..."

Dozens of masculine hands reached for the ceiling.

"Will the young man in black please stir up to the stage."

The doctor rose and moved forward with smooth and uncontrollable rapidity, aware only of an agitation of the air behind him. He landed smoothly before the aged pedant who slapped him on the face and turned him toward the cage. She gave him a liquid look. Excited in no small degree, he wanted to gently dab at her with his soft and spongy labella, touch the crackling flames of her lips with his own elongated structure which normally only savoured sewage or rotting garbage, but now quivered with hunger for the mucous of love.

"Be brave my boy," the pedant said, nudging Black forward. "Can't you see she is mad for you?"

The cage door swung noiselessly open, as if on magic hinges. He moved his lips toward hers, his head now engulfed, drowning in the exotic luxuriance of razor-entrenched tongue, of gums, of quasi-feminine uvula, that small piece of fleshy matter hanging at the back of slick warmth... of jubilant... desperate... struggle... sliding, kicking, heels touching the roof of her...]

"I really should not have eaten those mussels," the doctor murmured as he awoke. "They never do agree with my digestion."

III.

THE CITY OF ROME EMERGES FROM THE BANKS OF THE TIBER AT A distance of 1,867,214 inches from the mouth of that river, which makes a profound furrow in the plain which extends between the Alban hills, to the south; the hills of Palestrina and Tivoli, and the Sabine hills, to the east: and the Umbrian hills and Monte Tolfa, to the north. The city stands in latitude 41°54' N. and longitude 12°30' E. of Greenwich, a suburb of London east and west of which longitude is measured. It occupies, on the left bank, not merely the area of level country, but also the adjacent heights, namely, portions of the Parioli hills, of the Pincian, the Quirinal, the Viminal, the Esquiline (which are only the extremities of a mountain-mass of tufa extending to the Alban hills), the Capitoline, the Caelian, the Palatine (shapeless and enormous fragments, obelisks, porticoes of Nero's palace), and the Aventine. On the right bank is the valley lying beneath Monte Mario, the Vatican, and the Janiculan, the last-named of which has now become covered with palazzos and gardens; so envisage sweating amidst brushstrokes of Mediterranean vegetation. The Tiber, traversing the city, forms two sharp bends and an island (S. Bartolomeo), and within the city its banks are protected by the strong and lofty (high, noble) walls; bondstone, kiln-baked bricks (*testae* as opposed to *lateres*).

IV.

He spent thirty minutes at Santa Maria in Aracoeli, admiring the frescoes of Pinturicchio in the Chapel of San Bernardino of Siena, particularly the *Glorification*, which was really an admirable bit of work. The doctor then walked down from the Capitoline Hill, to the Roman Forum, to the Triumphal Arch of Septimius Severus; he stood for a moment beneath the imposing marble, and reflected on the glory of that great Emperor, and the Parthian campaigns the structure itself commemorated. Knowledgeable in numismatics, Dr. Black recalled a portrait he had seen of the emperor on a coin, the obverse legend reading L SEPT SEV AVG IMP XI PART MAX; then that emperor, laureate, with high cheekbones, low brow, short curling hair and beard, head indeed something like that of a satyr. He gazed at the relief of the arch, portraying the entire progression of battle, from its first phases, to its final outcome.

"If I had been conceived a couple of millennia ago," he thought, "it is not at all unlikely that a great general I would have been, a Caesar 'discussing amidst flying darts the declension of nouns, and the aspiration of words and their classification amidst the blare of bugles and trumpets'; quelling civil wars, trouncing pirates, subjugating barbarian tribes, making them hand over their best sons as hostages and pay tribute, making them, Dalmatians, Gauls, Macedonians, Syrians and so forth, each and every one humble, humbled by the perfect strategist, ever victorious;" (Dr. Black stands hip-shot, his chest encased in a golden breast-plate embossed with centaurs, griffons, many mythological beasts, one arm upraised, the other clasping shaft of spear; his idealised likeness reared in sculpture, in lumachella marble, in bronze, in chryselephantine, and placed prominently for all men to see); "a man greater than Trajan, than Claudius, eloquent as Virgil, Cicero, grave as Vespasian, Tiberius, fortunate, extravagant as Lucullus; writing memoirs, letters in Latin and Greek and overwhelming the senate with my power of elocution—oratorical rotundity;" imagining himself as: Pontifex Maximus dressed in the extreme simplicity of a toga woven from whitest Patavinian wool at a hundred sesterces a pound, with nothing beneath but a simple subligaculum; an early morning visit to the frigidarium, to bathe and converse with both wits and asinine fellows alike, the conjunction of off-hand erudition and luxurious hilarity; lunch with Marcus Cornelius Fronto discussing the different words for 'red' (id est: spadix, luteus, rutilus, phoemiceus, fulvus, flavus, rufus, ruber and rubidus), their meanings and origins, and the inadmissibility of using the word 'exsequiae' (obsequies) in a singular form, then a brief meeting with Dioscurides the Samian, in order to go over the plans for mosaics commissioned for Black's villa at Pompeii; subsequent night, suffering the most beautiful, refined and high-placed courtesans of the city to administer pleasure to him as he samples sweet wines from Leucas and snacks on Rhegian cucumbers,—for he would certainly refuse any refreshment offered from the ladies' own stores since, if Aretino is to be believed, it was a custom (surely very ancient) amongst the harlots of Rome to feed their lovers the rotting flesh of corpses stolen from the cemetery as an aphrodisiac. Them, those expert women, one her head a high honeycomb of Cypriote curls, the next with hair done up in an intricate network of braids, another wears a mitra with small coiling tendrils pulled out around the face, while a fourth has long tresses down her back as far as her flanks, the delicious fibres made blonde with spuma caustica; their brightly-coloured mamillaria attract the eyes to a diverse range of figures; their legs depilated smooth with essence of sea-scolopendra, eyebrows dyed with burnt rose leaves, one with her face carmine-coloured, made red with distilled strawberries, another purple, a third exceedingly pale; perfumed with marjoram, cypirus, fenugreek, all to spice his own private little excessive orgy.

"How I would enjoy those gentle hours without anxiety, that recreation."

He shook himself free from this daydream, large and powerful as an elephant conjured up by a magician. "Though unreal," he thought, "that magical elephant did have all the attributes of a real elephant; it behaved as an elephant, and therefore did exist. So, truly, was I not emperor for a few moments?" And, proceeding past the site of the ancient Basilica Julia, he pondered on the miracle of consciousness which, though unable to be directly perceived by the five human senses, could none the less take on the form of real matter. "So does the world created by thought exist, or not exist, or both exist and not exist, or neither exist nor not exist?"

He walked past a mother and her young and thought of that natural bond, milk, which unites the two, and the sad state when the child, turned man, must search for foreign food.... And Professor Galassio, was it incorrect to explore his private cupboard, to take hold of a few choice biscuits?... But when the cupboard itself invites.... And it was hard to have pity on a fool, a man with a head more empty than a snake's cast off skin.

Dr. Black was at the Temple of the Divine Julius. A little ahead, on his left, was the Temple of Antonius and Faustina. He thought of: instincts; mating patterns; polyandry; the breeding season, the natural course of things, when she requires more than one fertiliser.

V.

He, an always vigilant behaviourist, smoked on the steps of the Pantheon and observed the people. An old man with a face like one of Leonardo da Vinci's grotesques, another reminiscent of the *Ritratto Trivulzio* of Antonello da Messina. An interesting race these Romans, descended as they were from Homines feri, from those famous brothers Romulus and Remus who spent their youth without the traditional cultural matrices and whose personalities it should be assumed developed in exact proportion to the educative value of their environment. When Romulus abducted all those Sabine women it was positively rough stuff, typical wolf-boy behaviour.

The doctor gazed through the spirals of blue smoke that rose up from his cigar; he gazed at mankind, but with eyes that compared rather than contrasted that being with the inhabitants of the animal kingdom; and often saw in his supposedly fellow creatures resemblance to objects both organic and otherwise, heads like pumpkins or sometimes pineal, mouths resembling siphons, motions of progress often like the jerboa or small figures with jointed limbs moved by wires, an unthinking variety of predestined doll. Some men had noses turned up, snub, the two external openings wide, round, large as penny pieces; the organ of smell of another was long and thin like the beak of a kiwi bird; and he spotted one man whose proboscis was large and rough-hewn, as some primitive stone implement. Then women, some walking along on mincing little legs like those of fleas; others with legs extremely large and buttocks resembling those of pigs, packed tight in ill-fitting mass-manufactured pants that distorted the shape of the flesh making it appear like the thoracic segments of caterpillars or larvae. Verily it often seemed that the whole race suffered from a kind of zoomorphic condition. (Recalling Rousseau's *Discours sur l'Origine de l'Inégalité*, the *Systemma Naturae* of Carl von

Linne, Phillippe Camerarius's *Operae horarum subcisvarum sive meditationes historicae*, and other like books; then the cases, rapidly run over in his mind; the Irish sheep-child, Karpfen bear-woman, Peter, the wild boy of Hannover, Syrian Gazelle child, Assicia of Liberia, beings grown up with panthers, leopards, baboons; sow-girl, calf-child, snow-hen, wolf-fellow, Edith of Ohio, Tomko of Zips.) Men, dogs, birds, flies, fish and snakes; fauns, centaurs, grunting minotaur or lascivious mermaid; mix and match.

"The imagination need hardly be stretched," the doctor murmured to himself. And parading before him as might beings of the big-top there were men whose mouths were like those of the gibbon, with swollen bellies, then thinnish short legs similar to those of the orangutan; or others, with huge muscular torsos and legs short as the dachshund's; women with the convex body parts on their chests resembling the udders of prize cows, or them whose breasts stuck out like avocados; men ugly and virile as donkeys, walking as if their organs of copulation were dangerous weapons, scimitars, men with foreheads grotesque like the water-buffalo; hair done up like cocks' crests; their eyes round, expressionless concentric circles; sitting around like limpets; hardly different from lower animals, living in a sort of permanent hypnosis.

"The human race is certainly full of odd specimens," the doctor thought, lifting up his beard covered chin, running his thumb and forefinger over the base of his own huge neck. "... Of course the least intelligent of quadrupeds, when it comes to providing for their natural wants and protecting both themselves and their children, are far superior to these brutes of our species ... "

His cigar was half smoked. He rose to his feet, tossed it on the ground and crushed it with his heel. Then, with a slow and distinguished gait, Black walked along the Via Palombella, through the Piazza San Eustacchio and onto the Piazza Navona. He felt thirst. Aside from the large fountains, there was a smaller one before which stood several men in the dress of labourers. He watched the men, one after the next, stoop their heads beneath the waterspout, fill their mouths with that liquid.

"Is it fit to drink?" he asked.

One of the men looked up and gave the doctor a surly look. "We drink from it."

"Then it is undoubtedly not fit to drink."

The doctor turned and walked away. He looked at his watch and saw that it was just past five in the evening. There was a café and he sat down in one of the chairs outside. He ordered an orange soda, hooked one slender leg over the next and leaned his massive torso back, his whole form now lessening to some slight degree its stringency.

VI.

He dined alone at his hotel, avoiding lettuce, inclined to support the theory that it made men powerless for love, and instead indulged himself with a light but rich supper of soup made from those 'nuts that the sharp-leafed pine brings forth' (*Ars Amatoria*), shrimp grilled and heavily seasoned with fennel (the seed mentioned in the 3,600 year old Papyrus Ebers), and for dessert, simply melon.

At 22:00 he went to his room and read from Gjerstad's *Die Ursprungsgeschichte der rönischen Kaiserfora* for thirty minutes. He then turned off the reading lamp and closed his eyes. When he opened them again it was 23:05. He picked up the telephone, dialled the front desk and ordered a cab for 23:50. Then, after rising to his feet, he undressed and walked to the bathroom naked. Showering, he hummed an extract from *Don Giovanni* (*Notte e giorno faticar*). At 23:40 he went down to the hotel bar and ordered a caffé corretto, which he drank in three sips and then put a lozenge, a breath freshener, into his mouth, to cover up any unpleasant aroma.

VII.

The house was old, on a small street off the Viale Guido Baccelli, very near the Baths of Caracalla. The evening was cool and air moist so that dew gathered on the green fleshy leaves of the jade plants which grew in large pots on either side of the door; and the doctor noticed, with mild interest, sitting on the earth of one of these pots, a spectacled salamander (Salamandrina terdigitata), brown of back, crimson of ventral surface, the eyes of its broad head jutting out;—a strange sight, that miraculous European urodelan, normally found in shaded woodlands, there in that damp corner of Rome, probably hunting spiders or millipedes.

The doctor lifted his gaze, lifted his hand and rang the door bell.

"Ah, Doctor. . . . I was not sure if you would come."

"How could I oppose your invitation?"

"Few warm blooded men could. . . . But you. . . . I was not sure of *you*. I thought you might be impervious . . . to passion." She asked the doctor to enter. "Excuse me if I am awkward. . . . I am very excited. . . . And . . . what can I get you to drink?"

"Whatever is normally drunk on such occasions."

"Wine?"

"Sthenelus, the poet, says that it can bring even the wise to acts of folly."

"So?"

"So by all means open a bottle," Black said, seating himself on the couch. "I would not have come here if I was not prepared to indulge in a certain quantity of foolishness."

She turned; he watched the motions of her shapely caudal fin as she moved toward the liquor cabinet, bent over and plucked a bottle from the wine rack. "What sexual sorcery!" he thought. "The organic singularity of her physical structure certainly makes me feel attraction of a less than mental nature; as infants are taken in by bright colours and moths dazzling lights; even genius, great capacity of the mind or imagination, prostrates itself to beauty."

Mrs. Galassio filled two glasses half full of white wine, a Chardonnay, vin de pays de l'Île de Beauté.

"Salute!"

"Cheers," said the doctor, attending the pleasant tintinnabulation of the glasses making contact; then observing the creature at his side, balcony larger than that of the Venus de Milo, yet certainly with as much strength of purpose as Nike's of the Acropolis, body more lovely than that of Olympia, well formed as that of Samothrace; eyes inviting as any maenad's; lips, cheeks succulent as those of Poppea, who daily bathed in asses' milk; indeed, not dissimilar to the Aphrodite di Cnido, or Aphrodite Capitolina. He tasted the wine, riche et harmonieux, and thought: "She is at that state of womanhood most suitable for pleasure." And then several images promptly flashed across his mind: an open-mouthed pelican; a blade being driven into Santa Giustina dei Borromei; an advancing continuous curve winding around a central point; a mizzenmast; a lavishly decorated oinochoe dripping over with thin and transparent water; jets of plasma matter racing out of the ends of some swirling donut-shaped cloud of dust and gas.

The walls were decorated with framed cover-pages and illustrations from the old protofantascientific Italian periodicals, *Il Secolo XX*, *Psiche*, *Il Vascello*, *La Sfinge*. A bed, as large as a threshing floor, with head built up with downy cushions, sat in the middle of the room. She placed herself on its edge and revealed to him a long portion of her left leg and he at that moment seriously hoped that his ability would not prove to be the inverse nature of his desire. For Dr. Black, seeing the ripe beauty of her body, the wriggle of her smile, was quite ready to carry out test and trial with the mystic rights of love in order to study results, even possibly gain new knowledge. His person was a flask, some crucible or laboratory bottle, a corporeal vessel very ready to make extractions, assess combustibility with numerous roastings, him recalling that: even a dung-

Dr. Black in Rome

bath gives heat... but when an adult female human being is hotter than coal-fire. Thinking abstractly of: cementation in a bath of dew; commixtion; an operation of cohobation. Noting of his own person:
1) a slight rush of blood to the face
2) a throb or thrill of life or emotion
3) an unnatural degree of perspiration

Clelia: "Am I attractive?"

He began to give vent to a pompous parade of words.

"Oh, shut up and come here," she said.

One foot moved after the next and then he was there, suffocating her smile, sampling the liquescent fleshy edges of the opening of her mouth while simultaneously apprehending by means of all ten of his fingers both the depth and solidity of her figure.

She pushed him away.

"Oh, Doctor, I cannot breathe!"

Her massy hair, reddish-brown with henna, was undone and spilled over her shoulders.

"Come now... " murmured the doctor, moving in for a second assault.

"What sort of beast are you?"

"The sort... most hazardous."

"So you know what women like?"

"I know the requirements of your type."

"Your grip.... You are very strong!"

Him, abnormally misshapen and extraordinary of qualities, absurd yet feeling a violent desire to possess, the wife of another man, thus reasoning that he would without regret read another man's book; all houses he stayed at other men had stayed before; on occasion it was necessary to drive some other man's car; now sleep with his wife; while, physically, he groped not at random but obscurely and indistinctly as if plunging through thick fog or swimming amongst ten trillion floating balls of oxygen filled liquid to join, weave those strands of mortal substance together...

[... *while actions progressed (skirmishes, standards interwrapped without distinction, attempts to stave all buttresses to pieces, panic-stricken medley—one lighter and better adapted to blockading and darting about, the other broader and heavier, therefore slower, yet stronger to give blows and not so easily damaged) a fine considering of: the hermaphrodite as Plato described Apollodorus describing Aristodemus (of Cydathenaeum) describing Aristophanes describing: globular in shape, with rounded back and sides, eight limbs and two faces on a cylindrical neck and two privates;—these hermaphrodites Zeus, with his thunderbolt, split in half, to leave each bisection yearning for the other: Black, so descended, naturally attracted to women, as Theophilus said in* He Liked to Play the Flute *'in beauty beautiful, in stature stately, in art clever'—clipping and clasping as he advanced steadily, almost stubbornly, toward consummation . . .*]

. . . strands of mortal substance . . .

There was a sound from below.

. . . to splice, to weave the strands of one into the strands of the other.

"Did you hear something?" he asked.

There was a distinctive shout from below, a voice deep, surly. A pounding at the door.

Clelia Galassio scowled. "Damn! It is my lover!"

"I am your lover."

"No, you are *a* lover; this man pounding at the door is *my* lover. He is demanding entrance."

"But . . ."

"My dear Doctor, you do not live in Rome. For all I know, after tonight, I will never see you again. Gino on the other hand I *will* see again, and I cannot live with him angry at me. Please, be so kind as to step out that window."

"My pretty lady, I am not accustomed to stepping out windows, particularly when they are not on the ground floor!"

"A man who involves himself with a Roman woman grows quickly accustomed to many things. Now, away with you before Gino gets angry! You will find a very solid ledge out there to stand on." And so saying she guided him to the window and literally pushed him out.

There was a ledge, but it was not particularly wide, and more than half the available space was taken up by three or four flowerpots. Dr. Black considered leaping down from his post, but, due to the absolute darkness, was unable to determine, even with his supremely mathematical mind, the exact distance to the ground and if an aerial descent would be

Dr. Black in Rome

safe. He therefore took the opportunity to *a)* straighten out his necktie (below which it was apparently unwise for his passions to travel) and *b)* gauge the nature of the wall in which the window was set, using his sense of touch, his hands as the instruments of apprehension, so noticing that vertical structure of stone to be a decent example of *opus incertum*, not of a particularly high aesthetical status, but surely without great perishability; sturdy enough to have lasted many years, especially with the numerous iron clamps which his fingers reckoned, that wonderful Roman invention so long lost until they were re-invented by Brunelleschi. The doctor was indeed fortunate to be able to find objects of interest in nearly all situations... Now: hearing voices inside, he peered through the window; the curtains were drawn enough so that he could clearly make out the quadrangular face of Gino with its flat, rather course features, and the hair on the man's unsheathed chest which grew in abundant curls. When the doctor saw Clelia run her left hand, the fragile flanges of her fingers, through these same twists of hair, he turned away in disgust. After all, she might be an attractive, even a beautiful woman, but she was still merely a conglomeration of constantly changing atoms—atoms that might have once belonged to a dog or reptile, atoms that had washed through the gutter, been born through the latrines of Lepcis Magna or Timgad—a conglomeration of ten trillion times prostituted atoms that might very well have, in the extremely distant past, even belonged to some member of an alien race, some great mound of purple and oozing flesh, a lungless, heartless droxy, the butt of every space cowboy's disdain.... So love, when subjected to moderate cold, coagulates to indifference (thus now reasoning: that a man without a woman is like: *a)* Hasdrubal the Boëtharch with no rhomboid crystal hammer *b)* a quantum computer devoid of Pythionice *c)* a neopythagorist without a bobby pin).... He heard the sound of an automobile engine and then, off to his left down below, saw a set of automobile lights swimming in the distance. These expired. A car door slammed shut and he then heard footsteps pass below him.

The doorbell rang.

"It is past five in the morning. Who the devil is at your door?"

Clelia shrugged her shoulders.

"Damn you," Gino growled. "It is another one of your *ragazzi*.... As if I weren't twice as much man as you need." And saying this he pushed her roughly away and descended the stairs.

Now this Gino, though far from being a sophisticated man, was none the less endowed with a ready wit and an uncanny ability at mimicry, which had for long made him a favourite of the barrooms of the quarter.

When the doorbell rang a second time:

"Who is it," he murmured, very well imitating the voice of Clelia, that sweet, slightly husky cadence.

"It is Karel my dear. I know you told me it might not be safe to come, but I could not keep away—it was impossible for me to sleep. I saw that your husband's car was not here ... so he is not yet come back from the observatory at Monteporzio Catone! We surely have an hour or two.... Oh, please my love, let me in. I am desperate for you!"

Gino: "Oh heavenly heart, give me a simple kiss through the mail slot, which is just wide enough, and then I will try and open this door without making too much noise—because I cannot afford to alert the neighbours."

Van Oost was naturally eager to taste the lips of Clelia and so he lifted up the brass plate of the mail slot and applied his mouth, where it immediately came in contact with that of Gino, rather large, not delicate, and extremely eager and forceful.... The bibliomaniac was certainly not without intelligence and his senses were fully intact so that, by the stench which issued out of the opposite mouth, as well as the extreme thickness of its tongue, he easily guessed that it was not Clelia who was on the other side of the door, but an impostor. He had already noticed the spectacled salamander sitting on the moist earth beneath one of the jade plants, and forthwith grabbed it up in his hand and sighed softly through the door: "Oh my dear, your lips are so sweet, let me taste them again."

Gino, highly satisfied and thinking his joke was going very well, assumed once more the pleading voice of Clelia and then applied his lips to the mail slot. Van Oost, seeing the ready red flesh of the mouth, lost no time in slipping the salamander between the lips, and the creature, more than willing to be out of human hands, darted into the opening with alacrity and straight down the passage in Gino's neck which admitted air to the lungs and, normally, food to the stomach.... Clelia's adept lover was completely startled. Feeling something moving madly around in his belly, he jumped up and began to scream and bellow fiercely. He threw himself on the floor and writhed; his body lashed forward like a cracking whip (shout of triumph turned to shriek of despair), as inside him the creature frolicked, caressed the man's interiors with flips of its tongue and secreted large quantities of defensive liquid—all this being relatively harmless activity, the salamander in question not being that type (Salamandia maculosa) so feared by Pliny for its power to poison wells and the fruits of entire trees.

Dr. Black heard the commotion inside, saw lights going on in the neighbouring houses, and the first slight glow of the sun coming from the east (the ambition of 24:00 now more ephemeral than the shadow of smoke).... A lorry happened to be coming by, making its way slowly up the street, and he decided to jump down from where he stood, lest he be caught in broad daylight standing outside the woman's window like a burglar. He quickly took stock of his neuromuscular system, then bent his knees and (though missing velocity, certainly endowed with mass) ejected himself from that ledge, where he had kept his all-night vigil. He was momentarily airborne and then landed dramatically, skilfully in the back of the lorry, on top of a load of refuse.

VIII.

(*F**ADE TO: PROTAGONIST DESCENDING FROM LORRY, WHICH IS momentarily stopped. Sound of engine. Shot of receding lorry.*)

He looked around him. The rosy-pale somewhat polluted light of dawn showed the Via Appia Antica stretching before him, that ancient road commenced under Appius Claudius Caecus, 312 BC, that used to reach from Rome all the way to Brindisi; the principal highway to Greece and the East, on which Spartacus' men were crucified and Polybius, Publicola and Staberius set their feet.

The doctor took a cigar from his pocket and lit it. Normally he never smoked before noon, but his nerves were not entirely in order and so he allowed himself this lenience. He now proceeded to walk north-west, toward the greatest city on earth, admiring on either side the dark green of the old holm oaks and the lighter shade of the moist grass, glistening like an over-varnished oil painting of the Italian Divisionist school. And then there were other elements, the type certainly Romantic, the sort of things that would have been leaped on by men like John Sell Cotman or John Robert Cozens, very picturesque walls, antique and in disrepair, and he was in motion.

On that road, and at that hour of the morning, there was very little traffic and the doctor did not in the least hope to be favoured with any mode of conveyance exterior to the efforts of his own feet and legs. There always being space in this universe for a conditional context, a car pulled up along side him and a window was rolled down.

"Quid tu, inquit, tam mane, Black?"

The doctor looked and saw the smiling face of Professor Gallasio and then, opening his lips, replied quite calmly, "I am out for my morning constitutional."

"Your clothes are in disarray."

"The laundry service at my hotel is abominable."

"Would you like a lift back into town?"

"Being very interested in physical exercise, I normally would decline your invitation. It happens however, that three or four minutes ago I slightly stubbed my left large toe while tripping on a corner of the tomb built by Herodes Atticus in honour of his wife Anna Regillia. . . . The onychocryptosic condition I am prone to has now been aggravated, so placing myself in your car would probably be the wisest course."

The doctor sat shotgun and the car proceeded toward Rome, Black superimposing upon Professor Gallasio the image of Michelangelo's Moses, horned, due to an obvious misunderstanding amongst early Christian scholars regarding the Hebrew text, when Moses descended from the mount—for the word *kœren* means 'horn', and *karan* means 'to shine'. So some old scholars thought the man came down horned, instead of radiant; but Gallasio appeared both cuckolded and radiant; a professor in very good spirits.

"Tell me Doctor," he said, "are you very fond of jokes?"

"I do not consider myself completely devoid of a sense of humour."

"Would you like to hear about Quintus Caecilius Metellus Creticus and his slaves?"

"If you wish to tell me."

"I would."

"Then please do."

"Well, Creticus was on a sea voyage and there was a very dreadful storm. It seemed probable that the ship would sink and so his slaves began to weep. 'Don't cry,' Creticus said to them, 'for I have set every one of you free in my will.'"

"And?"

"And nothing. That is the joke. Since there are very few persons cultured enough to understand it, I rarely tell that one."

"So you have others?"

"Certainly. Not only have I memorised the entire *Philogelos* and but I also am about to publish many delectable fragments of an Attic joke book called *Travesties of Truth*, containing numerous riddles, personal insults and comic anecdotes, which I discovered in a palimpsest containing St. Augustine's commentary on the Psalms while I was doing research in the Vatican library."

Black: recalling internally the words *rained flesh upon them as dust, and feathered fowls like as the sand of the sea.*

Gallasio: "Did you ever hear the one about the Cymean doctor?"

Dr. Black had, but feeling pity for the man did not claim this knowledge.

"A Cymean doctor," Professor Gallasio continued, with a sly smile on his face, "operating on a man who was in terrible pain and screaming, switched to a blunter scalpel."

Black: *forced chuckle*; then: "Lucillius."

"Do you mean the one about Antiochus and Lysimachus' cushion?"

"No. I was thinking of this; listen: . . . Seeing another crucified on a higher cross than himself, jealous Diophon pined away."

(*Stock footage of: Circus of Maxentius, cork trees, Tomb of Cecilia Metella, Aurelian's walls, Roman traffic, the Colloseum in front of which stand contemporary rogues, unshaven, masquerading as gladiators and legionnaires, armour, swords, tridents, all of rigid Cheng Lee plastic.*)

Gallasio: "Once when he had been thrown into prison, indolent Marcus, being too lazy to depart, of his own accord confessed to a murder."

". . . More Lucillius?"

"Naturally."

Black: "Salute Aristides the rhetorician who has seven students: four walls and three benches."

Gallasio: "Little Hermogenes, when he drops something on the ground, has to pull it down to himself with a hooked stick."

Black: "Demetrius, when fanning skinny Artemidora in her sleep, propelled her straight out of the house."

Gallasio: "All Cilicians are bad; but among the Cilicians there is one who is good, whose name is Cinyras, and Cinyras is a Cilician."

Black: "Gellia has only one lover. The disgraceful thing is that she has two husbands."

Pan to (in rapid succession): Monument to Vittorio Emmanuele II, Palazzo Venezia (the balcony from which Mussolini made his infamous speeches), Palazzo Doria (Baroque Rococo), Palazzo Odescalchi, Piazza di Pietra, Temple of Adrianus erected by TITUS ÆLIUS HADRIANUS ANTONINUS PIUS, Piazza Capranica and then:

"Ah, here is your hotel!"

Dr. Black thanked the professor for the ride (his socially mundane words not even an echo of his somewhat depressed, somewhat degraded, geniusy and filth-splattered thoughts).

"And when are you leaving Rome?" the professor asked.

"This evening."

The two men shook hands (the delicate and alabaster right palm and fingers of Gallasio swallowed and then expectorated by the more robust hand of Black). The doctor removed himself from the car and entered the hotel. (There is no great general who has not endured their hardships, some variety of defeat; *Richard Egan impersonating King Leonidas in* 300 Spartans, *the bloody Battle of Thermopylae, a countless quantity of Xerxes' elite troops slaughtered, then 300 Spartans finally overrun and killed to the man; or Steve Reeves, Aeneas in* The Trojan Horse *w/John Drew Barrymore that skilful and cynical Ulysses; Marc Antony as played by Richard Burton routed at sea—an imitation of the burning of the Roman fleet in* Cabiria, *that 1914 epic starring the luscious Lidia Quaranta, another of Black's intellectual amours—strike a chord to Clelia; experiencing: the lingering taste of dashed expectations, hopes.*) He approached the elevator and pressed the button with the upward pointing arrow. He waited, reflecting on the third floor, on the room which there existed and the bed which was in that room, and the soft goose-feather filled pillow on which he would lay his gifted head.

Fragment

Group

D

I.

Inv. No: 675.4
Document on vellum; fragment; about 3 ½ in. by 2 1/8. Well-preserved. The writing is good Syriac.

> My father was an ape, my mother a dog. I am odious and I enslave and I grow and grow and grow. My father was an ape, my mother a dog. I am a great routinist and am odious and I enslave.

II.

He awoke in the night equally distant from the extremities.

Crickets. Rose, walked with arms extended to the library, liquor cabinet, where he secured a bottle of grappa, then out onto the lawn, barefoot *some far away lotus jewelled beings prescriptions of mirrors rivers of nectar cascade on the white bodies of little air beings bright colours of petals green. blue. yellow. showers of light beauty.*

III.

"Awake Sor Nero, for it is the time of the office of gluttony."

"Gluttony?" the good doctor repeated in a rather lost voice.

Three long deal tables were set end to end in the middle of the room around which were seated some forty sisters, all seasoned nuns except for one, Sister Martinez, whose withered, ghost-like frame was placed at the far end opposite the doctor. Huge platters piled high with bright-red pig bladders which were stuffed with fatty cuts and rolled in paprika and which they called 'bishops' were brought out. These the good Sister Francesca chopped with a huge blade and set afire, the oils of the meat being more than sufficient to provide fuel for the flames. Then came: an entire goat roasted on a spit. Rice with chicken feet. A pig's head resting on a bed of stinking cabbage boiled in lard. Wine and hard cider in abundance. And sausages made from:

cow tongue
offal
ox intestine
wild boar seasoned with ginger and garlic
goat's blood and pumpkin
pork livers
beef liver and juniper berries
lamb offal and lemon juice
sheep's lung and black pepper
rabbit's brain and fennel
pig spleen and parsley
veal and red chilli pepper

The women filled their faces, beat the table with their fists. Grease and wine dripped from the corners' of their mouths.

The most horrible sight however was Sister Martinez. Her famished lips wrapped themselves around a pig ear; her teeth showed themselves, biting into the soft, buttery article, as her throat opened, like that of a baby bird. Her mouth was loosened, a strange organ seemingly endowed with independent volition, magnetised towards hanging bits of chicken skin, old oysters bubbling like bits of a corpse rotting in a ditch. The food and wine seemed to have infused her with a sort of dementia. Belly thrust forward, hands clawing at scraps of cooked meat, she laughed hysterically, her eyes spinning in her head.

Dr. Black

at

Red

Demon

Temple

I.

"Ah ah ah!"
"Mmmm?"
"Your shoes. If you could remove them..."
....
"What's this?"
"Your plastic wristband."
"For?"
"You to find your capsule. Or your capsule to find you."
"Oh."
At night in plastic zôri lockers pink crumble incense dancing around the fire empty trance veil odour insect in florid skin peeling back metallic suspended ceiling cold formed spans in the village =
T
O
K
Y
O
Kenzô Tange's Metropolitan Government Office jutting into the sky mastering nearby Shinjuku Park Tower Park Hyatt occupying top 14 floors 40th floor wedding chapel led to by a by a circular Brazilian mahogany staircase
neon luxury
wire blossom
eight-fold petals
fall sadly to the side
crazy stillness
scream a man inside a bag ten thousand in dark blue suits writhe

millipede and, certainly, Mr. Clovis deserved no points for finding the doctor accommodation.

Black, that man whose beard and intelligence were in constant battle for the dominance of his head, had specified the Komagome Grand Hilton. Clovis had confused it with the Komagome Capsule hotel (no tattoos allowed).

But, a man can endure anything for a night.

Wrapped in a yukata, he lay in his 3 feet x 3 feet x 6 feet coffin-like cubicle. To his right controls: light, TV (big red button). A tiny window. A tiny view of the lights of Tokyo.

He turned on the transmission apparatus (picture tube) and, looking past the landscape of his belly, saw *Gojira, Mosura, Kingu Gidorâ: Daikaijû sôkôgeki.*

Involuntarily he opened his mouth with a prolonged and deep inhalation of air as he watched the monsters battle it out memories wandered along the edges of his brain young man in mid-70s New York films of Ishirô Honda.... *Mosura* (mighty winged monster); *Gidorâ, the Three-Headed Monster* (*San daikaijû: Chikyû saidai no kessen*) and then he glanced at the big red button to his right marked ¥3,800, but did not press (recollection: *Hanzô the Razor*) instead cutting off the device for castrating the mind.

"Sleep," he murmured, and closed his eyes.

Around 2 a.m. the drunken businessmen began to filter in from the surrounding bars. Voices dragged themselves through the hallways. Laughter. Suited men with short-cropped hair crawled into their kennels. The doctor turned on his side and grunted.

II.

Things for which Words Should Exist

A man who, finding it impossible to acquire ready-made clothes that fit him, must resort to a skilled tailor.

A homicidal maniac who kills people exclusively through psychic means.

Moccasins made of steel or any other alloy.

A child who refuses to eat lettuce.

An old teardrop.

A book or folio in which all the irregular verbs have been underlined.

A key which is constantly forgotten.

A dinner which begins in argument and ends in merriment.

III.

He was awakened at dawn by the sound of coughing; others rolling out of bed to pee[1] and shower. In the company of hungover salarymen—silent entities with averted gazes, some with cowlicks, some with fisheyes—he had his breakfast of miso soup, rice and strong black coffee.

The match was to take place in the afternoon, at 2 p.m.

With plenty of time before him, he hailed a taxi.

1) He changed hotels, to the Komagome Grand Hilton.
2) He issued onto the street, thronging with people / cars / bicycle / girl with mini skirt and yeti boots / man with long hair parted in the middle / gothic Lolita vs. kogal.
3) He recalled the six weeks he had spent in Japan many years before, under the guidance of Seki Rôshi[2].

1. As it says in the *Arya Sanghata Sutra*, "From food what emerges is excrement and what is drunk becomes urine."
2. Black sat down on a cushion and placed his right foot on his left thigh and his left foot on his right thigh with the soles of his feet turned up; spine erect; tongue on roof of mouth, teeth held together / sit like a great pine / in zazen. "Now, to pacify my mind," he thought. Observing the observer of shapeless consciousness. His mind alighted on a mote of dust floating through the air {*Piece of particulate matter containing five hundred quadrillion atoms an atom is how many millimicrons how many angstroms ten millionths of millimetres an atom of cadmium how did you get here one, two, three, forty-eight electrons.* Whack! Shock of pain. Seki was standing over him with a stick. "No matter how much you polish a brick, you will never make it into a mirror. Sit like that for an eon and you won't see reality." "Master!" Black said with delight, rising to his feet. "Machine-mind!" the other said, embracing him.

4) He bought a copy of the *Tokyo Gazette* and, going into an udon bar, split a pair of chopsticks and ate while reading:

In Ginza, after drinking too much saké, physician Tomikawa strangled his hostess while demonstrating the Heimlich manoeuvre.

> Ministers Takagi and Kirino resigned. Fisheries Agency chief Toshirô Mukai ended his life with a pistol shot. All of this over money-related scandals.

The six-car Mekagojira roller coaster at Expoland can travel up to 150 km/h. One dead and nineteen injured when it derailed this morning at 12:50 a.m.

> A poultry farm in Uwajima, Ehime Prefecture, has only 5,000 chickens. It had 10,000 more, until lightning struck an electricity pole.

Hiromi 84, after 50 years of marriage, became tired of her husband, Toru, 80. Last night at 10:05 p.m. she began to beat his head in with a hammer while he was asleep and stabbed him with a kitchen knife as he tried to run away.

> Tajima, Zushi and Imafuku hung by the neck yesterday. The latter, heart broken, killed himself. The other two were sent to the gallows by the Justice Ministry.

Ikuko Maki, a shop assistant of 38, was eaten by her two cats. Cause of death unknown.

> Use
> **SupesuMomo**
> Brand Chewing Gum
> *and smell like a*
> **Peach!!!**

1 tatami apt. now available. Ideal for large family or prophet. Call: 03-3503-1947

Are you not real? Come to Manga Joy Club for the finest selection of cartoon brides.

Learn to curl!
Tokyo Curling Society
seeks new members.
Reasonable annual fees.

Used axes bought and sold.
Highest prices paid.
Large selection.

Lost: red dot. Call 03-3269-0870 if you have information which might lead to its recovery. Modest reward offered.

Playing dice, womanising, drinking, dancing and singing; sleeping during the daytime; sauntering at unseemly hours... bring ruin to a man.
—*Singala Sutta*, 253

Like curling???
Join the Narasaki
Boys Curling Club.
Health benefits unmatched!

Found: four large beige dots. Come to Wataridori Sukiyaki shop, Rappongi St. for recovery.

ATHLETIC MEMORY
for future enjoyment
FAST!
SAFE!
LOW PRICED!
Give a bell: 03-5772-2839

> Try
> **Black Gun**
> Gum
> *&*
> *feel like a man*

IV.

At 1:30 he hailed a cab and was taken to the Tokyo En Passant Chess Circle:

Address: 1-14-2, Asakusa, Taitou-Ku, Tokyo
Phone: 03-3867-8196

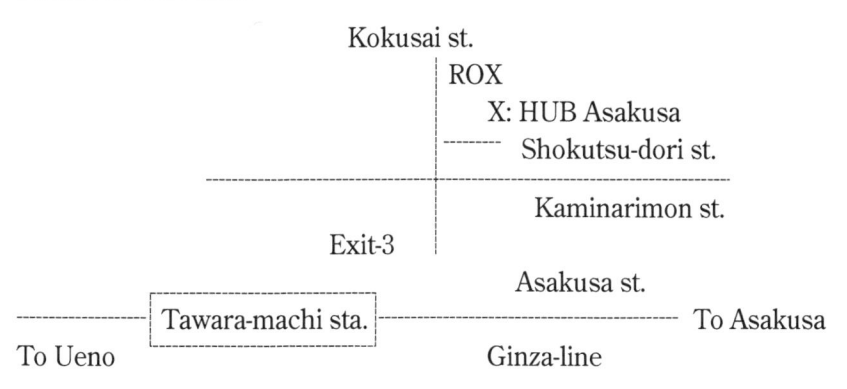

```
                        Kokusai st.
                        | ROX
                        |    X: HUB Asakusa
                        |------ Shokutsu-dori st.
                        |
                        |          Kaminarimon st.
                Exit-3  |
   -----------------------|       Asakusa st.
   ---------------| Tawara-machi sta. |----------------------------- To Asakusa
To Ueno          -----------------------         Ginza-line
```

It was upstairs, above a glow-in-the-dark raincoat factory. Present were almost all the members of the circle (Takashi Nakadai, physicist, Gonji Katô, son of industrialist, Fumio Ogata, classical scholar, etc). There was an air of excitement about the place. The doctor's hand was shaken and he was bowed to ceremoniously. Tajima[1] himself approached the doctor. He was a small, clean-shaven man with large glasses who stooped slightly. He had an embarrassed look on his face as he offered the doctor his hand.

"I am so glad you were able to come."

---

1. Ren Tajima, National Champion of Japan, an expert in South American politics and holder of a FIDE Master title.

"I could hardly refuse an opportunity to go up against Tokyo's best[1]."

The room was a spacious 16-mat room with leather couches and chairs along the sides and a chess table in the centre. Decoration was minimal. A fish tank. A few rare chess sets. An umbrella tree.

Before the game began, Tajima offered Dr. Black a shot of Jack Daniels whisky, which the latter gladly accepted.

"To your health," Tajima said.

The two men then sat opposite each other, with the board between them. Black was black, Ren Tajima, white.

White's opening move was P-K4. Black hesitated a moment, before responding with P-K3.

2. P-Q4　　　　　　　　P-Q4
3. PxP　　　　　　　　　.........

It is all about multiplicity. Everywhere you look, worlds are collapsing and worlds are being reborn.

3. PxP　　　　　　　　　PxP
4. Kt-KB3　　　　　　　Kt-KB3
5. B-Q3　　　　　　　　B-Q3
6. O-O　　　　　　　　　O-O

Tajima's mouth became somewhat tense. All that symmetry was probably beginning to annoy him.

7. QB-Kt5　　　　　　　QB-Kt5

Letting down the hook in the four seas.

8. QKt-Q2　　　　　　　QKt-Q2

---

1. His Japanese was extremely correct, though spoken with a strong Western accent.

Dr. Black at Red Demon Temple

Breaking in is twice as hard as breaking out.

| 9. P-B3 | P-B3 |
| 10. Q-B2 | Q-B2 |

Tajima rapidly crossed one leg over the next. This was an informal match, but he was clearly taking it very seriously. His fellow citizens watched in tense expectation.[1]

11. KR-K1	KR-K1
12. P-KR3	B-R4
13. RxRch	RxR

The Fire God comes looking for fire.

| 14. R-K1 | RxRch |
| 15. KtxR | B-Kt3 |

Black touched the edge of his beard lightly with the finger of his right hand, like an executioner checking the sharpness of his blade.

| 16. BxB | RPxB |
| 17. KKt-B3 | Kt-B1 |

White Queen:
    I ride out with my retinue
    trampling on the red leaves of autumn
    heart soaked with hatred.

Black Knight:
    Her heart is like a ripe persimmon
    its juice running down my arm
    as I thrust my fist towards heaven.

---

1. What did Tung Shan mean when he called the Buddha three pounds of hemp?

White Pawn:
   It was not so long ago that I was a seed, planted in the earth
   now, ripe grain, autumn wind makes me tremble.

Black Bishop:
   Rub wood against wood, and see fire.
   Pray to heaven,
   and your blood will turn to green jade.

White King:
   I tie my tear-softened sleeves and move along the shore
   the moon and I go together the moon and I.

The silence weighed a thousand pounds. The board between the two men was, in the universe, all that existed;—the pieces avalanches and whirlwinds, forests and mountains, planets tumbling through space and distant thoughts that cast themselves a trillion miles. When Black made his next move, it was like a gong being struck in an empty expanse.

52. P-R4   P-B6

For a long while Tajima sat staring at the board. Then, without displaying the least emotion, he resigned and rose from his seat.

"You have won," he said. "Perhaps you would like something to eat?"

His politeness was admirable. The doctor wondered if he would have behaved so well if Tajima had won.

V.

Black was taken to the Billy Kid steakhouse near Aoyama St.:

Address: KR-Bld., 3-2-2, Minami-Aoyama, Minato-ku, Tokyo
Phone: 03-5455-5411

```
                for Sendagaya
                      |
      Aoyama street   |   Bell Commons
   -------------------+------------------------------- for Akasaka
      Omote      MR   |   Gaien
      Sando      GF   |   Mae
      Sta        /    |   Sta.
                /x
                      |       MR: Magician's Residence
                      |       GF: Good Flour
                      |       X : Billy Kid steakhouse
                for Nishiazabu   1 min walk from the intersection
```

After a brief cactus tempura appetizer, a buffalo steak was put before him and he was regaled with highballs while the sound of Mel Tillis discretely played in the background.

Tajima's spirits seemed to have been elevated. He talked incessantly and kept repeating what an honour it was to have been beaten by Dr. Black. His effusion seemed exaggerated.

Afterwards the group piled into taxis, made their way beneath a blaze of neon (light citron, carnation, powder pink); went to the Wild Bar, famous for its hostesses, who all wore masks—some of pigs, others of giraffes. Plastic vines hung from the ceiling. The walls were decorated with pictures of gorillas. A jazz band played in the background. The lady who attended on the doctor, who poured ice-cold 100 Poems saké into his glass, had on a plush rabbit mask.

They got to talking and she tried her English on him.

"You speak very correctly," the doctor commented.

"Actually," she replied, bobbing her head and filling his cup, "I lived for four years in upstate New York. I got a master's in Middle English, but when I came back to Japan I couldn't find a job teaching, so here I am!"

She recited a passage from the *Harley Lyrics* (Brook 8; Ker 35):

> In a fryht as y con fare fremede
> y founde a wel feyr fenge to fere
> heo glystnede ase gold when hit glemede
> nes ner gome so gladly on gere

"Lovely," the doctor said and lifted his cup to his lips.

"Oh!" the young lady exclaimed.

"What is it?"

"You have something in your beard."

And bending over she plucked a small greenish dot from that sheath of hair. She showed it to him laughing.

"Where is Tajima?" someone asked.

"He got up to use the restroom about twenty minutes ago."

"And he hasn't come back yet? That's strange."

One of the men went to investigate and found Ren Tajima, the expert on South American politics, in the bathroom. He had stabbed himself in the calf with a fork and his sock and shoe were bloody.

"Ritual suicide is certainly not what it used to be," the doctor thought, upon hearing this.

VI.

Cigars Should Be Large

CIGARS SHOULD BE LARGE AND OSTENTATIOUS. NO ONE HAS respect for a man who smokes a small cigar. In fact, one should need to open one's eyes wide when looking at it and it should be unsuitable for a man with a small mouth. The smoker of a cigar should not be shy. He should talk fairly loudly and have a pompous attitude, especially in front of those who have not yet learned to smoke.

VII.

Early the next morning he took the Banetsu-West line. While in Japan, he wanted to see a bit of the country. There were also some unusual temples he had heard of, that he wished to visit as part of his research for his *A Key to All Gods*. The area that interested him most was around a village called Yohei. This was where the Zen poet Manzô[1] had lived.

A ball of molten yellow sat above the horizon, towards the east. The doctor gazed at and through the window: at the reflections of the interior

---

1. Manzô was born in Shirosawa, near Motomiya, though the year is uncertain, the son of a pharmacist of some means. While sitting outside, beneath a cherry tree, he had an enlightenment (gazing at the ripe fruit). It is therefore said that he received his transmission from the cherries—a pantheon of red deities. He took everything he owned, piled it onto a boat and, after rowing into the middle of a nearby pond, dumped it overboard. For many years he wandered from temple to temple, doing Dharma battle with the masters of his day. He wore dirty robes and had long, unkempt hair. A whole universe of lice lived in his beard. In fall he would help the farmers harvest their buckwheat. After many years he settled down in Yohei. Once an aspirant came to his hut to ask for the Dharma transmission. "Where have you come from?" Manzô asked. "From Edo." Exactly!" And he hit the other and broke his nose, upon which the aspirant had an enlightenment. Manzô practiced calligraphy for several hours a day throughout his life—taking as his teachers, not men, but birds and trees, mountains and lakes, whose flowing lines he imitated. Sometimes he wrote with his beard, at others, his wine cup. Unfortunately, though his work was valued by connoisseurs, few pieces remain—as he himself cared little for preserving what he wrote. His immediate disciple was a bun vendor named Atsushi.

Dr. Black at Red Demon Temple

of the train, through to the landscape outside: golf courses somehow surreal draped in haze and boxes on hilltops and they went through a tunnel. Reflection, a ghost, a vague, pale face. He turned. A woman, in her early twenties, was sitting on the other side of the isle. Full cheeks silkworm cocoon exfoliated skin reminded him of Utamaro's print of Oshichi the greengrocer's daughter. A swarm of cerebral cockroaches rustled through his mind:
- beaks of heavenly dogs
- water salad
- 500 monks brandishing white sticks, walking sleeve to sleeve, and chanting sutras
- demon

At Kôriyama he changed to a secondary train, a non-electrified rural line, which turned east. The seats were wooden and uncomfortable. There were very few passengers, and those few seemed to be farmers and peasants.

On a seat across from him sat a man around 35 years of age with a sparse and unkempt black beard and intelligent eyes who took out a Tupperware container full of rice balls and began to eat them.

The doctor wondered what their filling was, imagining:
- bolts
- hair-pins
- globs of green dish soap
- small rocks
- live snails

"Not many people on this line," he commented, when the conductor came to check his ticket.

"Unfortunately," the conductor replied. "They will abolish it in the spring due to lack of passengers—so enjoy the view while you can!"

The train moved slowly and gave the doctor the chance to admire the scenery, which was strikingly beautiful. He passed through paddy land and fields of buckwheat. Smoke wafted from the chimney of a dwelling. Its kitchen garden was full of flowering daikon.

The line had clearly been built on a budget, as there was not a single tunnel or bridge. The tracks wound around every hill, and went well out of the way to circumvent rivers, making it take a great deal of time to go just a little distance.

At Oshodomo he got off. A sad little city which long ago had been a post town and after that had had a boom due to the world's largest shoe-heel factory being set up there. But, half a generation earlier, the factory had closed and now the town was suffering from a depression. A man with a bandanna around his head wandered listlessly down the street. A dog sat gnawing at its own tail. In a café, a pair of old women sat eating day-old pastries behind a window that needed washing.

He got a taxi to take him the 10 km to Yohei. The driver was a young surly fellow who drove fast and carelessly. The doctor tried asking him questions about the area, but he only answered in curt monosyllables and shut his mouth tight, so the bottom lip overlapped the top.

The village was charming, the people simple farmers and noodle makers who smiled as he passed. This place had once been known for its hot-springs, but time seemed to have passed it by. The houses were for the most part small and deep-eaved.

At the inn he was greeted with great politeness and shown to a small but immaculate six-mat room, furnished traditionally. He ate a meal of soba and then walked around the village.

There was not much to see. Some houses, a small Buddhist temple, a stream along the banks of which willow trees grew.

He went into a bar and drank a couple of carafes of saké before returning to the inn, eating supper, going to bed and dreaming of:
- snow
- dried peony stems
- rebus

VIII.

THE NEXT DAY HE SPENT EXPLORING THE AREA.

In the morning he visited the Raijû shrine, 3 km distance, which was decorated with thousands of statues of weasels. He paid his respects to the officiating priest, a very tall, thin man of around 60 who greeted him with a bow and a smile.

"Manzô[1] once lived near here," the doctor said.

"Ah, yes, he did. There was a time when visitors would come here just to breath in the air that he had breathed. But these days people are very busy and no one has time to think of these things."

The doctor nodded his head in silence.

"If you would care to see it, there is a single piece of his calligraphy at this temple."

"Oh, yes? Please!"

It was a small, tattered piece of paper in a cheap frame that hung on the wall. The calligraphy, in semi-cursive script, was however still forceful, vibrant—the brushstrokes carrying with them an ineffable tenderness.

The doctor read:

> I awoke with the dew
> and couldn't find my bowl.
> In a hundred years
> where will my bones be?

1. A young man seeking enlightenment came to Manzô. "Where have you come from?" "From the South." "That's too bad," the calligrapher said, and went back in his hut.

In the afternoon, after lunch, he explored the nearby Blood Lake Hell—a large cave full of mud and steam. Red and blue hot water ran from the veins in the walls and little geysers violently burst out causing astonishment and horror—visions of the underworld and myriad suffering and in the bottom there was an acidic crimson-coloured lake with rafts of yellow sulphur floating on its surface.

And he recalled the line from the *Ksitigarbha Bodhisattva Sutra*, regarding the Avici hell:

> Their tongues are pulled out. Their intestines are ripped out and torn to pieces.

After leaving the cave, he made a quick stop at the Gonji Rock Shrine, which was nothing more than a very small building housing a large stone. It was said that the stone was the summer home of the androgynous deity Gonji, child of a primordial swamp spirit.

IX.

Beautiful Things that are Unpleasant

A rose with vomit-coloured petals.

Greeting an attractive woman and hearing her scream.

Moulds are unpleasant, but often pleasing to the eye.

Looking at a full moon from the bottom of a well.

Hornets are very beautiful but unpleasant when they sting.

X.

THE NEXT STOP ON HIS ITINERARY WAS YAHACHI[1], HOME OF THE famous Barrel-Maker Temple[2]. As the crow flies, it was only a little over 15 km (150 chô), but to travel there he would have to take a taxi back to Oshodomo, from there take the train to Tofû[3], where he would have to change trains (a two-hour wait at the station), go to Yuijirô[4], and from there finally take a taxi to his destination. He would spend the better part of the day using mechanised means of transportation.

"Is it possible to get to Yahachi by foot?" he asked the innkeeper.

"Certainly. The walk is long, but pleasant. Maybe three and a half or four hours. If you go to the north end of town, you will find a mountain trail. Follow it. After about an hour and a half or two hours, it will branch into an upper and a lower trail. Make sure you stay on the lower trail—otherwise you will never get there."

"Does the higher trail lead to the same place?"

"Yes, but you must take the lower one."

After arranging for his bag to be forwarded on, he took his departure.

He reached the edge of town, passed by an old man on a ladder picking persimmons from a tree. A group of children were playing by the side of the road. Behind them rose a field of high autumn grass. The trail was

1. The village is surrounded by mountains in all cardinal directions.
2. This is a temple dedicated to Hansuke, god of barrel makers. Followers of the god would practice *incubatio*—sleeping at the site after drinking a great deal of wine, in the hopes of gaining prophetic dreams.
3. The town has an estimated population of 11,640. It is famous for its green onions.
4. The town has an estimated population of 4,397, 56% of these being over 60 years of age. The remains of a Yayoi period moat attest to the town's ancient origins.

not difficult to locate, as, at its head, was a small stone statue of Batô Kannon, the Kuan-Yin with the horse-head crown. The doctor inclined his head slightly; his feet made their way over the dust of the trail.

He walked through beautiful mountain forest. Interlaced branches. A few maple trees stuck out like freshly spilled blood. The song of birds filled the air. Ahead, the mountains rose up, solid, dark-green humps which seemed to wrestle with the sky. The scenery was beautiful, and the doctor, whose intellect was perpetually at work, meditated on how nature often took on almost human characteristics: a ridge that looks like a bent old man; a rock that resembles a whore smoking a cigarette. A young woman's sigh: wild geese flying south. The embrace of lovers: the tide coming into a narrow bay. And the doctor himself: a black lake in lonely hills;—the mythopoeic aspect of all things: nature embodied with spirit—its trillion reflections: every atom in space containing every ocean, every river, every human, every god. He recalled Basho's words:

There is nothing you can think that is not the moon.

What mellow cogitations! Nature often had such effects on the doctor. In the city his mind computed. In the country his thoughts were prone to flow like water.

The path led along a sharp precipice. To the right, far below, the waters of Ôe River swirled—an intricate design of bluish-green and white curls. His calves strained themselves and he moved forward.

At around noon he came to a waterfall. He stopped and sat down on a rock, undid his lunch bundle. Tsukemono rice balls. He had an appetite and ate the simple food with relish while watching as thousands of silver streaks spilled over the cliff—which seemed to be split in two, as by a blade of silk. Music of the waterfall in his ears.

Having swallowed the last of it, the doctor fished in his jacket pocket and found a cigar. Lighting it, he gazed at a large pine which leaned over towards the water below. He thought:

"If this tree were a man, I imagine he would be quite lonely. But as a tree . . . ? What are the sentiments of plants? I have never really studied this enough. Reading Timiryazev. . . . Joachim Jung's *Plantes est corpus vivens non sentiens* could certainly be refuted. After all, Ken Hashimoto transcoding electrical signals from a cactus into musical notes goes a long way towards that. A weed or cactus in the desert. Genius could be locked in such entities. Being alone... truly the only time when one's mind functions at its fullest[1]."

Then recalling the line from *The Discourse of the Teaching Bequeathed by the Buddha Sutra*:

> Those who rejoice in the pleasures of company must also bear the pains of company.

"Yes, the inhabitants of this floating world were not always pleasant to be around," the doctor reflected as he expelled a generous puff of smoke from between his lips. But then he did need outlets for his speech, his intellect, and, occasionally, his violent desires. A real mundane view of life! In *The Lankavatara Sutra* it is said that if things are viewed in another light, through transcendental wisdom,

> they are beyond the reach of intellectual grasp...

"But then, one must consider what the intellectual grasp of your average human is. A few thousand words of diction, a gross or so of facts. What generally passes for knowledge is nothing more than a peripheral and feeble understanding of a very limited area of the universe[2]. And yet it has been proven that a man's mind, like a beaver, can continue to grow ad infinitum, if left unhindered by material forces."

And with this thought, he hoisted himself to his feet and continued on his way, over a precarious bridge and up a steep section of trail.

> Even in ancient days

1. Be careful not to depend on your own intelligence—it is not to be trusted. — *The Sutra of Forty-Two Sections*
2. The natures of ignorance and knowledge are the same, for ignorance is undefined, incalculable, and beyond the sphere of thought. —*The Vimalakirti Sutra*

> when gods ruled the earth
> their voices were not half so loud
> as the pine trees growing here.

He came to the split in the trail that the innkeeper had told him about. One part, clearly the less used, climbed up, the other meandered down.

"In another hour I should be there," the doctor thought continuing his way along the lower trail.

But as he turned a bend, he came upon a problem.

About 5 feet of the path was broken away—apparently by a recent landslide. There was no possibility to advance, without great risk to his life.

"Unfortunate! It is over two hours back to the village!... Of course there is the higher trail... which would probably be quicker than returning. And my baggage will be waiting for me in Yahachi anyhow."

He retraced his steps to the fork, and took the upper trail.

The path was steep and overgrown with weeds, sometimes spider webs stretched across it.

"Well... it is obviously not a popular route."

As he ascended, the air grew cooler, finer. Strange, scraggly pines stretched themselves out from crags—like monstrous, ugly claws. Prickly nezumisashi reached out their needly arms. An occasional white cedar loomed over him like a great green brain, the trunks effusing their bark in an excessive manner, like some bizarre moulting reptile. The trees indeed appeared deformed, monstrous and the doctor had the distinct sensation that they wished to touch him, grab him—cling to his skin.

"Undoubtedly some mechanism in the soil makes them grow in such an odd manner," he thought, hastening his steps.

The landscape itself was of striking, almost savage beauty. Thin waterfalls spilled from high cliffsides. Verdant slopes circumflexed to naked mountain peaks. Below, wreaths of mist crept like snakes—hiding the valleys, blanketing the forests.

Black was filled with an uneasy sense of wonder, elation, and was glad he had chosen this back-route. But time went on and the area he went through became more desolate. The only sound he could hear was that of his own footsteps; an occasional whisper of wind. It began to grow dark—and the doctor, truth to tell, somewhat uneasy. He was hardly equipped to spend the night in such a forlorn place. The mountains seemed to him unfriendly. The plants viperous. The trees now stood out in silhouette, like in a Bergman film.

A huge crow sat perched on a bare branch.

"What an ugly bird!"

The creature snapped its beak and let out a hoarse cry as the doctor made his way past it. Continuing along the trail, he thought he heard a noise behind him—muffled laughter or weeping—and turned around.

Now there was a full half-dozen of these strange, giant black birds. They looked at him ominously, flapped their wings, flew from branch to branch, tree to tree behind him,—followed him as he hurried on into the growing darkness, the sound of their wings behind him, like blades cutting through the air, guillotines springing towards his neck.

Then the trail suddenly plunged down, as did he, through a dense series of trees and thickets. The faint sound of running water. A clearing; and then his nose was met by a welcome smell. That of burning wood. A moment later he espied a small cottage.

"Ah, finally! A habitation!"

He approached with eager steps—a small dwelling stranded in the midst of mountain shadows.

A female figure was kneeling on the porch, in the act of washing a giant white radish.

"Konban wa," the doctor said.

The woman looked up in astonishment, raised herself to her feet. Her clothing hung loosely around her spare figure. She was in her early thirties, remarkably thin, with a long, though not unattractive face—pale as rice-powder, in which sat two black, somewhat frightened looking eyes.

"How far is it to Yahachi?" Black asked.

"To Yahachi? It is very far!"

"If you could just point the way."

"But it is almost dark. You will never find your way at night—especially through Ghost Hatchet Gorge."

"Well then—is there an inn near here? Some kind of lodging?"

"There is nothing—not for a number of miles."

"Then I will have to ask you for your hospitality."

Dr. Black at Red Demon Temple

The woman pouted. "But it is a little place.... My husband and I... "
"Might you ask him?"
"Yes, I suppose I can do that."
A bow-legged figure appeared from out of the darkness, hunched beneath a large bundle of faggots which he carried on his back. Silently he unburdened himself. Then, looking the doctor up and down: "Where did he come from?"
The situation was briefly explained to him.
The man scratched his head.
"Well—he will stay here for the night. And tomorrow he can be on his way. It is not like we are running a hostel."
Her husband was a profoundly ugly man. His lips were like those of a carp—a feature accentuated by an untidy little moustache made up of sparse, bristling hairs. He was bow-legged to the point of ridiculousness and his low forehead marked him as a man of limited intellect.
The doctor took off his shoes and entered the cottage. The place was quite small and not particularly clean.
The woman lit a paraffin lamp and set about preparing a meal. The three sat down on mats around a brazier.
Dinner consisted of turnip soup, chopped radish, dried sardines and pickled greens.
They ate in an uncomfortable silence only broken by the click of chopsticks, the slurping of broth. It was clear that they felt awkward in Black's presence. A moth fluttered about the room. Outside the crickets chirped in the depths of the night. The doctor thought he recognized in their sound the mitsukado-kôrogi, or Loxoblemmus doenitzi.
To break the silence, he mentioned his adventure with the crows.
"Those were not crows you met," the man said, looking up from his bowl.
"Oh?"
"Those were the hungry souls—of murderers, rapists, thieves."
The doctor smiled indulgently. "Indeed!"
"When they see you, they wish to rob you, kill you—do unspeakable horrors to your corpse."
The woman heated up a carafe of low-quality saké and served the two men.

The man drank greedily and the alcohol began to loosen his tongue. He told stories of ghosts and phantoms—of giant snakes and man-eating clouds—of beasts which roamed the forest and fed off the souls of birds.

"Up here in the mountains, things are not like in the city. We don't have such an easy time of it. Sometimes we don't talk to any other mortal being for months together. I forget to use my tongue. The trees are even afraid to talk to me, because when they speak I cut them down."

The spare room where bedding had been laid out for the doctor was small—a good bit of the space taken up by piles of half-rotted wood, a rusty cauldron, odd gear. An old futon had been placed in the centre. The room was cold. He stripped down to his underwear and lay down, curled up beneath the musty-smelling blankets. He could hear the wind outside as it whistled through the trees; and the couple in the next room, which he was only separated from by a paper shôji door, murmuring together in low, whining voices.

Though the conditions were not especially comfortable, he was tired and fell asleep quickly.

During the night he woke up. He thought he saw a shadow pass by the window—a bizarre shape, horns extending from a great shaggy mane.

"Dreaming," he murmured and fell back asleep.

XI.

He woke up the next morning with a heavy head, though he was unsure if it was from the sleeping conditions or the bad saké from the night before.

Getting dressed, the doctor noticed that his wallet was missing from his pants.

"Hmm," he thought, "then I wasn't dreaming. It seems that someone has appropriated my property."

He strode out of the room resolutely, his feet clad only in socks.

Outside the air was filled with mist, grey, white, vaguely pink.

"Ohayô!"

The woman bowed nervously and smiled somewhat coquettishly.

"My wallet appears to be missing."

"Your wallet, Doctor-*san*!"

"Yes, it seems that someone extracted it from my pants' pocket last night."

"But..."

"It would be appreciated if it were returned."

"How..."

"Obviously it is an embarrassing situation. I realise life must be difficult up here, and funds hard to come by. Of course I would be more than willing to offer a nice little reward for the wallet's return, and be more than happy to pay for my night's lodging. The cash is not what concerns me so much as the credit cards and identification papers."

"But I don't know where your wallet is."

"I saw a shadow moving past the room last night."

"Ah!"

"Yes."

"Red Demon!"

"Pardon?"

"It must have been the Red Demon from the temple!"

"He likes to pay by credit?"

"He is mischievous. He is the deity of the mountain and considers everything on it his property. Many years ago the inhabitants of the nearest villages would all make a yearly pilgrimage here and give offerings to this fellow. But modern times have made the people impious and now no one bothers with the customs of their ancestors."

Just then the husband came out scratching his belly.

"What's that you're saying?" he asked.

"I was just telling Doctor-*san* about the Red Demon Temple. It seems his wallet disappeared last night."

"I take no responsibility!"

"But this temple..." the doctor began.

"It's up on the hill."

"Is it possible to go there?"

"Well—I can take you there this morning. But then I think you should leave. You see... your presence disturbs my wife..."

"Believe me, I do not wish to stay any longer than necessary."

"Put on your shoes and we will go," the woodcutter said, wrapping a scarf around his head and taking up his walking stick.

They walked through a field, the grasses of which were partially dry—the colour of the whole a very pale green, tending closely to yellow, and then up an incline and into a very old cryptomeria forest, the grand trees shading the way, a few moths fluttering mystically through the air. Presently they found themselves on a definite trail. The doctor surmised that it was probably a very old off-shoot of the one he had been on the day before. It was lined with numerous old stone lanterns, some of them broken, strange, sad objects.

The path led through dilapidated wooden gates, myôjin torii, and then to the structure itself. The temple was old—moss-covered stones, with a tiled, sloping roof. Wooden statues of the Niô, Agyô and Ungyô, both manifestations of Vajrapani, flanked the door—large cracks appeared in their sides, most of the paint had long ago faded from their forms, and Agyô was missing an arm. But though worn, they still expressed a mysterious and savage beauty that affected the doctor as he admired their muscular physiques—their postures clearly showing a Greco-Buddhist influence.

The man pointed to a carving of a strange creature, half-monkey, half-lizard, which stood above the door.

"They say it was carved by Hidari Jingorô," he said.

The doctor looked about him with interest, the interest of a man of science confronted with an object worthy of study.

He was struck by a number of stone tablets lining the inner walls. They were engraved with a kind of tortoise-shell script arranged in a clearly logosyllabic system.

"I will take some rubbings."

"You do that," the man said. "You can find your way back. I need to go and do my work."

Using a piece of charcoal from a fire-pit he found outside, the doctor proceeded to rub selections onto sheets of his notebook paper (8 x 5" with handsome snake-skin-look hardbound textured cover and 20 lb. premium white bond paper).

> *The wife the husband whom it makes settle faithfulness, with the son of the parent mixed breed, we want the people depending upon the ruler. The wave does the war of the person of the stone, the wind, and the person with the sand. This does not mean the fact that the heaven is a defect. All limbs are the metaphor.*

"Ah, but I should start out so as to be in Yahachi by lunch time. I certainly don't want to be caught again on the trail at night!"

He left the temple and was quite surprised to see that a white mist had spread itself over the ground in the time he had been inside. The silence in the forest was almost absolute and, though it was still only mid-morning, the place seemed quite dark.

Then he heard the slow, methodical approach of footsteps.

"I suppose the woodcutter is returning to fetch me," the doctor thought.

A figure made its way forward.

His face was covered by long, orange-red bangs;—his hair was the colour of a nuclear sunset—which spilled from a helmet adorned with deer horns. He moved stiffly, with the motions of an automaton, feet resting on a pair of wooden clogs; spoke slowly, articulating every syllable in a deep and thick voice:

"Kono sato ni. Kono sato ni. I seem obliged to sleep. Forever. In this world of nothing. Kinô koso. Kinô koso. Only yesterday. Was I a man. Now a demon. I prowl the gates of hell."

He bowed ceremoniously. The doctor returned the salute.

"I have been taking some rubbings," he said.

Silence.

"Do you . . . live in the area?" he asked.

"No."

"Then you are . . . ?"

"Neither here nor there. Not living or dead."

"I am either in the presence of a hallucination, a madman, or a very rude fellow," the doctor thought.

"Some babble . . . about my big headstone. Humans are indeed frightful beings."

"I do not presume to know your antecedents, and therefore cannot claim to understand your bizarre prejudices."

"I am lonely."

"I imagine so. It is not as if you were living in a metropolis."

A fox came walking up with a tray, on which sat a cup of tea.

"A refreshment," the demon said, motioning for the doctor to be seated on a nearby stone.

Black sat down and sipped at his beverage.

"My antecedents . . . " the demon began.

"I am most curious to know."

And so the other told.

XII.

The Demon's Narrative

In my past life I was born into a family that had once been illustrious, but had fallen on hard times—demoted in status due to an indiscretion of an ancestor and the harsh whims of our clan leader. We were samurai, and I was a natural fighter. I took my first head at the age of 14. Later I studied for a brief period under Kamiizumi Nobutsuna, who taught me the secret Chrysanthemum Wind Strike. This I soon mastered and became known as a dangerous fellow.

Which was unfortunate for me, for I was asked to do all sorts of unpleasant tasks and treated like a guard dog. And then there were always fools who wished to challenge me and I was forced to spill their blood[1].

Finally, I had had enough. On the First Day of the Elder Brother of Wood, I slung my sword over my shoulder and with broad steps left. I wandered about, a rônin, a masterless samurai, through marshes and over hills. I still did unpleasant things, but could take or leave contracts as I saw fit. I was my own boss, though often a hungry one, it must be admitted.

One day I entered the village of Yohei and saw,

>sleeves wet with tears,

and heard,

---

1. A human body is difficult to obtain. One has to cultivate merit for innumerable kalpas to obtain a human body, so you should not use it to kill any living being.
   —*Sanghata Sutra*

> a brocade of lamentation.

The inhabitants were miserable as they were being terrorised by some local roughs led by a brother and sister team, who went by the names of Blood-Shot Eyes and Iron Tigress. The former was very skilled with a sword, the latter an adept in black magic. She could destroy crops with a gust of her breath and was in the habit of burrowing under the earth like a mole, entering the village at night and stealing young men's hearts.

It soon became known that I, a skilled rônin, had arrived in town, and I was invited into the hut of the village elder, a wrinkled little man, where I was treated to saké.

"Blood-Shot Eyes and Iron Tigress have demanded a tax of 250 koku of buckwheat," he told me. "On a normal year, this would be bad enough, but this year our harvest is going to be unusually poor. We will be lucky if we get 250 all told. If we give this to them, then we will starve this winter!"

"That's pretty tough luck."

"Listen, if you could help us..."

"What then?"

"We will give you 25 koku of buckwheat.—And maybe we could throw in three or five kan of coppers..."

At first I was going to refuse because, though I had little value for my life, I considered it still to be worth more than a pile of buckwheat. But then my eyes met those of the young woman waiting attendance on us, and I felt a sudden sense of happiness, as if I were,

> entranced by falling blossoms.

"We would be grateful, Sir, if you would help us," the young woman put in timidly.

I scratched my chin, and then replied:

"This brother and sister fancy they hold heaven and earth in their hands, but soon they will be wandering the shadowy roads to hell."

After sharpening my sword and drinking three or four carafes of wine to boost my spirits, I wandered into the hills, following the farmers' instructions on which way to go. After a while I came up to this mountaintop, which did in fact used to be their stronghold. It was the hour of the hare, and the light was already growing dim. Armed men grew like mushrooms beneath tall trees and, as I lay my sword into them, some became puffs of grey smoke to be taken up by the wind, while others exploded, like bubbles of pus.

"Who is it tampering with my men?" Blood-Shot Eyes said, issuing out.

He was a short, stout man with a huge beard. He wore a lattice-patterned battle robe laced with bright blue cords and in his hand he carried a long sword which he had drawn from a black lacquered sheath.

I told him my purpose.

"You bastard!" he replied. "I'm going to cut out your heart and boil it in water!"

So saying, he attacked.

We fought vigorously for five or six bouts, him lunging, me defending; me attacking, him blocking. I used my sword now like a falcon soaring in the air, now like a fish diving in the sea. He wielded his, first in an octagonal pattern, then like the wheel of a cart.

But in the end, my Chrysanthemum Wind Strike got the better of him and he was,

> cut down like ripe grain.

It was now time to deal with the sister. I looked about the place and found her sitting cross-legged on a stone. She was decked out in Ching-chow jewellery and wore a Chinese jacket and a skirt with a long train. In her hand was a six-string zither, which she plucked at as she sang,

> There in the sky,
> the clouds are like wool;
> a strong wind will blow you
> out of this world.

Then, getting up, she approached me.

"You have destroyed my brother," she said.

"I have."

"How impolite!" she griped, somersaulting forward.

She drew the pins from her hair, and attacked me with these sharp things, wielding them as deadly weapons. She spat fire from her tongue and a thick black liquid oozed from her sleeves.

Sweat rolled from my temples as I fought her, nothing existing in the universe but the two of us, her hairpins clattering against my blade.

I parried and tilted and she hissed and sprang. Sparks flew, and it seemed as if we fought far away from the world of men, with darkness lurching at us from all sides.

Finally seeing her cheeks flushed, I took my opportunity and knocked one of the weapons away from her. Then, bounding forward, I put my foot against her chest and pressed her against a wall.

"With my two hands I have cut off your brother's head," I shouted, "and now I will kill you."

I shoved the blade of my sword down her throat, leaning on it with all my weight, so that it pierced her all the way through. But sliding off it, she turned into a snake and slithered away.

I laughed for a moment and then gasped, for, looking, I saw that one of her hairpins had lodged itself deep in my neck and hot magma was running down my side. White waves poured over me as flames flashed and I realised that I was no longer a man as I belched out light and smoke from my lungs.

Though I had lived for some thirty years, my life seemed so short, like a single cup of saké.

In this world we travel from life to life, dream after dream.

The trees wept and the grass moaned.

It is said that when you kill a man you kill all men, and when you save just a single man, you save the entire universe. How much bad karma had I stored away—with only just enough merit to keep me from the flames of Avici.

The people of the neighbouring villages were grateful that I had freed them from the tyranny of those two and built a temple for me here. They used to regularly come—bringing gifts of wine and meat and burning incense in my memory.

Now no one brings me offerings. The rich men of the capitol cities seek to eradicate piety, so as to chain men's souls with money. No one

Dr. Black at Red Demon Temple 355

mourns my death but myself! My temple sits here unvisited, like a rotten log half buried beneath fall leaves.

Without sour plums, I sometimes grow hungry for human flesh and on the rare occasion when I am presented with a visitor, it is difficult indeed to resist.

XIII.

The doctor noticed a thin stream of drool running from the corner of the demon's mouth.

"I certainly hope that I am not the cause of this secretion of spittle," he thought. And then, in a voice calculated to be soothing, said aloud: "Well, our interview has certainly been enlightening. But I am afraid that I have tarried too long, for I have a considerable foot journey ahead of me."

He rose to his feet.

"If you could leave me a little something," the demon murmured, "I would be quite grateful."

"Leave you something? Well, yes, I suppose..."

"A little sashimi."

"I am not sure I quite understand."

"It you could leave me an arm or two, I would be most grateful. A little raw flesh which I can dip in soy sauce and eat with horseradish..."

The bangs that covered his face began to rise up, as if by the power of static electricity. First two red lips were revealed, set in ash-coloured flesh. Empty eye-sockets, the pits of which were tinged with vibrant orange, were oozing phosphorescent slime. A bluish tongue slapped itself against a set of black teeth.

"I can already feel the texture of your raw flesh on my tongue," he said creeping forward, fingers, out of which grew long, razor-sharp nails, extended.

The doctor, very distinctly, felt the hair on the back of his neck rise up. He stumbled backward, swinging his arms—a bizarre, monotonous screeching sound—an echo from some subterranean place of punishment—seeming to ring in his ears.

He turned and hurried away; hustled down the hill, his short legs moving with the utmost rapidity—arms pushing aside branches, feet slipping along stones.

Dr. Black at Red Demon Temple

After he had gone some distance, he stopped, with one finger wiped a dew of sweat from his forehead.

"Well, this certainly goes down as one of the more fantastic incidents in my life," he said to himself, straightening his necktie and then continuing on his way.

Suddenly he stopped dead in his tracks. A white cylinder lay across his path. He gazed at it with curiosity and it moved.

"A serpent," he murmured.

Slowly he stepped backward. Looking behind him he saw an identically shaped cylinder, apparently a continuation of what lay before him.

"Or is it very large and long worm?"

He let his eyes follow the shape, which began writhing and contracting. To his surprise, it terminated in the head of a woman, the woman of the hut, which now rose up out of the brush.

"I have been waiting for you."

"Indeed."

"We must fulfil our karma."

"And what sort of karma did you have in mind?"

"Kiss me," she said. "I long for you. I want to taste your tongue." Her neck wriggled like an eel. "Come now, my husband is an old fool and will never find out."

"Do you mind if I ask for a rain check?" the doctor said in an unsteady voice.

The neck wrapped itself around his left leg. The head rose to the level of his own. She smiled, in a sad, seductive manner and opened her lips: sharp, wet teeth complimented by purplish gums.

"Doctor-*san*, I have been dreaming of you . . . "

He felt the neck begin to contract and she pushed her lips forward to be kissed. The doctor, though quite frightened, did not lose his presence of mind.

"Look dear," he said, "I am as attracted to you as you to me. But romance is always best performed in a recumbent position. Let us relax beneath that pine, and I will very gladly put my mouth to yours."

"Ah, yes," she said in agitation, relaxing her grip and writhing off the trail, reclining beneath the tree.

"Just close your eyes, I am coming," he said, leaping away.

He arrived at the hut with pasty skin. The woodcutter sat on the porch, a pipe sticking from between his lips and his axe leaning next to him.

"My wife's not here," he said.

"Oh!"

"You have been touching her in the forest."

"My dear sir . . . "

"If you will just lower your head a bit," he said, raising his axe, "I should be able to sever it from your shoulders with a single stroke."

The clouds twisted and turned, like intertwining dragons, heads expanding, throats swelling, exhaling smoky breath, tails wrapping themselves around old pines.

The forest stopped abruptly and gave way to a wasteland. He walked through complete silence. The air smelled like rotten eggs. The earth was yellow, dry. Cone-shaped hills tinged with red. Steam seeped out from fissures.

He looked over the village. The sound of a man chopping wood met his ears. His eyes were greeted by smoke rising from a chimney.

woman water bird

Variety

A Gallery of Interesting Things

If you take a drowned fly, one dead up to twenty-four hours, put it the sun and cover it with salt, it will come to life again.

In Java it rains ninety-seven days a year.

On January 31st, 1889, an unexplained barometric oscillation took place over Central Europe.

The bodies of bees, when dried, powdered and mixed with oil, make an excellent cure against baldness.

Margaret Rich Evan, at the age of 70, was known as the best wrestler in Wales.

In October, 1909, Dr. A.P. Brigham proved that the maximum number of inhabitants that the United States of America could support would be 305,000,000.

On the 17th of June, 1278, two hundred madmen began to leap about on the Mosel Bridge in Utrecht. All fell in the water and drowned.

The Hipparchia Janira butterfly bears on its wings an exact likeness to Henry Peter Brougham, 1st Baron Brougham and Vaux.

If you hang branches of an elder bush in your house, flies will not come near.

On March 15th, 1860, a certain Mr. Goodman, between the hours of 10 a.m. and 7:20 p.m., smoked seventy-two cigars.

In Amsterdam, in 1682, a woman gave birth to a dog.

In Gloucester, Massachusetts, a goose lived to be 95 years old.

Take the skin of a young rabbit and cut it into two-inch wide strips. Gather mugwort on the first degree of the sign of Capricorn and sew it into the strips and then fold them in half and sew them up. With these make garters. When worn, you will be able to walk very fast.

Saturn is the most beautiful object in the sky.

The progeny of a single fly in a year is 2,080,320.

On May 27th, 1876, Commandant Tegrad successfully photographed a bottle using only his mind.

Suggested Reading

A Key to All Gods, in twenty-nine volumes. Printed by the Watson Ethnological Society, Boston, for its members

Regiae Biblothecae Matritensis Codices Graeci Manuscripti, Madrid, 1769

Conclusiones, Regulae Tractatus et communes Opiniones, Venice, 1568

Bible Wines, or, The Laws of Fermentation and Wines of the Ancients, New York, National Temperance Society and Publishing House, 1874

Supramundane Facts in the Life of Rev. Jesse Babcock Furguson, A.M., LL.D., Including Twenty Years' Observation of Preternatural Phenomena, London, 1865

A Table, exhibiting the Moon's age by Inspection, London, 1810

Annals of King David, London, 1823, Sudbury Printer, Gate Street, Lincoln's Inn Fields

Learn Syriac in 30 Days, Integrated Learning Publications, 1973

Telemetry Equipment Buyers Guide, 1970, Value Engineering Publications, Inc.

Balloon terms, their definitions and French equivalents, Washington, Government Printing Office, 1918

Sarvadharmasvabhāvasa-matāvipañcita-samādhiraja

Synagoge, Printed for the Booksellers, circ. 1860

Fiamme d'amor divino dell'anima desiderosa di fare tutto il bene e d'impedire tutto il male, 1681, G.C. Wagner

Jackson's gymnastics for the fingers and wrist, London, 1865, N. Trübner & Co.

try
𝔍𝔢𝔯𝔯𝔶'𝔰
World Famous
Moustaches
--Proven Effective!--

Questionnaire

Please fill in the following questionnaire and send it, along with a $1 (US banknotes only) processing fee to 525 Lolita St, Santa Fe, NM 87501, or deliver in person, on August the 3rd, between the hours of 3 and 4 p.m. at Piazza San Marco, Venice (give to the man with the small moustache standing in front of the Caffé Florian).

Please rate your level of satisfaction:

Extremely Satisfied ☐
Very Satisfied ☐
Quite Satisfied ☐

How much will you say under interrogation?

Everything ☐
Nothing ☐
Something ☐

Can you get the Tao?

Yes ☐
No ☐

Please explain, in ten words or less, the aspects represented in unity.

┌───┐
│   │
└───┘

Check your area(s) of expertise below

Second Temple Period ☐
Palaeography ☐
Gestalt Theory ☐
Mysticism ☐
Emotional Vampires ☐
Manusriptology ☐
Archaeoacoustics ☐
Shadow Theatre ☐
Paleoethnobotany ☐
Sargon of Akkad ☐
Eco-Gastronomy ☐
Cliometrics ☐
The Sun ☐

Invisible Hands
1 + 1
50% Off!
second pair